PENGUIN BOOKS

The Mysterious Affair
at Castaway House

Stephanie Lam was born and raised in London. She now lives in Brighton, close to the sea. *The Mysterious Affair at Castaway House* is her first novel.

D1040184

The Mysterious Affair
at Castaway House

STEPHANIE LAM

PENGUIN BOOKS

PENGUIN BOOKS

Published by the Penguin Group
Penguin Books Ltd, 80 Strand, London WC2R ORL, England
Penguin Group (USA) Inc., 375 Hudson Street, New York, New York 10014, USA
Penguin Group (Canada), 90 Eglinton Avenue East, Suite 700, Toronto, Ontario, Canada M4P 2Y3
(a division of Pearson Penguin Canada Inc.)
Penguin Ireland, 25 St Stephen's Green, Dublin 2, Ireland (a division of Penguin Books Ltd)
Penguin Group (Australia), 707 Collins Street, Melbourne, Victoria 3008, Australia
(a division of Pearson Australia Group Pty Ltd)
Penguin Books India Pvt Ltd, 11 Community Centre, Panchsheel Park, New Delhi – 110 017, India
Penguin Group (NZ), 67 Apollo Drive, Rosedale, Auckland 0632, New Zealand
(a division of Pearson New Zealand Ltd)
Penguin Books (South Africa) (Pty) Ltd, Block D, Rosebank Office Park,
181 Jan Smuts Avenue, Parktown North, Gauteng 2193, South Africa

Penguin Books Ltd, Registered Offices: 80 Strand, London WC2R ORL, England

www.penguin.com

First published 2014
001

Copyright © Stephanie Lam, 2014
All rights reserved

The moral right of the author has been asserted

Set in 12.5/14.75pt Garamond MT Std
Typeset by Jouve (UK), Milton Keynes
Printed in Great Britain by Clays Ltd, St Ives plc

ISBN: 978-1-405-91700-1

www.greenpenguin.co.uk

Penguin Books is committed to a sustainable
future for our business, our readers and our planet.
This book is made from Forest Stewardship
Council™ certified paper.

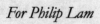

For Philip Lam

Prologue

The first time I ever saw Castaway House I knew it was meant to be mine.

I was only a kid then, in a dirty dress and unlaced boots. I'd gone to stand at the very end of the pier, where I could look up to the great cliff that marked the end of our town. Castaway House was the last one on the left, at the top of the terrace, bigger than the rest and painted buttermilk yellow, the colour of summer.

Of course, I knew I'd have to wait for it to be mine.

Still, anything worth having was worth waiting for, I thought. They said that the best things came that way.

I looked up at Castaway one more time, and made a promise.

Just wait, I thought to myself.

You just wait.

I

1965

A storm was breaking ten miles away along the coast, and thunder was cracking across the sky. Rainwater splashed down my neck and the back of my dress, leaking through my tatty coat. Above me, the air smelled of metal. I held on to the slippery railings and looked out over the deserted beach sixty feet below, its broken pier sinking slowly into the sea.

I'd just been on an ill-fated walk along the cliff. The rain had turned the ground into a mud slick, and I'd slipped over at the very top, nearly plunging to my death on the rocks below. Luckily, only the bungalows that lined the path had seen my undignified scramble to safety, and that was when I'd decided to give up on washing away my crimes, and come home.

I looked down; I was filthy with mud, and the rubber boots I'd borrowed were a mess. Still, like this I sort of fitted in with the general ambience of my current living accommodation. I turned, pressed my sodden back against the chilly railings and looked across the road at the building looming through the mist.

I squinted to block out the mildewing walls and peeling window frames. This way, all I could see were several storeys of grandeur, with a rooftop shaped like the turrets of a castle, pillars holding up the porch, and iron balconies on the first and second floors. The house had an almost authoritarian air about it, perhaps because it stood at the head of the terrace, or perhaps because it was the largest on the street.

However, once I opened my eyes properly and crossed the road, there was no escaping the rust eating away the balconies; and from the pathway I could make out the cracked basement window held together with masking tape, the scrags of tinsel up on the second floor, although it was nine months after Christmas, and the badly punctuated ROOM'S TO LET sign pasted to the door.

So here it was, my abode since August when I'd so hurriedly left home, shortly before the start of a fresh academic year as Miss Waverley's most promising pupil of the Upper Sixth; I'd spent the last month and a half trying to tell myself I wasn't missing it one bit.

I climbed the five steps up to the covered doorway, my feet sloshing inside the boots. As always, I stopped to look up at the oddly beautiful stained-glass window overhead. The hallway light was on, illuminating the vines and tulips that formed in red and green the name of my new home, *Castaway House.*

I dug muddy fingers into the pockets of the raincoat to find my keys. Inside, some sort of argument was going on. Two men: I heard the rumble of voices back and forth. I pushed my key into the lock and recognized Johnny's voice, telling someone to get out or else. I braced myself, wished there was another way in, and twisted open the door.

As soon as I stepped on to the mat, the timer light blinked off and I was left in the dark. I swallowed, punched the switch back on, and the hallway jumped into a dull yellow glare.

I was standing between the two doorways. The second one was always open, revealing a great expanse of hall, the dirty flagstones covered with a constant carpet of grit, sand, sweet wrappers and cigarette ends. Johnny was wearing his good suit, and his neck was red with irritation. Facing him was an old tramp, swaying against the snail-shell end of the banister. He turned to me as I came in, and said in a voice as rich as plum brandy, 'Please help me.'

'Oh!' I dripped across the hallway. 'What's the matter?'

'Stay out of this,' said Johnny, and then took me in properly. 'Bloody hell, Rosie, you look terrible.'

'I fell over in the mud, that's all.' I frowned at the tramp. 'Sorry, do I know you?'

The man shook his head. 'Indeed you do not. This is why I need your help.'

He was as pitiful a specimen as I'd yet seen grace the hallway of Castaway House. He had a tangled grey beard, a nose mapped with veins, and an overcoat that was giving off a hideous reek of stale alcohol and body odour.

Johnny growled. 'Look, pal, you don't live here and you're pissed, so do us a favour and get lost, all right?'

'Come on,' I said. 'At least let's hear what he's got to say.'

Johnny snorted a laugh. 'Please yourself.' He waved me vaguely towards the tramp. 'And you can get rid of him after.'

I smiled encouragingly at the man. 'Go on. What is it?'

He staggered slightly and cleared his throat. 'I have

made a journey,' he boomed. 'Across sea, across land, and this, mark you, this was my destination. And now I am here, I demand that you listen to my story.'

'Okay,' I said, a little uncertainly. Johnny winked at me.

The man smiled, revealing a row of rotting teeth. He patted the pockets of his overcoat. 'I have something here. Something to show you.' He glanced up at me fiercely. 'It is of the utmost importance!'

I watched the man transfer items from one pocket to another, peering at each of them in turn. This took some time, so while I was waiting I said, 'Listen, Johnny, I was just wondering if I could ask a favour . . .'

'No.' He readjusted his shirt cuffs below his jacket sleeves, and smoothed down his brushed-forward hair. 'Six quid on Tuesday, or nothing. If you ain't got the rent, ask your flatmates for a loan.'

I pulled a face, but he wasn't looking. 'Please. I'm just a bit short.'

He cackled. 'I know that.'

'Johnny . . .'

'Ain't my problem. Landlord's orders. I just hold this sodding place together, that's all.' His face softened slightly at my worried frown. 'How're you settling in, then?'

'All right.' I shrugged.

'Good.' Johnny glanced at the tramp, who was pulling from one pocket a heap of what looked like debris from the beach: an old shell, a bit of twig, a pile of sand-scattered bus tickets. 'You coming up to see Star later?'

I tried out a bitter laugh. 'Hardly. She was supposed to knock for me last night. We were going to go dancing at the One-Two, only she didn't bother to turn up.'

Johnny sniffed. 'You should've come up to ours. She probably forgot.'

'I did come up.' I shrugged away the wriggle of excitement at the thought of Johnny and Star in their love-pad; not even anywhere close to getting married, but with a double bed and everything. 'There was no answer.'

'Oh, yeah.' Johnny nodded. 'I think we went out for a drink. I dunno, Rosie, what can I say? My bird can't keep away from my side. One-Two's a dive anyway. You don't wanna go there.'

The light turned off again, and he leaned past me to turn it on. As the beam glowed, I saw that the man was peeling apart the innards of a tube of mints. 'Items from a newspaper,' he muttered. 'Five or ten items. Or seven. You will understand. You will see.'

'Well,' I said grumpily to Johnny. 'You can tell her from me that she can just . . . I don't know, find a new friend.'

'Yeah, yeah,' said Johnny wearily, as the tramp roared, 'Where have they gone?'

'Oh, they'll turn up,' I said, wanting to be gone now, with a hot bath already run and waiting for me.

'They contain the most dreadful news.' His brows beetled. 'As soon as I read them . . . I admit I cannot quite remember now what they contained, but as soon as I read them, I knew I had to return. I had to come back to Castaway House.'

'Back?' Johnny clicked his neck. 'What d'you mean, back?'

'I had to come back.' The man stared at the painted-over wallpaper. 'Had to come back.'

'Well, look,' said Johnny. 'If you been here before, you can rent a room again. I got one going in the basement.

Flat Four. It's got a lovely garden view. All mod cons. Then I won't have to kick you out, see?'

'Oh, yes,' I said. 'That's a good idea. And then he can have a proper look for his newspaper cuttings.'

'A room.' The tramp pulled out a much-torn manila envelope containing a huge bundle of dirty pound notes. 'Yes. A room. What are your rates, my good man?'

Johnny eyed the notes greedily. 'Um . . . we'll have a little chat about that downstairs.' He jerked his head as he sauntered towards the passageway that led down into the basement. 'This way, Grandad.'

'Wait.' The tramp eyeballed me. 'You have been kind to me, my dear. I would like you to be the first to know the truth.'

'Okay,' I said cheerfully. 'You just let me know as soon as you remember it.'

'First floor,' supplied Johnny from the dim end of the corridor. 'Visit any time. Rosie'll make you a cup of tea. Rosie Lee, ha ha.'

'How about I pop down instead?' I said, thinking hurriedly, glaring at Johnny. 'Er . . . tomorrow. You can show me those things from the newspaper.'

'Very good.' The man held out a filthy, calloused hand. 'My name is Dockie.'

I shook it gingerly, noticing that my own hand was likewise caked in mud. I had no intention of popping down tomorrow; I had a feeling that by then he'd have forgotten my very existence. 'Rosie Churchill.'

'After the great man.' Dockie nodded. 'I watched the funeral on Mrs O'Shea's television set. Most moving. And now, to rest.'

They disappeared into the darkness downstairs. I shook my head, relieved they had gone, and was about to go up to the flat when something about the telephone beside me caught my eye.

At first I wasn't sure what it was. The phone was an old-fashioned black Bakelite one, sticking out from the wall on a small plinth, and below it hung the money box with its A and B buttons and its slot open-mouthed for sixpences. Above the phone, somebody – probably Johnny – had erected a blackboard for messages. It had never been properly cleaned and was now a thick swab of grey chalk dust, although somebody had recently scrawled on it in pink. I looked at it for several seconds before I realized that the message was for me.

Rosy – yr mother called. Said shell call agane at 5.

I looked at my wristwatch; it was ten to. I rubbed off the message with the clammy duster that had been wedged behind one of the copper pipes that trailed floor to ceiling. As I was putting it back, I heard the whistling again.

It was a grating, tuneless sound that belonged to someone who was tone-deaf and had no sense of rhythm. I'd often heard it when I was out on the staircase, either rising or falling from one of the floors above or below me, but I now realized exactly where it was coming from, and that I should have guessed whom it had been all along.

Nobody had ever met the inhabitant of the ground-floor flat; at least, Susan, Val and I hadn't. The flat was certainly being lived in, because the girls had told me that sometimes the curtains at the front were closed at night. Whoever was there had access to the huge back garden, which we could see from our kitchen window, but none of us had ever seen anyone in it.

I realized that of course Johnny would know who was renting the place; he'd have the name marked up in his little black book, which he kept in a drawer in his and Star's flat on the top floor, but there was no point asking him anything. Johnny took great delight in denying all knowledge of anything we might want to know, and he loved to tease. I could have asked Star, but I wasn't speaking to her now. Anyhow, anyone who whistled like that was surely some sort of psychopath, perhaps with bodies in the larder like John Christie, so maybe it was better not to know.

I walked up the threadbare runner lining the stairs to the half-landing. The bathroom was empty, and the meter still had some go on it, so I thought I'd risk not feeding it one of my precious coins. I scrubbed the tidemarks out of the bath and turned on the hot water, the geyser whumping into shuddering life.

While I was waiting for it to fill, I climbed the stairs up to our flat on the first floor. I stepped out of Val's boots by the door; there was still a good quarter-inch of water in them, but I decided to drain and clean them later. At least the girls were out; Val and Susan were at the pictures watching *Help!* for the fifteenth time with Susan's boyfriend and one of the lads from their work. I slung my raincoat on the peg above, and walked in stockinged feet towards my bed.

There was a strict hierarchy of beds in the flat. Val's, which was the middling one, faced the door and was stacked with her soft toys like a first line of defence.

Susan's, the best, had a frilly pink coverlet and was behind the partition where we hung our coats, against the wall dividing this room from the kitchen. It was the warmest spot in the flat, and she'd positioned the bed so that whenever she got out of it, in a Jean Shrimpton stretch she had perfected in front of the mirror, her bare feet would land on the rug.

My bed was, naturally, the worst. Although its head was a few feet from the gas fire, this seemed hardly relevant as it was pushed up against the outside wall, and bubbles of damp oozed out of the discoloured wallpaper beside me as I slept. The bed lay alongside the furthest of the three floor-to-ceiling windows, which meant that the wind coursed in on chilly days, and on sunny ones it was like being roasted alive.

I stood beside the bed as I peeled off my sodden clothes and looked out of the window. Rain was still lashing down outside, forming puddles on the broken balcony. I pulled my padded dressing gown from the bed, where it lived as part of the covers, and wrapped myself in it. From the window, I saw Mrs Hale emerge from the gateway of the Bella Vista guest house next door and battle with her car door. She managed to wrench it open, although, as she climbed in, it swung away from her and she had to lean out and pull it closed. I heard the distant slam as she succeeded, and the iffy rattle of the car's engine starting up. She shuddered out and headed uncertainly down the cliff, wavering from side to side in the wind.

When I turned away, I caught my reflection in the huge gilt mirror that tilted at an angle over the disused fireplace. The mirror was tarnished and scratched, and the way it leaned meant whoever looked in it always felt slightly sea-sick. I'd lost weight in the short time I'd been here, which perhaps was fashionable, but there were dark hollows under my eyes, and my cheeks were gaunt. I ran fingers through my damp hair, and several strands came away in my hand.

Before I went down for my bath I pulled out R. C. from his hiding place amidst the stack of books I used as a bedside table. Star had given him to me; one of the fifth-floor tenants had found him folded and wedged behind a loose bit of skirting. 'Same initials as you,' she'd said. 'I was going to chuck it away, but, you know, you can have it if you want.'

That was one of the days when she'd been good: funny and generous and happy to seek my friendship. I smoothed out R. C. and studied him again.

It was a pencil sketch of the head and shoulders of a young man. It wasn't very well done, but there was something about the angle of his cheekbones, the tuft of uncertain hair, the bruised eye sockets, that reminded him of me. His face also had an uncertain look about it, or perhaps that was only suggested by the timid strokes R. C. had made with that pencil, forty-one years ago. Above the picture he'd scribbled, *Twenty minutes after my arrival!* and, at the bottom, *R. C., 10th June '24.*

It was the exclamation mark that intrigued me. The 'arrival' must have been at this house, but I couldn't work out if the *!* indicated excitement or disbelief. I thought the latter seemed more possible. I'd felt the same twenty minutes after my own arrival, having dragged my cases up the stairs and been told by Susan that we'd all get along just fine if I didn't consider myself their friend, they having quite enough to be getting on with, and that the bathroom would be out of bounds between seven and half past eight every morning, and that she usually invited her boyfriend over every Friday evening, so if I could make myself scarce then, it would be much appreciated.

From downstairs, the telephone pealed. I looked at my alarm clock, balanced on the books. It was five o'clock.

I replaced R. C. in his hiding place and reached under the bed to take my towel from the suitcase I kept there, which I used instead of a drawer. I went down towards the bathroom and stopped just outside, looking down the stairs at the jangling phone. I hoped nobody else would answer it. The house certainly felt empty, except, I supposed, for the murderer on the ground floor, Dockie in the basement muttering nonsense, and Johnny, sauntering along one of Castaway's many hallways.

Finally, the phone rang silent. I breathed out, as if I'd been temporarily reprieved, and opened the door to the bathroom. The tub was nearly full, and I twisted the tap closed, hung my robe on the hook and sank into the scalding water, determinedly not thinking about Mum tapping her nails, the receiver clamped to her ear.

I closed my eyes and concentrated instead on my mysterious R. C., his worried features and his exclamation mark. I mind-sketched arms and legs, gave him a suit jacket and a pair of trousers. I animated him, tried to see him climbing the stairs of Castaway House, but like a wooden man in a Swiss cuckoo clock he kept appearing and disappearing, his face a blank egg, even the features he'd drawn himself dissolving in the bubbles. I contented myself with writing our initials in steam on the tiles, and then held my breath and lay down under the water, the earth caking my body running back into mud, as if that would wash me clean of my sins.

2

1924

Both trains were packed all the way from Birmingham New Street to London, and again on the connecting service to the south. It seemed that in every carriage an elderly gentleman was smoking a cigar, and so I gave up my seat fairly early on and spent most of the journey in the corridor, pointing my nose towards the open part at the top of the window in an attempt to avoid a revolt by my lungs.

I had the letter from Alec folded neatly in my top pocket, inviting me once more to Castaway House, assuring me that he had meant what he had said at the funeral, and that I had merely to telegram the day and time of my arrival. I patted it again, feeling the crumple of it against my shirt. It had been my talisman all the way from my small Midlands town, and now, as I trundled through this unknown territory, it was a familial link that told me I was doing the right thing.

Mother hadn't wanted me to go; she'd had her tea leaves read and was convinced that if I made the journey I'd never come back. Father said it was for the best. 'Give those lungs of yours a chance, Robert,' he'd murmured around his pipe when I'd told them of the conversation we'd had at the wake. 'They need all the help they can get.'

'It's Alec,' Mother had said. 'He's always been a flighty one. I don't trust him.'

'They'll be all right.' Father had rattled his newspaper to indicate the conversation was over. We were in the back parlour, with the oilcloth on the table and Mother's heirlooms on the mantelpiece, and I attempted to smother my excitement at the idea of a whole summer in Alec's company by thinking of the rumoured Regency grandeur of Castaway House, my dead Aunt Viviane's family home.

'I wouldn't mind if he lived in a crummy boarding house on the seafront,' I muttered. 'I'd probably feel more comfortable there.'

'If he had a room in a boarding house there'd be no space for you.' Mother let out one of her practised sighs. 'I suppose you may as well make the most of it.'

So they had waved me off at the station, and I'd thought I'd seen a tear gleam in Mother's eye, which was silly because were it not for this year in the purgatory of my sickbed I would have been long gone anyhow. I pressed my forehead to the glass and watched the countryside of the South roll by in low-lying hills and broad streaks of meadow. A river snaked alongside us for a while, silvery under the June sun. We stopped at tiny country stations; I saw windmills bead the skyline and then, finally, the dotted cottages became terraced houses, heaped together and flung upon hillsides. A viaduct took us over a busy street thronging with buses and billboard advertisements, until finally we drew up alongside a platform heavy with trolleys and porters, beneath a vaulted glass-and-steel roof. A man in a square blue cap puffed alongside the train, pulling open doors and calling, 'Helmstone, ladies and gentlemen! Helmstone, your final destination!'

People were already pushing me against the window,

hurrying to the doors so they could be the first out. I waited until the rush had subsided, then went back into the carriage and retrieved my case from the rack, coughing on the lingering cigar smoke inside.

A porter approached me, his eyebrow raised hesitantly, but I smiled quickly and moved on, dragging my case and hoping he would not insist as I had no spare coppers for a tip. Alec had said he would meet me at the station, and so when I arrived inside the concourse I hovered and looked about, trying to make the smile I was wearing appear suitably nonchalant.

Between the two arches of the entranceway there was an advertisement that painted Helmstone as the Riviera, where beautiful people leaned on a bleached-white terrace under a gaudy Mediterranean sun. I stood beneath the poster, thinking it seemed like a prominent spot to be noticed, and watched the holidaymakers thickening the station concourse: cow-eyed honeymooners, fast girls in long scarves, doughty widows in fake pearls and elaborate hats.

After a while, I realized Alec must have been held up. Another train came in, expelling a few more hundred passengers like ants from a nest, and then another. My nonchalant smile became harder to maintain. I wondered if he were waiting outside.

I dragged my case through the wide tunnel, emerging at the busy entrance to the station. Motor taxis idled in a queue beside me. Friends and family enveloped each other in embraces and handshakes. A wagon staffed by ex-servicemen, medals pinned to their blazers, sold roses for sweethearts. I peered beyond them and saw the sweep of the road lead downhill and then, at the end, rising up like a flat wall, the blue slate of the sea.

I shivered when I saw it. I couldn't help but feel rather enclosed by the thing, as if there were no escape at the end, just that high, unforgiving wall. And still Alec had not come.

Perhaps he had misread the time. I knew the address; I could take a taxi and hang the consequences. Yet I thought of the pitifully few notes I had stashed in my wallet, and, remembering Alec had mentioned how the house gave on to a view of the sea, decided to head immediately towards it and ask for directions on my arrival.

I grasped my case and made for the end of the street.

The pavement was narrow and chock-full of people. I transferred the suitcase to my left hand and heaved it downhill, following two plump girls wearing skirts that brushed their calves. A man stood in the doorway of a shop with strings of postcards dangling ceiling to floor in his window. He was smoking a cigar. 'Luvverly postcards,' he called at me as I passed him. I saw flecks of spittle on his lips. 'Best photographic quality in town.'

'N-no thank you,' I said. 'Must get on.'

'You looking for an hotel, chum? I can sort you out. Beautiful little guest house, only half a crown a night.'

I was already a yard beyond the shop. 'I'm quite all right, thank you.' I hurried onwards, overtaking the plump girls, my case banging against my shins. I reached a junction where trolleybuses rattled back and forth. Straw-hatted schoolgirls waved down at me from the open deck of one. I smiled quickly, and looked away as they began blowing me kisses and giggling to one another. I crossed over, headed past a cavernous dance hall advertising four nights of hopping fun every week, and found myself at a busy promenade that spanned the length of the beach. I crossed over the road to the sky-blue railings, put my case down between my feet and looked to see what I could see.

I was standing about eight feet above the beach; uneven steps led down to a planked walkway that bordered the sand. Arches were set into the brick wall directly below me, and even from here the smell of fish drifted up from their open doors to greet me. Away to my left was a row of beach huts, outside which were gathered various family groups, the women sunning themselves on deckchairs, the men overheated in shirts and ties. A few, making concessions to the mildness of the day, had rolled up their sleeves.

Further along was a paddock of donkeys flicking their ears. A child, riding one, screamed, red-faced, while her mother waved from the shore. Out to sea, a few people were frolicking in the waves, mostly children of the lower classes. On the promenade beside me, a nanny was holding her charges' hands firmly and telling them that they were most certainly not allowed a bag of sweets from the scruffy seller by the pier.

I stopped her as she passed. 'Excuse me,' I said, and she turned a sharp eyebrow towards me. 'I'm looking for a place named Castaway House.'

'I know it! I know it!' shouted the little boy, jumping up and dragging on his nanny's hand.

'Quiet!' she said sharply. He ceased immediately and sulked, poking out his lower lip. She smiled tightly at me. 'I'm sorry, I haven't heard of any Castaway House.'

'It's on – er . . .' I pulled out Alec's letter. 'Gaunt's Cliff.'

'It's just there.' The little boy pointed his free arm behind him. 'D'you see that hill? That's Gaunt's Cliff, and the house is at the very top. Father showed me, and he told me an awful story about –'

His nanny cuffed him on the ear. 'I told you once, I'm not telling you again.' She sighed. 'I'm afraid I can't help you there, sir. You'll have to ask somebody else.'

'That's quite all right.' I smiled uncertainly at the little boy and tipped my hat to the nanny. 'Thank you.'

Gaunt's Cliff, according to the nanny's charge, and I was quite prepared to believe him, was a steep hill that led off the seafront. Where the promenade continued beneath, the cliff pointed at an angle all the way up to the headland overlooking the sea. At the very top, the boy had said. I flexed my fingers and picked up my suitcase again. If he was wrong, I thought, he quite deserved that cuff about the ear.

I turned right and headed along the promenade. Great queues of charabancs were parked along the seafront, like giant perambulators waiting for monstrous babies. One drew up beside me, and from it a phalanx of flat-capped men and shawled women clambered out in a mountain of chatter and excitement and snaggle-toothed grins. I thought of the slow tick-tock of the mantelpiece clock in the parlour and the quiet rustle of Father turning the pages of his newspaper. I was already overwhelmed by Helmstone, and I had only just arrived.

I dodged between the charabancs and crossed the road towards where Gaunt's Cliff launched into the sky. I craned my neck, peering up, and was just squaring my shoulders in preparation when a voice from above called, 'Hi, you with the suitcase! Put that down at once!'

I looked up, startled, and saw my cousin Alexander Bray coming down the hill towards me, as blond-haired and handsome as always in an ivory suit, colour-splashed with a magenta handkerchief. He had his hands in his pockets and was smiling broadly. 'Sorry about that, old chap,' he said as he approached. 'Read the time completely wrongly on the telegram. Found your way all right, then?'

He took my hand and grasped it in both of his. 'Tickled to death you decided to come. Can't remember a thing about the funeral, of course. Drunk as a fox that day. Bit emotional, you know, Mother finally popping her clogs and all that. Father reminded me afterwards that I'd invited you to Castaway for the summer.'

'Oh.' I swallowed. 'I d-do hope that's all right.'

'It's wonderful. Can't imagine anything better.' He took the case from me and batted away my protests. 'My fault entirely. Meant for you to be met at the station with the motor car, but, y'know, we don't stand on ceremony here. This is a modern house, Robert, you'll see. I'll even carry my cousin's luggage for him.' He gestured with the case and then grimaced at the weight of it.

'It's awfully kind of you,' I said, panting, as I followed him up the hill, my lungs protesting slightly. I hoped that over the summer they would improve.

'Least I could do. Had no idea you'd been at death's door. What was it, chest trouble?' He patted his own. 'Heard you had to put off university for a year.'

'Yes. I'm . . . hoping to go up . . . this autumn.'

'Good. I suppose you know I was sent down from

21

Brasenose. But we don't talk about that, ha ha. Anyway, you're off to – where is it, Magdalen? Glad Grandfather put a little aside for you. Least the old miser could do. By the way, Clara's at home.'

This non sequitur threw me somewhat. 'Clara?'

'My wife,' he said. 'The new Mrs Bray.'

He spoke in such a strange way I had no idea what he really meant by that. 'I don't believe I met her at the funeral,' I said.

'She didn't come,' he said shortly. 'Still, she's happy enough now Mother's left me Castaway.'

The effort of the climb and the strength of the sun were combining to form prickles of sweat at the back of my neck. I shrugged off my jacket and held it over my arm. All I knew about Castaway House was that it had been the family's summer home; while my aunt had been alive, none of the Carver branch had ever been invited down.

'You still have the flat in London?' I asked him, remembering rumours of Alec's wild years there.

'Gave it up.' Again, there was that odd twist to his voice. 'Castaway's the main residence now. One can't gad about having flats when one's respectable, you know.'

I supposed he meant that marriage had lent him that respectability, although I was not entirely sure why. They had wed pretty much in secret, and when the news had emerged it had caused a fair commotion. According to the family grapevine, his new wife had been a minor actress on the London stage, appearing in shoddy musicals and, before that, those revues where, apparently, girls stood in a line, naked or near enough. Mother, whose own marriage had caused its fair share of commotion in its time, took great relish in chewing over the details, especially in relation to her brother, my uncle Edward.

'He's such a terrible snob,' she had said, her voice salty with pleasure. 'Viviane too, of course. They thought *you* were beyond the pale. Heaven knows what they must be making of the whole thing.'

The *you* in question was my father, sitting in his chair in the parlour with his pipe clamped between his teeth. He simply nodded, and I could tell he wasn't listening. I, on the other hand, was imagining an apparition of my cousin's mysterious new wife, naked, on the London stage, and was forced to concentrate very hard on this week's copy of *Bystander* in my lap in order to distract myself.

Naturally, I was intrigued to meet her, although Alec's distinct lack of enthusiasm curtailed my excitement a little. If she had no connections and no money of her own, I thought, then she must be very beautiful to have snared him.

Alec had been the golden-haired wonder of my childhood: five years older and unaccountably sophisticated. As a youth, it had never occurred to me to question the differences in our backgrounds; we lived in a modest red-brick villa with a woman who came in to 'do', and Uncle Edward and Aunt Viviane owned a porticoed, pillared wonder of a place in Lancaster Gate, with a mighty network of black-clad servants traversing the back stairs to answer every ring of the bell, in addition to what they termed their 'beach house' in Helmstone.

We had seen them rarely; once a year Mother and

I made a visit to London for a quick tour of sneering relatives. Alec usually blazed in and out, on the rare occasions he was home from school. He was often being expelled for misbehaviour, and I, who at that time was still playing at conkers with the kids from the neighbourhood, thought the very idea of being expelled from school unaccountably glamorous.

One day, when I was ten, Alec, apparently on a whim, decided to take me out for the day, leaving Mother in the company of my frail, cut-glass-voiced Aunt Viviane and the rattle of china cups. I had yet to be parcelled off to Crosspoint on the largesse of my grandfather, and still spoke with the local accent, much to Aunt Viviane's distress. I marvelled at the way Alec tossed out instructions to the chauffeur as he loaded me into the motor car.

'Natural History Museum, if you please, Fenner,' he said, sliding in beside me, and I looked out of the windows in wonder as we whizzed through the streets. I had never been in a motor car before, and drank in every second of the experience. Alec ushered me in through the giant doors of the museum and past dinosaur skeletons, but the biggest prize of the day was being in the company of my cousin.

We returned to the diplodocus on Alec's request, and stood for a while looking up at it. He'd seemed a little distracted the entire day, although as I barely knew him I could not be sure that this was not just his way.

'I expect I'll be dead soon, anyhow,' he said. This seemed to be the conclusion of several minutes' internal questing, but I felt rather alarmed.

'Are you poorly?' I said. I knew that Aunt Viviane was

highly strung – nerves, Mother called it – but Alec had always seemed in the prime of health.

'If the war continues,' he said, by way of explanation. 'They're talking about conscription. Perhaps it'll all be for the best, dashed to smithereens in front of a German machine gun.'

'They won't make you go,' I said. 'Will they? Not until you leave school.' The war, to me, was an adult's preoccupation. I knew of classmates' elder brothers who'd gone off to France. Sometimes those same classmates had been absent from school, and the teacher had told us in a solemn voice that we had to pray for the fallen but never to mention the matter to Huggins, or Wilberforce, when they came back to school next week. To me, the war was happening somewhere else.

Alec shrugged. 'Who knows?' he said. 'I'm sure everybody would be happy if I disappeared.'

'I wouldn't,' I said stoutly, and he smiled and ruffled my hair.

'Thank you, Robert. When people have already decided you're a bad lot, you may as well continue in the same line, do you see?'

I did not see, not at all, but I nodded anyway and tried, unsuccessfully, to emulate Alec's shrug. 'Mother wishes I'd never been born,' he said darkly. 'She's found some new child to take my place, so I've heard.'

This sounded so unlikely, even to my immature ears, that I said squeakily, 'That can't be true.'

He smiled down at me coldly. 'She's always rather wanted someone who'd appreciate all her . . . her . . .' He waved a hand in the air to articulate the words he was unable to find. 'Anyway, I'm a disappointment, so I may as well go to war.'

'Please don't go.' My hand crept out of its pocket and felt his sleeve.

He smiled at me again, more warmly this time. 'All right, Carver, if you really don't want me to, I won't.'

As it turned out, Alec turned eighteen three months before they declared the Armistice. He was on the boat train to France when they held the entire battalion up at Dover for twenty-two hours before sending them to Gloucestershire, where he worked out his conscription stamping envelopes. Despite his gloomy protestations at that time, I had always considered him the luckiest of people, and even now, climbing up the steep slope of Gaunt's Cliff, thinking of the house he had just inherited and the actress he had just married, I felt privileged once again to share a space in his sunshine.

'Here we are,' he said finally. 'Welcome to our humble abode. It's only half the size of the Lancaster Gate place, of course, but I hope you find it suits you well.'

I breathed heavily, waiting for my lungs to come to rest. We were at the crest of the cliff. To my left, a railing separated us from the promenade far below, the waves breaking on the shore and the spindly finger of a pier glistening in the brisk sunshine. Ahead, the road ended abruptly and became a path leading along the cliff edge beside an ugly churned-over field. To my right, a long terrace of Regency houses spilled all the way back down the hill.

The topmost one of these was larger than the others and painted a buttermilk yellow, reflecting a mellow light in the early summer sun. It was about six storeys high, with a crenellated roof and a pillared doorway. There was a stained-glass decoration over the door in an art nouveau style, with a text I could not quite make out from across the road. As I was peering at it, the door swung open and an auburn-haired manservant descended the steps and came down the path towards us.

'Scone!' Alec crossed the road and put my case on the pavement, where it was picked up by the servant, presumably the butler. 'Take this up to the fifth floor, would you?'

Scone nodded. 'Shall I show Mr Carver the way also?'

'Good idea.' Alec ushered me on to the path. 'What d'you say I give you an hour or so to rest, and then I can take you for a drink in the town, and head back in time for dinner at eight?'

'That sounds . . .' I thought of the myriad chores bestowed upon me back at home, even during my long illness. 'Absolutely wonderful.'

'Good stuff. I'll knock on your door. Here, d'you like this?' We were walking up the steps now; he waved overhead at the stained glass, which I could now see displayed the name of the building. 'Mother put that in when she inherited Castaway. Loved the place, you know. Always hated London.'

I crossed over the threshold and found myself standing on an oriental-style rug, beneath which peeped the black-and-white chequered flags of a large hallway. Sunlight beamed in coloured lozenges through the stained-glass window. There was a mahogany sideboard upon which stood a silver platter for post, and above it was a mirror, curled about with cupids and leaves. So swiftly I barely noticed him, Scone took the jacket from my arm and hung it on the row of pegs between the first and second front doors.

'Dining room here,' said Alec carelessly, indicating a half-open door to his left. 'Scone'll show you the rest. I'm going to take a turn in the garden.'

He winked at me, and I watched him walk along the passageway and through a door further along. 'This way, sir,' said Scone, and I followed him past a gleaming brass gong at the foot of the stairs. The banisters were polished to a deep sheen and ended with a rather lovely snail-like flourish at the end. The stairs were carpeted a deep red, and the walls were hung with various paintings. I wondered if Alec had inherited the lot wholesale from his mother or if some of these were the new Mrs Bray's touches. I wondered what her taste, as a former actress, was like.

On the first floor there was a small landing, illuminated by a window behind the stairs, and a closed door ahead of us. 'The drawing room, sir,' said Scone, separating each word as if it were pickled in vinegar, and I frowned to wonder that a mere room could draw such disapproval. He pointed to the door to our side. 'And here is the library. Mr Bray wishes you to make full use of it.'

Up we went, Scone indicating Mr Bray's bedroom and the bathroom, which he showed me with some pride. 'Very modern, sir,' he said, indicating the hot-water geyser to fill the bath. He insisted on showing me how to turn the taps on and off, both there and on the wash basin. 'Right hand for the cold, left hand for the hot.'

'Excellent,' I said, as if I were used to such conveniences and not the freezing wash of school or the tin bath in front of the fire at home.

On the next landing, Scone merely murmured, 'The third floor here,' waving a hand at the closed doors, and I presumed this contained Mrs Bray's bedroom and perhaps some other private abode. We continued up to the fourth floor, where Scone indicated the study and 'Mr Edward Bray's bedroom'.

'How often does he visit?' I asked, maintaining a fake smile, hoping his stays were as infrequent as possible. My uncle was one of those men who enjoyed the state of being in a permanently foul mood, and being widowed so young had done nothing to improve his temper.

'He has not yet found the time,' said Scone mildly. 'We hope we will see him at some point during the summer.'

'Yes, quite,' I muttered, and thought with some relief that Uncle Edward would probably see it as an indignity of the highest order to have to stay on one of the upper floors of a house that had once been his own, never mind that he no doubt considered said mistress of that house to be several rungs lower than him, socially.

The fifth floor was the highest in the house, although at the top of another short flight of stairs was a closed door that I presumed led up to the servants' quarters in the attic. There were two doors on the fifth floor, one ahead and one to our right. Scone opened this one, and I found myself in a pleasantly furnished room, with a canopied double bed, a fireplace, a writing desk and a sash window that was slightly open, letting in a cool breeze. Scone placed my suitcase on the bed and said, 'Would you like me to unpack, sir?'

'No, no,' I said hurriedly, uncomfortable with the attention. 'I'm quite all right now, thank you.'

'Very good. Shall I send up some tea?'

I grinned. 'That would be marvellous.' I looked around. 'You're very kind.'

Scone snorted slightly. I suspected I had gone too far, and I blushed. I stepped back out on to the dark wood of the hallway. 'What's this door here?' I said to Scone as he came out to join me.

He obliged by twisting the handle and opening it. 'The nursery, sir.'

I caught a glimpse of a cot in one corner and a bed in another, presumably for the nanny. There was also a single ink-stained desk and a much-abused rocking horse, almost bald and with pieces gouged out from his face. One of his staring eyes had been coloured yellow, the other green, by a destructive childish hand.

I turned back to Scone. 'I didn't know they had children,' I said, although I supposed there was not any particular reason for me to know.

'They don't, sir.' Scone smiled, and I had the impression he thought I was rather slow. 'This used to be Mr Bray's nursery.'

'Ah. Of course.' As I retreated from the room and Scone silently closed the door, I wondered why it had been kept as it was; although of course, I realized, blushing once more as Scone descended the staircase with aplomb, there would be future inhabitants of this nursery. I thought they might want to replace the horse, though; its mad staring eyes had rather unnerved me.

I went back to my room and investigated it thoroughly. Alec was right: his parents' London house was twice the size of Castaway, but that one, with its myriad, cavernous rooms and echoing hallways, had always intimidated me. This place, with its elegantly twisting staircase, oblong sash windows and dark polished floorboards, fitted me to a T.

I went to the window and looked out at the garden several storeys below. It was agreeably long and broad, with paved walkways that led off into hedged arbours. At the back I could see an ornamental pond bordered with wooden recliners and, in one corner of the garden, a vine-covered stone summerhouse. Directly below me were a glass-roofed conservatory and a terrace containing several wrought-iron chairs and a table.

As I watched, I noticed Alec appear on one of the paved walkways. He was trudging along, hands in pockets, and seemed to be lost in thought. I leaned against the window and watched him, mellow with affection. I felt I had never really got to know him properly; perhaps this summer, I would.

Outside my door I heard a clatter and a muttered sigh. I pulled it open and saw a young girl with her head bowed, holding a tray upon which was slopping a quantity of tea.

'I'm sorry, sir,' she said in a voice barely above a whisper. 'I'll get you some more right away.'

'It's quite all right.' I took the tray from her, at which she flinched, and set it down on the dresser. A flannel had been laid out for me, and I used that to mop up the tea, lifting the little pot and the china cup and saucer. 'There you go, no harm done.'

Her chin was still stuck firmly to her chest. 'Thank you, sir. You're very kind, sir,' she whispered again.

I laughed. 'Let's not make a mountain out of a molehill, eh? What's your name?'

Her eyes darted left and right as if seeking some sort of escape. Her hair, tucked under its mob cap, appeared to be the colour of straw. 'Agnes, sir. I've only just been made parlourmaid, what with I was under-housemaid before, and I ain't that used to the trays, see . . .' She trailed to a halt, as if realizing she had said several sentences too many.

'Well, pleased to meet you, Agnes. My name's Carver. I'm Mr Bray's cousin; I'll be staying here for the summer.'

'Yes, sir.' Infinitesimally, she edged backwards to the door.

I felt thoroughly awkward now, as if I'd pinned her up against the wardrobe and attempted to ravish her. 'Well . . . er . . . I thought perhaps you didn't know.'

'No, sir. Is that all, sir?'

She barely waited for my nod before she vanished from the door. I sighed, and was about to dismiss her from my mind when, quite without warning, I found myself out in the corridor, calling, 'Listen, Agnes.'

She turned back in her hurry along the landing, looking rather like a sparrow trapped in a house. 'Yes, sir?'

I smiled. 'I'm sure you'll get used to everything in no time.'

She breathed, waiting for my next command, and when none came she allowed a nod of her head. 'Thank you, sir,' she whispered, and disappeared out of sight. I shook my head and poured a cup of tea. I could never quite get the hang of the whole servant etiquette thing; they seemed to take it as a personal insult if you tried to be too civil to them. Then again, the girl Agnes looked as if she'd be scared of her own shadow.

I drank my tea, unpacked and visited the bathroom. I washed my face in hot water, a little unnerved by the dreadful clanking noise this unleashed from the geyser. As I still had some time, I went back to the bedroom, pulled the chair up before the mirror and attempted a quick little self-portrait. I liked to think my skills were coming along somewhat, but all the same, when I had finished and compared the picture with the reflection before me, I wondered who it was I'd actually drawn. Determined not to let the failure of the sketch bring me down, I folded it away to look at later, and decided to walk down through the house to meet Alec.

I was reaching the first-floor landing, thinking only of what dinner at eight might consist, when the drawing-room door opened and a woman stepped out; the woman, presumably, whose marriage to my cousin had caused such terrible excitement in the family, Mrs Alexander Bray.

She breathed in sharply when she saw me. She was not as tall as I had expected, and had a pale, pinched face with an expression akin to a squeezed lemon. A pattern of spots dimpled her forehead. Her hair was shortish and dark, and hung in two lank folds either side of her scalp. She was wearing a jade-green gown in some floating material, with furred cuffs, and she wrapped it about herself now with nails painted the colour of blood.

I held out my hand. 'I'm so glad to meet you at last. Robert Carver, Alec's cousin.'

She looked down at my hand as if I were offering her a dead fish. 'I know who you are, Mr Carver,' she said in an ice pick of a voice.

'Oh, good,' I said, grinning foolishly. I let my hand

33

drop. Behind her, I caught a glimpse of a beautiful blue-and-gold drawing room, a huge gilt mirror leaning at an angle above the fireplace.

She pulled the door shut tightly against her back. 'You're the poor relation who's come to sponge off my husband for the summer.'

I stared at her. 'I . . . I assure you that I'm not . . . that I wouldn't . . .'

She raised a palm. 'Please. I really couldn't care less what your motives are. However, if my dear, darling father-in-law has sent you to spy on this house, then you can tell him from me that if that's the price of my husband's allowance, he can fuck himself up the arse with it. Thank you.'

And with that she glided past me and continued towards the stairs.

I gaped at the space she had left, a steady heat rising from my chest to my neck. I gripped the edge of the banister to steady myself. Horribly, I felt tears prick the insides of my eyes and blinked them quickly away. I swallowed and then, from below me, I heard Alec's voice and walked down the stairs, holding on to the rail as I went.

'You're here!' He was in the hallway, grinning up at me. 'Shall we . . . I say . . .'

I walked straight past him. I pulled open the front door, headed down the steps and marched along the path, out through the gate and across the road to the railings that held the cliff back from the sea.

'Robert! Robert, what's the matter?'

I heard Alec behind me. My breath was very hot and very fast. My knuckles were white on the rail. He landed beside me, his face half-amused, half-concerned. 'You marched out of there as if you had a hand grenade up your backside.'

Unwittingly, this brought forth the image Mrs Bray had evoked with her foul mouth, and I grimaced. 'I can't stay. I'm sorry, but I shall have to get the first train back tomorrow.'

'Why on earth . . . ?' His open face crumpled into a frown. 'Oh, no. Tell me she didn't. Tell me my wife hasn't said anything to you.'

'She . . . er . . .' I coughed with the force of the emotion. My lungs were stuck fast: the old problem, always recurring when I was under extreme stress. I felt the cool metal of the railing and used that to calm my breaths, in and out, in and out. Finally, I said, 'She accused me firstly of being a . . . well, a sponger, and secondly of spying on behalf of your father.'

'Oh, Lord.' Alec put his elbows on the railings and his hands over his eyes. Eventually he said, 'I'm so sorry, Robert.'

I shook my head, wanting to say it was quite all right but unable to find the words. 'If it had even occurred to me you might think I was . . . well, I would never . . .'

'Don't pay her any attention. She was only saying it to upset you. I mean, talk about hypocrisy. The woman's the biggest parasite I've ever met.' He looked up at me. 'I'm sorry to say this, Robert, but the cliché holds true. Marry in haste, et cetera, et cetera.'

I remembered once, long ago, going out with Grandfather to shoot rabbits and coming across one, its eyes stitched wide into its face as it looked down the barrel of my rifle. I felt like that rabbit now. 'I'm afraid I don't quite understand.'

'Don't you?' He fiddled inside his jacket pocket, took out a tin of cigarettes and offered me one. I shook my head. He fitted it inside his lips, lit it and said, 'I thought I'd show the whole stuffy lot of them – you know, Father, Mother, all the rest. If one loves the girl, I thought, who cares if she's an actress or a road sweeper or a bloody farmhand? She saw me coming, Robert, and now she's yoked to me and she hates me and hates anyone associated with me, and unfortunately you received the brunt of that and I'm sorry.'

I looked down over the rail at the dots of people on the promenade below and breathed a lungful of precious air. 'She seemed to think your allowance might be in jeopardy,' I said.

'Father's been threatening it ever since I married her.' Alec sniffed. 'She must be scared stiff about the chance of being poor again.'

'Well, anyway,' I said. 'You do understand that I couldn't possibly stay now?'

Alec put his hand over mine on the rail. 'You must,' he said. 'I've been feeling absolutely mad, shut up in that place with just the two of us and the servants chewing over every little detail. And look, she's either out of the house or gone on some mysterious errand she doesn't care to tell me about. You won't even see her.'

'I can't,' I said. 'I didn't realize ... that is, I wouldn't want to ...'

My inarticulacy was saved by Alec muttering under his breath, 'Oh, damn it,' and looking past me, down the hill.

'What is it?' I turned and saw a bearded, middle-aged man wearing a crumpled hat and round-rimmed spectacles striding across the street towards us. He waved exaggeratedly, although we stood only a few yards from him. 'Good afternoon, Mr Bray!'

Alec nodded dispiritedly. 'Dr Feathers.'

The man turned to me and beamed broadly. 'Don't tell me, this is the famous cousin. How d'you do? Awfully pleased to meet you.'

He pumped my hand vigorously. Alec sighed and said, 'Robert, this is our neighbour Dr Feathers. My cousin, Robert Carver.'

'Here for the summer, are you, Mr Carver?'

'Er . . .' I hesitated. Alec leaped in.

'Yes, he is, and we're both terribly glad to have him here.'

'Marvellous.' The doctor beamed. 'If you have any health problems, you know where to come. Surgery's directly next door.'

He turned and indicated the house attached to Castaway, a smaller mirror image of its neighbour.

'Oh – um – thank you,' I said, slightly unnerved.

'Actually, Robert's in perfect health, aren't you, Robert?' said Alec, nodding firmly.

'Indeed?' Feathers looked slightly crestfallen. 'How is the charming Mrs Bray? Is she well?'

'Quite well, thank you. We're all well.' Alec tapped his foot impatiently.

'And the servant situation? Doris . . .' And here the doctor turned to me. 'Our head parlourmaid; we're not blessed with a Scone, unfortunately. Doris says your under-housemaid's had a sudden promotion to fill the gap. What's her name? Agnes?'

Alec blinked. 'You appear to know more about our household than we do,' he said, attempting a laugh. 'Anyway, my wife deals with the servants. You'll have to ask her, I'm afraid.'

The doctor beamed, not fazed in the slightest by Alec's rebuff. 'According to Doris, the girl looks as if she might drop down dead any day now.'

Alec tightened his lips. 'If she feels unwell, we'll call you immediately, you can guarantee that.'

'Good.' Dr Feathers rocked back on his heels. 'We must take good care of our servants, or how on earth do we expect them to take good care of us, hmm?'

'Absolutely,' said Alec. 'Now, we must be getting along.'

He took my arm and tried to wheel me past the doctor, who said, 'Oh, Mr Carver . . .'

Alec rolled his eyes. I stifled a smile and said, 'Yes?'

'I'm sure your cousin has told you that the Featherses will be holding a modest dinner in a few weeks' time. We're expecting the mayor, by the way.' He nodded significantly at me. 'We would be extremely honoured if you would do us the pleasure of attending.'

'Thank you,' I said. 'Although I'm not sure if I'll still be in Helmstone.'

'He will be,' said Alec. 'And if the mayor's going to be there, I don't think Carver will be able to stay away.'

I coughed back a snort of laughter. Dr Feathers smiled broadly. 'I'll send the invitation over tomorrow.'

'Wonderful,' called Alec, dragging me downhill alongside him. 'See you soon.'

I was in time to see the doctor bow slightly before Alec pulled me out of sight. We walked down the hill in a dignified silence before spluttering into laughter once we were far from earshot. I laughed so much I was forced to hold on to the rail once more until my lungs had calmed down. 'The man's such a snob,' said Alec. 'Hated me when I was a kid, you know. Always complaining to my parents about my behaviour. Now I own Castaway he thinks I'm the cream of the crop.'

'Does he always tout for business like that?' I asked.

Alec puffed out his lips. 'He used to treat the servants for a pittance,' he said, 'back when Mother owned Castaway. I think his nose has been rather put out of joint we've not yet called on his services. It's my opinion he's a terrible doctor; probably killed more patients than he's saved.'

'That's why you didn't let on about . . .' I tapped my chest. 'The old problem.'

'You'll be all right,' said Alec. 'Fresh air and sunshine, that's what you need.'

'Not much of either at home,' I said. 'The house is riddled with damp; my own doctor said that was half the problem.'

'In which case,' he said casually, 'a summer spent by the seaside is exactly the tonic.'

I paused. 'Your . . .' I began. 'I mean, Mrs Bray . . .'

'I'm asking you as a favour,' he said. 'I need – well, I need somebody in the house who doesn't hate the sight of me. And do you know what? I can put up with her insulting me, but I won't allow her to insult my family. And if you do leave on that account I – well, I might just throw her back into the gutter where she belongs.'

'Please don't,' I said quickly. I thought of us standing in front of the diplodocus, and the way I had stared up at my hero Alec, goggle-eyed, thinking him the very paragon of worldliness. 'Look, there's no point in my leaving immediately, anyhow.'

Alec grinned. 'There's a good chap.'

'I can't promise anything,' I added, and he nodded, although I had the sense he was hardly listening.

'You'll like Helmstone,' he was saying. 'It's a small place, but it'll give you what you need.'

'Health and sunshine?' I supplied. We were approaching the bottom of the hill now, and stopped for a second. From somewhere unseen I heard an organ grinder's wheezy tune.

'Pleasure,' he said. 'Pleasure of all kinds. Mind you, I'm not saying that's necessarily a good idea.'

I wondered what he meant, but he was already walking away from me across the road. I hurried to catch up. 'The thing is . . .' I began, but he wasn't listening to me.

'That's enough sea air,' he said. 'Now let's have a drink.'

He disappeared inside a narrow opening between two shops and I followed him, the darkness swallowing up the sun. As I walked behind him down a tiny alleyway, I remembered the rabbit again, but this time after it had been shot. It had been hanging by its legs in Grandfather's barn, its eyes glassy as it waited to be skinned, and I had the unnerving sensation that I knew exactly what that was like.

3
1965

Twenty-four hours after the cliff-top storm had nearly flung me into the sea, I stood inside the tea kiosk on the edge of the fun park, shivering in my inadequate cardigan as the wind battered the tin roof and howled along the walkways between the rides.

To my left, the merry-go-round creaked in an endless circle to 'Camptown Races', one solitary rider clinging on to a pole spiked through a grinning porcelain horse. In front of me, through the kiosk's hatch, I could see the bored lad who worked the dodgems bounding from empty car to empty car. He waved at me as he jumped about, going faster and faster, and I waved back and felt bad that I'd worked opposite him for six weeks and still couldn't remember his name.

I looked at my watch. Ten more minutes until my job was over for good. It felt as if there were ten minutes until the end of summer, which was silly because summer had packed itself up a few weeks ago, high-kicking its way into the horizon, leaving behind it a squalling storm, a miserable dribble of coach tours, and day-tripping families marching along the prom with grim, workman-like faces.

There were still a few retired couples holidaying here, such as the ones approaching the kiosk now, wound into overcoats, she with a purple headscarf pulled tightly under her chin, and he with a pencil moustache. As I took two chipped cups and saucers down from the hooks over my head and held them under the tea urn, the husband eyed me narrowly. 'Are you a local girl, by any chance?'

'Not exactly,' I replied, topping up the sludgy tea with hot water from the other urn. 'I'm from – well, the suburbs, I suppose. Petwick, it's called.'

'Thought so.' His moustache twitched. 'You're far too well spoken to be from this dump.'

'Eric!' His wife gave me an embarrassed smile.

'It's true.' He hunched his shoulders inside his overcoat. 'This place – here, d'you remember it during the war, Frances? Really something, this place was, even back then when you couldn't swim in the sea.'

'It's fine,' whispered his wife, pink-faced. 'It's fine.'

'Is this what we fought for?' He took in the fun park with a sweep of his arm – the dodgems, the merry-go-round – and ended back at the kiosk with a limp shudder and a baleful glare at his drink. 'To be served tea in a chipped cup?'

'I'll change it,' I said, glad Mrs Hale wasn't around to hear, and that he hadn't noticed the sugar bowl, stuck fast inside a sticky ring of granules adhering to the counter.

'Hmm,' he muttered, barely mollified, and as he turned to his wife for her purse he said, obscurely, 'Now. It was Shipwreck.'

'No, no.' She handed me a two-shilling piece and, as they turned away with their cups and saucers to find a seat, I distinctly heard her say, 'Castaway. I'm sure it was Castaway House.'

'What's that?' I said, leaning over the counter, but the

wind whipped my voice away from them. They were talking about a scandal, a tragedy, some sort of mystery. My heart quickened; Johnny and Star – it had to be them, that mysterious pair.

'What a day!' Mrs Hale was approaching from the promenade, her fist bristling with keys, drowning out the couple's talk. 'Oh, Rosie, it would be wonderful if you could stand a little straighter. I don't want people to think I'm exploiting a cripple.'

'I am standing straight,' I protested, but Mrs Hale was not listening. The ties of her headscarf flapped in the wind, sending wisps of grey hair skittering across her forehead. She disappeared around the side of the kiosk and a second later came in through the door. Her stilettos rattled on the metal floor.

'How's it been?' she said, and without waiting for an answer opened the cash box. 'That's awful. Goodness, you didn't give anyone the wrong change, did you?'

'Of course not.' I handed her the paper bag upon which every transaction had to be written.

'That's terrible.' Mrs Hale studied the bag with a beady eye. 'How am I going to pay my bills on that?'

'Oh well,' I said. 'I expect we'll all be blown up in a nuclear holocaust soon.'

She gave me a sideways glance. 'Was that supposed to cheer me up?'

I shrugged. 'You know, live for the moment and all that.'

'I remember when I used to think the same,' she said to herself. 'Anyway, did you want this morning job at the hotel, or will you be too busy marching for unilateral disarmament to do some washing-up?'

'Oh no,' I said quickly. 'I still owe my rent this week.'

'It's only part time: half past six until half past ten. Tuesdays off. Start tomorrow if you like.' She handed me two ten-bob notes for today, and said, 'What's this cup doing in the bin?'

I tried not to think about getting up at dawn tomorrow, and pointed to the couple shivering at a table by the railings. At least I only had to go next door. 'They complained. Said it was chipped.'

'Some people are so fussy.' Mrs Hale fished out the cup and put it back on the side. 'By the way, do you want a tin of soup to take home?'

I paused, in the middle of untying my apron. 'I'm sorry?'

She was holding one of the giant wheels of soup tins that we heated up to serve customers on the tiny gas flame in the kiosk. 'I can't leave anything in here over the winter; you may as well have it.' She dumped it on the counter. 'It's not too heavy.'

This was a lie, but I only fully realized it once I had already left the kiosk and was staggering along to the beach. Still, it was soup. Not that I particularly liked tomato soup, but . . . oh well, it was soup.

As I passed the couple, I remembered their mention of my home. I hovered nearby, balancing the tin on the railings, and said, 'I was just wondering, what were you saying about Castaway House? It's where I live, you see.'

'I told you!' The woman made a nudging gesture with her elbow. 'I said it was called Castaway House.'

Her husband humphed, and I said, 'Has something happened there? I've only been in the place since August.'

The woman laughed. 'Oh, this was a long time ago,

love. I'm going back to when I was a little girl. We used to come to Helmstone for our summer holidays. Eating fish and chips, we were, and there was Dad, reading out loud from the newspaper they were wrapped in. I can't remember the exact details, but ooh, it was a fascinating story.'

I picked up the tin again, disappointed. 'I thought it was a recent thing.'

Her husband snorted. 'Anything that happened before these young 'uns were born is ancient history. Might as well be Roman times as far as they're concerned.'

His wife reached across the table and squeezed his hand. 'We're war relics, you and me, eh?' She smiled up at me, and I thought, as much as I didn't want to, that she was right.

I had a vague idea of donating my soup tin to someone in one of the beach huts, so I walked down the steps, a brisk wind rattling through my already knotted hair. Debris had been blown on to the sand overnight from the sea; chunks of bracken criss-crossed the beach like spidery handwriting.

The donkeys were clumped together, flicking sand out of their eyes, their garishly coloured saddles rather incongruous against the grey of the sky and the sea. A painted sign said, BEACH RIDES 5/-. A woman was sitting in a deckchair beside the sign, reading a paperback novel and eating a Chelsea bun.

I walked along by the abandoned fishermen's arches and then on to the walkways in front of the rented beach huts. A council sign stated that all of them had to be vacated by the thirtieth of September. I peered into one and saw a woman packing a gas stove into a wooden crate.

The rest were empty, and so I carried on along the sand, passing a father holding the hand of a child in a bonnet. 'Not until you apologize to your mother,' I heard him snap as they passed me, and he gave me a harried look, the child pouty-faced and miserable.

I turned and looked up at the fun park, the silent dodgems, the creaking horses. The kiosk was a lonely bunker from here, and with its corrugated tin roof it gave the impression of a wartime lookout post. People said there'd been barbed wire strung across the beach during the war, in case of invasion. I wondered what it must have been like on those boiling days of summer, when the sea turned turquoise and licked the fringes of the shore, barred from reach by looping cylinders of steel.

From here I could also see across the road to the skeleton of the new Majestic Arcade. Scaffolding was caged around it, but between the planking and metal struts a concrete butterfly was emerging from the chaos within. I'd seen the architect's plan pinned to the lower reaches, a silver dream of a pleasure castle with its name in lights across the door, and stick-thin young people looking up at it in wonder. Mrs Hale was very voluble on what she thought of the destruction of the grand old hotel, but I felt excited by the banner the council had had printed and put up on every new construction in the town: *A Brand-New Helmstone for a Brand-New Age*. I almost felt I was living in the future, when a mile of concrete walkways would span overhead and everybody would live on protein pills and yoghurt.

I walked as far as the broken pier, hacked in two during the war to stop aircraft landing and never again mended, and then I turned up the steps back to the prom. I thought I'd probably have missed Susan and Val, as they usually went home to their mums for Sunday dinner, but I was trying to make sure. I'd crept out of bed while they were still asleep, and hoped it would be a while before I had to listen to a lecture from Susan about not borrowing Val's boots to go out in the mud, or using her own Arôme de Violettes to fragrance my bathwater.

'Hey, dollface.'

I turned. Across the road, leaning against the doorway of Riccardo's with a cigarette dangling between two long fingers and her lips puffed into a pout, was Star. Her red-and-black striped dress bounced off her angular hips, and she had an oversized cap pulled over the new geometric hairdo she'd had done in London. She looked like a colour plate from a fashion magazine.

I scowled, but was unable to tear my gaze from her. She winked at me and jerked her head towards the coffee shop's interior, drawling in the same stupid put-on American accent she'd used just now, 'Why don'tcha come in and share some ice cream?'

I narrowed my eyes and marched across the road. 'You've got a nerve –' I began.

'Why the soup?' she interrupted, this time in her normal voice. 'Don't tell me; it's for a happening. We'll pass it round the room while reciting poetry backwards.'

'Eh!' Riccardo himself was coming past the door carrying three cups of coffee up one arm. 'You come or you go. You don't leave the door open so we all die of the hypothermia, okay?'

Star grinned sloppily. I thought she was probably

stoned. '*Va bene*,' she said, throwing her hands in the air. 'I'm over there, Rosie. I've got a booth.'

She turned and went inside. I transferred the tin into my other arm and stomped after her, determined I wouldn't let her get round me again.

At this time of day, Riccardo's was usually full of the after-school crowd: kids playing footsie with each other on the high stools by the counter, straggles of boys exclaiming loudly over the fruit machine. On a Sunday, however, the youth of Helmstone melted away and the coffee shop was a quiet hum of parents and well-behaved children in Peter Pan collars and velvet dresses. The steam from Riccardo's whirring coffee machine had bubbled mist up the plate-glass windows, making me feel as if we were on a ship bobbing on the icy waters of the North Sea.

'So . . .' I dumped the ugly tin out of sight on a chair and sat down, rubbing my arms to release the ache in them. 'What's your excuse this time?'

'*Ciao*, Antonia!' Star waved her cigarette at Riccardo's tatty wife, who nodded at her from her constant position behind the bulging trays of multicoloured ice creams beneath the glass cover. 'How're the *bambini*?'

She exchanged a few words in cod-Italian with Riccardo's wife, and I took the opportunity to watch Star, because even when I was annoyed with her, Star was still somebody you wanted to look at. It wasn't just her expensive clothes, which I presumed Johnny must fund as Star never seemed to have a proper job; it was the whole of her. She was tall, but not awkward; her limbs seemed to fold themselves around objects in just the right sort of way, and her face – well, it wasn't flawless, but it was beautiful all the same.

The brim of her silly cap was too large for her to see properly out of, so she lifted her head as she turned towards me. I caught a flash of her huge violet-coloured eyes. 'What were you saying?'

'I was asking you,' I said, as icily as I could, 'why you stood me up on Friday night without so much as a note. But it's all right. I've decided I couldn't care less either way.'

'Friday night . . .' She squinted at the cake stand and flicked her cigarette over the tin tray, scattering ash across the table. 'Friday night.'

All of a sudden, her brow seemed to collapse. She put her forehead on to the Formica. I was silent. From the booth beside us, a woman said, 'Give it here, Linda, you silly girl!'

After a while, still with her forehead down, I heard Star mumble, 'I feel awful. I'll never forgive myself.'

'You said that last time, remember? When we were supposed to go up to London for the day. And before that, when we were going to go night-swimming.' I shrugged, which was wasted, because she couldn't see me. 'But like I said, I don't care.'

I remained silent. She lifted her head slightly and pushed the ice-cream bowl towards me. 'You have it. It's pistachio.'

I looked down at the melting green gloop. 'Is that supposed to be an apology?'

She put her chin on one fist and looked up at me. 'Don't be like this, Rosie. What happened on Friday, it was un . . . un . . . oh, what's the word?'

'Unhelpful? Unutterably unreliable of you?'

She clicked her fingers. 'Unprecedented.'

49

'What d'you mean, unprecedented? You've let me down a ton of times before.'

'Oh, don't go all clever on me. I mean, I didn't know it was going to happen. I had a row with Johnny, and I completely forgot about our going to the One-Two.'

'Un-flipping-likely,' I muttered. Johnny and Star never rowed. They were the golden couple of Castaway House. All the same, I found I was picking up Star's spoon to scoop up pistachio ice cream, and licking it clean.

'I did, I really did.' She sat up further and ground out the end of her cigarette. 'And I'll make it up to you. Promise. We'll absolutely go this Friday, and we'll have a totally fab time. Okay?'

'You must think I'm some sort of gullible fool,' I said, finishing off the ice cream. 'I was knocking on your door for twenty minutes.'

'I don't think that, honestly.' She reached a hand across the table and stayed my fist, clamping it around the spoon. 'Don't be angry. I can't bear it.' Her eyes trembled, and I sighed.

'It's all right,' I muttered, 'I'm not angry.'

She smiled. 'Good.' Releasing my fingers, she snatched the spoon from me and pooled the last of the ice cream into her mouth, licking the steel clean. She clattered it into the bowl and said in a breezy tone, 'So you're coming upstairs? Johnny's out. We can make beans on toast and sit on the terrace.'

I *was* a gullible fool. I wished I could hold on to my bad mood, but I felt it melting just like the ice cream. 'Actually,' I said, trying to retain some aloofness, 'I've got commitments.'

'Commitments?' Star spoke as if the very concept were alien to her.

'I met an elderly man yesterday, in the hallway. I promised to visit him this afternoon.' I ignored the fact that not only had I absolutely no intention of visiting him, but I was sure he'd forgotten my existence the minute I'd disappeared from sight.

'You be careful. I know what these dirty old men are like.' She winked at me. 'Come up afterwards. We'll watch television tonight, and I'll be completely wonderful.'

The sunshine of her voice warmed me, despite everything – though it was no doubt also because Star and Johnny were the only people in the building who had a television set, and I missed *The Avengers* and *Ready Steady Go!* with an almost physical pain.

'Okay,' I said, 'but you'd better be,' and she giggled stupidly.

Afterwards, she pulled on her squeaky P. V. C. raincoat, tossed a few coins on to the table, and we left the café. Riccardo followed me out with the tin of soup, saying he most certainly did not want it as it would bring his reputation into disrepute, and I told her the story of dragging it with me from work, embellishing it and making her hoot with laughter. I realized that, despite all my good intentions, here I was, snared back inside Star's sticky net of friendship.

The wind notched up apace as we climbed Gaunt's Cliff, and I bent my head into it, battling my way upwards, holding the tin in front of me like a shield. Everyone said that you got used to the climb after a while, but I was still waiting for that to happen. 'Time to get out the winter woollies,' said Star, linking her arm through mine, and through the stale aroma of hashish and the new plastic of

51

the mac I found her real smell: cinnamon and cloves and blood orange.

'I haven't got any,' I said. 'They're all still at my mum's house.'

'We should go and pick them up.' She paused. 'If you don't want to see her, we can go when she's not in.'

'Hmm.' I didn't know how Star had intuited that. 'Maybe.'

She nudged me. 'By the way, you didn't tell me you had an admirer.'

I frowned. 'I don't. Unless . . .' I thought about my so-called commitment to that drunk, Dockie. 'You mean the old man? Did Johnny tell you what happened yesterday?'

She put a hand on my arm. 'Oh, God. Johnny never tells me anything these days. No, I mean the man in the white sports car. A Jag maybe, I'm not sure.'

I laughed, although my guts were creaking with unease. 'I don't know anyone who owns a white sports car.'

'Well, somebody knows you.' She sniffed a laugh. 'I was coming out of the house earlier on, and this chap was driving up the road and then back again, dead slow. I thought he was some sort of maniac at first, and then he stopped, leaned out and asked me if a Rosemary Church-ill lived at Castaway House.'

I wriggled free from Star and wrapped my arms around my chest as we climbed. 'What did he look like?'

'Erm . . . quite dishy. Dark hair. But old. Sort of thirty-ish.'

I felt as if the breath had been whipped from my lungs. 'Did you . . . did you say anything about me?'

Star shrugged. 'Just that you were at work. He said

okay, and thank you, and tootled off. Should I . . . ? I mean, was that all right?'

I looked out at the tossing waves below me to our left. 'It doesn't matter,' I said gloomily.

'Right. I won't mention him again, I promise.' I sensed behind her words an aching need in Star to discover exactly what was going on, but I stared fiercely ahead at the approaching Bella Vista guest house as if that were the only interesting thing in the world, with its faded red canopy drooping lopsidedly over the doorway and the sign on the pathway that said VACANCIES and had never, ever been changed.

'Disgusting,' muttered Star, and I jumped, startled, as if she'd seen into my soul, but she was looking at a herring gull in the middle of the Bella Vista's empty gateway, pecking at a fallen roof tile as if it were a morsel of fish. Either side of the gateway were two pillars in such a state of disrepair it was as if they were doing a dance of the veils, revealing crumbling brick innards within hints of grey plastering amid the mouldering paint on top. In fact, I thought, the entire terrace, all the way down the cliff, was falling to pieces, and it occurred to me that perhaps they ought to pull the whole lot down and start again, just as they'd done with the Majestic.

I saw a movement in the ground-floor window of the guest house. As I looked again, I realized an elderly man was standing there, watching us. I jumped, startled, but he merely nodded at me and raised his hand in greeting.

'Look,' I said to Star, indicating the old man. I raised my own hand and smiled at him.

'Mmm,' said Star. 'Listen, about that chap with the sports car –'

'Oh, God.' I looked up at the sky. 'It's starting to rain.'

I dashed ahead of her, not having a waterproof on, and ran up the steps to the house as drops started to fall. As I was fishing my keys from my bag I heard Star land beside me, breathy and curious.

'Are you all right?' she asked.

'I'm fine.' I blinked hurriedly up at her. 'Just, you know, thinking about my commitments.'

'Oh, the old man?' Star nodded at the tin I was resting on one hip. 'Hey, you could make him soup.'

I twirled the key ring on my finger until I found the battered brass one that opened the main door. 'I suppose . . . yes, I suppose I could.'

Star sighed. 'I wish I was like you. You're such a nice person.'

I wiggled the key in the lock and let us into the house. 'Oh, shut up.' I pushed on the light and wiped my feet on the mat. The blackboard above the telephone had no message, thank goodness.

She traced the snail-shell end of the banister with one finger. 'I mean it,' she said. 'You are nice. It's one of your best qualities.'

I glanced at her to see if she was teasing me, but her eyes were hidden beneath the brim of her cap. I thought about how I'd had no intention of visiting the old man, and revised my plan. A nice person would do what she'd promised to do, after all; at the very least I should check that he was all right.

Star was still avoiding my gaze; the air seemed thick with an odd sort of silence, but I wasn't quite sure how it had arrived. To break it, I said, 'Oh, by the way, you don't know who lives in the ground-floor flat, do you? Because whoever it is has the most awful whistle.'

'Um . . . no, I don't.' She climbed one stair. 'I meant what I said, you know.'

I looked up at her. 'About what?'

'This Friday. You'll love the One-Two. It's completely gear. For this old town, anyway.'

'You told me,' I said. 'It's in a basement just by the sea-front, and the walls are painted as if you're underwater, and the man who owns it is some ancient cat called George Basin.'

'That's it.' She looked at me now, from two steps up, and smiled. Her long fingers drummed the banister. I reached up, and as her fingers fluttered in my palm I felt an answering sensation in my belly.

'I'll be up shortly,' I said, and she grinned at me, before running up to the half-landing and disappearing at the corner, and I put the idea that I was a total idiot to a very small place at the back of my mind.

I peered down the dark hallway that led to the back of the building. I'd yet to go down to the basement; all the rooms there were singles, mostly occupied by people whom life had passed by, and consequently the social niceties too. I sometimes saw them in the hall, hurrying towards the back stairs with a half loaf of bread and a mad scowl on their faces.

Well, Star thought I was a nice person, and I would live up to that. I marched along the passageway and down the stairs, where the smell of old cabbage wafted up like the stench of despair. I climbed down into a long narrow hallway that continued behind me towards a chilly-looking bathroom with a mousetrap just over the threshold, and ahead of me all the way beneath the house towards the basement door.

To my right was another passageway, lit by one bare bulb attached to a looping wire pinned to the false ceiling. Flat Four, Johnny had said yesterday. It was the last door at the end on the right, with the number smeared on in white paint. Check he was still alive, I thought, make soup, leave. I took a breath and rapped with my knuckles on the bare wood.

There was no answer. I waited, and then knocked again. The timer light turned off, and I patted the walls between the door frames until I found the switch. 'Hello?' I called through the closed door. 'It's . . . er . . . it's Rosie. From yesterday?'

For a short while I thought my call might be met by yet more silence, but then I heard faint creaks from inside the room and a hacking cough that started and never seemed to end. Finally the doorknob turned, and a yellow eye beneath a wild grey eyebrow looked out. 'Is it the rent?' barked a cracked old voice.

'No.' I smiled at the yellow eye. 'It's me. Rosie.'

The door opened a shade further, revealing another eye and Dockie's red-veined nose. 'Were you sent by Mrs O'Shea?'

'Mrs . . . O'Shea?'

There was a noise from inside the room, a sort of strangled gargle. I heard a muffled oath, and then the door was flung open to its full extent, sending forth a reek of body odour and stale alcohol, and Dockie roared, 'Where the hell has my room gone?'

He was still wearing the stained overcoat he had worn

yesterday. Perhaps this was where the cabbage smell was coming from. He staggered out into the corridor and pointed a shaking finger towards the darkened space behind. 'My room has gone missing.' He clutched the wilds of his hair. 'Mrs O'Shea's. Tell me I am at Mrs O'Shea's. Ranelagh Road. Rathmines. Dublin. Ireland.'

I shook my head. 'None of the above, I'm afraid. You're in England.'

Dockie took in a deep, raggedy breath. His hand gripped the door frame. 'Oh, Lord,' he said, with a seashore of regret in his voice. 'What on earth have I done?'

He rested his forehead against the frame. I raised the tin and he blinked at it, trying to focus. 'I've brought soup.'

He grunted, and I took that to be an invitation. I entered the dark, foul-smelling room and said, with my breath held, 'I'm just going to open the window, if that's all right.'

He grunted again, and I put the tin down and walked to the lighter-coloured oblong at the end of the room. There were some nylon curtains covering the window; I yanked them apart, revealing a basement yard with nothing much in it but some corrugated iron sheets stacked against the far wall, rusting quietly, and an overgrown fern that was nodding under the weight of the rain.

I tugged at the sash window and pushed it up as far as it would go. A gust blew drizzle on to my face and rattled the curtains together on their flimsy runner. I pulled them apart once more, and turned back towards Dockie's new home.

I was standing in a small kitchenette, divided from the rest of the room by a half-partition. The kitchenette contained two gas rings, a sink, a few sagging cupboards and a small pull-down table, which was where I'd put the tin. Behind the half-partition was a single bed made up with a rough-looking blanket and one pillow, with planks for shelving overhead. Dockie remained in the doorway.

'You don't remember meeting me yesterday, I suppose,' I said.

He shook his head and ran his calloused hand across his eyes. 'I feel a little . . . my dear, could you tell me where I may locate the facilities of this establishment?'

'It's at the end of the hall,' I said. 'On the left.'

Dockie lurched into the hallway, then swung suddenly back towards me. 'I beg your pardon. Where did you say I was?'

'Helmstone,' I said. 'South of England.'

He squinted towards the end of the passageway. 'Helmstone,' he murmured. 'Helmstone.'

'Castaway House,' I said. 'That's the name of this place.'

He staggered away along the hall. I turned back to the window and gulped in lungfuls of damp air. I thought of how I could recount this tale of the confused old man to Star, already exaggerating the humour to make her giggle.

I investigated his lopsided kitchen cabinets and discovered the rusting spear of a tin opener in the drawer. I worked it into the metal of the soup can until I'd made enough of a hole to be able to pour some of it into the aluminium saucepan I discovered in the lower cupboard.

The gas sputtered into a squirt of flame and then died. I growled and leaned against the rain-spattered windowsill. Nothing else for it, I thought, as I opened my purse, pulled out a shilling and crouched down to slot it into the meter.

By the time Dockie returned, the soup was beginning to heat up nicely. He shuddered into one of the chairs at the pull-down table. 'I'm making you soup,' I said brightly. 'I put one of my coins in the meter.'

'Castaway House,' he said. 'I remember now. Helmstone, and Castaway House.'

'Oh, good.' I stirred the soup with a tarnished metal spoon. 'It was just a shilling, you know.'

'I stood at the wash basin. Right hand cold, left hand hot.' He held his hands out before him. 'I looked in the mirror, and I remembered.'

'Remembered?' I opened the cabinet and found a chipped cereal bowl.

'I remembered the gentlemen's facilities at Mulligan's.'

I poured the bright orange liquid into the bowl.

'I was there,' he continued, 'at the wash basin, looking in the mirror. A bright smear of graffiti on the wall behind. And that is when I knew, without a shadow of a doubt, that I had to go to Castaway House.'

I brought the bowl over to him. 'Ta-da!' I said, very proud of myself. 'Go on, eat it while it's hot.'

Dockie stared at the bowl. 'And from there, I took a taxi to the ferry terminal. That, I remember most clearly now. A one-way ticket. The coach journey to London. And another afterwards, to here. I remember all that, you see.'

'Good.' I handed him the spoon. 'If you don't eat, I'm going to be cross.'

'Oh.' He frowned at the spoon and then dipped it into

the bowl and ladled soup through a gap in his beard into his mouth. It appeared to take him some time to swallow, and then he said in a croak, 'I have a problem with my memory, you see.'

'Mmm, I'd noticed.'

He put down his spoon. 'My particular problem now is I cannot for the life of me remember *why* I thought it was a good idea to come here.'

'You said you had a story to tell. That's what you said yesterday.'

'That,' he said, 'is what a four-day bender will do to one. One wakes up having apparently rented a room in a strange town. I am an absolute fool. A stupid old bloody fool.'

'Well, you know . . .' I shrugged. 'Could happen to any of us.'

Dockie put the spoon into the soup again, raised it to his mouth and then lowered it. 'Castaway House, you said?'

'That's right. You said you'd been here before.'

'I know it.' He prodded his head. 'That name, it's as if a flower were blooming in my brain. I know the name so well, and yet every time I search for its origin, it escapes me. Do you understand? It's . . . I suppose one could say it's like a dream that runs away the more one tries to think about it.'

'You were talking about a newspaper or a magazine or something.'

'Ah.' He narrowed his eyes and then looked down at the overcoat he was still wearing, patting the pockets and taking things out, just as he'd done yesterday. I realized he was never going to eat the soup, and took it from him.

I left it on the side, just in case he fancied it later, as he laid upon the table the same collection of bus tickets, a grimy handkerchief, and the torn envelope containing the bundle of notes.

'What on earth . . . ?' He peeled through them and looked up at me. 'This is Frank's money. He left me all his savings in a strongbox when he died. To look after me in my dotage, he said. I must have brought the entire stock with me.'

'You shouldn't wave it around like that. People might take advantage.'

Dockie was tugging at his beard. 'I'm filthy. I must have travelled like this. Where are my clothes? Good God, this is awful.'

An idea wormed its way into my brain. I'd made soup, and while that had been a good turn, it was more of an accidental one really. Now I had the chance to do something properly worthy, to be the person Star imagined I was. 'I'll buy you some,' I said quickly, before I had the opportunity to change my mind.

He blinked at me. 'I'm sorry?'

'Clothes . . . and toiletries . . . and all those things you need.' I was already imagining Bradley's. I hadn't had the money to go into Bradley's for – well, for *months*. 'Oh, you must let me. I'll guess your size. It'll be so exciting.' I clapped my hands.

He swallowed, and pulled at his disgusting overcoat. 'Do I really look so terrible?' he murmured. 'Do I look like an indigent?'

'Well . . .' I peeled apart my thumb and forefinger. 'Perhaps a little.'

'Then . . .' He blinked at me again. 'You are right. I cannot go about like this.'

'I'll help you.' I nodded. 'You can trust me. I was Orchid Patrol Leader, you know. First Petwick Guides.'

'Of course, of course. You remind me of . . .' He frowned. 'I cannot remember who you remind me of, but you are trustworthy. That, I know.'

He flicked through the grubby wad of ten-bob and pound notes in the envelope. He muttered to himself and, I noticed with a giddy judder of excitement, added two fives to the collection before he held it out to me. 'Will this be enough? I am not yet cognizant of the cost of goods in this part of the world.'

I allowed the money to be crushed into my hands. 'That's . . . um . . . that's f-fine.' I hadn't handled this much money in – well, maybe ever. 'I'll have to go after work tomorrow. I'll come to you afterwards, okay? About midday. Guide's honour.'

He stumbled towards the bed and lay down full-length upon it, his badly laced boots still on his feet. 'By the way,' he mumbled, 'might there be any Buckfast around the place? Indeed any tonic wine, to revive me, so to speak?'

'I don't think *that's* a good idea,' I said primly, although I opened and closed cupboard doors, just for show.

'Then perhaps . . . I suppose you wouldn't want to make a purchase at the nearest public house, would you?'

I slammed one of the doors closed, and he added hurriedly, 'It was just a thought. Anyway, my dear, what is your name?'

His eyes were already shut. 'Rosie,' I said. 'Rosie Churchill.'

'Thank you, my dear Miss Churchill. My name –'

'I know.' I looked down at the rest of his money, spilling out of the torn envelope on the little table. 'Your name's Dockie.'

'Correct. I was born, you see, on the docks.'

There was a smudged square of paper on top of the pile of notes. As I looked closer, I saw it was a ruined photograph, sepia and almost obliterated by water or sunshine or just the passage of time.

I glanced at Dockie, but his eyes were still closed. Only the top right-hand corner of the dog-eared photo was at all clear, and it showed the blur of an ear and the mildewed top of a round forehead. That was all, but the proportion of the features – the tiny ear against the smooth head – was enough to convince me that the photograph was of a baby.

I eased the photo over. The back was a brown smudge, except for just one letter in the clear top left corner:

b

'Is this you?' I asked Dockie, but for answer I received only the steady in and out of a gentle snore.

I left the photograph on top of the pile of money and made my way out of the room into the dark of the passageway. As I pulled the door behind me, I realized I could hear someone crying.

I walked as quickly as I could back to the staircase, embarrassed that I'd overheard another person's misery. The sobs sounded like a woman's, although I couldn't be sure, and in any case I wasn't certain which sex would be worse. The crying seemed to chase me up the staircase, and I felt I could still hear it in the fresher air of the main hallway, although that must have been my imagination.

I climbed up again towards our flat, jangling my key to shake off the sound. It had been a desperate kind of crying, and awful to hear. I'd done a bit of it in my time, of course, but always silently, under the covers, while Susan and Val were asleep.

The kitchen door stood at a right angle to the bedroom door. I unlocked it, went in and closed it firmly, leaning my back against it and testing the silence for several seconds before verifying that the sobbing had been left behind.

The kitchen was my preferred room of the two, perhaps because the other girls were always in the bedroom, filling in 'What Type of Guy Is Your Man?' quizzes in their magazines or talking about how disgustingly fat they were. And now, although I had the flat to myself, I still liked the kitchen, with its large table in the centre, its rickety dresser against the left-hand wall, the floor-to-ceiling larder that needed a stepladder to get to its highest reaches.

I put my bag on the table and pulled out my purse. Dockie's notes crackled from within; it occurred to me what a very good con artist I'd be. In fact, I could filch some of his money right now. There'd been a pair of sandals in the window of Lady Lucinda for months, with white straps and a thick brass buckle, which I envisioned would turn me into the perfect dolly. Before I'd left home I'd nagged Mum for weeks to get them for me for my birthday; now it had come and gone, and every penny

I had was being spent on such boring essentials as food and rent.

I sighed and put the notes he'd given me at the bottom of my bag, where I wouldn't confuse them with my own. I was Rosie Churchill, and I was a good girl. I could be trusted.

I walked to the two sash windows that overlooked the back of the house, pulled one open, just as I'd done two floors below, and looked out. The basement well that Dockie's window gave on to was hidden from here by the old Victorian conservatory directly beneath me. The glass roof was covered in seagull droppings, and the paintwork was mouldering on the wood.

I leaned out further, clinging on to the underside of the windowsill for support, raindrops spattering the back of my head. The conservatory led on to a cracked terrace, and beyond that a garden overgrown with tangles of weeds and bushes. Plants splayed dangerously across paths; grass pushed up in the gaps between uneven paving stones. In an enclosed area was a stone bench encrusted with more seagull muck, overhung with the branches from the tree behind. Towards the end of the garden an ivy-laced stone storeroom sat in one corner near an empty oblong pond, the concrete lined with green slicks of slime. A deckchair had been left out there, abandoned on its side, and its canvas innards rattled back and forth in the wind.

The rain began pounding harder. I pulled myself back inside the room and remained by the window as the sky darkened further overhead. My fingers crept under the sill, tracing the grain in the wood, feeling ridges that had been gouged into it. The indentations curled, seemed linked together, and I realized eventually that they must be letters.

I sank to my knees on the gritty lino and peered at the underside of the windowsill. I was right: words had been etched into the wood beneath the sill and filled in with ink. They were very small, and I had to twist my neck at an awkward angle in order to make them out. It was dark in here; I should switch the light on but I was afraid of losing my place, and so I squinted at the awkwardly formed letters until finally, finally, they became utterly clear:

Robert Carver
is innocent

I straightened my neck, which clicked horribly. The words were a child's game, perhaps, or a silly joke. All the same, I wondered who Robert Carver might be, and who had etched the mysterious message.

Robert Carver. The name jumped into clarity. *R. C.!* Of course. I got to my feet, banged my head on the windowsill on the way up and staggered upright, clutching my scalp. It could be a coincidence, of course. They were fairly common initials – mine, for example – and this Robert Carver, innocent or not, might have nothing to do with the hesitant sketch made by the R. C. that I kept between the pages of an unread book.

All the same, I had a feeling. I looked again at the inked-in scribble. It certainly could be forty years old, although I supposed there was no way of knowing for sure. I got up and paced the kitchen excitedly, almost ashamed at being so eager over something that had happened such an achingly long time ago. So Robert Carver had arrived here, I theorized, and at some point someone had thought it necessary to tell – well, not the world, but certainly the underside of the window – that he was innocent.

But of what? That was the question. There were so many things a person could be innocent or guilty of – my crime, for one thing, although nobody would be scratching my name into wood in my defence.

I pulled out a chair and sat down, thinking about home and everything I'd left behind, the Sunday joint Mum would be cooking in the oven now, Frank Sinatra playing on *Two-Way Family Favourites*, me perhaps upstairs, chewing on the end of a pencil, frowning over how to conjugate a string of French verbs.

Rosie Churchill is innocent.

Not any more, I thought to myself. Not any more. All the same, Star thought I was a nice person, and Dockie thought I was good; and perhaps if they did, then I could believe it. And just in case we weren't all blown up by a nuclear bomb, maybe my future really would be space age and gleaming with concrete. I pulled my feet on to the chair, hugged my knees to my chest and imagined the disintegration of my past, wasting away like metal turned to rust by the relentless tide of the rain.

4
1924

I woke to a soft knock, mumbled an answer and then drifted back into the warm smell of fresh toast and the morning light on my face. I had the sense of velvet curtains being drawn back, I heard the slide and clip of them; and as my eyes shifted open I saw a shadow leave the room and close the door behind itself.

Beside me was a tray with buttered toast and a steaming pot of tea. All right, I thought, pulling myself to a seated position, this was all very ostentatious and unnecessary, but it certainly bested having to stumble downstairs for your first cup of the day. I sat up in bed, feeling rather like a roosting crow, in my nest at the top of the house. Perhaps in a moment I would wake up and be back in my tiny bedroom at home, with the noise of the milkman's dray passing in the yard below and Elsie, my mother's help, shouting across the wall to the neighbours.

After a while I hauled myself out of bed, and washed and shaved in the bathroom below. Alec had said I might encounter his wife at breakfast. 'I'm skipping the whole thing at the moment: the sight of her gives me indigestion,' he'd said last night. She had been absent for dinner as, apparently, was usual at the moment, and it had been a relief to get drunk with Alec and consume Mrs Pennyworth's excellent saddle of lamb without constraint.

In the hall, the dining-room door stood ajar. I braced myself, took a breath and entered.

It was a large-windowed, high-ceilinged room, with portraits of pastoral scenes hanging from the picture rails. The stench of the cigar Alec had smoked last night was gone, and in the brisk light from the sea the place appeared crisp and clean. There was a starched white cloth on the table, and at one end of it, reading a newspaper and eating a boiled egg, was Mrs Bray.

She was wearing a similar gown to the one she had been wearing yesterday, draped over a sort of Chinese pyjama affair, which most likely were not pyjamas at all. She had also styled her hair and done something to her face, because the sallow demeanour of the day before was gone. A gold locket with some elaborate engraving hung round her neck. She did not bother to glance up when I came in, and continued reading as if I were not there at all.

I was determined not to stoop to her level. 'Good morning,' I said, and was rewarded by a murmur from the parlourmaid, Agnes, who was placing cold meats on trivets that stood on the polished sideboard, but a silence from Mrs Bray. The stutter that had been the curse of my school life trampled my tongue for several seconds before I managed to say, 'Is th-th-th-that coffee fresh?'

Agnes picked up the pot. 'I'll be back immediate,' she said, and left the room, leaving me alone with the witch. Previous trips to Lancaster Gate and various other relatives' houses had instructed me with the breakfast-room modus operandi, and I sat down as far from Mrs Bray as possible, helping myself to slivers of bacon, a couple of eggs, two plump sausages and a spoonful of mushrooms.

From the hallway, there came the faint sound of crockery smashing and a hurriedly hushed-up commotion. Mrs Bray shook her paper and looked at Scone as he entered, bringing the scent of fresh coffee before him. 'Everything all right?'

'A broken teacup, madam.' He set the coffee and toast on the table.

Mrs Bray pulled a slice of toast from the rack. 'I suppose that's the girl again.'

Scone nodded. 'I shall dock her wages, of course.'

She smeared jam on her toast, the flat of her blade crushing the bread. 'Just tell her that if she can't manage to hold a tray properly I'll boot her all the way down to kitchen maid and she can bother Mrs Pennyworth instead.'

'Very good, madam.' He left the room, presumably to give poor Agnes a dressing down on his mistress's behalf. I wondered what bad luck had led the mite to serve in such a graceless household, but I forbore to comment and instead managed to eat my extremely delicious bacon, which melted under my tongue in a way it never did at home.

After a while, however, I sensed I was being watched, and looked up. Mrs Bray was drinking her coffee, appraising me. 'I see you're not on the train back to the hinterland yet,' she said. Her blood-tinted nails tapped her china cup.

The bacon caught in my throat. I swallowed it with difficulty. 'My health requires me to stay.'

She rested her elbows on the arms of her chair. 'Very good. I suppose I should feel guilty now for upsetting the poor invalid.'

I speared a mushroom. 'Not at all,' I said. 'You didn't upset me in the slightest.'

She put her head to one side and surveyed me. 'Perhaps not,' she said. 'Perhaps you're so grateful to be in these fabled rooms that you'll put up with anything.'

I felt myself turning purple but tried to keep my voice low as I said, 'I never much notice my surroundings, to be honest.'

'Oh, come on now.' She leaned her chin on her hand. 'The first time I saw the inside of Castaway I nearly wet myself. Do you know, Mr Carver, you and I have a lot in common. We're both outcasts, after all.'

I glared at her. In my lap, my napkin was scrunched in my fist. 'I don't believe I'm an outcast,' I said. 'And I wouldn't presume to speak on your behalf.'

She widened her eyes. 'But Alec's told me all about it. How your mother was cut off from the family fortune because she got herself up the duff by a minor official. Still, I'm sure it was a thrilling romance, wasn't it? And all worth it in the end.'

Irony gleamed coolly in her gaze. I squeezed my fork with my left hand, longing to plunge it into that delicate white forearm which was turned towards me now.

'She loves goading people,' Alec had said last night. 'And she's bloody good at it. Likes nothing better than to set the cat among the pigeons.'

I forced myself to breathe steadily and, keeping my voice at a calm pitch, said, 'As thrilling a romance as yours with Alec, no doubt.'

'Oh,' she said, 'we've certainly had our thrills all right.'

She stood up, her gown swirling about her, snatched up her newspaper and left the room. I stared at the buttery mushrooms, my heart beating fast, my breath scratchy in my throat, ashamed but relieved that I had survived the skirmish; and if there were to be more – well then, I would be ready.

Slowly, my heartbeat returned to normal. I ate the rest of my breakfast in peace, looking out of the bay windows at the cobalt-blue sky, and I thought of the sketchbook and pencils in my case. A different maid came back to clear the dishes, and curiosity got the better of me. I said humorously, 'Cup broken earlier, was it?'

'Sorry about that, sir. It was the parlourmaid.'

'Agnes?' I ventured, and she nodded. 'A new job for her, isn't it?'

'New for all of us,' said the maid. 'Since Sally disappeared so sudden the lot of us've been moved about. One of those things, sir.'

'Disappeared?'

The maid nodded. 'No note or nothing. Just vanished. I mean, it's not on, is it? Well, she won't get a reference like that, is what I say.'

She bundled the napkins inside the tablecloth and left the room. I supposed that servants were often prone to disappearing; I certainly would have been unable to stand working in this house for more than five minutes. I went back upstairs to collect the leather bag containing the tools of my hobby, thankfully avoiding Mrs Bray, and thought no more about it.

The sun was rising to a warm pitch by the time I left the house. I walked down the hill to the promenade, turned a sharp right and followed it along, under the cliff towards the pier, slotting my coin into the turnstile and walking along the planks. Below me, a few families were starting to set up camp on the sand, unpacking their luggage of parasols, blankets and picnics.

I walked to the very end, passing elderly ladies and gentlemen on their morning perambulations. I settled on the furthest view, facing to sea, and took out my book. I had watercolour sketches inside, painted during my year of recuperation: the view over the rooftops from my bedroom window, the brightly coloured barges on the canal. I flipped to a new blank page, possibilities darting about as always, rested it on the rail and, pulling out a ready-sharpened pencil, attempted a rough sketch of gulls bobbing on the waves.

'Mr Carver!'

The voice in my ear startled me. The pencil scored a thick grey line across a gull's beak. I growled to myself and looked round for my attacker.

It was the neighbour of yesterday, Dr Feathers. He was leaning over my shoulder in a far too intimate manner, and smiling at me through his beard. 'I was calling you from the other side of the pier,' he said. 'But you were lost in your own world.'

'I was,' I said, hoping he would infer from this that I wished to remain lost, but it seemed that Dr Feathers was not attuned to the subtleties of communication. He waggled a finger towards the sea. 'Sketching the view, eh?'

I realized I would be unable to continue while the doctor was standing behind me, and so I put away my pencil and turned to face him. 'That's the idea.'

He stroked his beard as he peered at it. 'Jolly good,' he said. 'No paint, eh? Wish I were a painting man myself. Always fancied a little dabble in *les beaux arts*. What do you think of the Paris scene? Can't abide them meself. All those horses without heads and mechanical elephants. No, give me your Monet or Manet or Degas any day. Now, they were geniuses.'

Beyond the doctor, a little further along, I noticed two girls leaning on the rail. One, blonde and pretty, flicked me a blue-eyed glance and then turned back to her friend and giggled. I blushed cadmium red and felt very conscious of how I was standing and the position of each hair upon my head.

'Tell me, how is Mr Bray at the moment?'

It was just as well, I thought, that I had Dr Feathers to talk to. At least I had a purpose, so to speak, and appeared fully occupied.

'Um . . . he's very well, as far as I know.'

'Dear Viviane's passing was a terrible loss.' The doctor stared mistily out to sea. 'Insisted on consulting that charlatan from London. A terrible loss.'

'Alec seems to be coping fairly well,' I murmured, closing my sketchbook.

The doctor raised his eyebrows, causing his glasses to wobble on his nose. 'Did you know, Mr Carver, that the month after it became clear Viviane wasn't going to make it, Mr Bray jumped into marriage with the Tutt girl? Have you read Freud? Quite marvellous, the whole psychology aspect. Know Mrs Bray well, do you?'

'I only met her yesterday, actually,' I said, as breezily as I could.

'Aha,' he said with a triumphant air I could not quite fathom. 'Of course, I've known Clara Bray since she was a child.'

I frowned. 'I'm sorry?'

The doctor beamed. 'You didn't know that she grew up in Helmstone? She was a wild kid, almost feral. I used to see her hanging around outside Castaway, hoping for . . . well, who knows what?'

'Oh.' I wondered why Alec had not told me. 'I'd heard she was an actress. I thought they'd met in London.'

'I wouldn't know about such a thing,' said the doctor artlessly. 'All I know is, she left here as dirty little Clare Tutt, voice of a fishwife, and returned as Clara Bray, with a plum in her mouth and her nose in the air. Obviously the servants all despise her; *she's* below *them*, you see.'

'She must have had elocution lessons,' I murmured, and felt oddly guilty for discussing Mrs Bray in this way. After all, she had given me no reason to defend her cause. Yet somehow it did not feel quite right, and so I turned and peered up to where the crenellated roof of Castaway could just be seen poking out from the tip of the cliff, and beside it the Featherses' slightly narrower one, reducing in size all the way down the hill. Castaway did look rather lonely, I thought, stuck out on the end like that, with an expanse of nothing to its left.

But all I said to Feathers was, 'It's quite a marvellous old building, isn't it?'

'Too big,' snapped the doctor. 'Only families with pretensions would buy it. Of course, that was the Devereaus all over – Viviane's family. Always banging on about how they could trace their lineage back to the Normans, as if being descended from that rabble was something to be proud of.'

'She was always rather a Francophile,' I said, wondering

exactly how much Dr Feathers knew of our family. 'Alec told me she installed that lovely art nouveau glass over the door.'

'I'm sure. Viviane was a beauty in her day, of course. I often think if I hadn't married Mrs Feathers . . . but there you go, one can't go about regretting the past, eh? After all, I'm sure the current lady of the house doesn't.'

I mumbled non-committally and surreptitiously glanced at the girls. They were quite openly staring at us now, as if they were trying to listen in on our conversation.

The doctor turned and saw them. 'Ah!' he exclaimed. 'Lizzie, Maddie, come here and meet our new neighbour.'

At the realization that these were the doctor's progeny, my stomach sank a little. The girls walked towards us; and the younger one, who looked about fifteen, with mousy hair spilling out from an untidy bun, darted towards me, while the prettier, blonde one, who was, I thought, about eighteen, hung back, her cheeks blooming vermilion.

'My daughters.' Feathers pulled them both towards him and shoved them at me. 'This is Madeleine, and this here – come here, Lizzie! This is Elizabeth, my eldest. Go on, shake hands with Mr Carver.'

'How d'you do?' I said, amused at her shyness.

'Are you an artist?' said Madeleine, the young one, peering with unabashed curiosity at the sketchbook nestled in my bag. 'We've always wanted to know an artist, haven't we, Lizzie?'

'Maddie!' hissed Lizzie, elbowing her sharply in the side.

'Mr Carver is a gifted amateur,' said the doctor. 'No modern rubbish here, you see?'

76

Maddie pulled a face at me. 'Father thinks I've terrible taste.'

'I don't *think*,' said the doctor. 'I know. Go on, Mr Carver, show my daughters what you've achieved this morning.'

'Hardly anything,' I said, embarrassed now myself. I never enjoyed displaying a work in progress, but three pairs of eyes had turned eagerly my way and so I reluctantly retrieved my sketchbook and showed them what I had made of the gulls.

For a few seconds they peered at the page, and then Lizzie said in a tight little voice, 'Rather decent, aren't they?'

'There you go!' The doctor beamed. 'And Lizzie's the cleverest one in the family, so you ought to take her word for it.'

Maddie rolled her eyes, as her sister said in that same voice, 'I'd love to draw. Only I'm afraid I'm utterly talentless.'

I smiled at her, glad now that she was the doctor's daughter and I'd been afforded an introduction. 'I'd be happy to talk you through some techniques.'

'Yes, why don't you let Mr Carver do just that?' The doctor put an arm round his younger daughter. 'While I take a turn with Maddie.'

'Can't I stay?' said Maddie, but Feathers wheeled her about and marched her down to the other side of the pier. I groaned inwardly at the contrivance, but all the same I was rather pleased.

I showed her a pencil drawing I'd done a fair while ago, of trees along the canal. 'You see, the important thing is to look at the shapes between the solid objects,' I began, afraid I sounded terribly pompous.

'Oh, gosh, yes,' she said vaguely. She was knotting and unknotting her hands. 'Father said you were spending the summer in Helmstone.'

I stopped, my finger still on the page. I realized that, of course, she had no interest in drawing whatsoever. I also realized that I must have been discussed, perhaps at the Featherses' dining table after our encounter yesterday. 'Yes. That is, I hope to.' I decided not to mention the proviso of Mrs Bray keeping a civil tongue in her head for the duration. 'I'm a cousin of Alexander's.'

Of course, she knew that too. She peered up at me through the frame of her sandy lashes. 'Maddie and I say that they ought to be in the pictures, Mr and Mrs Bray. They're glamour personified, don't you think? And they love each other so much.'

'Well . . . um . . . that is, I'm sure they do,' I said, as Lizzie blushed again. She really was a very nervous young lady, and made me feel rather protective of her. 'So tell me about Helmstone. I've only just arrived, you see.'

'Well, it's terribly dull, of course.' The sun, moving from behind a cloud, caught her eyes and she shaded her forehead, looking over to where her father and sister were standing, peering through a penny telescope. 'But I suppose the old quarter, the Snooks, is rather sweet. All cobbled streets and antique shops, that sort of thing.'

'Ah yes,' I said, remembering the dark alleyway Alec had dragged me along yesterday towards his favourite haunt, the Walmstead Arms. 'Anything else?'

'Um . . .' Her eyes really were the most astonishing

shade of blue, I mused. 'Of course, we've a ton of picture houses, and the Majestic Hotel's quite grand. Oh, and there's Bradley's, the department store.'

In the distance I saw the doctor and his daughter heading back this way and, seized with a sudden rush of confidence said, 'D'you know, I really need somebody to show me round. My cousin hasn't the least interest in that sort of thing, I'm afraid.' Or rather, I thought, Alec's interests limited themselves to evening entertainments.

'Oh,' she gasped. 'Oh. Oh yes. That is, I mean . . . I could. If you'd like.'

I smiled down at her and was rewarded by an answering smile that lit up her face. 'Are you free tomorrow?'

She nodded. 'After lunch. Um . . . three o'clock?'

'Then I'll be at your door at three.'

She breathed a long sigh, as if she'd been holding air somewhere deep inside her. 'That would be wonderful,' she said in a whisper.

And then they were upon us, and I chattered, delighted with myself at my foray into this land of the female. After I waved them off I returned to my sketchbook, although I had to stop intermittently as I mused on Lizzie and what we might get up to tomorrow. My experience with girls was fairly limited, more through lack of opportunity than lack of desire, and my knowledge of them was spliced together from what more worldly friends had imparted. All I really knew was that there were 'good-time' girls, of whom Mrs Bray had no doubt been one, rather masculine in their outlook on life, sex-mad and cold-hearted, certainly not romance material, and there were regular girls like Lizzie, feminine and delicate, whom one had to handle carefully as they were likely to spring forth tears at any moment.

I was interrupted in these musings by the growling of my stomach, and I realized with a start that it was well after two o'clock. Scone had informed me that luncheon was usually a cold buffet anyhow as neither Mr nor Mrs Bray had much appetite at the moment. I thought this was rather so they could avoid sitting together for yet another meal, and I hoped that if I set off now Mrs Pennyworth might be persuaded to knock me up some meat sandwiches.

Along the length of the pier were benches set into the ridged column of its spine, facing both ways out to sea. I walked along the far side, where the empty cliff line continued for several miles until, in the distance, I could make out the afternoon sun twinkling on windows of the next town. I was ensconced in my own world and feeling fairly peaceful, so the sharp sobbing beside me intruded like a funeral bell.

I turned. A girl was crouched on one of the centre benches, face in hands, elbows in lap, crying. I glanced down at her, embarrassed, and was already moving on when I realized that it was Agnes, the young parlourmaid I had encountered yesterday on my arrival – the girl on a warning from Mrs Bray.

I presumed this was why she was sobbing and, not wanting to intrude, was about to walk on when she looked up, puffy-eyed, and saw me.

'Oh no.' She sagged downwards on the bench. 'Don't tell no one, please, sir.'

I hovered awkwardly in front of her. 'Is . . . is everything all right?'

'I'm f-f-fine.' She sniffed. 'It's my afternoon off. I can do what I like, can't I?'

Somehow that note of defiance set her on her crying spree again. I dug about in my pocket and pulled out a handkerchief. 'Here,' I said, dangling it in front of her. 'It's clean.'

She looked at it suspiciously, then took it and blew her nose. An elderly lady tottered past, eyeing us beadily, no doubt thinking I was the one who had made her cry. I sat down on the bench next to hers, with an arm of sculpted metal between us.

Finally, the sobs subsided into sniffs. 'Thank you, sir,' she muttered eventually, folding the handkerchief into a sleeve of her dress. 'I'll wash this and give it back.'

'It's a shame to be crying on your free afternoon,' I observed. 'Especially as the weather's so nice.'

She was staring out to sea, at the grey waves licking the sides of the cliff. 'I'm off to my sister's now,' she said in a monotone. 'I'll be fine.'

'Good.' I wondered how I could politely leave without making her feel abandoned. 'Are . . . are you sure you're all right?'

She swallowed lumpily. 'You said . . . you said you were staying here for a while, sir.'

I nodded. 'That's right. Did you want me to . . . I mean . . . ?' I stopped, because I had no idea what to say next.

'I think . . .' She paused. 'I think you should be careful.'

'What?' I smiled. 'Is that a threat?'

She shook her head once, sharply, as if trying to dispel an insect. 'You seem nice,' she said. 'I just wanted to let you know you ought to be careful.'

I laughed out loud now. 'But why, for heaven's sake?'

She turned to me, her eyes flat. 'There's evil in the house,' she said. 'And if you ain't careful, sir, it'll get you too like it got Sally.'

'You'll have to explain further, I'm afraid,' I said humorously, but Agnes's gaze was anything but. 'What happened to Sally?'

She pinched her lips together. 'I'd best be getting on to my sister's.' She got to her feet and began fussing with her coat.

'Agnes . . .'

'Thanks for the handkerchief, sir.' She tottered off on her boots along the planks of the pier. I watched her retreating figure as I stood up and dusted flecks of dirt from my trousers. She was very young after all, no more than sixteen or seventeen. I recalled myself at that age, blindly believing all that was presented to me about the world. Thank goodness I had reached nineteen and was now in full possession of all the facts I needed to know.

For some reason, the image of Mrs Bray came to mind as I walked along the pier; not as she was now, but as a street urchin, dirty-faced, hanging around outside Castaway, hiding from the servants. Strange that no one in the family knew of this extra twist in the tale of Alec's impetuous union, but I supposed this would only have added fuel to the gossipy fire, and my aunt and uncle were very keen on appearances.

I returned to the house and spent a pleasant afternoon alone in the garden, reading on one of the stone benches that dotted the various shaded arbours leading off the central winding path. As the sun dipped down I went up to my room to dress for dinner, and on entering the dining room was pleased to see Alec there, at the sideboard, mixing some drinks. 'Robert!' he said, his face lighting up. 'I was worried after I missed you at lunch. Thought you might have run out on me.'

'Not a chance.' He handed me a gin Martini. 'I bumped into Dr Feathers on the pier.'

'Surprised you managed to get away. People have never been seen again after falling into conversation with Dr Feathers.'

I smiled. 'Well, he does have a rather attractive daughter. The eldest Miss Feathers – do you know her?'

Alec pulled a sour face. 'Lord, don't do it, Robert. Feathers'll have you married off to her within the week. He's petrified some rogue is going to take advantage of his dear precious, and he wants to secure her future before that happens.'

'He doesn't know I'm not a rogue,' I observed, settling myself at the table. Scone, whom I had not noticed in the room until that point, darted forwards to pull out my chair, and seemed most disappointed when he was foiled.

Alec pondered on my observation. 'Not with your face,' he said. 'You've the physog of a vicar.'

'Thanks very much.'

Alec burped. 'You're welcome.'

'God, you're an oaf.'

This last sentence came from a cool voice in the

doorway. We both turned and saw Clara Bray entering the room. She allowed Scone to seat her and said to him, 'We'd better start eating straight away. Something needs to soak up all the alcohol my husband's consumed.'

Scone nodded and withdrew. Alec leaned across the table and tickled her under her chin. 'Any chance for a little dig, eh, my dear?'

She withdrew her face sharply. 'Please stop that, darling, or I shall be forced to dig properly. By which I mean at your testicles, with a blunt spoon.'

Alec snorted. 'Oh, they went a long time ago, as well you know.' He slugged at his wine. 'I don't suppose you feel like telling me where you've been this afternoon?'

She picked up the glass Scone had just poured for her, looked at him over the rim of it and said, 'No, I don't.'

Alec misjudged the distance of the table and thumped the wine down; it tipped on to the cloth. 'It doesn't matter,' he said, his eyes sliding towards me. 'I can guess.'

'I doubt it, my dear.' She gave him a shark's smile. 'But cast all the aspersions you like; I really couldn't give a shit.'

Alec winked at her. 'And with a mouth straight from the sewer. How perfect.'

Throughout this entire spat I had been affecting an interest in the dragon's head decorating the mantelpiece, and wishing I were anywhere else, even in my sickroom back home, rather than having to listen to this.

However, through the doorway of the dining room came Scone carrying the entrées, little squares of pâté on toast, and as I chewed on them and gulped down wine, Mrs Bray got out a book and read it at the table, much as she'd done this morning, seemingly completely unconcerned by the insults she and her husband had batted back and forth. I sensed a certain settling in the room, a cessation of hostilities while the servants were around, and I breathed a little more easily, wishing nevertheless that I could be afforded the same courtesy as they.

The courses came and went. Alec ate little and drank a lot. The silence in the room was as thick and loaded with menace as a gathering storm. I noticed him watching his wife through narrowed eyes, his face growing redder and redder. I attempted to engage him in conversation, but to my questions he gave only monotone answers. I tried to think of pleasant thoughts, such as the bloom in Lizzie Feathers' cheeks and the smell of the brine from the sea.

'So this is to be it, then, is it?' he said after a half-hour in which I had given up attempting to leaven the atmosphere with small talk. 'Honestly, Clara, I thought you might at least make an effort, seeing as we've a guest here.'

Without looking up from her book, Mrs Bray said, 'He's no guest of mine, darling, as you well know.'

Alec threw down his napkin, startling one of the maids clearing plates. 'He's my cousin, damn it!'

'Mmm,' she said, 'guilty by association.'

Alec was practically purple with rage.

'Please,' I said to him. 'Don't be concerned on my account.'

He wasn't listening. 'Now then,' he said, 'say what you like about me, but Robert's a decent chap and he doesn't deserve any of this.'

'Well, perhaps you shouldn't have invited him to stay, then.'

'I'd rather he stayed than you.'

I sensed the servants shrinking back against the walls, eyeing each other, retreating rapidly from the room.

'Now you're upsetting the servants, dearest.' She snapped her knife and fork together on her plate and got to her feet, drawing a cardigan around her shoulders. She turned to me and with a red-lipped, cold smile said, 'Don't worry, Mr Carver. You may have my husband all to yourself now.'

And, with that, she swept out. We waited in silence as she rapped out an order to Scone in the hallway, and we heard the sharp creak of the stairs as she went up.

We sat back in our seats, both breathing rapidly. I had the sense of emerging, scarred and weary, from a field of the dead. Alec wiped his forehead with his handkerchief. 'How are you?' he said eventually.

I grimaced at the fruit salad which had materialized in front of me. 'This wasn't exactly how I'd planned to spend my summer.'

'Do apologize for that, old chap.' Alec ran a hand through his hair. 'She's been having meals in her room for weeks. Probably only emerged so she could goad me further.'

I put a stoned cherry in my mouth. 'She certainly doesn't want me to stay.'

He leaned across the table and put his hand on my arm. 'Well, I do.' He grinned at me. 'I think she's jealous.'

'Of me?'

Alec glanced towards the door, and then whispered in my ear, 'She hates me because I've seen through her.'

I turned to him. 'What on earth do you mean?'

'Shh.' He looked at the open door, and then, loudly, 'Let's go out. I've something to show you.'

86

'Show me?' I asked, heavy with food and wine and not particularly willing to leave the house. 'Is it important?'

He squeezed my hand. 'Life-threatening,' he growled, and then sprang to his feet. 'And what's more, it'll be fun. *Carpe diem, veni, vidi, vici*, et cetera, ad nauseum.'

I laughed at the way Alec could switch his mood on a sixpence. He swung on the dining-room door, and I heard him tell Scone in the hallway that we would not be needing coffees or port tonight. I put my chin on my hand and sighed, wishing that Mrs Bray had decided to take a motoring tour of the Lakes for the duration of my visit.

The air was warm and scented with violet-coloured four o'clocks unfurling in the front gardens as we descended the cliff. We crossed the road at the bottom and I followed Alec down the slippery steps that led to the beach. There were no street lights here, and I clung on to the handrail.

'Isn't this rather dangerous?' I asked, but Alec was far ahead of me, marching across the boards alongside the brick wall of the promenade. I followed him gingerly, the fish-smoking houses spiking shadows upwards against the dusk. I heard the sea washing in and out at the end of the sand, and felt my feet dampening inside my inadequate shoes. Alec was a shadowy glint ahead of me; I hurried to catch up.

Hammered out of the wall beside us were arched doorways, some open and empty, others doored and barred. The open doorways swallowed darkness and I hurried past, practically bumping into Alec as he turned to me, dangling a long iron key on a length of string.

'Are you ready?' he asked.

We were outside a padlocked doorway with '231' above its entrance.

'You said this would be fun,' I grumbled.

'It will be. Just wait.' He fitted the key into the padlock, turned it and pulled back the bolt. The door opened with a shudder, and Alec stepped over the raised threshold and into the black space beyond.

I hovered in the entrance. The dusky beach now seemed fairly benign compared to the emptiness beyond. I remembered that Alec had always had a fondness for practical jokes; had told me about putting frogs in his teachers' desks and pinning messages to his classmates' backs.

'What is this?' I asked impatiently.

'Come on,' he said, his voice a little faded. He must have moved well within the interior of the arch. 'I've a lamp here somewhere; just looking for it.'

His matter-of-fact voice finally convinced me, and I stepped over the wooden ledge and into the arch. 'I can't see a damn thing ...' I began, when a gas lamp was switched on and a bearded man leaped at me.

I yelled and lashed out. The man toppled backwards. I heard an oath and saw a dark shape as Alec crouched over the figure. 'Well done, Robert,' he said, his light ranging over the figure's head. 'You've just knocked over the King.'

He heaved the man back to a standing position, from where he stared at me with glassy, imperial eyes. On his military chest were pinned several medals. His face was a smooth pink, except for two rosy cheeks. 'Here,' I heard, and the lamp was thrust into my hands. I held it up by the handle and looked about me at a hundred bodies peering back through the dark.

'Oh my God,' I whispered. 'What is this?'

'Hold that steady.' I saw Alec flitting about the room. 'I can't . . . ah, here it is.'

Another lamp flared on. My cousin picked it up and grinned at me. 'What do you think?'

We were in a tunnel that stretched far back under the road, and the various bodies were stacked along both walls. Beyond the King there was the Queen and a figure dressed in a Grenadier Guards' uniform that I presumed was the heir apparent. To my right was a little man with a moustache and a bowler hat wielding a cane, and past him a girl with a cascade of ringlets and a dress made of rags.

My heart still pounded, and my chest was constricted with the fright and the musty air of the tunnel. 'Why didn't you tell me you were taking me to a waxworks?'

'Precisely that.' He leaned on the shoulder of the little man with the bowler hat. 'I wanted to see your reaction first. They're good, aren't they?'

I looked at his companion. 'I suppose that's Charlie Chaplin,' I said. 'But I couldn't tell you who this is. Lillian Gish?'

'It's Mary Pickford, you fool,' he said somewhat impatiently. 'Come through. I've tons more to show you.'

His lamp slid off into the darkness and I followed, not wishing to be left behind with the present company. Alec called out names as we headed further into the tunnel. 'Gloria Swanson, that's Sarah Bernhardt over there – I expect we'll have boys peeking under her skirt to see if she really has a wooden leg – Mr Baldwin here, the Kaiser, Mata Hari . . . d'you like the artfully placed sheet? Rudolph Valentino . . . the ladies will all want to pose next to him, no doubt.'

The tunnel turned the corner and became another archway, heading back down towards the beach. At the rear of the tunnel was yet another empty doorway. 'That's going to be the Cellar of the Dead,' he said, pointing. 'But at the moment it smells of fish.'

I put my hands in my pockets and circled round a bare-chested Douglas Fairbanks, curtain rings dangling from his ears. 'Is all this . . . yours?' I asked, rather faint from the whole experience.

'Yes. Well, mine and Bump Mason's. Bump's an awfully good chap; whole thing was his idea, actually. But we're in it together. Mason and Bray's Hall of Fame, that's what we're going to call it, when it's done.'

'I see.' I frowned at Fatty Arbuckle. 'Rather reminds me of a famous waxworks on Baker Street.'

'Exactly,' said Alec. 'That's where Bump had the idea. Now, Robert, I want you to picture the scene. Imagine you're a family man, working in some evil little job that keeps the wheels of industry going. You have your week's holiday and you take the wife and the two brats to Helmstone, along with your savings. And what d'you know, one day it just pours with rain. Now what is there to do in a seaside town when it rains? Go to the pictures? Maybe. Go to a museum? Not if you've a brace of run-around kids.'

'Or go to Mason and Bray's Hall of Fame?' I supplied.

'Adults two bob, children sixpence.' He grinned hugely and reminded me of a child himself, with a very expensive toy. 'You're in a small minority, Carver. Not many people have seen the show so far.'

'Obviously.' I squinted at the mannequins. 'Although I have to say, if it wasn't for the get-up I'd be hard-pressed to tell who any of them were.'

'Oh, who cares about that?' Alec jumped off the table and joined me in inspecting Fairbanks. 'That's what the clothes and the wigs are for. And the props. That'll be half the fun, working out who they are. We'll have plaques, anyhow.'

'Mmm,' I muttered, not entirely convinced. I had been to Madame Tussaud's myself, once, as a child, and had gasped at the lifelike representations of the great and good. Here, in three arches under the seafront road, I was not quite sure that tourists would be so impressed by a marble-eyed figure in a headscarf. 'You haven't invested all your money, have you?'

He sighed. 'Now, Robert, you're in fearful danger of sounding like Mother, and as much as I miss her, I'd rather not have her back in your body. That would be far too complicated.'

'All right.' I looked about. 'It's a marvellous idea. But listen. Are you really going to have all these models just standing about like this? Because it's rather ... higgledypiggledy, if you don't mind my saying.'

Alec folded his arms and put one hand to his chin. 'Continue.'

'Well ...' I looked about me. 'It sort of seems as if they're queuing for a bus, and I don't think that's the impression you want to be giving of Rudolph Valentino, do you?'

I walked up to the figure and turned him a little. He was leaning forwards, his dark eyes heavily rimmed with black pencil. His sheikh's robes brushed my hands as I moved him, and I jumped.

'Don't worry, that happens to me all the time,' said Alec. 'Easy to believe they're touching one. Rather creepy, until you get used to it.'

Now I moved Gloria Swanson so she was facing him. She had her head thrust back as if declaiming, and so the scene now looked as if she were resisting his attempts to ravish her. 'There you go,' I said. 'A tableau. Gives one more of a complete picture, don't you think?'

Alec put his arm about Gloria's waist and looked over her shoulder at me. 'That,' he said, 'is utter genius.'

'Good.' I said. 'Can we go now?'

He moved behind Valentino and peeked over his head-scarf. 'You don't fancy being our artistic advisor, do you, Robert? After all, neither Bump nor I have a clue about aesthetics.'

'Artistic advisor?' I looked about at the dank, smelly room, thinking that the first thing the place needed was a good airing.

Alec came out from behind Valentino and leaned on a carpenter's workbench stationed opposite. 'I'll be frank with you. I . . . well, with one thing and another I've incurred a few debts over the years.'

I nodded. Of course. Cards, I supposed, and perhaps that was the least of it. 'You're in trouble?'

'Not at all.' He shook his head rather vigorously, and

I realized he was still drunk. 'But Mother's inheritance has . . . frankly, it's been used up, and this is the last of it. I've finally decided to be sensible, you see. Invest in my future, for once.'

'With Mr Mason?'

'Mason-Chambers actually, but that wouldn't fit on the sign. No, Bump's the ideas man, and I'm the hard cash. Clara was . . . that is, she was supposed to help us with the other side of things.'

He folded his hands under his armpits.

'Help you?' I said.

He waved his hand. 'You know, tableaux and so on. Paint pigments. Artistic whatnots. That's all gone down the pan now. I mean, actually, when I think about it, this whole thing's been quite a help for me,' he continued blithely. 'Taking one's mind off the domestic situation.'

I went and sat next to him on the workbench. 'I am sorry,' I said softly. 'About, you know . . .'

He shrugged. 'My own fault, Robert. Bump told me. You should meet Bump; he's a wise old saw. By all means fuck them, he said, but for God's sake don't fall in love with them; they'll eat you alive.'

I goggled at him. 'Sorry?'

But Alec was in his own world. 'It was through Bump I met her. Dragged me along to some third-rate musical one night because of the so-called Greek nudes. Lot of bunkum, anyway; a queue of silly girls wearing fig leaves. But the lead – Clara – well, I'll give her this, she lit up the whole stage when she came on.'

'Oh yes,' I said carelessly. 'I'd heard she was an actress.'

He smiled. 'I went to see her twelve times before I

decided I was going to talk to her.' He glanced at me. 'You know going to bed with an actress is as easy as falling off a log, don't you? If you've the cash for it. And by God, they want paying.'

I thought of Clara Bray, in a grubby dressing room in a shabby theatre, waiting for a man to knock on her door, legs crossed at the knee, gown folded across her cleavage, and then dashed that thought away. 'I see.'

He looked at me. 'No, you don't. Clara wasn't like that. At least, I thought she wasn't. I was completely wrong, of course. Turns out she's been to bed with half of London, but she made out she was this very simple, sweet, inno-cent girl, and I believed it. I mean, she really is a very good actress, I'll give her that. Fell for her completely, married her in this sort of haze of love, everything's peachy . . . I take her down to Castaway for weekends, show her the whole town, not a word said. She puts off meeting the parents – understandably, perhaps – but then one day we're at Castaway and Mother gets a little better and decides to show up, with Father. We're sitting round the pond with friends and cocktails when Mother's wheeled up the path, looks at Clara and says, "My word, Clare Tutt, what on earth are you doing in my garden?"'

Alec turned to gauge my reaction.

I attempted a show of surprise. 'She'd grown up in Helmstone?'

He frowned at me. 'Wait a second. Who have you been . . . ? Oh, don't tell me. The Feathers town crier. Didn't take him long, did it?'

I pulled a face. 'He told me she used to lurk outside the house.'

Alec nodded. 'Mother insisted that none of the family should know. Well, you're the first. I don't remember her at all from those days – I was at school, you see – but apparently she wormed her way into Mother's affections, playing the poor little orphan card, and Mother, being a soft touch, took pity on her, used to bring her in for tea and so on.'

'I remember,' I breathed. 'When you took me to see the dinosaurs. You said something about another child taking your place.'

'Exactly,' said Alec bitterly. 'Of course, I was a terrible disappointment all round and Clara – well, she fooled me and before that she'd already fooled Mother. She'd been on the rob every time she'd been invited into the house. Stealing from Ma's handbag when she wasn't looking, that sort of thing. Father was the one who found out; gave her the old heave-ho. Clara used to tell Mother she'd love to have a house as beautiful as Castaway. She must have decided she'd get her hands on it one way or another, the spiteful little bitch.'

I suddenly thought of Agnes sobbing on the pier. 'The parlourmaid,' I began, and Alec looked up sharply. 'She was talking of evil in the house. I mean, I hadn't a clue what she meant.'

He sighed. 'They all know who Clara really is,' he said. 'Of course they do. Not that she cares; she's as hard as nails.'

He put his hand on mine and entwined my fingers with his.

'I'm so sorry,' I said.

He squeezed my hand. 'I fell in love with a chimera,' he

95

said softly. 'Clara Bray doesn't exist, and now I've seen through her she hates my guts. You've seen the locket she wears?'

I nodded, remembering the elaborate engraving upon it. 'A gift from you?'

'It was my mother's. After she . . . well, when she first became ill it hurt her to wear it, and she gave it to me to look after. Back when I was spoony over Clara, I presented it to her with a lock of my hair inside.' He grimaced. 'The day I realized she'd told me a pack of lies, we had the most enormous row. She tore the thing open and emptied out the contents. Didn't hand back the locket, of course. Far too avaricious to let that go.'

'I'm surprised you allow her to stay here,' I said. 'Considering all of that.'

'Still trying to work out what to do for the best.' He looked at me with his wide, open face. 'It's all rather new and raw, I'm afraid.'

I felt suddenly thrust into the adult world, and with that came a welter of emotions I had little idea what to do with. I smiled with more confidence than I had and said, 'I know what we should do.'

He looked at me hopefully, and I remembered when I'd gazed at him below the dinosaurs and thought him the repository of all the world's wisdom.

'What's that?'

I jumped off the table. 'We should go for a drink.'

He grinned, and the old Alec was back in the room. 'Now, that is what I call a bloody good idea,' he said. 'I'll stand you a beer in the Walmstead Arms if you'll agree to help us out.'

I frowned, but realized he meant helping him out with this project, not with his marriage. The latter problem seemed insurmountable. I swung off the workbench and flicked Valentino's headscarf as I walked past him, the glassy stares of the mannequins upon me as I went.

5
1965

I stood in the basement kitchen of the Bella Vista guest house, elbow-deep in grey dishwater, the white belly of the Ascot by my head sweaty with condensation. To my right, Mrs Hale rattled pans on the blackened stove, muttering under her breath when the scrambled eggs turned gritty. I was trying not to think about the note Val had left for me last night, and yet every time I planted another soap-streaked plate in the rack, I found myself drifting loose and going over it once more.

'Rosie?' said Mrs Hale from behind me, and I jumped.

'Sorry. I was just . . . um . . .' I picked up a butter knife. 'Scrubbing.'

'Is that what you call it?' Mrs Hale was scraping burnt bacon off the frying pan with a fish slice. 'Perhaps you could turn your attention to all the piled-up plates in the breakfast room, instead.'

'Oh yes. Absolutely. On my way.' I looked longingly at the stone-cold cup of tea I'd not yet had time to drink, wrestled with the beaded curtain that separated the kitchen from the breakfast room, and lumbered through, my left shoe sticking to something nasty on the carpet tiles.

Of course, I'd stayed up too late at Star's last night, sneering at *Sunday Night at the London Palladium*, taking the mickey out of the performers, eating Spam and baked beans and then playing Beggar My Neighbour with a torn pack of cards. But it hadn't helped that after I'd seen Val's note in her bubbly handwriting I'd lain awake in bed for hours, thinking about how one could never really run away from the past.

The breakfast room was murky with the metallic daylight filtering through the barred windows at the end. Mrs Hale's transistor radio in the kitchen burbled out Mantovani on *Housewives' Choice*. I piled up abandoned plates, scraping congealed egg on top of cold toast. Most of the guests had already left to battle the wind coursing along the seafront; only the fake Mr and Mrs Smith remained, hands entwined over the plastic tablecloth, giggling idiotically.

'Excuse me, miss.'

They were even younger than me, and she was twirling a curtain ring on her finger. The pale yellow walls made them both look sallow, and they were hollow-eyed and sated, perhaps with food but more likely with sex.

'What d'you want?' I asked ungraciously, the plates weighing heavily on my wrists.

'My – er – my wife was just wondering if she could have some more tea.'

'Peter!' She giggled again.

'More tea. Okay.' I snatched up the teapot and stalked back to the kitchen, the words of the horrible note rearing their ugly head once more.

Rosie, Val had written. *Someone named 'Harry' called by to see you. He says he'll come back <u>every day</u> until you're in. You MUST tell us who he is!!! You dark horse, you never said you were somebody's girl!!!*

'They want more tea,' I announced to Mrs Hale, jabbing the tap on the urn. 'It's disgusting. They're not even married.'

Mrs Hale emptied the plates into the pig bin. 'You'll fall in love one day, Rosie, and everything will feel entirely different.'

'Love!' I snorted, flipping down the hinge to the pot and thrusting apart the beaded curtain once more. I dumped the tea in front of them. 'Any more toast for you?'

'Judy?' He stroked her hand. 'More toast?'

She shook her head, simpering, and he turned to me with a wink. 'She says she's stuffed, thanks.'

I growled and lurched back to the kitchen, where Mrs Hale was smoking a cigarette beside the window to the yard. She began talking to me, but I found myself drifting loose yet again, wondering what time Harry was likely to come by and how best I could avoid him.

'. . . so can you take him up some tea when you've finished?'

'Of course.' I narrowed my eyes in an attempt to knit a meaning out of half a sentence. 'Which room?'

'Room One. He's always in Room One.' She rolled her eyes and blew out a plume of smoke. 'When he's here. Luckily, all of us siblings have him on rotation.'

'Oh, your father.' And now I remembered earlier talk from Mrs Hale, back in the kiosk, monologues that I'd ummed and ahhed to, but to which I hadn't really paid any attention at all. To cover up, I said quickly, 'I think I saw him yesterday. He waved to me through the window.'

'Very sociable, is Father. Be careful or you'll be trapped there for hours.'

I laughed, because I had no intention of staying at the guest house for any longer than Mrs Hale was paying me, even if it meant I ran the risk of seeing Harry. 'I will,' I said, as she loaded me with a tea tray, and I took it up the stairs to the empty lobby.

Josie, the receptionist, was absent, although the smell of her cigarettes hung like a cloud of flies in the blood-red hallway. There were a lot of notices behind her desk, which Josie had typed up herself on Mrs Hale's old Imperial machine. They said things like KEEP NOISE TO A MIN-IMUM and NO SAND IN THE WASH BASINS and DRUNKS SHALL NOT BE ADMITTED, which Josie imagined lent the place some class, although I thought any holidaymaker who saw them was bound to feel rather dispirited.

I balanced the tray under one arm and knocked on the door of Room One. I heard a lot of shuffling about before the door finally opened, and a shrivelled elderly man with a small white beard looked nervously out, leaning heavily on a stick.

'Ah,' he said, and beckoned me in with a shaking hand. 'Please come in.'

I walked into the room, which had a tattered old arm-chair facing another tattered old armchair in the window, and a single bed with a green coverlet. 'Over here?' I asked him, indicating the low table that stood between the two chairs.

'That's the one.'

I set the tray down and watched him make a slow, trem-bling journey across the carpet towards the chair. Finally he arrived and sat down, although his head still shook uncontrollably.

'I wonder if you would be so kind,' he said, 'To fetch me a glass of water from the basin.'

'Of course.' I let the water run cold before filling the glass, and brought it back to him.

'Thank you,' he murmured, and sipped at it. He took a breath, rested his hands on his cane and looked up at me. 'Are you a new girl?'

I nodded. 'I'm Rosie. I'm helping Mrs – your daughter – with the breakfasts.'

'Good for you.' He swallowed with what appeared to be a painful effort, and stretched his face into a smile. 'How do you do, Rosie. My name is Dr Feathers.'

I shook his trembling hand. 'How do you do, Dr Feathers.'

'In name only now, I'm afraid.' He coughed timidly. 'Would you play Mother for me and pour the tea?'

'Of course.' I tipped in the milk and poured the tea through the strainer. 'Sugar?'

'Two, thank you. You seem very young, Rosie. How old are you, if you don't mind my asking?'

'I've just turned eighteen.' I glanced at the books lining the window seat beside us. I had an awful habit, the moment I entered a person's room, of judging them based on their reading material. Val and Susan owned no books and thought, probably rightly, that I was a terrible snob. Johnny and Star had a collection of James Bond novels and a John Le Carré. Harry, I remembered, owned *How to Win Friends and Influence People*. That should have told me everything I needed to know about him.

'Eighteen! I remember when my daughters were

eighteen.' He nodded at the books. 'I see you've noticed my – ahem – oasis of sanity.'

Dr Feathers' books appeared to be an eclectic bunch: some Shakespeare plays, a few nineteenth-century classics, an illustrated guide to birds of the British Isles – appropriately enough I thought, given his name – a George Orwell, a Graham Greene. Even though he was as old as the hills and we clearly had nothing in common, I highly approved, and pointed to a leather-bound copy of *Measure for Measure*. 'We were going to study that this term.'

'Justice and truth.' Dr Feathers nodded. 'Not the most famous play, but one of the most profound, in my opinion. Would you like to borrow it?'

'Oh no. I mean, thank you, but I couldn't possibly.'

He grimaced with pain as he shifted in his chair. 'But you said you are to begin studying it at school?'

'Well, they are. But not me.' He frowned. 'I've left school.'

There was a pause. 'Oh,' he said. 'I assumed you were working here as a holiday job.'

I shook my head. 'Term started two weeks ago,' I said. 'I should be in the Upper Sixth, but I decided not to go back after the summer.'

He leaned forwards on his stick, peering up at me. 'And why is that, may I ask?'

'I – er – I left home. I needed some . . . independence.'

'Independence.' Dr Feathers said this as if it were an entirely new concept for him. 'You're not having a baby, are you?'

I gasped. 'I beg your pardon?'

His eyelids drooped; his head continued to shake. 'I'm

sorry, dear. I was a doctor, you know. I'm used to asking direct questions. Forgive me, there is no requirement to answer.'

'No, it's quite all right. I was just – um – surprised.' I bit my lip. 'No, I'm not going to have a baby.'

'Well, that's something.' He gave a tight little smile. 'Of course, I am assuming you left home because of a boy, and if there's a boy, there's often a baby involved. I've seen it all before. A hundred times before. You see, my dear, it could be worse. Much worse.'

I smiled back, although I wanted to tell him he didn't know the half of it. 'Things could always be worse, I suppose.'

'Please. To make up for my rudeness.' He waved at the books on the windowsill. 'Take one of these. Yes. I saw you perusing them; it takes one aficionado to know another.'

'No, honestly, there's no need.'

'I insist.' He leaned forwards and pulled a handful of books towards him. 'Have a look. It would make me feel better.'

I took the books from him, to be polite, and looked over the covers. *Nineteen Eighty-Four*, *Northanger Abbey*, *Little Dorrit*. I flicked through a few dusty pages. They were all rather dog-eared, and some had scribblings in the margins and on the flyleaves. I opened the back cover of *Northanger Abbey* and looked at it awhile, trying not to show my astonishment at what it contained.

He beamed at. 'Ah, Austen. Yes, please take it. A favourite of my daughter's. In fact, I think it belonged to her.'

'Mrs Hale?' I said, and as I spoke the door to the bedroom opened and Mrs Hale herself walked in.

'No, another daughter.' Dr Feathers turned a creaking neck and saw Mrs Hale at the door. 'Ah, Madeleine! We were just talking about you.'

'That's nice,' she said absently. 'I just wanted to tell Rosie that it's half past ten and I've her wages in the safe if she needs to go.'

'Of course.' Dr Feathers nodded. 'She doesn't want to carry on chatting to this old fogey, does she?'

'No, no,' I protested, but he winked at me and made a shooing motion with his hand. 'Enjoy the book,' he called as I left the room.

'Thank you.' I held it to my chest, and Mrs Hale looked at it curiously as I walked past her.

'Has he been pressing things on you?' she said, closing the door and following me back into the lobby. 'He's always doing that, the silly old fool.'

I supposed it was a daughter's prerogative to insult her elderly father, and I supposed I didn't know what it was like to have to look after him, but all the same I thought she was being a little unfair. I remembered what I had seen scribbled in the book. 'Did you – um – grow up in this house?' I asked as we walked back to the reception desk, where Josie had returned, tapping her brightly lacquered nails on the counter.

'Oh yes,' said Mrs Hale mildly. 'That was my father's office, you know.'

'You know what curiosity did,' said Josie to me, batting her false lashes, her out-of-date beehive wobbling. Josie was forty-seven and dressed as if she were eighteen, and she petrified me.

'I was just interested,' I squeaked, and she snorted.

Mrs Hale lifted up the flap on the counter, bundled herself beside Josie and bent down. 'Now, what's the combination of the safe?'

Josie rolled her eyes. 'One-five-oh-six-three-four.'

'Of course.' She straightened up with a red cash tin and squinted at the bundle of keys she always carried with her. 'Now, which one is it?'

Josie puffed out her lips and picked up the library book lying face down on the counter. 'Best doctor in town, Dr F. was, according to my mum,' she said, as if reading out a line of prose. 'Before the bomb blast. Where was it, Southend?'

'A plane offloading ballast before flying back home, apparently.' Mrs Hale fitted a small key into the lock, turned it and picked through the cash inside. 'He might've been all right, but then getting the news about Anthony being killed just about did for him. Here you are, Rosie.'

I held out my palm and she folded a note into it. 'Ten bob for today, seeing as it's only four hours.'

A memory flashed into my mind: yet another present from Harry, a silver chain with my name engraved on it. That had been one of the first; back in January, the day after Churchill's funeral. 'Ten bob for your namesake,' he'd said, 'but you're worth it,' and the second he'd gone I'd taken it from my wrist and hidden it at the bottom of my jewellery box.

'Don't know the meaning of work, your generation.' Josie sniffed. 'Once you've picked shards of glass out of some poor sod caught in a blast, you'll know what hard graft is.'

Mrs Hale glanced at her. 'V. A. D., were you?' she asked, surprised.

'Do I look like a mug?' Josie snapped. 'It was my Derek. Come home one night looking like a chandelier. I said to him, if you will go gallivanting about Princes Street, what do you expect?'

'Terrible.' Mrs Hale sighed. 'All those pointless deaths . . .'

'Well, Derek didn't die. More's the pity, I sometimes think.'

'And Rosie's father.' Mrs Hale turned to me. 'Did you say he was shot?'

I nodded. 'He was all right then; it was after I was born the pneumonia got him. The doctor said his whole system was too weak to take it.'

'Your poor mother.' Mrs Hale shook her head and sighed again.

Josie snorted and pulled another cigarette from her black leather handbag, which lived on the desk like a malevolent tomcat. 'When my mum got the telegram about my dad being missing at Passchendaele,' she sniffed, 'she thought he was still alive, soppy cow. Two weeks later, one of his mates knocks on the door. He's on crutches, holding a shoebox. Gives it to her and says, "That's all we found of Bill." She opens it up and there's this finger sticking up at her. Six months pregnant with me, she was, and she goes and faints on the doorstep, banging her head. When she wakes up she says, "I knew it was his finger straight off. Never would clean under his nails, the dirty bugger."'

Mrs Hale gave a patient smile and handed me my coat

and handbag from behind the desk. 'See you on Wednesday, Rosie,' she said as I left. 'Enjoy your day off.'

I waved her goodbye, excited at the prospect of no work for nearly forty-eight hours. I practically ran down the steps on to the street. The wind was racketing along the cliff top, blowing my hair about my face as I walked towards town, and the clouds were yet again threatening rain; but I was so glad to be free from work that I skipped my way down the cliff, and forgot about the note and Harry and all the rest of it, in the delight of being alive, and the delicious sense that all of life was bursting out before me, a hundred avenues, a thousand possibilities. I had cash in my handbag and was going shopping at Bradley's.

I turned left on to King Street and then right on to Wellington, passing Lady Lucinda with my head turned the other way so I wouldn't have to see the sandals I knew were still gracing the plinth in the window display. I trotted past a headscarfed housewife wheeling a giant pram, and at the plate-glass doors followed a lady in a camel coat and stilettos over the marbled step and into the hallowed entrance of the department store, passing under the huge three-sided clock that hung from chains lashed to the ceiling of the ground floor.

The six storeys of Bradley's had been the engine of my childhood, with its lift operator punching buttons, its block letters proclaiming such exotic names as *Haberdashery* or *Lingerie*, its coffee shop at the top where you could look out over Helmstone while lacy-aproned girls served grated-cheese sandwiches. It had been our treat, Mum and I, back when she was the centre of my world, the pavements of Petwick its cosy perimeter, and a day trip into town the highlight of my week.

I took the new escalator up to the top and worked my way down, starting at Menswear and perusing the racks of shirts and slacks with the eagerness of an explorer, embarrassedly gathering up underpants and flinging them into my basket, covering them up with packets of socks. A pleat-skirted salesgirl saw my numerous items and offered to pack them up for me. She added, with a superior, lipsticked smile, that they could be delivered for a small charge.

'Of course, if you'd like extra help to find any more goods,' she said, eyeing the huge quantity of notes I still held in my hand, 'we'd be happy to oblige.'

'That would be wonderful,' I purred, and so, for a short, happy hour I was once again a member of the moneyed classes. A young lad raced about the shop for me picking up toiletries and groceries, while I found myself drifting towards Ladies' Clothing. The new autumnal range was in stock; I fingered polo neck jumpers and wool skirts, wishing I'd thought, on leaving home, to pack for future seasons, and not just the one I was in.

After Ladies' Clothing came Ladies' Footwear and the special Modern Girl section, and of course they were there, the same fab white sandals that had been gracing the window of Lady Lucinda all summer. They had a thick round buckle and a low heel, and the tiny price tag attached to it read, in discreet handwriting, *45/-*.

I caressed the shoes furtively. They were five bob

cheaper than they were in the shoe shop, not that it made any difference to me: I wasn't about to buy them. Despite myself, my thoughts returned to the mountain of Dockie's notes still squashed into the bottom of my bag, and I knew that he'd never notice how much I returned to him. He hadn't even asked for a receipt.

I wrestled with my conscience for several minutes, as another pleat-skirted, red-lipsticked salesgirl hovered discreetly nearby, waiting for my nod. I had helped him, after all; more than anyone else would have done. I would never, ever be able to afford the shoes. I would never be able to afford anything decent ever again – or, at least, not for years and years, which was the same thing. And what did he need the money for, in any case?

'Can I help you, miss?' The salesgirl took a step closer.

'I'm not sure.' I thought of the day before I'd thrown everything up in the air, when I'd gone into town with my schoolfriends and had bumped into Harry, purely by coincidence, and he'd made them giggle and I'd said nothing at all. He'd tagged along, even though I hadn't wanted him to, and as we were exclaiming over the white shoes in the window, he'd offered to buy them for me.

'What, now?' Sheila had said, and I'd caught the puzzled look that passed between her and Mary, and I'd known that it wouldn't be long before they caught on.

'It *is* my birthday in a month,' I'd said archly, and they'd nudged and teased me for the way I'd said it, and I hoped I'd distracted them enough that they wouldn't twig that all the little extra things I'd come to school with – the gold-nibbed fountain pen, the bound copy of *Madame Bovary*, the lipstick applied in secret at break time – hadn't come from my non-existent savings but from the pocket of the man trailing us around town right now.

Well, I was glad I was finished with that, although the presents had been nice, and I sort of wished I hadn't got used to them.

'Let me know if you need me,' the salesgirl said a little wearily, clearly thinking I was a time-waster.

'Wait,' I said as she turned to go. 'You wouldn't have these in a size three, would you?'

Sometime later I headed out of Bradley's, several paper bags clutched in my fists, one of them containing a rather beautiful pair of expensive white sandals. The plate-glass door was opened for me, I was waved off with cheerful smiles, and I bounced back along Wellington Street, grinning at the shoes in the window, turning left on to King Street and then right at the seafront up Gaunt's Cliff, pleased that I'd done a good turn, not only to the old man but also to myself.

When I got back to Castaway, I went straight down to the basement and knocked on Dockie's door with a confident fist. 'Hello!' I called. 'Rosie here. I've got some things for you.'

Just like yesterday, there was no answer, although this time as I hammered again I heard somebody behind the door opposite snarling at me to shut the fuck up. After several more knocks, which were again greeted with insults from across the way, I realized, belatedly, that he must not be there.

I looked at the bags in my hand and glanced down the passageway. I had a feeling that if I left them outside his door they would be gone within half an hour, and so I tried the handle to his room. When it gave, I opened and stepped in.

The smell of yesterday had lessened slightly, perhaps due to the open window. The closed curtains billowed inwards, rippling grey daylight across the dim room. I made out the shape of the table and went to put the bags on it.

'Who's there?'

I yelped and turned, my heart hammering. The shape on the bed was shifting. In the dark I could just about see Dockie's tangled head and lumpy body.

'You scared the living daylights out of me!' I dropped the bags, went to the window and pulled the curtains open. Dockie was lying on one arm; he had removed his overcoat and boots at least, which were lying on the floor, but the blanket was cramped around his much-darned stockinged feet. His eyes were half-closed and gummy.

'Whassgoinon?'

'It's me. Rosie.' I returned to his bedside and looked down at him. 'I've brought your shopping.'

'Ugh.' He put a hand to his brow to hold back the light.

'You asked me to buy you some things. You gave me money.' I opened my handbag and took out his change, putting it on the table where the torn envelope still lay. No, I decided, he would never, ever notice the missing forty-five bob.

He grunted something which sounded like, 'My head,' and rolled over on to his side.

'There's more being delivered later,' I said brightly, conscious of the shoes in their clean white box, wrapped in tissue paper. I was still holding this bag in my hand, and placed it carefully beside the door. 'But look, I've brought you some groceries. Shall I make you a cup of tea?'

'Tea.' He snorted. 'Tea.'

I thought that might be some sort of assent, and took one of the bags to the kitchenette, filling the kettle at the sink and setting it on the gas. 'You do remember, don't you?' I said, lighting the flame with a match.

'Mmm.' There was a pause. 'You're the girl. You came before.'

'That's right. I'm Rosie. You're Dockie.' I looked over at him; he appeared to be hanging half off the bed now. 'You left Dublin?'

I heard another 'Mmm', but it sounded more certain now. I busied myself with spooning tea into the battered metal pot and setting a chipped cup and saucer on the side.

'The house,' he muttered. 'The name of the house.'

'This place? Castaway House?'

He grunted. 'Yes. Oh, God, my head.' There was a squeak of bedsprings and he shuffled himself up to sitting, resting his back against the wall. 'I have a problem . . . with my head. It doesn't allow me to . . . to breathe.'

I glanced at him. 'To breathe?'

'To think. To remember.'

'Yes,' I said, as the kettle whistled and I poured boiling water into the pot. 'You said you'd been on a bender.'

'Ah. Of course. The bender.' His gummy eyes peeled open further and appeared to take me in for the first time. 'You . . . went shopping?'

'You asked me, as a favour.' My cheeks burned as I poured the tea and spooned in powdered milk, wondering if he'd notice my mangling of the truth. 'To, you know, buy you some clothes and whatnot.'

'I think I remember.' He breathed slowly, as if unsure of his lungs. 'Thank you.'

'That's all right.' I opened the packet of sugar and shook some into the cup. 'Here's your tea.'

I brought it over to him and he took it from me carefully. I pulled out a chair from under the table and sat on it sideways. 'Do you want me to call a doctor?'

'Absolutely not.' He blew on his tea. 'I shall be fine very shortly.'

'It's just that you don't seem . . .' I paused. 'At all well, really.'

He sipped his tea and sighed. 'I have a problem with my memory,' he said. 'It's not the booze, you know. The booze is medicine, to stop these headaches. I am plagued, you see, by terrible headaches.'

'Okay,' I said slowly. 'If you say so.'

'I don't expect you to understand.' He glanced up at me. 'The tea is excellent. You will make someone a good wife one day.'

I barked a sour laugh and put my chin on the back of the chair. 'So you still don't know why you're here?' I asked.

'Castaway House . . .' He sighed. 'A tattoo on my heart. Castaway House.'

'Items from a newspaper, you said.' I recalled mentioning that to him yesterday, although this time he forbore from going through his pockets yet again.

'Ah. Yes. That rings a bell.' He frowned. 'I believe it was the reason for the bender.'

'You read a newspaper and went on a bender?'

'I'm not sure. Perhaps. I suppose I read something important.' He shook his head. 'It's gone, I'm afraid. Maybe it will return.'

I glanced at the table beside me, where I'd laid the money. Beside it was the tatty envelope. 'That photograph, from the envelope,' I said, sliding it out and showing him. 'This isn't what you meant, is it?'

He looked at it. 'I have always owned that,' he said. 'I was born with it.'

I put it back inside the envelope. 'I thought it might be you as a baby,' I said. 'But I wasn't sure.'

'Ah, now, as to that I have no idea. If it is indeed a baby, I am at a loss as to which baby it might be.'

I frowned. 'But you said you were born with it.'

'On the docks. I was born with it on the docks.'

'You were born on the docks?' He'd muttered something about this yesterday, but I hadn't been paying attention.

His red-rimmed eyes flicked in my direction. 'By which I mean,' he added, 'that I was found on the docks.'

'Really? How odd.'

'By Frank. He found me on the docks, wrapped in a torn blanket, clutching this photograph, and there I was born, because prior to that moment I have no memory at all.'

I leaned forwards on my chair. 'What do you mean, no memory?'

'I mean exactly that. Of what happened to me before,

there is nothing but smoke and fog.' He shrugged. 'But it was a long time ago, you understand. It is of little consequence now.'

'But that's . . . but that's . . . how old were you? I mean – you weren't a child?'

'Not in physical form, no.' He breathed heavily. 'But in many other respects, that is exactly what I was.'

I put a hand to my mouth. 'That's incredible.'

'And ever since then . . . you see, the headaches. They get in the way of my remembering. I have a brain somewhat akin to a Swiss cheese.'

'But you must have been told, surely. I mean, who you are, what your name is.' I frowned. 'You know what your name is? Your real name.'

He shook his head. 'I know nothing. As I said, I was born on the docks.' He took another sip of tea.

'Yes, but . . .' I hesitated. 'People don't just turn up. Somebody must have been looking for you.'

He shrugged. 'Alas, not in my case. It appears that nobody wanted to recover me at all.'

'But that's awful.'

'Not at all. Who needs memories? Weighing one down with a lot of nonsense.' He nodded firmly. 'Frank was of the same opinion. He used to say that if I'd ever wanted to remember my past, it would have come back a long time ago.'

I looked down at the table top and thought of my own nonsense and how if I could erase my memories – at least, certain ones – then I surely would. Another thought occurred to me. 'So when you came here before, to Castaway House, it must have been before you lost your memory.'

Dockie shook his head. 'Not necessarily. I could have been here last year and forgotten about it. Frank remembered things for me, you see, but now Frank is dead and I have to rely on myself. And, as you see, I am not very reliable.'

'Perhaps if you knew who the photograph was of . . .' I stood up. 'Perhaps that would help?' I trailed off, feeling inadequate, as if nothing I could say would ever match the enormity of losing who you'd once been.

He waved a hand in the chilly air. 'I need no help. When one has a faulty brain, one must learn to adapt to the flow of the river.' He frowned. 'Except that I find myself here, without the slightest notion of why, when I could be in my own room with Mrs O'Shea bringing me soup on a tray.'

'I made you soup yesterday.' I went to the kitchenette and looked through one of the bags. 'By the way, I brought you this.'

Dockie squinted at the bottle of Wincarnis Tonic Wine in confusion. 'Hmm.'

I put it on the side. 'You've some more things arriving this afternoon. Look, the money's on the table, okay? You can count it.'

He gave a dismissive shake of his head. 'You're a good girl,' he murmured, and as I went past he held out a hand. 'Thank you.'

I smiled at the hand, not really wanting to touch it. 'You're welcome.'

'And now, to rest.' He put his cup of tea on the floor.

I opened the door and swung back on it, looking down at him. 'Do you want me to . . . I don't know, pop down tomorrow? Make sure you're all right?'

'Oh no. You've done quite enough.' He nodded, and guilt curled my spine because I really had done quite enough.

'I shall be fine now,' he went on. 'I have food and clothes and a good wine. What more could I want?'

'Well.' I waggled my fingers. 'Bye-bye, then. I mean, I'm sure I'll bump into you in the hall or something.'

'I shall return to Dublin as soon as I am fit.' He wheezed out a sigh. 'What a foolish adventure.'

I left him staring blearily at his holey socks, twisted into the end of the bedclothes, and climbed the stairs back to the ground floor. I was walking along the passageway towards the hallway when I realized I'd forgotten the shoes. They were still in their pristine box, wrapped in tissue paper, in an innocent-looking Bradley's bag sitting beside the door.

I closed my eyes and leaned on the snail-shell end of the banister. I should go back now, make up some excuse about just checking if he was still all right, then whip up the bag and high-tail it away. 'I didn't know he was ill,' I muttered to the painted-over Anaglypta below the dado rail, scuffed by a hundred passing bodies.

At that moment the telephone pealed into life and I jumped out of my skin.

I stared at it, frozen, as it rang, accusing me. I felt unable to take a step towards it or away; instead I clung to the banister like a life raft, as the overhead light clicked off and I was left in the dim milky light of the afternoon.

The phone continued to ring and then I heard a growled, 'All right, all right, I'm coming.' The door to the ground-floor flat burst open and I steeled myself, gripping the banister harder, as Star emerged with an apron over her Mod-girl striped top. She switched on the light, darted to the phone and, as she picked it up, saw me and gasped as loudly as I'd done when Dockie had surprised me just now.

'Shit,' she muttered as she pulled the receiver towards her, and shook her head sharply before barking into the phone, 'Helmstone 4895.'

I smiled a weak apology, but she frowned at me and said into the receiver, 'Who's that? Rosie?'

I shook my head frantically and waved my hands. Star continued to look at me as she said, 'No, I'm sorry, she's just gone out . . . No, no idea. Sorry.'

Thank you, I mouthed to her. She nodded at me and curled the telephone wire around her long fingers. 'Okay. Do you want me to ask her to call you back?' She paused. 'Oh. Well. Look, I'll make sure she sees it, anyway.'

I took a step away from the stairs towards Star as she took the chalk from its shelf and scrawled on the board, *Rosie – your mother called. Again.* 'On the top floor, yes,' she was saying. 'Yes. Yes, I know her.'

I leaned my head on the wall as Star turned slightly away from me. Odd notes had been scribbled all over the area beside the telephone, perhaps in the days before the blackboard, and they loomed in close-up: *Carry Me Home 5:2 (D'cster 3.18), Oral 15/-, Full £3, Tel. Mr Rattle 8390 (urgent!)*

'Um . . . well, fine, I suppose.' I noticed two spots of pink light up Star's cheeks. I had never seen her blush before. 'As far as I know. Yes. I suppose. Very happy . . . No, no, carry on.'

I heard the tinny chip of my mother's voice speaking through the wire, and felt my own cheeks burn red. I looked away from Star, towards the open door to the ground-floor flat, through which I could make out a small hallway and, beyond that, what seemed to be a bedroom.

'Well, the thing is, you see, I don't really know her all that well,' said Star, turning slowly back towards me. 'A boyfriend?'

I shook my head again, my eyes bulging inside their sockets. Star nodded slowly, listening. The telephone wire spun long waves about her fingers. Her sharp haircut gleamed under the overhead light. It suddenly occurred to me that Star belonged even less to Castaway House than I did. She'd have fitted in more on a yacht, holding a glass of champagne in one hand, wearing a one-piece swimsuit and laughing at the spray kicked up by the turns of the boat.

'No. Not that I've noticed.' Star looked me up and down and said, in a careless sort of way, 'Not at all. She doesn't seem the sort . . . Oh well. I'm sure she's fine . . . It's – um – it's Star . . . as in, you know, the night sky.'

I waited, my heart hammering, as Star said, 'I'll tell her . . . All right then . . . Goodbye.'

She placed the receiver carefully back on the telephone and surveyed me, her head to one side. 'She wanted to know if you had a boyfriend.'

I smiled. 'You know what mothers are like. Always worrying.' I spread my palms out. 'Anyway, you know I haven't.'

Star leaned one elbow on the end of the banister. 'And she asked if you'd broken up with anyone. If I knew about any man who'd upset you.'

I pressed myself back against the wall. 'My mum!' I laughed. 'She thinks there's some big secret behind it all. The Reason Rosie Left Home.'

Star reached out and touched my shoulder. 'You can tell me, you know.'

'There's nothing to tell.' I drew away from the wall, into her touch. 'Nothing important. Anyway, *you've* got secrets.'

Star snatched her hand back as if I were fire. 'What do you mean?'

I smiled. 'You know . . .' I said teasingly.

'You don't know what you're talking about,' she said rapidly. 'And if you listen to stupid gossip, then you're a bigger idiot than I thought.'

I gaped. 'What? I only meant that you told me you knew nothing about the flat, when you clearly do.' I nodded at the open doorway opposite.

Star glanced over. 'Oh.'

I narrowed my eyes. 'Then why am I an idiot?'

'I didn't mean it.' She smiled hurriedly. 'I'm sorry. I was just . . . It doesn't matter. You're not an idiot. You're the opposite.'

'But what gossip? What do people say?'

'Nothing.' She glared at me, daring me to pursue my line of enquiry, and I realized that we were at an impasse.

I nodded. 'Okay. So tell me about the flat.'

She looked back at it and her body sagged. 'It's the landlord's, all right? And I'm supposed to clean it. That's my job.' She waggled her head to indicate the irony of the final phrase.

'So why didn't you tell me yesterday?' I wondered what the gossip could be, what people would have dared to say about Star.

She pulled a face and tugged at her apron. 'Cleaning, all that housewife stuff: it isn't good for my image, do you know what I mean?'

She caught my eye, and we both smiled at the same time, and our truce tightened. 'That's funny,' I said, 'I was just thinking that you belonged on a yacht.'

'Oh, that's nice.' She sighed wistfully. 'We could sail out into the ocean and dive for pearls. Johnny could steer the boat for us.'

'Mmm,' I grunted, pleased she'd included me in her daydream but irked she wanted Johnny there as well. 'I'd always imagined the landlord to be that sort of wealthy tycoon – you know, yacht, permanent tan, beach house in Rio. I had no idea he lived downstairs.'

'Oh.' She nodded at the doorway. 'The landlord doesn't live there. He – er – just comes to stay every once in a while. Keeps an eye on things. Luckily, he doesn't come very often.' She winked.

'Then who's been driving me nuts with that awful whistling?' When Star frowned, I added, 'It's definitely coming from the flat.'

'I think you've already gone nuts. There's been no one in the flat for weeks.' She laughed suddenly. 'Perhaps it's mice.'

'Whistling mice?'

'Or – I don't know. The wind. Yes, it's probably that. You know what old places are like: full of holes.'

'Listen.' I indicated the telephone plinth. 'Thanks for speaking to my mother. For telling her – I mean, for not telling her – I mean, reassuring her, okay?'

Star shrugged. 'No problem.'

'I'm just . . . not in the mood for speaking to her right now, that's all.'

'Hey, none of my business.' She looked down at me as unspoken words hung in the air.

'And I don't care about any . . . gossip, or whatever it was, whatever people have said.' All the same, I yearned to know the details. Perhaps another time.

'Good,' she said fiercely. 'I knew you were better than that.'

'If you say so,' I replied, and on impulse I leaned towards her and pressed my lips to her smooth cheek. 'Thank you.'

'Oh!' she said, surprised. She gripped the edge of the banister. She indicated the open door to the flat and smiled uncertainly. 'I've – erm – got to get on. See you later, alligator.'

And then she was gone, the door closing behind her with a thud. I continued on up the stairs, the memory of Star's cheek still imprinted on my lips. I let myself into the kitchen, made myself a cup of tea and a cheese sandwich, and I'd been sitting at the table for fifteen minutes listening to the crackle from Radio Luxembourg on Susan's transistor radio before I remembered I still hadn't picked up the shoes.

I moulded crumbs back into dough with my fist. The thought of going back to Dockie's room made me shudder, with his rotten smell and his tales of brain injuries and boarding houses, all wrapped up inside an old man with holes in his socks and his mind. The whole thing made me feel unutterably sad, and I was relieved he'd mentioned returning to Dublin, away from any place I could help him.

All the same, I had stolen money from him: two pounds five shillings to be precise – or four if I took one back for the gas meter. Stealing from an old man with a handicap – I'd actually done the reverse of a good turn. I drank the last of my tea, remembering that he had oodles of cash and I had none, and he'd never notice, and – well, it was done now, for better or worse.

Thinking of that – *For better or worse, for richer or poorer*, all of that – reminded me of the copy of *Northanger Abbey* Dr Feathers had lent me, and I reached into my handbag for it. Maybe tomorrow I would ask Mrs Hale all about it; if she'd known Robert Carver, what he'd been like, why somebody had scratched a belief in his innocence into the underside of the windowsill.

The book was an old hardback, in a much-worn green material, cracked at the spine and with loose pages that tried to flutter out when I opened it. There was a line drawing on the front of a young girl, and the title caressed the cover in what had once, I supposed, been a gold colour but was now a dull brown.

However, none of this interested me. Neither did the contents of the book; or, at least, not as much as the inked scrawl that covered the flyleaf at the back. The handwriting was perfectly neat, in a calligraphy I had never managed to achieve, but the words themselves darted about the page in a random order, like butterflies:

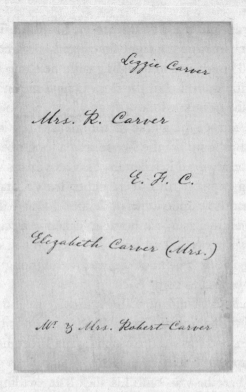

Lizzie Carver

Mrs. R. Carver

E. F. C.

Elizabeth Carver (Mrs.)

Mr & Mrs. Robert Carver

One floor below, the doorbell rang in three harsh bursts, but I ignored it. I went to the underside of the windowsill and found again the protestation of Robert Carver's innocence. I squinted at the words etched into the wood, trying to work out if it was the same handwriting, but there was no way of telling for sure.

The doorbell rang again. I took the book with me as I opened the kitchen door and stepped out on to the landing. From here, I could see nothing but the central stairwell disappearing to the ground floor, but I heard footsteps cross the tiled hallway and the crunch of the door being opened. Distantly, Star's voice spoke.

I went as quietly as I could into the bedroom. The place smelled musty from the night-time breath of three pairs of lungs, still lingering and mingling with the damp bubbling through the walls. I shut the door behind me and tiptoed towards the nearest window, from where, beyond the balcony, I could see the whole of the street.

Parked in front of the house was a long-nosed white car with beady-eyed headlamps. I sat heavily on Val's bed, squashing her soft toys. It all depended on Star, I supposed, and how much she understood that I definitely, most certainly, was not at home to callers, especially ones in white sports cars. I wondered if I could just refuse to answer the door if he knocked, and then I thought that he was only bound to come back.

Yet the idea of talking to him stuck in my throat. *Don't want to*, I thought, like a child. The front door crunched shut again, and I stood up, watching the street, hoping I'd see him appear. I held my breath.

Yes. There he was, with his slick hair, twirling keys in his hand. I could even hear the faint jingle of them from up here. At the gateway to the house he stopped and turned, and I stepped backwards away from the window and from view. I listened for the sound of the car door opening and closing, and then the roar as the engine started. I watched it dart down the hill, and breathed out again.

As I stood there in the silence of the room I heard the whistling once more.

My thoughts skidded to a halt, and I strained my ears to listen.

Yes. It was the same grating, off-key whistle as before.

It travelled through my bones from somewhere else in the house, making me shiver.

Holes in the walls, Star had said. Perhaps she was right and it was only the wind making the noise, because it certainly wasn't coming from the ground-floor flat any more. If anything, it was coming from just outside the door, and it was a lonely, pitiful sound, similar in tone to the desperate crying I'd heard yesterday.

I walked to the door and opened it, one ear cocked for the direction it was coming from. Yet now I was in the hallway, the sound was fainter. I shook my head and was about to go back inside the flat when I noticed the package just outside the door.

It was a thick paper bag with string handles, and as I picked it up I saw the legend on the side: *Lady Lucinda Boutique.*

There was a click as a door below me closed, and I thought of Star darting up the stairs to leave it here, gathering my secrets like desiccating leaves. I took the bag inside the flat and put it on my bed, my stomach knotting as I removed the box inside, opened the lid and saw, nestling among sheets of tissue paper, a pair of white, thick-buckled sandals in a size three.

There was a label attached to the string handle. I turned it towards me and read: *Rosie – happy belated birthday. Reckon you'll look a proper little sexpot in these! Harry xxx*

I collapsed backwards on to my bed, my head resting against the chilly windowpane, my feet trailing to the floor.

Tomorrow, I thought. I would deal with everything tomorrow. I brushed my right hand across the bed cover, and it collided with *Northanger Abbey*. I drew it towards me and opened it to the back flyleaf, holding it above my head and reading again the various versions of a name, feeling oddly soothed by the repetitions: *Lizzie Carver, Mrs Robert Carver, Mrs Elizabeth Carver, E. F. C.*

I could still hear the whistling, and it grated on my teeth. I elbowed the box of shoes on to the floor, where it fell with a satisfying clatter. *Nothing matters*, I thought to myself, concentrating on the names in the book and thinking of Robert Carver and a girl who imagined herself married to him, remembering a time when I'd done the same thing with another name, scribbled in pencil in the margins of my diary, my cheeks burning now with the shame of it: *Mrs Harold Bright, Mrs Rose Bright, R. C. 4 H. B.*, over and over and then rubbed out so fiercely I'd scored a hole in the page, and gone to bed, dreaming of things I had no right to be dreaming about at all.

6

1924

The weeks passed, and as June blended into the deeper warmth of July, Helmstone revealed itself to me in slow bursts of colour, from the weather-gnarled fishermen gutting sprats on three-legged stools outside their arches, to the young shop girls queuing excitedly outside the enormous dance halls that flung fast jazz from their temple-like doors. As summer blossomed, the population of the town swelled accordingly, packing out the guest houses that lined the front and thickening the promenade and beach. All movement slowed, so that one ended up ambling in a shoal of humanity, buffeted by the tides of holidaymakers who joined and left the swarm, laden with picnics, parasols and the constant anxiety of the Englishman away from home.

I occupied myself in helping Alec with his nascent Hall of Fame, which appeared to be coming on much more slowly than I'd imagined, sketching odd views as they occurred to me, and avoiding Mrs Bray. This last was not so difficult, as since that first hideous skirmish in the dining room she had absented herself for every meal except breakfast, and was indeed out of the house most of every day. I remarked to Alec that it was almost as if she had a job, to which he roared with laughter and said he'd believe a hundred unlikely things before that.

I had also been seeing a great deal of Lizzie Feathers and, over the weeks, she had overcome her nervousness. In fact, she was fairly forthright at times with her opinions. She was also, naturally, quite undeserving of the lascivious thoughts I entertained about her while sitting side by side in the cinema. I knew I was wrong to have these thoughts; and yet, as they came unbidden, I let them run their course.

One blue-skied, mid-July afternoon, we went to a showing of *Faint Hearts over the Amazon*, and as Lizzie watched the screen, rapt in the action, her hands clutched in her lap, I watched her – or rather, the shape of her breasts beneath her blouse. Her bosom was large, and I had spent many happy hours at night imagining it unsheathed. My fantasies were informed by the French photographs passed around under the desks at school, and so doubtless were not particularly representative of the average female form, but they were all I had to go on.

Afterwards, standing on the steps of the Regal Picture-house, I had the odd, out-of-kilter sensation that often comes from sitting in a darkened room for several hours and then emerging, squinting, into bright sunshine. Lizzie was still deep in the world of the film. 'Wasn't he just the most handsome thing you've ever seen?' she said in a hushed voice as we climbed down the steps, referring, I imagined, to the jumped-up lead actor and, I also imagined, not requiring a reply from me. I had no idea what the film had been about as I had been looking at Lizzie during the entire picture, but this was never really a hindrance where Lizzie was concerned.

We repaired to a tea room in the old quarter of the

town, a maze of alleyways known locally as the Snooks, packed with tiny shops where antiquarian booksellers plied their trade, shoulder to shoulder with jewellers and chocolatiers. I bought Lizzie a slice of cream cake and we sat at the counter in the window, watching the day-trippers pass by.

'You're still coming to Father's dinner party next week, I hope?' She sectioned off a piece of cake with a glinting fork and folded it between her lips.

'I daren't miss it,' I said. 'Whenever I've met him it's all he's spoken about.'

She shook her head and pulled a wry, adult sort of expression that I supposed she was trying out. 'He's driving Mother round the twist. He's most worried that Mr Bray won't come. I suppose he thinks he's the cherry on the top.'

I smiled, although I could understand Feathers' point of view. Alec would lend a certain glamour to what would otherwise no doubt be a terribly dull evening. Merely the fact that he was from London seemed to infuse him with a raffish, debonair quality in the eyes of the Helmstonites who knew him.

'I'm sure Alec will be there,' I said, although I could quite equally imagine him changing his mind at the last minute.

'Father wants to smooth over rough ground with him, you see.' Lizzie's eyes narrowed, and she said in quite a different tone, 'I wish that girl wouldn't keep looking at you.'

'What girl?' I turned, suddenly intrigued; at the other end of the counter were two overly thin females drinking

tea and talking in loud, affected voices. However, which-
ever girl it was to whom Lizzie was referring, they both
appeared to be interested only in themselves. I shook my
head and turned back. 'Rough ground, you said?'

A frown clouded Lizzie's brow. 'She obviously thinks
she can have any man she wants, and never mind if he's
with someone else already. They're probably laughing
right now about how grossly overweight I am.'

We had had similar conversations like this previously,
each time plunging me into a state of confusion, although
I had by now developed a strategy for such an occurrence.
I privately thought Lizzie utterly deluded, but I had learned
that to suggest such a thing was to invite hours of conversation on the matter. 'Firstly, you're not fat,' I said, 'and
secondly, I don't find those sorts of girls attractive in the
slightest, as well you know.'

The frown lifted slightly. 'But they're so *thin*. And, you
know, completely fashionable.'

I glanced at them again. 'They look like scrawny chickens to me,' I said, which in all honesty I did not exactly
think, but it cheered Lizzie up no end and so I was able to
return to the subject of Alec and the rough ground to be
smoothed over.

'Well, according to Father, he was quite a tearaway
when he was younger,' said Lizzie, allowing a smile to
creep on to her lips, especially once the girls had left without a backward glance and she was able to relax.

'He was,' I said. 'Spoiled to death by my aunt, no doubt.
I'm sure he terrorized the town when he was here for the
summer vacs. It's all right; he had the same reputation in
our family too.'

Lizzie held out her smeary, licked fork to me, a question on her face, but I shook my head.

'Father was always going next door to complain about him, and then raging to us that the boy was "completely undisciplined".' She puffed out her bosom in a passable mimicry of her father. 'Although I don't suppose your cousin has particularly fond memories of him.'

I shrugged. 'Alec forgives everybody. I'm quite sure he deserved any dressing-down he got, and I'm sure he knows that too.'

'Well, Father wants to mend any broken bridges. Especially as . . .' She tilted her head to one side. 'As we're neighbours, I suppose.'

I thought privately that if Alec had not inherited Castaway and a sizeable amount of money from his mother then Dr Feathers might have left those bridges broken. Then again, maybe I was being prejudiced against the bumptious fool.

Afterwards, I walked Lizzie along the seafront to show her the Hall of Fame. She had been begging me for weeks to give her a tour, but Alec had made me promise to wait until it was at least in some sort of presentable condition.

The door was open, and the sound of hammering came from inside.

'Hello?' I called, sticking my head in, and the carpenter emerged, scratching his chin.

I had met him before, and he smiled easily enough and said, 'You're Mr Bray's mate, ain'tcha?'

'I'm his cousin,' I said. 'And his artistic advisor.'

That sounded idiotic now, but the carpenter simply

stood back and said, 'You taking the young lady to have a look round?'

'If that's all right.' I stepped over the raised door frame and held out my hand to Lizzie to follow.

The carpenter pulled his tobacco tin from his top pocket. 'You take your time.' He winked at me in an extremely seedy manner.

I led Lizzie into the entrance way of the Hall of Fame, which now boasted a fresh coat of paint and the beginnings of a turnstile. 'Oh, how exciting,' she said. 'I say, who's that?'

She pushed through the turnstile and inspected the royal family, peering up the King's nose as if a beetle had got stuck there. She turned uncertainly to me. 'Lenin?'

'Not quite.' I adjusted his glued-on beard. 'Let me take you round the corner.'

The second half of the Hall of Fame was illuminated by a frosted window at the end of the arch. Blurred shapes moved across the hazy blue. The electric light was still a little temperamental, so I kept the room dim and showed Lizzie the tableau of Rudolph Valentino with Gloria Swanson.

'How darling,' she said. 'But they weren't in *The Sheik* together. It was *Beyond the Rocks*.'

'Well, don't tell Alec,' I said. 'He thinks I'm a genius because I'm the one who arranged them.'

'You are a genius,' she said stoutly, and loyally inspected the rest of the exhibits. 'And I'm sure you're going to make lots of money.'

'Not me,' I said. 'Alec and his business partner will.

They're the ones who've invested in it; at least, Alec has. His inheritance, I believe.'

Lizzie turned on her heel. 'I suppose he knows what he's doing.'

'Ye-es,' I said doubtfully. 'I'm sure he does.'

'Of course, it should be open now, for the summer.' She rearranged Valentino's headscarf. 'Still, don't ask me. I'm utterly clueless.'

I approached her softly. For weeks now, I had been wondering how I could be in a room with Lizzie, alone, and now I was I did not quite know what I should do. 'Lizzie . . .' I began, unsure of what to say next.

She turned. 'Oh!' she said, not realizing I was so close behind her. Then there was an adjustment in her features. She blinked, half-smiled, and said, 'Yes?'

I took her hand. She wanted me to kiss her; I felt the urge in her rise up through me like a heat, taking me by surprise. I swallowed, and she inched towards me, and I bent my head to hers, miscalculated my descent and kissed the side of her nose.

She snorted a giggle. I put my hands around her waist and she relaxed into them. 'Those girls *were* awful, weren't they?' she murmured.

'Hmm?' I had no idea what she was talking about. I bent my head again, and her lips pressed against mine. They were soft and pleasant-feeling. This was going better than I'd hoped.

I wasn't sure how long one should continue kissing for, and her nose was nudging the side of my cheek, and I felt a little too hot, and awkward with my hands, but perhaps any second now I'd begin to get the hang of this, and then her tongue pushed against my lips, parting them slightly, and with a gasp she spun away from me and said, scarlet-faced, 'I'm so sorry,' whirled down the arch, around the corner, and was gone from view.

I ran after her, emerging through the archway on to the beach. The carpenter, leaning against the wall smoking his cigarette, turned to me, pushed his hat back up his head and said, 'You went too far there, mate.' He cackled unpleasantly.

I ignored him, scanning the beach for her. However, she had sprinted faster than an Olympic runner and was nowhere to be seen. I walked up the steps to the promenade to get a better view, but saw only a galaxy of children swirling like tiny stars towards the Punch and Judy man just starting to set up his red-and-white stall on the edge of the sand.

I touched my mouth, the memory of Lizzie's tongue still imprinted between my lips. I began walking, ostensibly looking for her but in reality attempting to allow my sensations to settle. I headed towards Gaunt's Cliff and then changed my mind, resting against a wall and letting the day-trippers and holidaymakers shift past me in waves of excitement, gabbling and arguing and squealing.

Somebody passed me who was not gabbling or arguing or squealing. I was struck by her, but at first I was not sure why. She was wearing a plain brown dress and an old shawl, and was carrying a straw basket. Her hat was dull and shabby. It was only when she turned her head to cross the road and I saw her unmade-up face tilt against the sun that I realized it was Mrs Bray, and that was why I had noticed her – not because she stood out, but precisely because she did not.

I stared. I had never seen her so . . . well, so ordinary-looking. As I watched her go in her inconspicuous get-up, I realized that she was heading to wherever she usually headed off to, and, the memory of Lizzie's tongue in my mouth still inside me, I knew with an absolute certainty that, right now, Mrs Bray was heading for an assignation with the man who was making my cousin a cuckold.

Rage boiled my head. I darted after her across the busy street. I would follow her, and then Alec would have proof, should he need it, should he wish to divorce himself from her. At the very least he should know, I thought, what a wanton slut he had married, and as I followed her past the chemist's advertising its 'Cure for Male Baldness' on King Street and then right along Wellington, I did not even stop to wonder why the thought of her infidelity enraged me so, only that it did.

She stopped suddenly, staring inside the window of Dacre's Meat Shop ('Only English Meat Sold Here'). I halted to match, and stepped inside the doorway of the Lady Lucinda Boutique. She was looking up at a man, possibly Mr Dacre himself, climb a stepladder with a leg of ham and hook it on to the rail, next to all the others that formed the window display. She called up to him and he brushed his hands on his starched white apron as he climbed down. She disappeared inside the shop and I knew I had her.

I faced the boutique window while I considered my plan. The legend 'Best Paris Fashions!' mocked me with its sneering lie, sucking in young would-be flappers through its black-wood doors. The whole town was a lie, an act, and Mrs Bray the biggest act of all. I imagined her inside the butcher's back room now, amidst the hanging sides of beef, one bare leg wrapped round Mr Dacre's waist, her tongue probing his lips just as Lizzie's had probed mine, and as I paced up and down, I realized I had worked myself into quite a state of excitement and I had better calm down before marching in there to confront the hussy.

Then, as suddenly as she'd stopped, she emerged and continued on her way down Wellington Street, her heels clipping the pavement, a joint of meat wrapped in paper emerging from the mouth of her basket. I started after her, blinking at my mistake, realizing that of course she was on her way to her assignation still and had merely stopped to buy him some meat. Perhaps their furious lovemaking woke some sort of savagery in them, to be tamed only by animal flesh. There was certainly some sort of insidiousness occurring, as the meat orders for Castaway were undertaken by Mrs Pennyworth at pain of death of anyone else interfering, including Mrs Bray.

She slowed outside Bradley's, the department store that imperiously surveyed the rest of the street from its position at the base, like a much-upholstered maiden aunt, and under whose curlicued three-sided Victorian clock I had met Lizzie and realized how much she bloomed when her father was not by her side.

Across the road from the end of Wellington Street was a small green with a fountain at its centre. Mrs Bray headed towards it, and I scanned the various benches that surrounded the fountain for a lone man pretending to read a paper. I wondered, again with a rising excitement, if there were some particular bench well known as a spot to meet strangers with a view to disappearing to a cheap hotel. However, Mrs Bray walked straight through the crowd of people without looking left or right and crossed the road at the other end.

I hurried so as not to lose her. On the other side of the green was a terrace of run-down houses, broken by a narrow street opening in the middle. It was down here that she disappeared and I, desperate by now not to lose her, plunged across the road and followed her inside.

Instantly, I was in another world. A closed-in, dark, fetid little world.

The road here was cobbled still, a relic from an earlier time, and the cobbles sloped from both sides of the street to form a drain in the centre. Arched alleyways broke the two-storey terraces at regular intervals, leading to who knew where. Washing was pegged across the streets from the upper floors, and a foul smell permeated the air – of latrines, coal dust and rubbish.

The slums.

I had never entered streets such as these. I was aware of their existence in my home town, but I had never even been close to them before. In my imagination they were pockets of depravity and crime, where housewives emptied bottles of gin into their gullets and babies squalled their way to death behind walls oozing damp.

I should have known that this would be where my cousin's wife chose to commit her act of adultery. She had a mouth as unpleasant as the stench I was breathing in now; it was only natural she would feel at home here. I was tempted to turn tail and go straight back the way I had come, but I told myself that only a coward would do such a thing, and so I continued walking. Although I occasionally lost sight of her round a corner, the steady clop of her heels told me she was only slightly ahead, and I knew it would simply be a matter of time before she entered the house she was making towards.

I was somewhat surprised that these very houses were cleaner than I had imagined; in fact, several women were on their doorsteps as I passed, bent double and scrubbing them, a tin bucket of water by their side. Two more, neighbours, were cleaning their adjacent windows with red-raw hands and old grey cloths. As I passed they turned and nudged each other. 'Lost something, dearie?' called out one.

'I . . . I'm quite all right, thank you.' I tipped my hat to them as I passed, rather scared of their thick wrists and tree-trunk legs.

'Don't worry, darling, she'll help you find it!' shouted her friend, as they both hooted with laughter. I continued on my way, scarlet-faced, realizing now why Mrs Bray had stripped herself of the usual fast make-up and couture outfits, the better to blend into these crooked little streets.

'Mister, you from the Corporation?'

There was a gaggle of young boys swarming about me.

'No,' I said. 'I'm not from any Corporation.'

'You got a farthing?' asked one, a cheeky little beggar with dirty blond hair.

'No, I haven't.' I turned my walk into a stride, as if I had some perfectly legitimate business here and that, once conducted, I absolutely knew where I was going and how to get out of this hellhole.

Yet every street I followed Mrs Bray down seemed to bring me further into the maze of the slum. The smell here became more intense, and I attempted to take as few breaths as possible, resulting in my lungs constricting further and panicking me even more.

I nearly collided with a man emerging from one of the arched alleyways, a black book in his hand, a sense of self-importance in his step although his shoes were worn and his hat was bent. I wondered if this was the mysterious man from the Corporation.

I proceeded cautiously to the next alleyway, and, on looking down it, I saw Mrs Bray being embraced by a tiny, malnourished woman in a pinny.

I could almost believe I had imagined the scene, that Mrs Bray, with her bobbed hair and eyebrows shaped into a permanent sneer, could bear to be touched by such a creature – and yet she had. Perhaps the woman was the procuress, I thought, although it hardly seemed feasible that Mrs Bray would have the need of her services. Yet I had led an innocent life and had no idea of the depths to which the vicious could sink.

A sharp object hit my back and, as I turned, another stone now hit me square in the chest. A group of older boys – in reality, more like young men – stared at me, hands in pockets, expressions of malignancy on their faces.

I stared back at them and, as I did so, one of them pulled back his hand and lobbed another stone at me. I held up my arm and the stone bounced off it. 'What you doing here?' one of them jeered.

I put my arm down. 'I was going about my business,'

I said firmly, determined not to be intimidated. They were younger than me, after all.

The leader of the men, who wore his shirt unbuttoned at the neck and had his cap pushed back on his head, spat on the ground. 'Going about your business?' he mocked. 'We don't want your fucking business here, ponce.'

'Yeah,' said another. 'Fuck off back to the Majestic.'

A stone hit me again, and a sharp pain spiked my cheek under my eye. I staggered backwards, holding up my hands to protect my face, and said, 'You could have blinded me, you fool!'

'I'll fucking get you next time.' I sensed another stone being prepared. I was against the wall; I could not even run. They had me surrounded; they had heavy-looking boots and fists trained by manual labour. My lungs constricted and I cursed them for letting me down just when I needed them the most.

'What the flaming heck is going on out here?'

The youths turned. The malnourished woman I had seen in the alleyway was out on the street, arms akimbo, glaring from me to the boys.

As one being, they shrugged. 'Nothing,' they muttered.

'Nothing, my arse!' She jabbed a finger in my direction. 'He's bleeding, you not see that?'

'What's he doing here anyway?' said the ringleader, defiantly. 'Ponce.'

The woman turned to him and said, 'And you, Ted, you should know better.' She made a shooing motion with her hands. 'Go on, get yourself back home and lend your mother an 'and instead of hanging about here causing trouble.'

There was a general embarrassed shuffling. Backs were turned, shoulders hunched. Ted muttered something vague about getting me another day.

The woman shook her head at me. 'You,' she said firmly, 'you're coming in here so I can take a look at that.'

She walked into the alleyway, beckoning me to follow with one finger and shouting behind her, 'And if any of you're still here when I come out, I'll box the ears of the lot of yer.'

I followed her into the depths of the alley. 'Thank you,' I said to her back, feeling that the words were somehow inadequate. 'Honestly. Thank you.'

'No blinking work, that's the trouble with that lot,' she muttered, almost to herself. 'All they got to do is hang about being bored. You something to do with Clare? Cos she never told me no one else was coming.'

'Er . . .' I began, as the alleyway turned a corner and we were suddenly in a small yard.

The smell of sewage here was overwhelming and appeared to be coming from what I assumed was the privy, tucked into one side of the yard. More washing was strung across the cobblestones, and facing each other on either side were two houses, the mirror of the ones on the street. On the step of the left-hand one a child dressed in a scrubby little dress was playing with a rag doll: some sort of make-believe game. She walked her doll first one way and then the other along the low step, sing-songing imaginary conversations to herself.

As I stood in the yard, watching the girl, I had the odd feeling that I was looking down on myself from above, and the image I saw made me cringe. Here was a young man in good clothes marching through the poorest quarter of town as if he had the perfect right to be there. Not only was he obviously a cretin, he was a frightful snob to boot. No wonder those boys had attacked me; in fairness, I deserved nothing less.

'Not there.' The woman jerked an elbow at the right-hand house, bustling her way towards its open door. 'This way. I'll need to dress that wound.'

I swallowed and entered the house, ducking my head to fit under the low doorway. The entrance gave directly on to a tiny bare-walled room, which had a stone sink, a lung-tightening, smoking black range and a wooden table, one of whose legs was propped up with a pile of news-papers. Sitting at the table was Mrs Bray, smoking a cigarette and looking as incongruous in the room as a poppy in a rubbish tip.

Her eyes widened with shock when she saw me. Her mouth gaped open around her cigarette. 'Oh my God,' she said. 'What the fuck?'

'Found him outside being set on by that Ted Barker and his mates.' The woman had pulled a clean scrap of cloth from some hidden drawer and was holding it over a small bottle, tipping it upside down. 'Throwing stones at him. Can you believe it?'

'I'd throw a grenade at him if I had one handy.' She eyed me with as icy a look as I'd ever seen on her.

The woman turned, a question on her brow. 'You two know each other?'

'Unfortunately.' Mrs Bray tipped ash into the tin tray in front of her. 'Following me, Mr Carver?'

'Ooh.' The woman cackled and looked up at me,

delighted. 'You do know she's a married woman, don't you?'

'He certainly does.' She sucked on her cigarette. 'He's my husband's cousin.'

'I see.' The woman clearly did not see, but covered her confusion with a brisk, 'Right, sit down, you, so I can have a look at that wound.'

She dragged me on to a chair by my jacket and I sat down with a thump, facing Mrs Bray. I wished, with a fervency that I had never previously experienced, that the floor would open up and take me into the bowels of the earth for ever. I wanted somehow to present an acceptable explanation for my presence, but none occurred, and so I simply said, 'Yes, I'm afraid I was following you.'

The woman held the cloth to my forehead; the alcohol she'd soaked it in stung horribly and I winced.

'Hurts, does it?' asked Mrs Bray. 'I really hope so.'

'Come on now,' said the woman, dabbing at my wound. 'We all know what it's like to be lovesick, don't we?'

Mrs Bray snorted and poked a finger in my direction. 'He's not lovesick, Dotty. He's been sent to spy on me, either by my husband or my father-in-law. I presume Mr Carver followed me because he thought I was on my way to visit my lover, like the brazen little whore I am.'

The woman she'd called Dotty laughed. 'That's a good one,' she said. 'Got a lover in here, have you? Wouldn't mind one meself. Pass him over when you're done.'

'I'm not a spy,' I whispered, in between winces. She gave me such a look of scorn I added, 'I – I mean, Uncle Edward didn't send me ... and Alec ... Alec knows nothing.'

'That's true enough,' she said sourly. 'They'll inscribe that on his headstone.'

'Please.' I knew I was scarlet-faced. I lowered my head, only to have it whipped upright by Dotty. 'I am so sorry. Allow me to apologize.'

'For what? Thinking I'm an adulteress, or following me, or having far too much interest in your cousin's wife than is appropriate?' She stood up and ground out her cigarette in the ashtray.

Perhaps I could die right then and there, I thought. That would solve the crushing shame that was forcing me lower and lower in my chair. 'I can only apologize,' I said again.

'Oh, grow up, you little boy.' As she swished past me, the wool of her shawl brushed my neck. 'Bye, Dotty. Sorry I couldn't stay.'

'That's all right, my love.' Dotty's voice was as strained as my own. 'And thanks for all the stuff. You shouldn't, you know.'

'I absolutely should.' I heard the soft collapse of a cheek-to-cheek kiss, and then, like a subsiding storm, Mrs Bray was gone, clacking back over the cobbles, and I found that, once again, I was able to breathe.

Dotty whistled. 'Ooh, you really upset her and no mistake. Like a tiger when she's riled, ain't she?'

'To be honest,' I winced again, 'I've never seen her any other way.'

'Ah, she's a pussycat really.' She leaned close to my cheek as she inspected the damage. 'But then, I've known her since she was born. Can't get away with nothing with old Dot.' She laughed.

Despite myself, curiosity forced a question from my lips. 'She grew up here?'

'Princes Street girl, through and through.' She turned her back to me and bent down, pulling apart a flimsy curtain that hid shelves of neatly stacked boxes. 'That's the main road, Princes Street. It's what we call our area. You never been before?'

'No.' I coughed. 'I – ah – I'm not from Helmstone.'

She turned to me with a roll of gauze, measured it with her eyes and ripped off a piece. 'Well, me and Clare was neighbours, see. She grew up in that house there, across the yard.' She nodded, and I turned to where the line of sagging washing half-obscured the doorstep where the little girl was still playing. 'Her mum died when she was only a kid, so I used to keep an eye out, you know, what with her dad being such a useless idiot. Cor, she was a wild one though.'

'Really?' I wondered what Mrs Bray would make of Dotty spilling all her childhood secrets. I supposed she'd been so angry she'd stormed out without thinking of what the consequences might be. 'I had no idea.'

Dotty prodded the wedge of gauze against my face. 'Hold it there while I stick it down,' she ordered, picking up my hand and placing it against the cotton. 'Hard as nails, she was. But anyone would be, with her life. It's either get on top or drown, and she got on top. Always said she was going to get away from this place, even when she was a littl'un. I must say, I never thought she'd come back, but she's done good. Visits nearly every day, she does, and brings stuff. I mean, it ain't charity, know what I mean? Cos I wouldn't accept that. It's like payment for all the times I fed her and that when she didn't have nothing herself.'

She snipped off a tiny piece of tape and fixed the gauze in place.

'I think she hates me,' I muttered.

'She probably ain't even thought about you enough to hate you,' said Dotty. 'I'm sure she's got other things on her mind.'

'Well, this certainly won't help,' I said gloomily; and then, conscious of whom I was speaking to, 'Sorry. I've taken far too much advantage of your good nature already.'

'Oh, do be quiet, Mr . . . What's your name?'

'Carver,' I said. 'But call me Robert, please.'

'Well, I'm Dotty. Dotty by name, dotty by nature.' She cackled. 'You staying up at the house, then?'

I nodded. 'At my cousin's request, I hasten to add.'

Dotty bit her lip and gathered the debris of her make-shift first aid into her palms. 'I won't go there. She's invited me enough times, says she'd love to set the cat among the pigeons, have me up there for dinner, with all the servants yes-madaming me and all that, but I won't go.'

'Yes, I can imagine that might be rather . . . awkward.'

'Not for that.' She waved a hand. 'Since you-know-what happened, I can't help but think about it whenever she talks about the place. I mean, just hearing the name Cast-away House and I remember all the stories and get the right heebie-jeebies.'

I frowned. 'I'm sorry, I have no idea what you're talking about.'

She looked at me. 'You don't?'

'No. What happened at Castaway?'

She tightened her lips and shook her head. 'Sorry, if you don't know, I ain't going to be the one to tell you. Not if you're staying there.'

'Come on.' I smiled, and the gauze tightened on the wound. 'Whatever it was, it must have been years ago.'

'Only nine.' She nodded sharply. 'Not so long, really.'

'Nine years ago? But that would have been . . . I mean, that was when my aunt and uncle owned the place.'

'Well, of course it was,' she snapped, and sighed. 'Look, I'm sure you'll find someone to tell you, if you're desperate, but it ain't going to be me.'

My interest was piqued, but Dotty's voluble mouth had shut tighter than a clam. She dropped the scraps into the range and said, 'So, now you're here, you want Clare's cup of tea? I didn't even have time to put the kettle on before she rushed off.'

'No, but thank you.' I got to my feet, scraping the chair on the rough stone floor. 'And I am so sorry for spoiling your afternoon.'

Dotty looked up at me, shaking her head. 'The way you posh people talk: it's like you all got sticks up your spines.' She made the same shooing motion to me that she had done with the youths. 'Come on, then, I'll walk you out of here. Don't want you getting lost and running into Teddy, eh? Not that he's anything without his little gang around him.'

'I . . . I assure you I'm not that posh,' I said, attempting a laugh as I crossed the threshold and stood in the yard waiting for Dotty to emerge and shut the door. Across the way, a young expectant mother appeared behind the little girl. She was almost at her time, and she stared at me with unabashed curiosity. I tipped my hat and smiled at her daughter, who jumped up, unnerved, and clung to the woman. 'Good afternoon.'

She nodded at me, her hands on the little girl's shoulders. Dark shadows bagged under the woman's eyes, and her cheeks had an old lady's hollowness. Dotty waved to her as she crossed the yard. 'I'll be back in two ticks, Lorelei.'

Lorelei nodded herself into a semi-smile and then coughed, a sharp hacking sound I recognized only too well. I cast around inside my mind, wishing there was something I could do to help, but Dotty was already wheeling me back down the alleyway towards the street. 'Poor cow,' she said. 'Won't make old bones, that one.'

'I know the problem.' We walked swiftly back along the cobbles, Dotty waving and calling to most people she passed. 'I nearly died myself last year.'

Dotty glanced at me sympathetically, and I felt uncomfortably aware that had I been born in Princes Street, I almost certainly would have died, if not from the bronchitis, then from the pneumonia that had followed.

'I reckon them back-facing houses're the worst,' she said with a healthy sniff. 'Cos you don't get the fresh air, see. Mind you, I wouldn't want to live in the front-facing ones, having to walk all that way round to the privy in the morning, not when you're busting. All right, Sarah?'

A woman dragging a heavy-looking bucket along the street winked at Dotty. 'Who's the boyfriend?'

'Hands off, he's mine.' Dotty put her arm through mine as we walked. 'You don't mind, do you, eh, Robert?'

I did not see that I had much choice in the matter, and so I merely shrugged and mumbled something off-hand.

'By the way,' I added, 'I don't want you to think that I ... I mean, I come from a fairly humble background myself, nothing like my cousin's. It's just that my grandfather paid for me to be sent away to school. They pretty much beat a demeanour into you from the age of eleven.'

'Well, you coulda knocked me down with a feather when Clare comes back here with that la-di-da voice. Lessons, she had. Not just in speaking, but in all sorts. Books, history, French, all the stuff she says you need if you want to speak to the gentry. I mean, you wouldn't know now, would you, to listen to her that she was born down here?'

'You wouldn't, no.'

'So you two got something in common, eh?' Dotty squeezed my arm. 'Don't worry, I'm sure she'll come round in the end.'

'Hmm.' I was not as confident as Dotty. Previously, Mrs Bray had hated me without good reason; now she had one, I could not see that she would relinquish her scorn.

We were almost at the end of Princes Street; the road was becoming wider and better maintained. The dwellings I had initially taken to be shabby seemed magnificent compared to the mean little roads I had now encountered.

'How long are you staying at the house for?' asked Dotty.

'For the summer, hopefully. If – well, if everything works out for the best.'

She sighed. 'Rather you than me, if you don't mind my saying.'

I nodded. 'The atmosphere has not been particularly ... but it is good for my lungs, at least.'

She stopped. Ahead, a trolleybus thundered past the junction, and I knew I was nearly free.

'Do you believe in ghosts, Robert?'

'What?' The question was so unexpected it took me several seconds to understand it. 'Er . . . no. No, not at all. Why?'

'Castaway House.' She narrowed her eyes and tightened her lips. 'The way it's stuck out on the end like that: lonely, watching the sea. I wouldn't be surprised at more than a few restless souls up there.'

I tried not to laugh. 'Well, I've never experienced anything supernatural, and I've never heard of anything untoward occurring there, either.'

She tossed her head. 'Men never notice a blessed thing. But I tell you something: you won't catch me within ten feet of it. And if I was you, I'd clear off as soon as I could. Full of nasty little secrets, that place; it's cancerous, d'you know what I mean?'

I rather resented her implication that the house had been the cause of my aunt's fatal illness, but Dotty had been so kind to me I felt I could say nothing but, 'If you won't tell me what this awful thing was that happened nine years ago, how can I make any sort of decision about staying or going?'

She shook her head, muttering, 'Oh, ignore me. I'm just a mad old hag,' and laughed, revealing blackened teeth that made her look exactly as she had described herself. 'Go on, you'd best get yourself out of here while you still can.'

'Thank you.' I shook her hand, which surprised her rather. I felt the bones through her fingers.

'You're welcome.' She watched me walk down the cobbles. At the end I turned to wave goodbye, but she had already disappeared behind the curve of the road.

I emerged at the busy thoroughfare and crossed on to the green, noticing for the first time how pleasant this place was. Two small boys played wooden soldiers on one of the benches, lining them up for battle, and I saw how healthy the children looked with their filled-out cheeks and clean caps. A pair of nursemaids on the adjoining bench murmured together, one pushing a lace-edged perambulator back and forth. Sunlight beamed warmly on to my shoulders, and I felt the mire of Princes Street shedding from me like a second skin, aware of the astonishing good fortune that I, unlike Dotty or Lorelei, was able to do so.

I had first thought of returning to the house, but the idea seemed to have lost its appeal. I headed towards the seafront, deciding that I might take in the Punch and Judy show after all: however evil Mr Punch was, at least one knew what one was getting with him. I attempted to dismiss the woman's superstitious mutterings from my mind: surely what had happened nine years ago was of little consequence, or we in the family would have heard about it. In fact, that was probably why she had refused to divulge it, because secretly she knew that it was no doubt a rumour blown up to the status of a truth. Perhaps my uncle Edward had been accused of violence, I mused, thinking of his irascible temper, or my aunt Viviane had snubbed an important person at one of her many garden parties – that, I could imagine – who had then revenged themselves in slander.

Or perhaps Alec . . . and then I remembered the dinosaurs again, and Alec's uncharacteristic gloom that day, talking of going to war as preferable to his current position. I would have been – yes, about ten years old, and so that was nine years ago, or thereabouts.

And of course, that was when he had spoken of the 'other child' his mother preferred, who, I now knew, had later turned out to be Clara Bray. I wondered if Mrs Bray had had anything to do with the mysterious incident. Although surely in that case Dotty would have mentioned the connection, if only to defend her surrogate daughter from possible denigration.

I realized that I was in danger of considering Mrs Bray in the worst possible light yet again, once more without a shred of proof. In any case, I should be devoting my attention to Lizzie, and I had not thought about her or our kiss for some time.

I continued on my journey towards the beach, deciding that if I could not find her there I would hunt her out at the Featherses' house. I presumed she had run away on some misguided notion of shame; I would seek her out and reassure her that she had done nothing wrong. On balance, after all, I had behaved in the shoddier manner this afternoon, although I would never tell Lizzie of my misguided trip into Princes Street.

I thought then of Mrs Bray growing up across the yard from Dotty, a grimy little kid, who no doubt had never played with dolls on the step the way Lorelei's daughter did. All the same, I growled to myself as I strode along; just because she had grown up poor hardly made her any less of a cold-hearted bitch. What of it, that her regular disappearances were to bring food to her old neighbours? It meant nothing. She was still obnoxious, and sewer-mouthed, and everything a decent woman was not. In such a way I attempted to boil up my usual hatred of her, but found it harder to come by right now.

It would be all right, I mused as I walked seawards. After a few days I would be able to properly despise her again; and, as the gulls wheeled and called overhead, this thought comforted me slightly, while alongside me, in my mind's eye, trotted a dirt-encrusted, motherless little girl, growing armour plating round where her heart ought to be.

7
1965

I dozed slowly into Tuesday morning, luxuriating under my heap of blankets and coats, as the girls rushed around the flat, Val spooning fruit yoghurt into her mouth, Susan fastening her stockings to her suspender belt, la-la-ing along to Radio Luxembourg on her transistor, which was balanced at a specific angle on her chest of drawers to catch the intermittent crackle.

After they'd gone I stretched myself properly awake and lay in bed with the curtains peeled apart a fraction, watching the sunlight struggling to pierce the clouds, and trying to prepare myself mentally for doing what I knew I had to do. I planned my outfit in my mind: perhaps my prim pinafore dress and a long-sleeved blouse. Nothing too exciting; nothing too provocative.

I dressed in front of the hissing gas fire, searching for my clothes on the free standing rail amidst Susan's nylon dresses, and then buckled my plain black shoes, picked up the paper bag from its hiding place under my bed and left the house. I planned my little speech as I shivered along the seafront road, and how I would enter and exit with my head held high, as classy as Julie Christie and twice as unreachable.

'All right, darlin'?'

I was shaken from my reverie by the builders overhead,

who were climbing the carapace of the Majestic Arcade like monkeys. One was leaning over the railing, winking at me. I ignored them, as I usually did, and was rewarded with cries of 'Frosty knickers!' and 'Give us a smile, then!'

Directly across the road, beside the promenade, was the fun park. The closed kiosk stood a little self-consciously out on the end. Some kid had written in large black ink over the faded drawings of lollies *Anne Watson is a Slag.* The lad who worked the dodgems was still there, hanging half off one of the poles, talking to someone. As I neared the end of the arcade I saw that it was Johnny, in his bespoke suit and neatly brushed-forward hair.

'I don't half fancy a coupla grapefruit.' Without meaning to, I looked up and saw one of the labourers clutch his hands to his chest, guffawing.

'Oh, shut up,' I said, conscious all the same of my breasts inside my bra, joggling as I walked.

'I'm only having a laugh, love. Lost yer sense of humour?'

'Sod off,' I muttered, but quietly, thinking of the further gauntlet I still had to run.

I walked as far as the little harbour and the black points of the fish-smoking towers. A couple of old men in sou'westers were sat on three-legged stools beside one of the boats, complaining in loud voices. One of them had a pipe clamped between his teeth, and I thought that if I squinted this could be two hundred years ago, so little did things seem to have changed in this particular corner of the world.

I turned up Regency Road, away from the seafront, and headed towards the green, where the dribbling fountain stood and the old ladies gathered on the benches with their shopping trolleys. To my right, across the street, was a ten-foot-high fence that stretched across a dusty, uneven road. Behind the fence a huge placard had been erected. The same artist who had depicted the shiny new arcade had also done some work here, although this time the people had been drawn in full colour: a husband and wife with gleaming copper hair, and two freckle-faced children, all looking up in wonder, open-mouthed, at the magnificence stretching above them. The sign banded below them read PRINCES STREET ESTATE: *A Brand-New Helmstone for a Brand-New Age.*

There was a gate set into the fence; I opened it and went through.

Behind the placard was a broad expanse of dusty brown earth, and springing up at regular intervals were semi-constructed blocks of flats rising like stubby fingers from the rocky ground. Like the Majestic, they were surrounded by frames of scaffolding, except for one, completed and gracing the clouds at its peak. The building seemed all windows to me, broken up with plain slates of concrete, and its height took my breath away.

'Excuse me, love. You ain't allowed here.'

It was the foreman, a grizzled man with tufts of unshaved beard, wearing an old shirt with the sleeves rolled up, a safety hat pushed back on his head.

'It's Ted, isn't it?' I said with my brightest smile, and held out my hand. 'Rosie Churchill. We've met before. I'm just here to see Mr Bright.'

Ted reached up to scratch his head. He looked about

him. 'You should probably wait here. We don't want any rubble landing on you.'

'Oh, I'll be all right.' I strode past him towards the clutch of small huts at the centre of the weird landscape, and after a second I heard Ted panting to catch me up.

'They're going up a treat, aren't they?' I indicated the finished building. 'Last time I was here they'd hardly begun.'

'Fast workers, my lads.' Ted sniffed proudly. 'Hoping my daughter's going to get a flat when they're done. Not that we get special treatment, mind.' He wagged his finger.

'Of course not.' I thought of living at the top of that skyscraper, with the whole of Helmstone laid out before me; a bit like being a crow in a nest, perhaps.

'I used to live here, you know.' Ted nodded at a man operating a mechanical digger, a pile of twiggy earth in his scoop. 'Before it all got bombed to smithereens. Ooh, I was a right little tearaway in them days.' He chuckled throatily.

'Really?' I said, not at all interested, but not wanting Ted to keep me from my goal of the steadily approaching huts. The central one, on a sort of raised platform to show it was special, had a window, made grimy from all the dust flying around, and through it I could see the dim shape of Harry's head behind his desk. Just the sight of his silhouette made my stomach clench with nerves.

'You've moved to Castaway House, ain'tcha?' Ted said suddenly, and I turned to him, startled. 'Mr Bright told me. Soon as I heard the name, I remembered.'

I stopped at the base of the wooden steps leading up to the hut. 'Remembered what?'

'About Clare.' He shook his head, as if amused by some far-distant joke. 'Girl from our area; I used to play with her brother, till he got the old T. B. Rough as a cock's arse, she was, and she only ends up marrying the poncey sod who lives there, don't she? Goes all la-di-da, gets herself an education from somewhere, changes her name to Clara, as if that'd help. You wouldn't credit it.'

I climbed the steps. 'Well, thanks for that, Ted.'

'Ah, I know you ain't interested. You get along now.' He waved a hand.

'I am, honestly. But I've got to . . .' I waggled my head. 'You know.'

'Course, it all went wrong in the end.' He was walking away now, speaking more to himself than to me. 'It always does.'

I watched him go, something in what he had said unnerving me slightly, although I wasn't sure why. Still, I had other things to think about, and so, without knocking, I turned the stiff metal handle of the door to the hut and went in.

There was a sort of anteroom before Harry's office, with a shatterproof window laid into the door, criss-crossed into squares, so I could see him before he could see me. He was sitting at his desk in his usual manner – leaning so far back as to be almost horizontal, sideways on – and looking up at the giant plan of the Princes Street Estate pinned to the wall.

I opened the door.

Harry switched his gaze to face me, and when he saw who had entered his whole body jerked upright. 'Rosie!'

His teeth formed its crooked smile. 'What a lovely surprise!'

He got to his feet to welcome me in. I strode towards the desk, trying not to notice his looks. Even his uneven teeth gave him a sort of flawed perfection, and his permanent five o'clock shadow appeared somehow to enhance his features rather than detract from them.

I dumped the shopping bag on his desk, the shoes in their box still inside, and said, 'I don't want you to buy me any more presents. I don't want ever to see you again. Do you understand?'

Harry gaped at the bag. From behind me there came a discreet cough, and a voice said, 'Erm . . . should I step outside for a moment?'

I turned. A pale, blond man in a frayed suit was standing just there to my right; he'd also, I saw now, been looking at the map of the estate.

'Sorry, Joe,' said Harry, with an easy charm, as if this sort of thing happened all the time. 'Look, let me introduce you. Rosie, this is Joe Prendergast from the council. Joe, this is Rosie Churchill. My stepdaughter.'

'How d'you do, Miss Churchill?' The man held out a nervous hand, which I shook, my face burning hot shame.

'Sorry about that,' I mumbled. 'I didn't know you were here.'

'That's quite all right.' He smiled at both of us, still a little unsure of the situation. 'I have nieces your age, and I hear all about the fracas between the girls and their parents.'

'Rosie's left home,' said Harry, by way of inadequate

explanation. 'She's living in Castaway House – you know, up the top of Gaunt's Cliff.'

'Oh yes, the Regency terrace.' Mr Prendergast nodded. 'Or was it just after – William IV, perhaps?'

'Um . . . I don't know.' I wanted a hole to open up and swallow me into the dusty floorboards.

'Joe's in charge of planning at the council,' informed Harry. 'He's got a vision for the town, haven't you, Joe?'

I knew Harry's ways: it was a distraction for the man, but it worked.

'Absolutely.' Mr Prendergast's pale blue eyes widened. 'You see, we have people desperate for housing, and nowhere to put them. Take your terrace, for example, Miss Churchill – or Rosie, if I may. How many people live in your building?'

'I'm not sure.' I sensed Harry on the other side of the desk working out strategies and manoeuvres. 'Maybe twenty?'

'And I suppose it's terribly draughty and damp, isn't it?'

I flicked a glance at Harry. 'It's fine,' I lied. 'I don't notice it, anyhow.'

'Well, anyway,' continued Mr Prendergast hurriedly. 'I want you to imagine, Rosie, a whole row of skyscrapers just like these ones your father is in charge of, on that hill-side, leading down into the town. Picture the whole city from the sea, utterly transformed.' He pointed out of the obscured window at the rising stacks.

'I don't know,' I said, having spent the last six weeks cursing the house. 'I think the terrace is quite beautiful.'

Joe wagged a finger. 'Ah yes, but beauty does not house people. We could fit two hundred people in a building the size of yours! With piped-in gas and fitted kitchens. Children could play on the walkways. Lifts to every floor. A city in the clouds. Now, tell me you prefer your damp, draughty home to that.'

I folded my arms, determined to annoy Harry. 'Well, I do,' I said. I sensed Harry rolling his eyes. 'It's got . . . character.'

Mr Prendergast shook his head. 'You didn't tell me your stepdaughter was one of these preservation types,' he said. 'Although I suppose it behoves the youth to rebel against their elders.'

'Less of the elder, if you don't mind,' said Harry. 'I'm only thirty-two.'

'It's got history,' I said. 'And a funny castle bit on the roof. And . . . a lovely stairwell, with this snail-shell at the end of the banister. And . . . well, I'd rather you didn't pull it down, thanks all the same.'

'I see this is where the young are going, then. Back to the past.' Mr Prendergast smiled. 'But you can't stem progress, Rosie. Concrete and aluminium: these are the materials of the future. And we must all live in the future.'

'Speaking of which,' said Harry, coming out from behind his desk, 'I think Ted's going to sound for tea any second now, and I shall take the opportunity to have a quick chat to my stepdaughter, if she doesn't mind. Rosie?'

'No,' I said sourly. 'Of course not.'

'Ah yes.' Joe Prendergast looked at his watch, muttering incomprehensibly, 'Time and motion, time and motion.'

Harry came past me and scooted up his jacket from its peg by the door. 'Come on, girlie. Let's go for a spin. I'll show you my new Jag.'

We all left together. The whistle sounded and the build-ers downed tools; I noticed a few of them looking over curiously as I walked with Harry to his car. It irked me that it was only his presence and, earlier, Ted's, that had prevented them leering at me just as the builders outside the arcade had done, and I was even more irked that I couldn't laugh it off, take it as the joke it was supposed to be.

'What d'you think, then?' Harry twirled the keys in his fist as we approached the car. 'Only got her last week. E-Type. Four-point-two litres. Thought to myself, *Y'know, Harry old boy, you deserve a treat.* I tell you something, she drives like a dream.'

He got in and leaned across to open the door for me. As I climbed in, sinking down with my knees up high, I knew I was making a mistake. I should have stalked in, dumped the shoes on his desk and stalked out, and never minded whether a man from the council was there or not. I cringed at my own eagerness to not make a fuss.

We drove slowly along the wide, rutted track towards the vehicle gate, past an abandoned concrete mixer. The men had gathered in clumps, sitting on pallets or leaning against the beginnings of walls, filling plastic cups from flasks of tea and watching me, as I sat hunched in Harry's car while he hopped out to open the gate with the engine still revving, and then drove us through.

'I'm glad you came along,' said Harry after he'd closed the gate and got back in. 'I've been coming up to the house all week, trying to catch you in.'

'I know,' I muttered, as he roared out into the traffic

and then right along the seafront, stuttering to a halt behind a bus as soon as we got there.

He banged the steering wheel. 'For Christ's sake!'

I jumped, but Harry was only referring to the traffic jam. 'Bloody buses.'

The car was waiting directly beside the fun park, with the Majestic Arcade opposite. I turned away from it and faced the stationary merry-go-round and the idling dodgems. As I gazed, nervous, preparing for the encounter I knew was coming, I saw Johnny emerge from round the back of the ride, adjusting his trousers and squaring his shoulders. I grimaced at having seen him, realizing he must have been for a pee, and then was surprised to see the boy who ran the dodgems also emerging from the same place a few seconds later. He swung up on to the platform in one quick move and lifted a hand. I switched my gaze to Johnny, who was now striding along the seafront, one hand also lifted in farewell, although if I hadn't seen both of them I'd never have realized they were waving to one another.

Odd, I thought, and then the bus lumbered forwards and we followed in its wake.

'Don't take me back to Castaway,' I said. 'I don't want you ever to go to my house again.'

'Your home's in Petwick,' said Harry, but he obeyed me, and instead of turning up the cliff we continued along the promenade, past Riccardo's ice-cream parlour and the barred entrance to the pier, all the way along to the sheer wall of rock rising up in front of us. Harry nosed his car to a spot beside the pavement, turned off his engine and looked at me. 'Now then, will you stop playing silly buggers and move back in with me and your mother?'

I stared out through the windscreen at the black face of the rock. 'Is that all you wanted to say?'

He paused and then leaned across me. I stiffened, but he only flipped open the glove compartment and took out his packet of fags. He pressed the lighter button on the controls and sat back. 'It's killing Grace, all this nonsense.'

'She'll get over it.'

'It's your education, that's what she's worried about. Throwing up your schooling like that. There's no need for it.'

I tightened my lips and continued staring straight ahead. 'Is that everything?'

'She knows I've been coming, you know. Practically sent me round there. She's worried about you, living by yourself.'

'I'm not living by myself.'

'Not returning her phone calls.'

I turned to him now and opened my mouth, but he spoke before I could.

'She only wants a chat.'

'All right.' I gripped the seat edge. 'I'll call her tomorrow.'

'Not tomorrow. She's visiting your auntie. Sorting out the sale of the farm; said she won't be back till late.'

'Okay. Thursday.' An idea took hold of me: Mum would be out all day tomorrow. The house would be empty, and Thursday was a whole other day away. 'Tell her I'll call her on Thursday.'

'And not before time.' The lighter popped out. 'If you ask me.'

I watched him as he lit his cigarette and blew smoke into the confined space of the car. 'The reason I left home was because of you,' I said. 'The reason I haven't been returning her calls is because of you. Because I don't know how I can talk to her any more. And when she asks me why, I don't know how I can lie.'

'Jesus, Rosie, you're such a drama queen.' He wound the window down a fraction and tipped ash out into the breeze. 'I don't know why you're making such a big deal out of things. We were having a bit of fun. Where's the harm in that?'

'Fun for you,' I snapped.

'Hey.' He tapped my arm and, despite myself, I shivered. 'You were more than willing, as far as I can recall. Christ, you nearly gave me a heart attack when I came home from work and your mum was in bits, saying you'd moved out. If we'd actually . . . you know . . . well, you know what I mean . . . I'd have been petrified you'd got yourself up the duff.'

I switched my gaze back to the cliff. A pensioner, an elderly man, was hobbling on a stick past the car. I watched him move slowly all the way to the end of the pavement and lean on the rail for breath. 'I feel bad enough already,' I said. 'Don't make me feel worse.'

'No need to feel bad.' He leaned closer towards me; I smelled his familiar smoky breath as he murmured, 'As long as she never finds out, where's the harm?'

'You should never . . . We should never have . . .'

His face was very close to mine now. I turned towards him and he eased his lips on to mine.

'There you go,' he whispered, pulling away. He was

clever, Harry, moving back while I still wanted more. A small kiss, and he knew he had me hooked back in. 'Just a bit of fun, see?'

'No.' I hugged my arms around myself. 'It's not fun, it's wicked. It's evil.'

'Bloody hell.' He sighed heavily, and I was relieved, because while he was frustrated he was less attractive to me. 'Look, I like you, you like me. You'll be off to university soon, won't you? And we'll say no more about it.'

I looked at him now, feeling stronger. 'Listen, I don't care whether you think I'm being stupid or childish or whatever, I don't want to see you again.'

'Well, that's going to be a bit difficult, eh, seeing as how I'm married to your mother.'

'You could go.'

He laughed at that.

'If you leave,' I continued, 'I'll move back in.'

'And how's that going to help? Devastate your poor mother? Ruin her life?'

'You're not that special,' I said. 'If you really loved her, you'd do the decent thing.'

'Hey.' He jabbed a finger towards me, and this time I didn't shiver. 'You're her daughter. You're the one with her blood. If you had any sort of loyalty you'd never have tried it on with me in the first place.'

I spluttered for a bit, almost inarticulate with rage, before saying, 'It was you! You made a move on me.'

'Don't be a silly bitch. Swanning around in that itsy-bitsy school uniform, giving me welcome-home kisses. I mean, look at what you're wearing now, all sexed up. What was I supposed to think?'

I was helpless with the awfulness of it all. I tugged at my prim pinafore dress. 'But . . . but that was just my school uniform,' I said. 'And this is just me. Being me.'

'You're so full of crap.' He flung the end of the cigarette out of the car. 'You're a little minx, and you know it.'

'Stop it!' I put my hands over my ears. 'Just stop it!'

'I'm a man, Rosie. I have urges.'

I grappled with the car door and swung it open. As I picked up my handbag, he said, 'Don't be like this. You're a special kid, you know?'

I scrambled out of the car. 'Don't call me. Don't come round,' I snarled, my head full of rage. He was smiling at me, not bothered by anything I'd said, anything that I'd told him I felt. I pulled my house keys out of my bag and slammed the door closed. Holding one of them between finger and thumb, I put it against the door and scratched a line along his paintwork, moving all the way along to the end of the car and then back again.

As soon as he realized what I was doing, he honked long and hard on the horn. 'Stop that, you slag!' he roared distantly, from inside the car. By the railing, the pensioner looked up, startled.

I bent down and saw his enraged face. I was still holding my keys in my fist. 'I never want to see you again!' I shouted, and then turned and clattered into a heeled run along the prom. Behind me I heard his engine start, and I'd only gone a few yards before he drew up alongside me. He leaned across and rolled down the window.

'You're a frigid cow!' he yelled, and then he stepped on the accelerator and Harry and his E-Type Jag leaped down the seafront and finally disappeared from view.

I held on to the rail. I was beside the entrance to the hacked-in-two pier, with its walkway leading to nowhere. I saw its bolted entrance, the steel bars on the plinth overhanging the damp sand. The pier itself, ten yards further from shore, seemed to be listing into the corrosive sea, splintering under the relentless, daily wash of salt and seagull droppings.

A wave of despair for that poor old pier engulfed me, and I found myself exploding into sobs, shaking with the force of them, bent double over the railing as tears and snot dripped on to the sandy rocks below. I groped blindly inside my bag for a handkerchief, but had none, and this calamity drenched me further, until I felt as if I too were rolling about in the icy water, flailing and drowning, my skin flaking from sea salt, my hair twisting into a coiled rope, gasping for air and sinking beneath the scudding tide.

'Here.'

I jumped, as a handkerchief was thrust into my hands. Johnny Clark was beside me, and I cursed him for being there, even as the tears continued to fall.

'It's clean,' he added, and so I took the handkerchief from him and blew my nose and dabbed my eyes and wished he'd go, but he stood there and waited until finally my tears dried and I was left with tired, gritty eyes.

'I don't want it back.' He held his palm towards me. 'Seriously.'

I swallowed back the last of the sobs. 'Thank you.'

'Nobody likes to see a damsel in distress, eh?' He leaned on the rail a foot away and we remained like that, in silence, watching the sea crash against the sand. After a while he said, 'D'you want me to – I dunno – get Star or something? You know, have a chat?'

'No!' I said frantically. 'Please, don't. I'm fine now. Honestly. It was nothing.'

'All right, all right, keep your knickers on.' He turned and leaned with his elbows against the rail. 'Between you, me and the deep blue sea, eh?'

'It's just a – you know – time-of-the-month type thing.'

'Ugh.' He grimaced. 'Here, this ain't to get out of paying your rent, is it?'

'Of course not,' I croaked, my throat raw from sobbing. And then, a spasm of fear twisting my guts, 'Oh, God, it's today, isn't it?'

'I'll be down this afternoon.' He banged the rail with his palms. 'With my little book.'

Too late, I remembered I still owed the tin a pound. I had fourteen shillings in my purse, and that was it. 'I'm six bob down,' I said frantically.

He shrugged. 'Not my problem. Ask your flatmates for a loan.'

I ran a hand through my hair. 'I can't. I mean . . . oh, Lord . . .' I pictured Susan's sneer. 'Please, just give me until tomorrow. I'm paid daily. I'll come up as soon as I've finished work, how about that?'

Johnny narrowed his eyes at me and said, 'I'm too bloody soft, that's my problem.'

'Oh, thank you. Thank you.'

He jabbed a finger at me. 'Before midday, okay?'

'Yes, yes, absolutely. Before then, even.' I sniffed, and stuffed the handkerchief up my sleeve. 'Thank you so much.'

'All right, don't make a meal of it.' He started walking to where Gaunt's Cliff twisted to the left and climbed steeply upwards. I followed him as he swung around the street sign that marked the start of the hill. 'You coming to our party on Thursday?'

'Party?' My stomach slithered uncomfortably. 'What party?'

'I thought Star would've told you. Yeah. We're having a party at our flat. It's gonna be ace. We'll have some proper ska, and I got a mate coming with some party starters, and – oh yeah, you got to bring some booze. You should come.'

I swallowed on my raw throat. 'She didn't invite me.'

'So what? I'm inviting you now.'

I rubbed a hand over my swollen eyes. 'I suppose she doesn't want me to come.'

Johnny huffed. 'What is it with you girls? You're always so touchy. It's like that other one she was mates with last year.'

I peered at him. 'What other one?'

'Oh, some bird called Gill. I dunno, it was back when me and Star were all part of the same gang, before we got together, you know. Her and Gill, they were like best buddies, then they had some stupid row over nothing and off that one goes to London and Star's all in tears over it.'

We were approaching the top of the hill now; outside the Bella Vista, I saw a taxi pull up, its engine ticking as the driver got out to open the side door. I remembered my conversation with Star yesterday, and wondered if that row with Gill had had anything to do with the way Star had flared up at me. There was something there, some truth I wasn't quite able to put my finger on.

'I'm not touchy,' I said. 'And I'm coming to the party, okay?'

'Ooh, Lady Muck.' Johnny snorted. 'Grace us with your presence, why don't you.'

'Shut up.' I grinned anyway, and watched a plump woman in early old age climb out of the car with difficulty, leaning on a stick the driver was handing her.

As we approached them on the opposite side of the road I said, 'By the way, how d'you know what's-his-name – you know, the boy who works on the dodgems at the fun park? I worked opposite him for weeks, only I never saw you then.'

'I don't know him,' snapped Johnny. 'Who told you I knew him?'

'Nobody. I saw you when we were – when I was – oh, just now. I was going along the prom and I saw you. Chatting,' I added, although that wasn't exactly what I had seen – at least, not the second time.

'What are you on about? I was just passing. He asked if I had a light.' Johnny spoke rapidly, swallowing hard. 'I mean, I know him. I know everyone. Adam, his name is.'

'Adam, right, that's it.' I saw the woman across the road standing about imperiously as if she expected something dramatic to happen on her arrival.

'He's just . . . you know. Nobody special.' Johnny clicked his neck left and right, as the woman waved at somebody in the doorway of the guest house.

We crossed the road towards Castaway, and I saw Mrs Hale come down the steps and along the path to the pavement. As we drew level alongside the woman, I heard her say, 'There you are, Maddie,' and a half-acknowledged assumption gathered substance in my brain. The woman had that sort of blonde hair that never really greys, just fades away, and a mottled complexion. She was carrying a handbag with a garish brass clasp, and had a shawl thrown over one shoulder, fastened with an amber-coloured brooch.

Mrs Hale handed the driver a note, murmuring, 'Keep the change.'

'Thanks, missus.' He climbed back into his cab, and Mrs Hale turned to the woman and said, 'Lizzie! I thought you weren't ever going to come.'

'Some people have things to do,' said the woman coldly, and I breathed in with the full knowledge that *this* was her. This was the girl who'd signed her name as Robert Carver's wife.

As I hovered, Johnny said, 'Yeah, well, tomorrow with the rent, all right?'

I turned to him, as both Mrs Hale and her sister saw us beside them on the pavement. Johnny was already backing away, heading up the steps towards the house.

'All right,' I called after him. 'I promise.'

'Rosie!' said Mrs Hale. 'Let me introduce you. This is my sister ... and ... oh, Lizzie, this is one of our employees.'

Lizzie looked at me as if I'd crawled out from under a stone. 'Indeed,' she said. 'Well, if you don't mind, Madeleine, I'd better get inside and see to Father. Heaven knows you've probably been leaving him to stew the entire morning.'

She hobbled towards the house, leaning heavily on her stick. Mrs Hale watched her go with a stricken look and said, 'Sorry, Rosie. My sister's not been . . . very well. It affects her mood. I'll see you tomorrow, all right?'

'Did she . . . ?' I began, and Mrs Hale paused in her scurrying up the path. I wanted to ask about Lizzie and Robert, but I didn't know how to put my question without seeming horribly rude and nosy. 'It doesn't matter,' I said, and watched my boss follow her sister up the steps, attempting to lend her an arm and being shaken off irritably.

I turned back to the house. Johnny had disappeared inside, leaving the front door swinging wide open. I was about to follow him when I happened to glance over into the basement area and saw Dockie hunched on the steps, wrapped in his coat, looking up at the porticoed entrance and muttering to himself.

'Dockie!' I called, my heart sinking a little as he turned his head and saw me. 'Are you all right?'

'Rosie. My dear, dear Rosie.' He staggered to his feet and climbed the few steps back to ground level. 'Thank you for saving my life.'

He came towards me and clasped my hands in his own, too quickly for me to escape, although I noticed belatedly that the grime around the nails was gone, and they were clipped clean and short. The nasty smell that had been surrounding him had also more or less lifted. 'I owe you everything,' he murmured, dropping his head, and I thought for one awful second he might be about to kiss my finger, as if I were the Pope.

'Oh no,' I said, horribly embarrassed. 'Please don't. It was nothing.'

He continued to grip my hands. 'You have brought me

back to life,' he said. 'I arrived here with nothing. You contrived for me a room, and made me food, and bought for me the symbols of a civilized human being. Soap. Clean clothes. I am indebted, my dear. Indebted.'

I understood from this that he had not yet noticed my purloined shoes still in his room. I really had to pick them up before he saw that he might not owe me exactly everything. 'It's the least anyone would do,' I muttered, noticing he had yet to tidy up his shaggy beard, although it did seem to bristle with a cleanliness that I hadn't noticed the day before.

'Certainly it is not.' He stood up straighter and tapped his head. 'Your care, dear Rosie, has brought back clarity.'

'It has?' I wondered whether he'd drunk any of the tonic wine I'd provided. He certainly seemed in much more buoyant spirits than yesterday.

'I woke in the night, you see, with a moment of absolute remembrance.' He gestured to the house. 'I dashed outside, and stood looking up, just as we are doing now, and I remembered it all, Rosie. I remembered it all.'

'Oh, good.' I wondered when I could politely leave him to it. I glanced around, looking for an escape route, and saw, in the distance, the unmistakable, long-legged gait of Star, making her way up the hill towards us. She hadn't seen us yet, and as I watched her a confused tumble of emotions jostled for the upper floor of my mind.

'I remembered Castaway House, and its significance,' Dockie was saying, and I turned reluctantly away from Star. 'You see, my dear, I realized that this place holds the key.'

'Okay.' I wondered if I'd missed something. 'The key to what?'

He tapped his chest. 'The key to myself.'

I heard Star's footsteps approaching up the pavement, and, distracted by the sound of them, it took me several seconds to understand what Dockie was saying. When I did, I wished I'd paid him more attention. 'What? Do you mean your memory came back? From all those years ago?'

He nodded, his eyes gleaming. 'Last night, I found the newspaper clippings, and the world was unlocked. They were in my boot. Can you believe that? In my left boot.'

I could quite certainly believe it. 'That's wonderful,' I said, his enthusiasm buoying me up, because surely this was more important than Harry's insults or Star's oddness.

'I knew everything. Who I was, why I was here, and what Castaway House meant to me.' He shrugged. 'It was just a flash though. For a brilliant, electric moment, I understood it all. And then, almost as suddenly, it was gone.'

The footsteps paused, and I knew Star was arriving.

'What? You mean . . . ?'

'But I knew it then. And if I knew it then, it will come again.'

'Your memory went? You can't remember any more?' I said to Dockie. Behind me, I sensed Star hovering on the walkway, the magnet of her drawing me into her orbit. I tried to ignore her. 'What about the newspaper clippings?'

'Ah.' He held up a finger. 'I put them in a safe place. Unfortunately, I can no longer remember where that safe place is. But I shall find them again, never you worry.'

'No, Dockie. No. We must find them. This is . . . this is terrible.'

'Absolutely not.' He grinned broadly. 'I do not want an artificial aid. I want to remember properly, truly. This is why I have been sitting where you found me, waiting for the knowledge to strike inside me again.'

The idea of this seemed so desperately sad I hardly knew what to say, although Dockie seemed enraptured. He looked back up at the house again, and jumped when Star said, 'Sorry, can I just get past?'

He stared at her, his face bulging with shock, and I turned. She was closer than I'd realized, and she smelled of something sweet: honeycomb, perhaps. I nodded at her politely and said, 'I didn't notice you there.'

She smiled at me. 'That's all right. I'll leave you both to it.'

Dockie was making a sort of gurgling noise in his throat, and looking at Star with wild, mad eyes. 'Clara,' he whispered. 'Clara.'

'Eh?' Star took a pace backwards.

Dockie gripped my arm. 'I . . .' he began, and his beard quavered. 'I must . . .'

'What's the matter?'

'I must think. I must think about Clara.' He was panting hard, as if he'd been running. 'Come with me, Rosie. Come and listen to me. Help me make sense of it all.'

'All . . . all right.' I glanced quickly at Star, who had her hands on her hips and a fascinated look on her face. 'Where do you want to go?'

'Anywhere.' He peered up at the house and then let go of my arm. He walked down the steps on to the pavement. 'Into town. Not here. I must make sense of the thing in my head. You will help me, won't you, my dear?'

'Of course. I . . .' I looked again at Star.

'Oh, don't mind me,' she said cheerfully. 'You carry on.'

'All right,' I said. 'I just wanted to let you know how much I'm looking forward to your party on Thursday.'

Her face slackened. 'Uh?'

'Yes, thanks for the invitation, seeing as we're friends and all that.'

'Rosie . . .' She pulled a face. 'Listen, can we talk?'

I knew I ought to go with Dockie, I knew I ought not to give in to her, just as I always gave in, but I couldn't help myself. 'Wait for me,' I called to him. 'I'll be two minutes.'

He waved and turned so his back was against the stone wall that bordered the front garden of the house. Star was leaning against the railings that bordered the basement steps, and I followed her. 'Well?'

She shrugged. 'Y'know, I thought you might not like it. The party, I mean.'

I looked at her, took her in properly, the force of her presence over me now. 'If you've got some . . . problem with me, just tell me, okay? But I can't bear all this push-and-pull stuff. I'm not cut out for it.'

'I don't mean to be push and pull.' She put out a hand and touched my shoulder, as she'd done yesterday in the hallway. 'You're my friend.'

'Then why didn't you invite me to the party? Are you embarrassed of me, is that what it is? Do you think I'll show you up in front of all your friends?'

'No,' she said with a pout, but so vehemently I felt there was some truth there. 'Of course not.'

'I suppose I'm far too square for you.' I shrugged. 'Well,

Johnny doesn't think so, and he's invited me, so I'm coming anyway.'

'You're not square.' She let go of my shoulder and held on to the spikes of the basement railings. 'I mean, you are a bit, but that doesn't matter. I like it. I'm glad you're coming. Honestly.'

I put my hand around the spike beside hers. 'Is this anything to do with Gill?'

Her lashes closed once. 'Gill was just a stupid cow.'

'Well, I'm not her, okay? I mean, whatever sort of row you had . . . You can trust me.'

Star shook her head. 'You don't understand.' She stole a glance at me. 'I didn't want it to spoil things. The party – I didn't want it to spoil our friendship.'

I frowned at her; I had no idea if she was telling the truth or just saying it to get round me, just as she always did. 'Don't be silly. Of course it won't. How could it?'

'I don't know.' She inched a little finger over to mine. 'I'm glad you'll be there.'

I linked our fingers on the warm metal of the railings, the black paint flaking under my grip. A shiver ran along my arm. 'I've got to go.'

Star looked over to where Dockie was still leaning against the wall, gesticulating to himself. 'He's a madman,' she said. 'Don't go anywhere near him.'

'He's not.' I peeled myself away from the railings. 'He's just a poor lost soul.'

Star frowned. 'Are you okay? You look as if you've been crying.'

I shrugged. 'Time of the month.' She still looked concerned. 'It wasn't over your party, if that's what you're wondering. It's not the event of my life.'

She grinned. 'No. All right. Me and my ego.' She took a step towards the path. 'But listen, there is something funny about that chap.'

I lowered my voice. 'He's had a brain injury.'

She shrugged. 'Either he's completely mad or he's one of those prophets – you know, dressed in rags and performing miracles – and we all ignore him until it's too late.'

I snorted and started to head towards Dockie. 'I'll see you later, okay?'

I was almost out of reach when she grabbed my arm and whirled me back to face her. Her breath still had that sweet smell to it, and she looked down at me and said in a whisper, 'He is, or otherwise how on earth did he know my real name?'

'What?'

She winked at me and then, on an impulse it seemed she could not control, reached forwards and touched my cheek. She traced my jawbone with a finger and then snatched her hand back, her eyes darting up at the house.

'Bye,' she whispered, and was gone, up the stairs to the main entrance and in through the front door.

My face tingled where she'd touched it. 'Clara . . .' I murmured to myself.

Dockie had moved to the pillars in front of the Bella Vista. Dr Feathers was sitting in the same chair in the window, with Lizzie opposite him. She was talking rapidly, but he appeared not to be listening. I raised my hand and he dazedly lifted his own hand in return.

'Clara,' Dockie murmured when he saw me, tugging at his beard. 'Who is Clara?'

Surely its being Star's real name was just a crazy coincidence. I remembered that Ted the foreman had mentioned a similar name . . . but I must have got that wrong. I wished I'd been listening more carefully now.

'Come on,' I said. 'Maybe if we try hard enough, we can get back that memory of yours.'

He nodded at me and smiled, and we matched pace with each other as we walked down the hill towards town. I still glowed with the memory of Star's touch, and the way she'd looked as she'd caressed my face, her pupils flaring black, almost eclipsing the violet of her eyes.

8

1924

After my trip into the slums in the erroneous pursuit of Mrs Bray there followed several days of rain, and I spent the time either skulking in the library or staring at the screen in darkened rooms at the town's various picture houses. Luckily, I had not seen my hostess once, and now that the weather had suddenly turned fine again, I received a message in the afternoon, delivered by Scone, that I was to meet Alec 'in front of our beach hut'. When I questioned Scone further on where this might be, I was told that Mr Bray had assured him that Mr Carver would be able to find it without too much difficulty, being a 'clever sort'.

That was why five o'clock found me stumping along the beach, sand burrowing into my shoes, peering at each hut in turn at the holidaymakers slouched there in various states, from fully clothed to semi-naked. The sky was puffy with clouds, although that hadn't stopped the London weekend hordes descending on Helmstone in their thousands. I tripped over feet and parasols, begged apologies, sweltering in my clothes yet feeling that familiar tug on my chest all the same, and I was thoroughly red-faced and annoyed by the time I heard a voice call, 'Robert!'

I turned. Alec was waving at me from further along the beach, where a larger line of chalets clung to the edges of the sand. A decked area was laid out in front, and outside one of them, its doors open to the sea, sat Alec on a wicker chair, a low table beside him upon which stood an ice bucket and two glasses. On the other side of the table, thoroughly filling out another wicker chair, was a fat young man.

I slunk through sand towards them and breathed heavily. 'What an awful day,' I said. 'Give me overcast and dull any time.'

Alec shaded his eyes with his hand. 'Honestly, Robert, anyone would think you were a hundred and three. Here, come and say hello. Bump, this is my cousin, Robert Carver. Robert, my old school coeval, Hugh Mason-Chambers.'

The fat man leaned forwards and enveloped my hand in two plump sweaty ones. 'How d'you do, Carver? Just call me Bump. Glad to meet you at last; Alec says you've been a real help with the old Hall of Fame.'

'Not . . . not really,' I said. 'Just lent an artistic eye, I suppose.'

'Heard the tableaux were your idea. Jolly good one.' He twisted in his chair. 'Sampson!'

From nowhere appeared a man with sleek hair and an athletic build, a champagne flute in his hand. In one move he lifted the bottle from the bucket, poured a glass of fizzing liquid and handed it to me.

We toasted the Hall of Fame's success. Sampson disappeared as quickly as he'd arrived.

'Damn good, ain't he, my Jew?' said Bump proudly, as if speaking of a grandchild. He bent out of his chair, holding his glass to where I stood awkwardly on the sand. 'Anyhow, to future riches!'

'I certainly hope so,' muttered Alec, and then, recovering his usual cheerful demeanour, added, 'I mean, with Robert on board, it's practically guaranteed.'

I shifted under the weight of this extra responsibility. 'When are you hoping to open?'

'Not long now,' said Bump airily. 'Always a hiccup, isn't there, Bray?'

'Teething problems,' said Alec. 'Of course, it's all *her* fault. If she'd helped us, as she was supposed to, we wouldn't be behind at all.'

A short silence followed. Bump turned his champagne flute round by the stem and studied the bubbles. I looked out to sea.

Finally Bump coughed and said, 'Coming out on the razz tonight, Carver?' I turned towards him and he winked heavily. 'Bray and I are painting the town red.'

'But it's the Featherses' soirée,' I said. 'Or have you turned it down?'

Alec closed his eyes. 'Bugger. Completely slipped my mind.' He opened them again and winked at Bump. 'Robert wouldn't have forgotten. He's taken a fancy to one of the Feathers girls. How is all that going, then? Does she defy her pure and innocent appearance?'

'Not at all,' I said, attempting to sound shocked. Bump and Alec roared with laughter.

'Don't tell me,' hooted Bump. 'You go to the pictures and spend the entire night with your hand creeping up her arm, and by the time you get anywhere interesting she does a sort of wriggle and you're back to square one.'

This was not exactly the truth, but I was certainly not about to tell him that after my and Lizzie's secret kiss beside Rudolph Valentino, and our eventual red-faced conversation afterwards, pretending that nothing had ever happened, *she* had been the one inching closer to me at the cinema. Strangely enough, for some reason I had found myself actually watching the films, and had been almost annoyed that Lizzie's fingers were fluttering inside my palm.

I had by now taken a thorough dislike to Bump, and so I merely drank my champagne as if the idea of discussing a lady's behaviour was far beneath my dignity. I cast about for a new topic of conversation. 'Is the chalet yours?' I said to Alec, who was busy winking and smirking at Bump.

'Er . . . rented.' He burped and put his hand over his mouth, a second too late. 'Clara usually moons about in here, flicking paint on her dreadful canvases, but when she heard Bump was coming down she took off.'

'Can't stand me,' said Bump, attempting to look rueful. 'No doubt I'm a bad influence.'

'You do your best,' said Alec, and they smirked again.

'She paints?' I said, squinting at the grey interior of the hut, trying to see canvases. 'I didn't know she painted.'

'If you can call it that.' He made a humphing sound. 'I call it daubing.'

'No harm in having a little hobby.' Bump nodded. 'For the ladies. Men, though. Let me tell you, I've met a number of male artists. Bunch of pansies, the lot of them.'

Alec coughed and glanced at me. 'Of course, Robert's an artist.'

Bump glanced at me with distaste. 'Yes. I'd forgotten that.'

I put my glass down on the table. 'Thank you for the

champagne,' I said, and then, to Alec, 'I must get back and change for dinner.'

Alec groaned as if the effort of even thinking about dinner at the Featherses' was too much for him. 'What time do we have to be there?'

'Seven, for eight,' I said.

He wrinkled his nose. 'I'll be there at five to.'

'Blow them out,' roared Bump. 'They sound like a lot of bloody bores anyway.'

I left them as Bump called for Sampson to pour more champagne, and wound my way back up the hill. I sincerely hoped I'd never have to meet Alec's business partner again: he was just the sort of boy I'd hated at school, always trying to screw one's head into the ground during rugby, flicking one's backside with a wet flannel in the changing rooms, the kind who thought knowledge and learning were seditious weapons best avoided at all costs.

A couple of hours later I left Castaway, alone. The evening air held a pleasant little breeze, and I ran up the steps of the Featherses' house wishing I'd had further to walk to get there. The parlourmaid Doris, dressed in black for the occasion, opened the door and led me into the hallway. It was much narrower than Castaway's, although every time I had been here I had had the sense of life spilling over itself behind the closed doorways.

In fact, as I stood in the hallway a door there burst open and a young boy I had never seen before ran towards me, brandishing a wooden sword, a sticky ring of something round his mouth. 'Ngah,' he snarled at me. 'You go away now.'

Doris groaned. A buxom woman in a starched uniform leaned over the upstairs railing and said, 'You little devil! I'm going to smack you so hard, you won't see next week!'

The child looked momentarily distressed and then turned tail and ran towards the servants' stairs at the end of the hallway.

'You wait there!' we heard, as the nanny ran down. 'I'll skin the hide off him,' she muttered at us, before making away after the boy.

'Sorry about that, sir.' Doris headed for the staircase and I followed her. 'If you'd like to come this way. Some of them are already here, you know. Arrived too early,' she added with a sneer.

From the basement, I heard a distant squawk.

'Was that the youngest Feathers I saw?' I asked.

'Master Anthony. Runs Nanny Woods ragged, poor thing.' This last was said with some malicious amusement in her voice, and I suspected the two did not get on.

The first time I had visited Lizzie at home, I had been struck by how the Featherses' house was a perfect reverse copy of my cousin's, only smaller. Now I had got to know it a little better, I almost preferred it. The drawing room here, at the top of the first flight of stairs, had a permanently opened door – unlike at Castaway, where Mrs Bray had claimed it for her own – and Doris led me inside.

A few people were dotted about the drawing room, murmuring politely to one another. A gramophone player in the corner cranked out an inoffensive tune. I looked round for Lizzie, but saw only Dr Feathers, who approached with his arms drawn wide as if to embrace me.

'Mr Carver! How good of you to be so punctual. A highly underrated virtue, if I may say so myself. Elizabeth and the other girls will be down shortly; there have been tears today because I am only permitting Lizzie to stay for the dinner. Girls, Mr Carver, cause one nothing but trouble. Tamsin! Tamsin! Mr Carver is here.'

I shook Mrs Feathers' ghost-like hand. She was a pale, faded woman – if one were asked to describe her as a colour, she would have been beige. I had wondered before how on earth she could put up with Dr Feathers' monologues without wanting to strike him on the head with the poker. However, I had come to realize immediately that had she ever had any life in her the good doctor had long ago bled it dry.

'Wonderful to see you again, Mr Carver,' she said in a voice like autumn leaves. 'Lizzie says such nice things about you.'

'Yes. Good of you to take her on,' said Feathers. 'She was moping about the house like a lost soul for months after the Frederick Sponder episode.'

'Honestly, Father!' said a sharp voice behind him. He turned and Maddie stood there, her brows knotted. 'You . . . you can't . . .' However, here her nerve failed her and she trailed off before turning and stomping across the room.

'I'm sorry,' said Mrs Feathers weakly, as I wondered of what exactly the Frederick Sponder episode had consisted. 'I don't know what's got into her recently.'

'She's fifteen,' muttered Dr Feathers. 'That's explanation enough.'

And then Lizzie was in the room, her hair arranged in a complicated sort of chignon, and her eyes flashed when she saw me, and I was utterly relieved that we were over that awkward kiss a week ago. 'Good evening, Robert,' she said demurely, and I sensed the snare of her gaze even as I looked away.

'Ah! You're here! Good. Now, Lizzie, I want you to circulate. Talk to our guests. Don't stick to Mr Carver like a stray puppy all night. Get you a drink, Carver? You look like a Scotch man to me.' Before I could refute that, he was waving a tumbler of the hideous stuff over towards me.

Lizzie bent her head towards me. 'Must go,' she whispered. 'Sorry. Doctor's orders.'

'It's fine,' I whispered back. 'I've plenty to amuse myself with here.'

I walked to the floor-length window, from where I could see mist wreathing the waves. The guests were, I imagined, the great and good of Helmstone: the promised mayor, a few town councillors, probably a headmaster or two, plus the inevitable spare women. There was a clump of them by the other window, wreathed in flowers and perfume; I observed that they seemed rather jolly to be spinsters, and were knocking back their sundowners with gossipy abandon. I smiled genially to hide my disapproval at the sight of them larking about.

I had a sudden thought of Mother and Father in the dining room with the oilcloth on the table and the doily dead centre, the mantelpiece with the jade figurine that Mother had been given on her seventeenth birthday. We weren't a noisy household; even as a child I'd been tamed and quietened, but I felt all the same that they might be missing my presence, for without me all they had in common was their deepest, most heartfelt desire not ever to make a fuss. I presumed this was because of all the fuss that had occurred when they'd eloped together twenty years ago. They'd been retreating from it ever since.

'How d'you like the parents' collection, then?'

I turned, startled. Madeleine Feathers was standing next to me, her hands behind her back, rather in the manner of her father, nodding at the wall of paintings that I had been unconsciously staring at.

'Oh. Yes. Very – um – very . . . I'm sorry, I hadn't even paid them any attention.'

Maddie laughed. 'Come and have a look. Do you think this is proper hostess behaviour? Mother says if I'm good I may even be allowed to stay to dinner next time.'

'You're doing a marvellous job,' I said, and allowed her to lead me over to the wall. I had been in the drawing room a few times since my arrival next door, and yet I had always felt rather constrained from looking round the room. I took the opportunity to have a good peruse now I was here in company. There were various portraits of, I assumed, the Feathers brood, framed in the usual velvet, including one of Lizzie and Maddie as young girls, holding white feathers in their palms, which struck me as almost grisly in its mawkish symbolism. There were others, possibly of deceased household pets, and one, at the edge, that seemed not to fit at all.

It was of a sunrise over the sea, a common enough subject, but the splashes of vermilion and ochre on the churning waves suggested anger, as if the brushstrokes had flicked over the canvas again, again, again.

'What do you think of this one?' asked Maddie. 'Don't

worry, it's not one of ours, so you may give your true opinion.'

'Mmm.' I frowned in mock-seriousness, as if I were conversing at the Royal Academy. The painting did have something about it, and so I said, 'Rather undisciplined, but it has a certain wild passion, don't you think?'

Maddie chuckled. 'Can you guess who did it?'

I peered at the signature and, as I did so, a voice over my shoulder purred, 'Admiring my painting, Mr Carver?'

Maddie blushed. I turned to Mrs Bray and said, hoping she hadn't heard me earlier, 'It's very nice.'

She raised an eyebrow. 'Nice?'

I saw that Alec was behind her, swaying slightly as he surveyed the room.

'Would you get me a gin and tonic?' she rapped out to him, and he sighed heavily, put his hands in his pockets and lumbered across the room to the drinks table.

She looked like a sharp-toothed carnivore in that sheath of a dress she was wearing, along with her scarlet lips and glittering eyelashes, and her perfume smelled of crushed cigarettes.

'So tell me, Mr Carver, have you been back to Princes Street lately?'

I had been expecting something like this, but felt wrong-footed all the same. 'N-n-no,' I said. 'Of-of c-course not.'

'Strange. I thought you might have formed an attachment to the place.' There was a mischievous slant to her voice I had not heard before. 'You were quite the talk of the area, you know. Everybody thinks you're desperately in love with me.'

I did not mind her teasing. It meant, I presumed, that she could not be as furious as she had been before. The gong sounded, and so before she was stitched back to Alec's side I said, 'I'm n-n-not a spy.'

She widened her eyes. 'I beg your pardon?'

'As you accu-accus . . . said I was.' For some unknown reason, my speech was splintering as badly as it ever had done in my first nightmare years of school. 'N-Nobody in the family's asked me to rep-p-port back to them. About you, I m-mean.'

She nodded. A servant held out a silver tray with a drink clinking ice upon it, and she took it and raised it towards Alec, who was hovering at the other end of the room. 'All right. I believe you.'

The turnaround stunned me. 'R-really?'

Past us, people began drifting down to the dining room. I saw Lizzie make her way across the room.

Mrs Bray sipped her drink through a straw. 'If I didn't know better, I'd therefore surmise that the only reason for your following me is that you were sexually attracted to me and, as you despise yourself for that, you have convinced yourself that I'm a blatant little slut who deserves everything she gets.'

'Then,' I snapped, 'it's just as well you do know better, isn't it?'

Mrs Bray smiled round her straw and flicked her eyes leftwards. 'Elizabeth!' she exclaimed. 'How lovely to see you. I'm so glad you've been entertaining our cousin. Alec and I have been far too busy, and I'm afraid we've quite neglected our duties.'

'Oh no, it's been fun.' Lizzie gave Mrs Bray a cow-eyed

look. 'I love your dress by the way,' she added, as she blushed a deep crimson.

'You are a sweetie. You must come round sometime, and we can have a jolly girls' chat in the garden.' She shone her teeth at me. 'Anyway, I'll allow you two to go down. I believe my husband's coming this way. Ah. Here he is.'

And nobody would know, I thought, as I descended the stairs next to Lizzie, the frosty silence that reigned at home. True, Alec and his wife hardly said a word to each other the entire evening, but as they were placed at opposite ends of the dining table this went unnoticed, except by me.

The Featherses' dining room was a curious affair. I had never been inside it before, but I was surprised to see that there were various locked cabinets on the walls, shelves with untidy files heaped upon them, and items of furniture shrouded in lengths of white cloth. It was my misfortune – or perhaps both of ours – that I was placed next to Mrs Bray at dinner, but I immediately turned to my neighbour, one of the spare women, and began chatting to her about the first nonsense that came into my head.

'Lovely room, isn't it?' I said.

She sneaked a glance at the senior Featherses. The lady of the house was nodding wearily while being subjected to a monologue by one of the town councillors, and the doctor was occupied with waving in the clear soup course. 'It's his consulting room,' my neighbour hissed to me, indicating our host.

'Is it?' I looked round. Across the table, Alec drained his glass and held it up for more.

'The front part's the office, the back's the doctor's den.' She waved her soup spoon towards the shrouded furniture. 'I've spent many an invigorating session on that couch. Rather strange to be back here enjoying oneself, so to speak.'

The doctor settled himself on the other side of Mrs Bray, and my neighbour immediately changed the subject. We chit-chatted amiably as the soup was followed by grilled mackerel stuffed with fennel. It was during the roast pork that I heard Dr Feathers say, seated on Mrs Bray's other hand, 'How's your parlourmaid doing? What's her name? Agnes, is it?'

My neighbour was at that moment expounding on the delights of some country estate that I simply must visit now I was in the area. ('The delphiniums are just a delight at this time of year.') I tried to nod and smile while holding an ear to Mrs Bray's answer.

'Oh, I don't care any more,' she said.

('You employ a chauffeur? I see. Well, the drive is quite spectacular.')

'If you ask me, she was making the whole thing up.'

'But it was . . .' I heard the doctor cough. 'I mean, it is the same room?'

'Possibly. I don't take much notice of the arrangements.'

('Tell him to head past Walmstead Hall – no, no, that's not right. Turn left just before it, that's the one . . .')

'But thank you for asking. She's a hysterical little child, to be honest, and saying that she's homesick won't wash with me, and she knows it. I left home when I was fourteen. Best thing I ever did.'

'Well, as you know, I don't hold for any sort of superstition, and thank goodness Mrs Feathers is of the same opinion as me. But here's the thing, Mrs Bray: it's rather interesting that what occurs in the head can have quite physical effects on the body.'

('I do believe the National Trust is perhaps the most important institution this country's produced in the last fifty years.')

'Oh yes. So just because there's no basis to it doesn't mean she's not in severe pain.'

'Pain!'

('What a marvellous cook they have here. I shall have to have words with Mrs Goode.')

'The girl doesn't know the least thing about pain. I think I might have to send her home. I'll give her a reference . . .'

And then I was forced to answer a direct question from my neighbour, at some length, and the next time I was able to eavesdrop, Dr Feathers was talking to his other neighbour, and Mrs Bray was now free.

I quickly turned back, but my applauder of the National Trust was now engaged in the same monologue on her other side, and so I was thrust once more into the shark-infested waters of social chit-chat with my cousin's wife.

I wanted, of course, to ask all about Agnes, but as that would have shown I had been listening in, and as I had already denied the charge of spying, I felt that that particular conversational gambit was not on the cards. Casting about for a safe topic, I said, 'I didn't realize that you painted.'

'I don't really,' she said. 'Daubing.' And this was so close to how her husband had disparaged her that I nearly smiled.

'You've probably a greater talent than me,' I said, thinking of my timid pieces.

She narrowed her eyes. 'Yes, probably.'

I looked at my wine glass. 'I see you've no room for false modesty.'

'I haven't. Although I don't think it's false. I think you're right.'

'I had an exhibition once,' I snapped. 'At the local library.'

'Good for you.' She scooped a last piece of potato into her mouth. 'My circle would no doubt approve of your public-spiritedness.'

'Your circle?' Round the room, plates were being cleared and orange compote served. Alec stared at his dreamily.

'My painting circle. We meet once a month and drive into the countryside. Watercolours, mostly. We're meeting tomorrow, actually. If you'd like to come.'

I stared at her. She dipped a spoon into the compote as if nothing untoward had occurred.

'Y-you'd like me to come?'

She continued not to look at me. 'It's of no consequence to me. I just thought you might want to improve your skills somewhat. You probably need to.'

'Well.' I looked at my dessert. 'Well. I . . . I suppose. One could . . . I mean I could . . .'

'I shall be outside the front at nine o'clock sharp tomorrow morning.' She dabbed her lips with her napkin.

I saw the red smear left on the white linen cloth. 'It's up to you.'

I couldn't help but wonder whether this was some sort of elaborate trap, as revenge for my curiosity, but as she seemed entirely unconcerned whether I went or not, I decided I would wait and see how the evening progressed and if she defrosted any further towards me.

Yet I was unable to find out. Hardly had dinner finished and the ladies gone up to the drawing room than Alec, jumping to his feet as if pulled by strings, announced, 'Sorry to leave you, chaps, but Robert and I have to go.'

I stared at him, a fat unlit cigar in my hand. He gave me an elaborate wink, witnessed by every other man in the room and therefore pointless. I had been rather looking forward to partaking of this ritual, denied me at home on account of the trouble it caused my lungs. I'd already brewed up several opinions on the new government that I was hoping to air. 'Now?' I said. But my voice was swallowed up by Dr Feathers, who said, 'What? Is there some sort of emergency?'

'Well . . . that is . . . no. Not really.' Alec blinked down at the assembly, like a schoolboy caught out in a lie. 'I've arranged to meet an old chum, you see. My business partner, actually,' he added, as if that made it all much more acceptable.

'Do I know him?' Feathers chomped enthusiastically on his cigar. My stomach sank at the thought of having to deal with Bump again, and I wondered how I could edge out of Alec's arrangement without upsetting anyone.

'Prob'ly not.' Alec attempted to lean on the sideboard,

then realized that would be a bad idea and tried to straighten himself again. 'He's the Duke of Cowray. Tenth-richest man in England,' he continued, smiling broadly.

I noticed a general rustling round the room as this information was absorbed. Dr Feathers looked pleased with himself, as if knighted by association. 'Well, well. Of course, in that case you must go,' he said, looking across the table to make sure everybody had heard. 'But must we also forgo the pleasure of Mr Carver's company?'

'I'd be happy to stay,' I said immediately, staring at Alec as if I could convey my message telepathically.

Alec waved his brandy balloon. 'Unfortunately . . .' He trailed off, staring at the clock, and seemed almost to fall asleep standing, until he blearily returned to the room. 'Hmm. It's a business meeting. Robert is our artistic advisor. We are in desperate need of his services.' He gave a high-pitched giggle.

I was about to argue, but I saw that the rest of the room was quite as happy to get rid of me as Alec was to take me away, and so I reluctantly got to my feet and went about shaking hands with bigwigs I was never likely to meet again.

Doris was dispatched to fetch Lizzie, and she came down into the hallway to say goodbye. Alec was already outside the front door, leaning on one of the house pillars for support. I thought perhaps the night air might be sobering him up, but I did not have much hope in it.

'Do you have to go?' she pouted, as the men barked at each other from the dining room next door. 'Surely you can get out of it if you really want to.'

'Not for showing Alec up to be a dreadful liar.' I added quickly, 'Don't say that to your father.'

'Well, you did promise you'd be here.' She beetled her brows. 'Although I'm sure going off with Mr Bray will be far more fun than listening to dreary old me play some dirge on the piano.'

'I'd much rather stay!' I protested, feeling unfairly got at. 'And I did come. You didn't tell me you were going to perform.'

She was still pouting. 'One of Chopin's nocturnes. It was supposed to be a surprise.'

'I'm sorry, Lizzie. Look, I'll make it up to you, all right?'

She sniffed. 'I suppose you could come for lunch tomorrow.'

I thought of the painting circle, but decided to be circumspect, at least in her current mood. 'It'll have to be later, I'm afraid. How about tea at four?'

Her pout threatened again, but I did not waver, and finally the lower lip retreated and formed itself into a reluctant smile.

'Come on, Carver!'

Alec was in the doorway, a black silhouette against the indigo sky outside.

Lizzie blew me a sly kiss and headed for the stairs. I called goodbye, but I heard the click of the drawing-room door opening, and knew my words were lost amidst the murmur of female voices that emerged, among them a scratchy, hoarse burst of laughter that sounded as if it had been swept off the factory floor.

'There goes my wife,' said Alec, jerking his head towards

the sound. 'Apparently one can rub it all out except for the laughter.'

'Rub all what out?' I echoed as we went down the steps together.

Adopting a sneer, he said in a terrible cockney accent, 'The old fishwife voice, y'know.' Reverting to his usual manner, he continued, 'You see, there are some things elocution lessons can't erase. Laughing's one. Of course, there's another.'

I wondered what the other was, but he was already striding ahead of me down the cliff. 'I hadn't actually heard her laugh before,' I said, running to catch up.

'Never in my presence, old boy. Never in the house. Only with her "friends".' He tossed the word out towards the waves. 'Still, we're off to have a jolly time, eh?'

'The thing is . . .' I said.

'Thought I was going to die of boredom back there,' he said, weaving left and right across the pavement. 'Worst thing of all having to turn up with one's wife when one can't stand her. You did all right, did you, sat next to her? She didn't rip you to shreds?'

'No. At least, not exactly.' I paused. 'She actually invited me on a trip with her painting circle tomorrow.'

Alec hooted. 'Oh, she's a devil, all right.'

I narrowed my eyes at him. 'Why's that? I might not go, you know.'

'Oh, you should. Have a whale of a time, as long as you keep your wits about you.' He laughed again, and I wasn't in the least comforted.

At the bottom of the hill we crossed over the road,

walked past the entrance to the Snooks and carried on. The Majestic Hotel reared its wedding-cake façade beside us, and Alec roared good evening at the liveried doorman, clasping the man's meaty hand before trotting up the steps to the revolving doors. I followed at a slower pace, fearful we might be thrown out, although the doorman, whose broad red face and veined nose betrayed his habits, merely beamed at Alec's disappearing back.

In the large, chandelier-lit lobby of the Majestic, a nonagenarian with a handlebar moustache tinkled the piano and clumps of holidaymakers sat in huge enfolding chairs and pretended not to be falling asleep. Alec strode to the desk, leaned one elbow on its polished surface and said to the clerk, 'We're here to see Lord Hugh Mason-Chambers. He's expecting us.'

'Mr Bray and friend?'

Alec pointed to me and nodded heavily, like a dog.

'Room Eighty-Two, sir. Top floor.'

As the lift ticked down to meet us, I said to Alec, 'So what are we doing here, exactly?'

Alec put an arm round my shoulders. 'Having fun, dear boy. Isn't that what life's all about?'

It seemed pointless to say that I'd been having fun before. I allowed Alec to lead me into the lift. 'Is he really the tenth-richest man in England?'

'God, no.' Alec peered at himself in the mirrored walls that lined the contraption. My stomach churned as we ascended, and I realized I'd had more port than I'd intended.

'Bump's the youngest of the tribe. Hasn't a bloody bean to call his own, except for the old man's allowance, and I tell you, it requires some financial jiggery-pokery to convince him it all goes on essential needs. This is the plan, y'see, with our little dummies under the arches. Goin' to make us a fortune.'

'What about Sampson?' I said, as the lift jerked to a nausea-inducing halt on the eighth floor.

'Duke of Cowray pays for him.' Alec flicked my collar. 'That's the old man.'

Not Bump, then. 'So you lied to Dr Feathers.'

Alec widened his eyes. 'Me? Lie? I won't have it, Carver. I bite my thumb at you, cuz.' Which he did, as the lift doors opened. 'See how well studied I am, eh, quoting the Bard? Come on.'

He dragged me along a parqueted corridor to a room and hammered on the door. 'Let us in, you fool!' he bellowed. 'We've been waiting here for hours!'

The door was opened, not by Bump, but by a girl with a feather in her hair and so much make-up smeared on her face she made Clara Bray seem positively demure. She was holding a cocktail in one hand and peered at us short-sightedly, then leaned back into the room and said, 'Oi! You got a coupla mates out here! Shall I let 'em in?'

There was an answering roar, and the girl stepped back, waving us through exaggeratedly. 'You look like nice boys,' she said, 'or I wouldn't bother, know what I mean?'

I entered the room gingerly. We were in a sort of ante-room, carpeted wall to wall, and through an open doorway we spied Bump spread out on a huge sofa, a girl draped on either side of him. They were all drinking the same cocktail, a bubbly concoction spiked with mint leaves. One of the girls, I noticed, was wearing just a petticoat.

'There you are.' Bump cast aside the girls and lumbered to his feet. 'Thought you'd pansied out. Come in. Right. This is ... sorry, I've forgotten their names. Anyway, they're damned pretty, don't you think?'

I hardly knew where to look. Alec, however, went straight to the sofa, sat down and said, indicating the cocktails, 'How about you get me one of those? A man could die of thirst in here.'

Bump snapped his fingers at the girl who'd just let us in and was now hovering in the doorway. 'You! Go and tell Sampson to knock us up a couple more of these things.'

The girl clipped two fingers to her head in a mock-salute and staggered off through yet another doorway.

Alec watched her go. 'How many bloody rooms d'you have here, Mason?'

'Whole bloody suite of 'em.' Bump waved his arm. 'Bedroom's the size of a swimming pool.' He winked at the girls on the sofa, whose bored expressions flipped back into simpers as he turned to them.

I sat on the edge of the armchair, torn between horror and fascination. Bump resumed his position between the two girls.

'Now, where was I?' he said, holding out his arms along the sofa back, allowing a female to fold herself into him. 'What d'you think, Bray? Sampson doesn't even know this backwater, and look at the beauties he's picked.'

The girls giggled with dead eyes. Not a single one could be described as beautiful, but I supposed Bump was attempting to be chivalrous. The one wearing more than a petticoat shuffled over to where Alec was sitting.

'Hello, sweetie,' she said. 'What's your name then?'

'Don't tell 'em!' commanded Bump. 'No names, no pack drill, what?'

The girl stuck her tongue out at him. 'You're full of it, ain'tcha, Oscar Wilde?'

'Calling me a fairy, you strumpet?' Bump turned away from her in rather an affected way. 'I shall talk to you, little flower,' he mumbled, stroking the neck of the petticoat-clad girl.

The girl with the feather in her hair came back into the room. 'Ta-da!' she said, holding a tray of drinks, which rattled dangerously as she weaved her way towards us. She bent towards Alec, who took one with a mumble of thanks, and then made her way towards me. 'Here y'are, darling.'

I took it and sipped. It was extremely strong. I should go, I thought. The whole situation was so immoral I could barely take it in. And yet my rear appeared to be rooted to the armchair, even when the girl with the feather sat on the arm of it, her perfume drifting in and out of my lungs.

'You got a special friend, sweetheart?' she said. 'I wouldn't be surprised, good-looking man like you.'

I coughed. 'I'm . . . um . . . yes,' I said, hoping that would encourage her to leave me alone, and then hoping that it wouldn't. 'That is, I'm, um . . . well, she's called Liz-zie.' I wished immediately I hadn't told the girl her name.

'Sounds lovely.' She put her lips near my ear. 'Bet she don't put out for you though, eh?'

I swallowed my drink with difficulty. 'Um . . . I'd rather not . . . rather not say,' I said weakly. The girl laughed and tickled my ear. 'Wh-what about you?' I asked. 'I mean, are you married, or – er . . . ?'

The girl laughed out loud. Recovering herself, she said, 'No, darling, I ain't. No time for a beau, know what I mean? And all these handsome men about, seems a shame to tie yourself to one of 'em, don't it?'

This last was shot across the room to the other two girls. The one who was talking to Bump looked up. 'I reckon I got the handsomest here,' she said, stroking Bump's face.

'Stop talking, you.' Bump stood up and held out his hand. 'Come with me.'

She squealed with delight and allowed him to pull her to her feet. She trotted after him towards the bedroom, waving goodbye at the others, and I thought all of a sudden, and quite unbidden, about Clara Bray, and if this had been her life before she'd married my cousin. Everybody knew what third-rate actresses were like, and Alec had confirmed it. Yet I couldn't quite square it somehow, these brazen girls with their harsh voices and tipsy manners, and Mrs Bray at her dining table in a lozenge of morning sunshine, shaking the newspaper and pouring coffee.

I looked at Alec. He had his eyes closed and was sprawled on the sofa. The girl beside him watched for a while, then shrugged and stretched herself out on the spot recently vacated by the other two. From across the room, I heard two sets of rhythmic snores.

The girl on the arm of my chair laughed. 'Listen to the pair of 'em,' she said. 'Like a soddin' express train, eh?'

'He's . . .' I hiccuped. I looked at my glass and realized it was empty. 'He's a married man.'

'I see,' said the girl disinterestedly, and then, in a flurry of excitement, turned to me. 'Listen, is that the one I think it is?'

I looked up at her. Her perfume was giving me a headache. 'I'm sorry?'

'You know, what all the scandal was about all that time ago.' She peered at him. 'The fat feller, your mate, he mentioned something and I thought, *Hang on a minute, I'm sure it's him*. I mean, I know he was all like, what's the word, exonerated and that, but anyway, is it him?'

'I . . . er . . . I . . .' I found it hard to answer her at this point because she was rubbing her hand up and down my inner thigh. I wondered if she would be beautiful without the make-up and the heavy perfume.

'Dreadful,' she said thoughtfully, still moving her hand. 'That poor, poor girl. I mean, I know it was nothing to do with him, but still. That poor girl.'

'I don't know wh—' I began, but was forced to stop because she lunged at me, planting her lips upon mine and putting her tongue in my mouth.

She tasted warm and wet and of tobacco. Her kiss was nothing like Lizzie's experimental manoeuvre; this was professionally done. My head spun. I was drunk – I was aware of this, and aware of her hand travelling across the surface of my trousers, and of the cheap scent of her, and, somewhere far distant, the sound of snoring, and, beyond even that, a steady grunting accompanied by high-pitched squeals, and I thought of the pigs on my grandfather's estate farm rushing for their food, and then all thoughts of any kind receded in importance right the way to a very small spot at the back of my brain.

There was a confusion of limbs, and the girl clambered on top of me. I heard my glass hitting the carpet and the crackle of ice cubes spilling out. She released my tongue and nibbled at my ear, then undid the top button of my shirt. Her hand was still scrabbling about over my groin and I set my jaw, tried to control myself, to think grim, miserable thoughts, but then her fingers were curling round the buttons below my waist and, with a sudden burst amidst shouts and other noises, it was all over, quite, quite suddenly.

'Oh.' The girl looked down, then back into my face, a smile on her lips. 'You was having a great time, wasn't you?'

'I ... I ... I'm terribly sorry.' My face was burning. My trousers were sodden. Now my thoughts truly were miserable. From across the room the pairs of snores still emerged, and from the bedroom the grunts and squeals, and as a whole they appeared to mock me.

'You ain't got nothing to apologize for, sweetheart.' She kissed my forehead. 'My fault for getting you all excited too quickly. I don't know my own power sometimes.' She dimpled a smile.

I thought I might burst into tears, and struggled to contain them. 'I'm so awfully embarrassed,' I whispered. 'This is all ... I mean, I would never do this sort of thing usually.'

She shook her head, eyes wide. 'Promise I won't tell a soul,' she said. 'Anyhow, means I still left you pure and unsullied, eh?' She winked.

I hardly knew what to say to that, but she lifted my chin with her hand and said, 'Or we can wait and try again in a bit.'

'No, no.' I struggled to sit upright. She removed herself from my lap and returned to the armchair as I did myself up again. 'Thank you. But no.'

She shrugged. 'Your fat mate's paid for us for the whole evening. Ain't no skin off my nose.' Then she turned back and stared at my groin. 'Can't see a thing, sweetheart. You'll be just fine.'

I looked down. We were in dim light, but I felt the liquid drenching my underclothes all the same, and wondered how on earth I would get home. This was my punishment, anyhow, for being so utterly wicked. 'I am sorry,' I whispered. 'I have used you in such a vile way, I . . .'

'Oh, shut up, darling.' She leaned away from me, beside the armchair, and returned with a silver bag from which she pulled a cigarette and a lighter. She offered me one, but I shook my head. 'Your sweetheart – you said she was Lizzie, right?' she asked as she lit her cigarette.

'Yes.' Blackmail, extortion. I wondered how I could tell her I was completely broke. I trembled.

'Then who's Lara?'

I blinked. 'Lara?'

'Ain't that what you was saying? Just now. Lara or Clara. Something like that.'

'No, no,' I said, thinking quickly. 'It was C-Cara . . . Caravaggio. The . . . the quality of light in his work is ever so . . . moving.'

She tapped the ash into my now empty glass. 'Killed a man, didn't he?' she said. 'Funny, ain't it, to have all that beauty inside you, and all that violence too.'

I felt nauseous. 'I have to go.'

I left her just like that, without even a farewell, and lurched towards the anteroom. Even from here, I could hear the crescendo of noises as Bump reached the peak of his personal mountain, and the cry as he fell off the end of it. I opened the door and stumbled into the corridor, walking blindly along until I found the staircase, thinking I could hardly bear to see myself in the mirrored brightness of the lift.

The eight flights offered me a steady rhythm within which my brain bobbed a little more comfortably than it had before, but as I reached the lower floors the lights flared more harshly and I was suddenly aware of the awful state of my appearance. On the first floor I removed my tailcoat, folded it in front of myself to hide the damp stain on my trousers, and took the rest of the stairs like a fugitive.

The lobby was quiet now: the nonagenarian had packed himself off to bed, and the concierge on the desk was nodding asleep over a book. He looked up when I came down and I forced myself to keep a steady pace, smiling goodbye, even lifting a hand, and emerging into the cool night air with a sense of blessed relief.

I met nobody on the walk back to Castaway. The events of the evening continued to swirl about my head. Thank goodness Alec had been asleep as I'd called his wife's name; what had I been thinking of? A moment of madness, no doubt. I would have to blow out the trip tomorrow; I could hardly face her. Then I thought that I would have to go, or else she would suspect something was up.

In such a way my thoughts revolved and repeated one another. It was only as I was climbing up the cliff towards the house that I remembered what the girl had said about Alec and the scandal. I should have asked her for more information, I thought, but it was all too late now. I climbed the steps to the door of the house, pushed at it and realized that it was shut tight.

I closed my eyes and rested my forehead against the wood. After a while I leaned back and looked up at the front of the building, but I knew immediately that there was no way in without knocking. Why hadn't Alec asked for it to be left on the latch? Of course, he must have a key. I had never been back later than the servants' bedtime before.

I sat on the front step and stared at the black night above me. Alec would be home . . . well, he would be home at some point, surely. Or I could knock, but I shuddered at the thought of Scone opening the door to me in my dishevelled state.

To my left were the area steps, bordered with sharp black spikes. I peered through them; it was ridiculous to think that they would have left the basement door unlocked, but I thought I might as well try.

I climbed back to the ground, went around to the little gate, and took the stone stairs down. I rattled the door handle, but it was of course locked fast. The area was dank and chilly, but perhaps, I thought, I could rest here, at least until Alec came home. However, I was just curling my lip at the thought of it when I heard the shaking of bolts and the door opened.

I was too late to run up the steps, so I stayed to await my fate. A pale face peered out from a crack in the door, and a small voice said, 'Was you wanting to come in this way, sir?'

It was Agnes. She opened the door further, and I had no choice but to enter the long dark passageway. 'I was in the servants' hall,' she said, 'and I sees you coming down the steps, and I thought, *Of course, but you don't have a key, do you?*'

To my left an open doorway led into the servants' hall. I caught a glimpse of a long table and a few chairs and lamps. 'Thank you,' I said, and then, curiosity getting the better of me, 'You're not working now, are you?'

She shook her head. She was wraith-like in the dim light coming from the room. 'Oh no, sir. I'm too scared to sleep in my room, so I comes down here.'

'In the servants' hall?' I pointed, my hand accidentally pushing the door further open. As it swung back, I saw that two of the chairs had been placed together with a blanket on top. 'You can't sleep in here, Agnes.'

'I can.' Her lip trembled. 'And you ain't going to tell no one on me, sir. Not after I let you in. You can't. It's not fair.'

'Shush,' I said. 'I'm not going to tell anyone. But you're shaking, look at you.'

'Just a bit cold, that's all. Nothing I can't get used to.'

I held a finger. 'Wait there,' I said, and was rewarded with a shiver instead of a nod. I headed down the stone-flagged passageway under the length of the building, lit by the dim bulb of an electric lamp in the wall. I had never been down here before; it smelled of damp and must, and the walls had been painted a cheap-looking brown up to the halfway mark, with a green-tinged distemper on the rest.

I resisted the urge to snoop into Mrs Pennyworth's kitchen, and instead continued past the row of bells set into the top of the wall, spotting my own ('top back bedroom'), and climbed the linoleum-lined stairs up to the warmth of the ground floor.

The lacquered cabinet in the dining room revealed a quarter remaining of Alec's good cognac. I poured a largish amount into one of the tumblers that lined the glass shelf above, thinking it a pretty poor substitute for a warm bed, but it was the only comfort I could conceive of that would not involve a hue and cry the next day.

When I returned, she was no longer in the passageway but had retreated to the servants' hall, where she had tucked herself into a rocking chair in the corner and was wringing her hands. I hesitated, aware of the questions that would arise were anybody to find out, but feeling that I had behaved so immorally tonight, one more transgression would hardly make a difference. Besides, it was Agnes that was running the risk, although I felt that the girl was so at the end of her tether she no longer cared about propriety.

Inside the room, a small fire was still burning, and I noticed that it was indeed very cold in here, despite the warm summer evening outside. I sat down on a chair opposite her, still keeping my tailcoat folded carefully across me, although Agnes was too distracted to notice anything about my appearance. I put the brandy on the table and pushed it towards her.

She shook her head vehemently. 'Oh no, sir, I can't.'

'Drink it,' I said. 'Then I'll take the glass back upstairs and, should anyone ask, it was mine.'

She paused, and then picked up the tumbler, held it to her lips and took a sip, pulling a face and screwing up her eyes in a manner that under usual circumstances would have been much cause for amusement. 'Tastes like fire,' she muttered, wrinkling her nose at the glass.

I watched her. 'You can't continue like this, you know.'

She frowned. 'I will if you don't tell no one.' She took another cautious sip. 'Sir.'

'Well, perhaps I can help. How about if you changed your room?'

'It's Madam,' she said sulkily. 'She'll send me away if I start causing a fuss.'

'I'm sure she won't,' I said, only recalling, after I spoke, her determination to do exactly that at the dinner tonight. 'But perhaps I can . . . I don't know, speak to her.'

'Would you, sir?' For the first time, Agnes's eyebrows lifted in hope.

'That's no guarantee, by the way.' In fact, I thought, any intervention of mine was perhaps more likely to secure Mrs Bray's mind in the opposite direction, not least because any interest I showed in the female servants' sleeping arrangements would implicate me as some sort of depraved beast. 'But I don't understand. Why on earth would you be scared of your room?'

She looked down at her hands. 'It was Sally's room. When I got promoted they gave it me, and I tried to say I didn't want it, only they said I had to now I was parlour-maid, that it wouldn't be proper for one of the others to have a room to herself.'

'Sally? The girl who disappeared?'

She nodded. 'That room's evil, and it brings evil on everyone who sleeps there.'

I remembered her melodramatic talk on the pier the

day after my arrival at Castaway. 'What do you mean, evil? Sally may just have . . . I don't know, had a better offer.'

Agnes moved her lips sulkily. 'But before that, sir, it was Gina's. I mean a while before, but still. I know she slept there, because Sally told me.'

I stifled a yawn. 'And who is Gina?'

Tears welled in her eyes. 'She was parlourmaid, like me. See, I'm scared, sir. I'm scared that what happened to Gina'll happen to me, and . . . well, Sally caught evil too.'

She was making no sense, but then, all of a sudden, a thought struck me as I remembered Dotty's half-told tale in the tiny back-facing house. I sat upright. 'Gina . . . Was she here about nine years ago?'

'Something like that. I wasn't here then, of course. But we heard about it, in the town. Most people heard about it. I was a kid then; didn't think nothing of it. Then I started here and it's like I can't get it out of my head.'

'Tell me,' I said, urgently now. 'Tell me what happened.'

She cradled the brandy glass in her lap. 'Gina was . . . she was going to have a baby.'

'I see.'

'No, sir. I mean, sorry, sir, but you don't see. She never told anyone. She kept it a secret.'

'And who . . .' I paused, and took a breath. 'Who was the father?'

Agnes looked at the ground. 'Nobody knows, sir. They . . . people will talk, won't they? But nobody ever found out for sure. She kept it a secret.'

'A nasty little secret,' I muttered, a chill rattling my spine, remembering Dotty's odd warning last week. 'What happened?'

Agnes sighed. 'Well, one day she was down late for work, and they sent the under-housemaid to knock her up and . . . and . . .'

'And?'

'She'd hanged herself in the wardrobe in my bedroom, sir, and I keep thinking I can see her in the night, swinging from the rail.' Agnes's voice quavered. 'I daren't sleep in there, sir, and it's making me almost mad.'

I sank further into my chair. I was dog-weary with tiredness, but despite that a fear was stirring my heart. 'Oh, God,' I muttered, and prayed that the suspicion my mind was forming was completely, utterly untrue.

9
1965

I finished off the corned beef and ketchup sandwich I'd made myself for lunch, and traced a finger down the much-creased bus timetable that was taped to the kitchen wall by the door. I still smelled of old egg and bacon fat, but I had no time to wash. I'd spent long enough dithering about whether to go as it was, and now it was midday already. Not that she'd be back for hours, but I didn't want to run any risk of bumping into her. That, I already knew, would be disastrous.

There was another half an hour before the next bus to Petwick was due, so I picked up *Northanger Abbey* again and traced over Lizzie's handwriting. I'd been trying to mention it, casually, to Mrs Hale all morning, but every time I talked about her sister she rapidly changed the subject. In the end I'd given up.

I wouldn't have been so bothered, had it not been for my conversation with Dockie yesterday in the pub, his beard in his drink and his head in the past. Somehow, he'd bound me into his quest to discover himself, despite my best intentions, despite the present tense being my current concern. I thought over what he'd said to me, and spent a few minutes musing, rocking back on two legs of my chair at the kitchen table, when I remembered with a jolting start that I still had to pay my rent.

'Bugger.' I looked at my watch. Before midday, Johnny had said, and I was late, and the girls had already flipped when I'd told them I'd had to ask for an extension. I scrambled to my feet and pulled out the rent tin from its hiding place in one of the cabinets, emptying out notes and coins into my palm. I added the rest from my purse and put the whole lot in my pocket.

I ran up the stairs to the top floor, past more bath-rooms on the half-landings, past flats that held the faint strumming of a guitar, the whistle of a kettle boiling, the clacking of a typewriter's keys. At the final half-landing, where a dangling phone extension was clamped to the wall, a short linoleum-floored passageway led towards a nar-row, winding flight of stairs. It was lit by one tiny window and had a closed-in, musty smell.

At the top of the stairs was the white-painted door that led to Johnny and Star's flat; I knocked hard, hoping he hadn't gone out. Last Friday I'd waited here for twenty minutes, knocking like a demon, dressed up dolly-bird-style while I waited to go dancing with Star. I'd been convinced she was inside, because I thought I could hear somebody crying from behind the door, even though crying was the last thing anyone would imagine Star doing. However, as I waited now I thought I heard it again, that faint sobbing sound, and realized it must be some quite other sound: pigeons in the eaves, perhaps, or the wicked cackle of seagulls.

Finally, I heard footsteps and then Johnny pulled open the door and looked down at me. He was wearing his work-ing outfit of trousers and a paint-spattered shirt and was wielding a dangerous-looking spanner in one hand. From behind him I heard the faint whisk of ska music playing on the turntable and, even more faintly, smelled the sweet-edged aroma of pot. He grunted when he saw me.

'You're taking the piss,' he said. 'I was just about to write you an eviction notice.'

'I was held up.' I was unsure if he was being serious. 'I really appreciate this. Thank you.'

'You owe me one.' He jerked his head. 'Better come in.'

I entered the narrow hallway, the sobbing sound disappearing as I followed Johnny down the corridor, past the intriguing double bedroom on my right, and the fridge, which for some reason sat opposite the bathroom beneath one of the skylights, before I finally emerged into the wider space of the flat.

I'd become used to Star and Johnny's flat by now, but the haphazard nature of the place managed to take me by surprise every time I saw it. There were different-sized kitchen units along two of the walls, one overhanging an armchair whose stuffing was spilling out from various tears in the fabric. Beside the armchair was a stately looking cooker with encrusted rings, its grill pan thrusting forwards like an Edwardian lady's bosom. Linoleum had infected the entire area like bindweed, bulging around the two small empty fireplaces, and scored black from where furniture had been dragged across it. In the battle between the living area and the kitchen, the kitchen was winning.

The record came to an end and revolved silently on the turntable. 'Can I put a new one on?' I asked, handing the notes to Johnny, who slapped them on to the draining board along with the spanner and picked up the end of a joint from where it was resting in an ashtray.

'Huh?' He looked up in the middle of relighting it. 'If you want. But none of Star's shit, all right?'

He moved the joint around his lips as he puffed on it, attempting to count the notes. I knelt down by the portable Dansette, which stood on a table beside the door to the spare bedroom, and flipped through the records resting on the floor beneath. I showed Johnny a Prince Buster L. P., to which he nodded his approval. I peeled it from its case and slipped it on to the player.

'Take it.'

I looked up. Johnny was holding out a badly scrawled receipt for six pounds.

'Okay. Thanks again.' I pocketed it and stood up to go. If I was to catch my bus I'd have to leave sharpish.

He squinted at me through his bleary eyes. 'You might have a word with my girl.'

'Star?' I said stupidly, as if there might be any other.

'She's been in a right mood all morning. Won't speak to me.' He handed the joint to me, but I shook my head. 'Nah,' he said. 'It's for her. Tell her . . . tell her I'd give up if I could.'

I took the soggy joint between my first finger and thumb. 'Where is she?'

He jerked his head towards the window. 'Outside. Listen, I got to go. Bloody pipe's leaking on the second floor. Just . . . y'know, cheer her up and that.'

He shambled off through the flat. Seconds later, I heard the door bang shut. I peered at the window on the other side of the room, where I could just about make out a dim shadow on a chair. I walked across the bumpy lino, under the steeply sloping roof and the bare bulb that dangled from the ceiling, scrambled on to the table at the far end, and stuck the still-smoking joint through the window.

There was a scrape of metal on concrete. 'I said I didn't want any,' I heard Star snap and then, in a different voice, 'Oh, it's you, Rosie.'

She shifted her chair so I could climb through on to the tiny terrace. Star was on one of the two chairs, her legs stretched out, feet folded on to the sculpted holes in the wall in front. I crammed myself against it. 'Hello.'

'Hi.' She squinted up at me and I flushed, remembering yesterday, her finger tracing my jawline as we stood by the basement railings. She turned her attention to the joint end, which I'd left on the floor of the terrace, picked it up and threw it over the wall. I turned to watch its descent, leaning over the wall with the whole of the cliff falling away before me, the sea spread out in a tapestry of blues and greys, the sun sending feeble rays out through the thick cloud overhead.

'He said he'd give it up if he could.'

'Eh?'

I twisted my head back towards her. 'Johnny. He wanted you to have the joint, and said he'd give it up if he could.'

'What the hell's he talking about?' She shook her head impatiently. 'Has he gone out?'

'Fixing a leak.' I looked again at my watch. 'Um – listen, I've got to head off now. Just popped by to pay the rent and say hello, you know.'

'Oh.'

Her violet eyes flickered, and I saw with a jolt of surprise that she was disappointed; that she wanted me to stay. I thought of the soft crush of her lips on my cheek and said rapidly, before I had time to think, 'You can come with me if you like.'

She raised an eyebrow. 'Where are you going?'

The instant the words were out of my mouth, I regretted them. If she came, there was a chance she'd find out everything, and if she did that, I'd no longer be the nice person of her imagination. 'Nowhere special,' I said quickly. 'Just going back home to pick up some of my clothes, that's all.'

'Petwick?' She uncurled her legs from the wall. 'Can I really come too?'

'Um . . .' I smiled glassily. 'Um – of course. But it's dead boring, honestly. Nothing ever happens there. I mean, I'm just going in and going out again.'

'Great.' She hopped to her feet. 'Do we get the bus?'

'Gosh, yes. It takes ages,' I said, futilely, as Star edged past me to climb back into the flat, her hand brushing my arm. I closed my eyes for a second, wondering if I could suddenly change my mind. But this was my only opportunity: today was the only day I knew for sure that Mum would be out. I sighed, and followed Star through the flat, waiting as she disappeared inside her bedroom to collect her things and reassess the state of her make-up in front of the mirror that hung to one side of the door, then button her grey cape around her neck.

We walked to the main part of the house and down the stairs to the ground floor. 'You really don't have to come,' I said, once we were out and walking along the path.

She turned back. 'I want to see the place that made Rosie Churchill,' she said. 'Anyway, I need to get out of the flat before I murder Johnny.'

'It's that bad?' I pointed to the right. 'The bus stop's up here.'

'Worse.' We walked to the junction, across from which were the bungalows and the cliff-top path where I'd nearly tumbled to my death on Saturday. The bus stop was further up, on the corner of Shanker Road and Duckett Lane, and when we got to the concrete post Star leaned against it and said, 'Also, I'm dying to meet your mum.'

'Oh, she won't be there.' I felt myself reddening. Already I'd given away far more information than I'd intended. 'I mean, that's why I'm going now, to avoid her.'

However, Star merely nodded and then said thoughtfully, 'You know, I left home when I was fifteen. Went to live with my grandmother. My mother treated me as if I'd put her effigy on a bonfire.'

She gave me a swift glance, almost as if she were afraid of the effect this information would have on me.

I said with a laugh, 'Because you went to live with your grandmother?'

Star waggled her head. 'My father's a vicar.'

I did laugh now. 'You're joking.'

She grimaced. 'Sadly not. And my grandmother . . . well, she's very different. She doesn't get on with my mother. I mean, what I'm saying is, I'm not very welcome at the family home either, at the moment.'

On the other side of the road, the bus approached its final destination at the stop opposite ours, and its three passengers spilled out. I wanted to tell Star that it wasn't that I was unwelcome, exactly, but I didn't know how to do that without telling her the truth about Harry. 'Mum didn't get on with my grandma either,' I said. 'They had a farm, Grandma and Josh – that was her husband. He always sort of resented Mum, you see, thought she had airs above her station, that she was too good for them.'

'Her stepfather?' asked Star, and I nodded, as the bus travelled to the end of the road, turned about and came back up again. 'Stepfathers can be very awkward, so I've heard.'

I glanced at her sharply, but she was already getting on to the empty bus and had her back to me. We paid our fares and bumped on bad suspension all the way along, from Duckett Lane to Petwick Lane, past the closed-down farm and the old stone-built village, turning right at the petrol station into what the old folk called New Petwick, with its Grammar School and its Crescents and Avenues, its parade of shops ribboning the high street.

Nothing had changed during my six weeks' absence. The Eastway chippie was still next to Dodds & Sons' butcher's; the ironmonger's, with its yellow-and-green sign advertising lawnmowers to hire for fifteen bob, still remained on the corner beside Coster's sweet shop. I took Star inside to buy a bag of sweets from Mr Coster, and we plucked cola bottles and spaceships from little paper bags to chew on as we walked.

'I'd heard there was a lake,' said Star, biting the head off a jelly baby. 'Can we have a look?'

'I suppose so.' I looked at my watch, but it was still early. 'It's nothing special.'

She shrugged. 'There's a painting of it at the house, in the third-floor bathroom. I don't even know who did it, but it looks quite nice.'

'If you say so.' I took her to the lake via a pathway

which ran along a narrow gap between two houses in one of the roads off the high street. The lake was still sign-posted, although the white-painted writing that showed you where to go had faded away over the years, so it merely said TO PE   AKE now. We walked in single file along the overgrown pathway, tramping on nettles poking out of the fencing either side, until we came to a small opening and then, further along, a padlocked metal gate with KEEP OUT! in red pinned to it.

'Sorry.' I turned back to Star. 'It's not usually locked up. I suppose they must think it's dangerous.'

I stood back to let her peer through the gate at the muddy path leading to the brown waters of the lake. The shopping trolley was still there, rusting gently into the rip-ples, and broken glass trodden into the path led to whole beer bottles camped around the edge. Just beyond the locked gate fluttered a greying, deflated balloon.

'Nice.' Star indicated the balloon. 'I suppose it's changed quite a bit, over the years.'

'I suppose so.' I clung on to the holes in the fence and thought of Mr Prendergast. 'Perhaps they'll build houses on top of it.'

'Perhaps.' Star opened her bag and produced a battered-looking joint. She waggled it and said, 'Fancy a smoke?'

Star had offered them to me before, and I'd always refused. Now, though, thinking about the task ahead of me, I looked at it and said, 'Okay.'

'Good. Me too.' She put the joint between her lips, took a box of safety matches from her bag and struck one, holding the flame to the twisted end of the paper.

I watched it catch, mesmerized, and she looked at me from over the top of it. She smirked.

'Better than Johnny's soggy roach-ends, eh?'

'He's not doing a very good job of giving it up,' I replied, as she pouted to blow out smoke and frowned at me. 'Well, that's what he said he wanted to do, wasn't it?'

She shook her head and leaned against the gate. 'He wasn't talking about this.' She indicated the joint.

'Oh.'

She handed me the joint, and our fingers collided.

'Then what?'

She paused, as if weighing up a decision in her mind and then said, with a little sigh, 'Johnny . . . he's queer.'

I paused, the joint halfway to my mouth. 'What?'

She folded her arms across her chest. 'That's what he wants to give up. At least, that's what he says. I don't even know whether to believe him any more. I think he's just saying it because it's what I want to hear.'

Slowly, jigsaw pieces slotted together. Adam, the dodgems boy; a half-wave, barely acknowledged, on the promenade. 'Oh my God. Are you sure?' I sucked on the end of the joint.

'That day when we were supposed to go dancing, remember? I came home and they were – well, he was with . . . he was with somebody, all right?' She bit her lip. 'I threw a plate at his head. That's why I completely forgot about, you know, the One-Two and all of that. Ended up drinking all night in the Walmstead Arms; there was a lock-in. Me and Johnny, talking for hours, going round in circles.'

'Wow.' I blew out smoke as I'd seen Star do. I found the

thought of Johnny being queer curiously exciting. 'You wouldn't know, would you? I mean, that he's one of them. Not that I've met one before.'

'Rosie!' she snapped, and I looked at her, startled. 'He's supposed to be my man. He might, you know, end up in prison or in the paper or something. Never mind that it's totally against all the laws of nature. You have to swallow.'

'What?'

She patted her throat and gulped down air. 'That's how you inhale.'

I sucked and swallowed; my lungs burned and I coughed violently. 'Yuck.' I stole a glance at Star, wondering if I dared to ask a particular question to which I'd always been nervous of the answer, and so airily, as if it meant nothing to me either way, I said, 'I suppose you love him very much?'

'That's got nothing to do with it,' she said tightly, and I thought to myself with a ripple of anticipation, *Perhaps she doesn't.* 'Imagine if people found out. Nobody would ever speak to us again. Or worse, they'd feel *sorry.* I'd hate that. To be pitied.'

Then again, I thought, my head spinning already from the effects of the tobacco, maybe she did and she didn't want to discuss such a soft-centred concept with me. Shrugging casually, I said, 'Maybe you should, you know, split up.'

'I don't think you understand how serious this is.' She snatched the joint back from me and sucked on it viciously. 'Come on, let's go.'

She ground the end out in the mud and stalked back along the path.

'Wait a sec,' I said, my legs wobbling a bit as I hurried after her. 'You don't even know how to get there.'

But Star didn't stop.

'And the worst thing is, he's not even ashamed,' she was muttering as she marched back towards the high street.

'I'm taking it seriously, honestly,' I called, although the further we walked the less serious I felt, and as we turned on to the road I'd grown up on, all mown grass verges and plane trees, I felt the effects of the hashish shredding my brain. 'I think I'm stoned,' I said to Star in a stage whisper.

She finally slowed and turned back to me, her face softening, a smile curling her mouth. 'For goodness' sake,' she said, 'you've only had a couple of puffs.'

'I'm new to this game.' I nodded at the garden gate. 'This is it.'

Star nodded. In a BBC announcer's voice she intoned, 'And so we arrive at the childhood home of the great Rosemary Churchill.'

This struck me as idiotically funny, and I collapsed into giggles as we staggered together up the path.

'Come on,' hissed Star, 'you can do it,' and this made me giggle even more.

The spare key under the flowerpot felt solid and satisfying in my fingers, and it turned nicely in the lock. Then we were inside, in the narrow hallway, and it all looked so familiar and unchanging that I could hardly believe I'd been gone all this time.

Star took off her cape and hung it on the peg next to the telephone stand. 'Mind if I have a look round?'

I waved her off. 'It's not very interesting.'

'Let me be the judge of that,' she said as she walked

towards the kitchen. I leaned against her cape, breathing in the scent she'd left behind. I closed my eyes and remembered how it had been here, in the hallway, where I'd first met Harry, when Mum had invited him over for Sunday lunch one day and I'd opened the door to him.

'Ah, the famous Rosie!' he'd exclaimed, and had presented me with a bunch of roses as a gift. I'd been goggle-eyed, fourteen years old and already half in love with this stepfather-to-be, with his raucous sense of humour, his generosity, his listening to my opinions as if I really did have something to say.

'All mod cons,' I heard Star call from the kitchen. There was a noise like grinding knives; I peeled open one eye and saw her repeatedly pressing the button on the waste disposal unit at the sink. Harry had bought the kitchen with his fat chequebook when he'd moved in; nothing was too good for the new ladies in his life, he said, and Mum had her evening dresses and pieces of jewellery, and I got taken out to the Golden Dragon to try Chinese food, and to the pictures like a proper grown-up, and thought Harry the best thing since sliced bread.

I was sixteen when I began scrawling his name in my diary, wishing I'd met him before Mum, because she was too old for a proper love relationship. They were more like friends, I supposed, and when I began noticing his eyes lingering upon me I kept the observation to myself, bubbling with suppressed desire.

It was in the kitchen, when I was seventeen, that Harry had kissed me for the first time, the night he and Mum had come home late from a party, both of them a bit squiffy, and Mum had gone up to bed, leaving us alone.

He'd pinned me against the Royal Houses calendar, his tongue pressing through my teeth, and then he'd pulled away from me, his lips still glistening with my saliva, told me I was a very naughty girl, and went upstairs to bed. The next day he came home with a present for me, a fountain pen wrapped in tissue paper, and said he'd seen it in the stationer's window and had just known I would adore it, and he was right.

I shook myself into the here and now. Star had disappeared from the kitchen, and I heard a thump from the front room next door to the hall, where we never usually sat except for when we had visitors. I remembered suddenly what was in the room, and panic assailed me. 'Wait!' I called, and flung open the door.

She had spread herself horizontally on the sofa, her legs raised, her skirt falling back over her thighs. I stood in the doorway and watched her, remembering how Harry had beckoned me to join him on the same sofa, that night when Mum was away at the farm sorting through my dead grandma's bits and pieces, telephoning at ten o'clock to say there was so much work she was going to stay overnight.

'Just you and me then, eh, Rosie?' he'd said, offering me a beer and patting the space next to him. He'd bought me more presents since that first time, and had given me more kisses too, and sometimes fondled my breasts through my clothes. He was my secret sweetheart, nibbling my ear in his dusty office that day when I'd gone to visit him at the building site, telling me how beautiful I was.

I'd been kissing him a while on the sofa before he put

my hand in his lap and had said, 'That's what you do to me, Rosie.'

I'd stared at him, not properly understanding, and then he'd said thickly, 'We've just been playing toy houses up till now, haven't we?' He'd stood up and held out his hand. He'd drawn me to standing and led me out of the room and up the stairs.

Star beamed up at me, stretching first one arm, then the other, like a cat. 'Lap of luxury, this. Not at all like the vic-arage, you know. That's about two hundred years old and it's always freezing.'

She hadn't seen the sideboard. To prevent her spotting it, I came over and sat on the sofa next to her. 'Enjoying yourself, are you?'

'Mmm. I think I'll stay.' She giggled.

I sensed she was about to look round the room, so I leaned over her, pinning her wrists to the sofa's cushions with my hands.

She gasped a soft, 'Hey!'

'I'll make you stay.' I bent down, my hair trailing in her face. 'And you can be the best daughter ever.'

She relaxed into my grip. Her elbows framed her face like a portrait. Her lips bowed into a smile. 'You'll make me?' she whispered.

I nodded. I leaned closer, and Star's eyes switched sud-denly, nervously, her gaze skittering around the room. She squealed, 'Oh, photographs!' and pushed aside my grip, jumping to her feet.

I watched her approach my mother's sideboard, my guts slithering. It had always been the repository for our important photographs, all the frames placed at an angle to avoid the bleaching of the afternoon sun through the net curtains.

Star picked up one and showed it to me. 'That's you, isn't it? Aren't you adorable?'

I nodded mutely. She picked up the photograph of my father in uniform, and cooed over his moustache.

'And this one!' she said, picking up another. 'Is that your mum? And who's this with her?'

'My stepfather,' I said miserably, as Star frowned at the handsome face, the face that she had seen twice already this week, and, beneath the photograph, the telltale inscription *Harold & Grace, 11th April 1962.*

She turned to me, still holding the photograph. 'Rosie . . . ?'

I pounced on something. 'Oh, God, what's this?'

'Eh?' Distracted, she watched me pick up a small framed photograph at the back of the collection.

'This wasn't here before.' I looked at the sepia snapshot of the baby in a crib, with a blurred speck of grass behind.

'Okay,' said Star. 'Can I ask you something?'

'No, but . . .' I peered at the photo in my hands and looked up at Star. 'I've seen it before, I'm sure of it. Recently. Very recently.'

'Yes, well, all babies look the same.' Star took the photograph from me and set it back with a soft *tock* on to the counter. She pointed to Harry's face. 'It's him, isn't it? The chap in the sports car who brought you the present.'

Her eyelids flickered, and I knew she was thinking of the note Harry had left with the shoes, the sort of note no proper stepfather would ever write. I flicked a glance at the clock on the wall. 'I must get upstairs and sort out my clothes,' I said, as breezily as I was able. 'Otherwise I'll completely forget, you know, and that was the whole point of my coming.'

I darted out of the room, muttering something about being back in a minute, and ran up the stairs, leaving her behind.

My old bedroom looked exactly as it had done when I'd left it at the height of summer. My schoolbooks were still lined up in a row on the edge of my desk. My pencil pot held a filigree of dust inside each compartment. I opened my wardrobe and found an old travel case inside, and as I put it on the bed to fold in jumpers, I remembered how I'd sat here beside Harry, and he'd said, 'Are you ready to be a proper grown-up, Rosie?'

I'd shrugged, scared of what he'd meant by that, but he'd calmed me down by kissing my hands, then my mouth, and running his fingers along my arm, and I'd gasped with that ripple of desire he always managed to spool out of me. He then unhitched my blouse from its moorings in the belt of my skirt, and undid all its tiny buttons. He peeled the sleeves from my shoulders and slid a finger under one of the straps of my brassiere. 'Take this thing off, won't you?'

I did as I was told. I was glad to, anyway, because it was a horrible Marks & Sparks one, but once I was topless and sitting in front of him I felt a little bit like being at the doctor's. I watched from above as he caressed my breasts, and concentrated hard to feel that ripple of desire again. It was there all right, but very faint, almost as if it had gone to sit in a back room while it worked out exactly what was going on here.

He reached around under my skirt and fingered aside the edge of my knickers. The ripple vanished into a seam of marble, and I wriggled away. He waited a second, staring at me impassively, and then said, 'Don't worry. We can take our time.'

I'd smiled gratefully, glad he wasn't annoyed with me for being so gauche. 'Thanks.'

He winked. 'Still, you could help me out here, or I might be in trouble.'

'Yes, yes. Of course.' I had no idea what he meant. I watched as he unbuckled his belt, freed himself of trousers, underpants and socks, all in one go, and then dragged his shirt over his head.

His neck had a ring of red from its exposure to the sun when he'd been out on the building sites. His chest and stomach were pale, but tightly packed with muscle. His penis looked like nothing I'd ever imagined. It leaned upwards, listing to one side as if drunk. Underneath, his balls hung like two jowls. I felt a second of panic.

Harry took my hand and guided it towards his penis, unfurling my fingers and wrapping them around. 'Like this,' he murmured, moving my hand up and down. 'That's it. That's it, baby.'

I moved my hand up and down as he'd shown me. He closed his eyes and rested his hands on the candlewick bedspread. I felt goosebumps prickle my chest. I tasted beer on my breath. I tried to give in to the moment, but instead found myself looking at my textbooks on the chair, my end-of-year revision notes pinned on to my bookshelf, my framed O-level certificates on the wall.

Harry shuddered. A milky substance shot from the end

of his penis and I stared at it as it spurted out over my hand. Stupidly, I hadn't even known about that. I supposed it was the baby-making side of the business. 'Oh, God,' he mumbled, and collapsed backwards on to the bed, releasing my grip.

I looked at the sticky stuff all over my hand. Harry still had his eyes closed, so I wiped it on my bed sheet. It smelled odd, sour almost.

'You're beautiful.' Harry was looking at me through half-closed lids. He stroked my arm, and I felt as cold as winter. I sat still, until he'd sighed, pulled on his clothes and left, kissing the top of my forehead just as he used to back in the more innocent days.

Afterwards, I heard him moving around downstairs, opening another beer, going into the lounge to watch television. I'd pulled on my nightie and picked up the hidden base of my jewellery box where I'd put the chain he'd given me, holding it against my manhandled breasts as evidence of Harry's love.

Now, as I stood in the bedroom, folding a jumper into a tight roll in my arms, I heard the click of a key turning in the front door, and then a thud as someone entered the house. The door closed with a tight bang, and my heart shot into my throat.

Five seconds later, I heard the door to the front room open and my mother's gasp – no doubt as she came across a strange girl with her shoes on the sofa.

I stuffed my clothes any old how into the bag and struggled to close the zip. Voices rumbled back and forth below me, my mother's fast and frantic, Star's slow and laconic.

I finally closed the zip, picked up the bag and hurried

downstairs. My mother was just inside the front room, and I almost walked into her in my rush. She turned with a startled yelp and said in an almost whisper, 'Rosie.'

She was wearing a matching wool skirt and jacket; I supposed she'd dressed up to see the solicitor. Her hair was ruffling loose of its curls. She'd put on a dash of make-up: pearly lips and cream-edged eyes. I squeezed past her into the room. Star was on her feet, some sort of excuse on her lips.

'Mum,' I said. 'This is my friend Star. I invited her to . . . um . . . to . . .'

But Mum was already taking in the zipped bag in my hands. She put a hand to her chest and bit her lip. 'Oh, Rosie,' she said. 'Do you really hate me all that much?'

A blur of guilt heated my head. It hadn't even occurred to me that she'd think that. 'No, Mum, no. Of course not.'

'I'll just . . .' Star walked to the door, squeezing past Mum. 'I'll be outside, okay?'

I wanted to ask her not to go, but I stayed silent as she left. We listened to the front door opening and closing and I said, utterly inadequately, 'I came back to pick up a few things.'

She sat down heavily in the armchair. 'You want to avoid me that badly,' she said, staring glassily at the coffee table. 'You knew I was going to be out, so you came by.'

'It's not how it looks,' I croaked, sitting down too, on the sofa arm. But then again, it was exactly how it looked. 'I'm so sorry.'

She glanced up at me. 'What did I do? That's all I want to know. What on earth did I do to drive you away?'

'Nothing.' I put out a hand towards her, and she whipped her own back. 'Of course you didn't do anything.'

'Then why all this?' She waved a hand. She'd lost weight; the jacket hung loose on her frame. 'And before you left. Don't think I didn't notice you avoiding me, leaving the room if I came in. I mean, God, Rosie, I can take it, but I need you to tell me the truth.'

I shook my head fiercely. 'I just needed my independence.'

'What, am I so smothering? I'm not as strict as . . . well, as lots of people.' She got to her feet and walked towards the sideboard, hugging herself. Absently, she began putting the photographs back in their proper places. 'You must think me a complete bitch.'

'Of course not.' I blinked away my shock at Mum swearing in my presence. I stood up too. 'I'm so sorry. I never wanted this.'

'What did you expect?' I noticed she was holding the photograph of the baby, the one I'd picked up earlier. 'That I'd say, "Oh well, my daughter's suddenly left home in the middle of her A levels and won't tell me why. Never mind, I'm sure it'll all come out in the wash."'

'That photo.' I indicated it. 'Is it you?'

'Mmm?' She glanced at it. 'Yes. I found it when I was going through Mother's things at the farm. My uncle Peter took it with a Box Brownie just after I was born.'

'I think I've seen it before,' I said. 'Very recently.'

'Well, you can't have, dear.' She sighed. 'I haven't seen it myself for years.'

'There's something about it . . .' I began, but I saw I

wasn't going to get away with changing the subject that easily. 'I can't talk about what's going on, that's all.'

'I thought you might be having a baby.' She looked down at my stomach. 'I've been asking around, you know. I've spoken to all your school friends. They said you'd been acting a little strangely recently.'

I shook my head. 'I'm not having a baby.'

'Then there's a boy involved.' She tilted her head back and looked at me, and I had the feeling she saw straight into my warped little brain. 'I thought so.'

'No . . .' I said miserably.

She turned and walked a few paces away, throwing her arms in the air. 'I'm not some innocent, Rosie. You can talk to me about . . . about boys, or sex, or . . . well, you know.'

'Not this,' I whispered. 'Not this.'

She sighed, and when I looked up saw she was leaning on the doorway. She took me in slowly. 'You've lost weight,' she said.

'So've you,' I said.

She tugged at her skirt. 'Oh, I've been trying to do that for years. Very fashionable now, isn't it?' She rested her chin on the edge of the door. 'How are you doing in that draughty old place?'

I shrugged. 'Fine. I'm working. Paying my rent.'

'And that girl?' She indicated the hallway, where Star had gone. 'Is that the one I spoke to on the telephone the other day?'

I nodded. 'She lives on the top floor. She's . . . um . . . she's nice.'

'I'm sure she is,' said Mum, with just a hint of scepticism in her tone. 'A little self-obsessed, perhaps, but I'm sure I was the same at her age.'

'I've made a heap of friends,' I said earnestly, nodding the white lie into truth. 'There's an old man in the basement.'

'An old man?' Mum coughed.

'I mean, he's adorable. He's sort of . . . um, grandfatherly.'

Mum took a step towards me. 'People aren't always what they seem, you know.'

'No.' I wished I'd never said grandfatherly. 'But he is. I mean, he's rather a lost soul. He can't remember things, you see, and he turned up with a ton of money and a photograph . . .'

I trailed away as I looked again at the sideboard. 'Perhaps you ought to keep yourself to yourself a little more,' Mum was saying, but I wasn't properly listening, because I suddenly twigged where I'd seen the photograph of the baby before.

'Oh my goodness.' I picked it up and showed it to her. 'He has the same one. I mean, his is ruined, but still . . . it's the same.'

'Don't be silly.' She stalked towards me, snatched it back and returned it. 'Why would some old man have a photograph of me as a baby?'

'I don't know. It just looks . . .' I squinted at it, remembering a splash of grass, a blurred hint of a baby's forehead. 'So similar,' I ended lamely.

Mum held my chin and turned my face towards hers.

'Come home, Rosie,' she said softly. 'It's not too late. The school will take you back. I've spoken to them: Miss Waverley's very anxious about you.'

My stomach sagged, because the thought of waking in a warm bed, with nothing more to worry about but unravelling the origins of the Hundred Years War, was so appealing I nearly burst into tears right then. I shook my head. 'I'm sorry,' I said. 'Tell them I'm sorry.'

She let go of my chin. 'Wait there,' she said, and clipped away to the kitchen on her heels. I picked up the photograph again and peered at it. Perhaps she was right. After all, Dockie's photograph was almost completely obliterated.

When Mum came back into the room she was holding a roll of notes held tight with an elastic band. She pressed it into my hand. 'Take it. Please.' She smiled in a wobbly way. 'Buy yourself those sandals you wanted.'

I swallowed, and took the money. 'Thank you.'

She held me by the shoulders. 'Look, if you can't bear to move back, at least return my telephone calls.'

I nodded. 'I will. I promise I will.'

'And you could visit, you know? Just to let me know you're alive.' She paused. 'How about on Sunday? You could come for lunch. I'll pick up a joint of beef from Dodds. Just the three of us: you, me and Harry.'

'I can't. Um . . . not Sunday,' I said, my heart racketing hard in my ribs. At her disappointed face I said, 'I could come on Tuesday. I get Tuesdays off. I could come for lunch. How about that?'

'But Harry won't be there,' she said, frowning.

'No. Well . . .' I trailed off, and then in half a second saw her face change as a new idea lit up her brain. Before it had time to plant itself, I leaned forward and groped her into an embrace. 'I love you, Mum,' I said, and she laughed, startled, because I wasn't the sort to show affection usually.

'I love you too.' She hugged me back and kissed my cheek. I pulled away from her as quickly as was polite, and picked up my bag. 'Just a second, Rosie,' she said.

'I've got to go.' I made a show of looking at my watch. 'The bus'll be here any minute.'

She stayed me with a hand on my arm. 'Harry . . .' she began.

I pulled my arm away. 'I'll call you,' I said, forming a telephone shape in the air. 'About Tuesday, okay? See you later.'

And with that I dashed into the hall, pulled my jacket from the peg, opened the door and hurried down the path, swinging through the gate, past a surprised Star, who was leaning on the wall, and walked rapidly down the street.

Star found me at the bus stop outside Drover's News. I tapped a nervous tattoo on the post, pretending to look down the street for the bus. 'Should be here any minute,' I muttered.

She gazed down at me. 'I take it that didn't go too well,' she said.

'I didn't think . . .' I said quietly. 'It just didn't occur to me how upset she'd be that I'd left home.'

She laughed softly. 'Hey, if you can't go through life without devastating your mother at least once, then you're not really normal.'

I leaned on the pebble-dashed post. 'The thing is, I didn't have a choice, but of course I can't explain that.'

'Then I take it you haven't told her about you and Harry?'

I grimaced and looked away. 'Let's not talk about it,' I muttered.

'God, Rosie, I'm not judging you.' I looked up; she was balancing the soles of her feet on the edge of the kerb. 'Remember when I spoke to your mum on the telephone a couple of days ago? She said your stepfather had been coming by to see you. And I thought, *Oh, God, not the chap in the Jag who'd shag a tree if it had tits?* Plus that saucy note, of course. I worked it all out then.'

'Well done, Miss Marple,' I muttered. 'Now you see what kind of a nice person I am.'

'But you are.' Star flung her arm out in a dramatic gesture. '*He's* the filthy pervert.'

I shook my head. 'It was both our faults. Worse for me. I'm . . . you know . . . I should have known better.'

'How old were you when it started?'

'Seventeen,' I mumbled. In the distance, I saw the bus rounding the corner.

'Then he's the one who should have known better.' She put a hand to the post and swung on it. 'I suppose he told you a load of lies, did he?'

I wrinkled my nose. 'I was an idiot.'

The bus drew closer. Star stuck her arm out to hail it. 'Don't be daft.'

'I was. I thought he really liked me, you know? That I was the one for him and he'd only married Mum by mistake. And all the time I was just . . . I was just . . .'

'Just a challenge?' suggested Star, and I nodded. The bus drew level and we climbed on to pay our fare back to Helmstone. Star threw the driver some coins, saying, 'My treat, and no argument.'

We settled at the rear of the bus against the rickety back of the seats. 'The worst thing is,' I said in a hushed tone, although as we moved off my voice was drowned by the rattling of the engine, 'I didn't even leave straight away after we . . . well, I mean, I didn't . . . you know . . . that is, maybe we would have . . .'

'Spit it out,' said Star. 'Which, by the way, I hope you did.'

She chortled, and I wondered if I felt as she had an hour earlier when she'd accused me of not taking her problem with Johnny seriously enough. 'I went into Mum's bedroom to borrow her hair irons,' I said crossly. 'And in her drawer I found all these notes and cards – all from him.'

Star dug in her bag for a cigarette. 'You hadn't realized they were having a full relationship, so to speak.'

I blushed. 'I was such a fool.' As soon as I'd read Harry's messages to my mother, the language in them, much dirtier than anything he'd ever written to me, all the things I'd witnessed and ignored slotted back into place. A memory of Harry pinching my mother's bottom as she hung out the washing, of her squealing hysterically as they sat in the front seats of the car while I read a book in the back, of the muffled noises that came through the bedroom wall at night.

If he'd professed love for her, I wouldn't have minded: I'd have thought he was lying. But all the references to

243

body parts and what he wanted to do to her where – I'd read them and flung them back, feeling sick at the thought of it: partly at the thought of my mum as a sexual being, partly at the thought of them together in bed, but mostly just because I'd been weaving a fantasy in my own head. I couldn't even blame Harry for that. The illusion of the two of us as star-crossed lovers fractured as quickly as the time the cinema reel caught fire and melted Sean Connery's face in Technicolor, right in front of us on the screen.

'The thought of living in the same house as them,' I said to Star, as we bounced up and down on the bad suspension while Petwick passed by, 'I just couldn't bear it. I got the bus, just like this, saw the notice in the window of Castaway, rented the room and went back home to tell Mum I was moving out.'

'Of course,' said Star. 'That's normal.'

The whitewashed, crumbling houses of Helmstone began appearing and I felt, strangely, as if *now* I was really coming home.

'And now Mum might have guessed,' I said, as the bus trundled towards Duckett Lane, and I pulled the bell wire in the ceiling to stop it. 'She asked me about Harry, and I had no idea what to say.'

'She won't guess if she doesn't want to know.' Star swung up to standing and we walked the length of the bus. 'But come on, you're her daughter. She won't blame you.'

'Of course she will. I'll have ruined everything. She'll never speak to me again.'

'Perhaps she'll just kick him in the balls instead, and throw his things on to the street.'

I snorted as we climbed off the bus on to the windy road. 'Of course she won't. She's in love. And he's a fantastic liar.'

'I thought he was a slimy git from the first moment I clocked him.' She flung an arm around my shoulder as we walked back, along the giant side wall of Castaway House and round to the front. 'I said to myself, "Rosie can do better than *that*, surely."'

'How wise you are,' I said teasingly, nestling under her arm, feeling oddly safe in her embrace, as if nothing could harm me there.

We walked along the path and up the steps to the front door. Once we were in the hallway Star said, 'Listen, fancy popping upstairs for a cup of tea and a smoke?'

I hesitated. Johnny might be there and I didn't want to share Star with anybody, not right at that moment. 'Come to mine,' I said. 'The girls'll still be at work.'

She looked down at me, and nodded. 'Yeah. We don't want anyone interrupting.'

Her cheeks spun pink almost immediately, and I wondered why she'd be embarrassed. I continued up the stairs, around at the half-landing and then up to the kitchen door. I turned my key and let us both in.

The place was as I'd left it, the remnants of my corned-beef sandwich still on a plate on the side, although it seemed as if everything had changed. I put my bag of clothes on a chair and filled the kettle at the sink. Star leaned against one of the window ledges and looked out at the garden. 'Nice view from here,' she observed. 'It's a bit depressing only being able to see the sky from those dormer windows upstairs.'

'You've got the terrace,' I said, plugging the lead back into the kettle and switching it on. She turned and shrugged a smile at me, and I added, 'By the way, there's something quite interesting down there, where your hands are.'

Her cheeks bloomed pink again. 'What's that?' she said, removing them.

'Just there.' I went over to her and took one of her hands. I moved it back below the windowsill, inching along the ridges and grooves scored into the wood. 'Here. You feel it?'

'I'm not sure.'

I closed my fingers around hers and moved them over the words.

'Okay,' she said, 'yes, I can feel something.'

'It says . . .' I traced the letters with her, our fingers in tandem. 'Robert Carver is innocent.'

She frowned. 'Robert Carver?'

'Yes. Have a look.' I pulled her down, and she came with me so we were sitting on the floor, our backs to the wall, peering up at the underside of the windowsill. I kept my hand around hers, and used it to point at the lettering. 'There.'

She shuffled herself closer to me and peered up, flapping her long lashes. 'Oh yes.'

'Remember that sketch you gave me? The self-portrait. R. C.? I think this is him.'

'R. C.' She hugged her knees in towards her. 'The same initials as yours. God, do you think so? Wasn't that, like, absolutely ancient though?'

'Forty-one years. And then . . .' I paused, wondering

246

whether I ought to share all this with her, if she'd laugh and say I was silly to even spend a second's thought on a time way back in history. But she was waiting for me to speak, and so I ploughed on and said, 'And Mrs Hale next door – you know, my boss – her father gave me this book, a really old one, and inside it was all this . . . well, I'll show you in a minute. It's in my room . . .' I trailed off, because Star looked as if she was somewhere else entirely.

'Sorry,' she said. 'What's in your room?'

I shrugged. 'Don't worry. It's not very interesting.'

'No, no. It's not that. I was just thinking that that name, Robert Carver, I've heard it before.'

I sat up. 'Really? Where?'

She shook her head and frowned. 'I can't remember.'

'You know Dockie?' I said in a rush. 'The old man from yesterday, the one who called you Clara?'

'Oh yes. The crazy mystic. What about him?'

'Well, we ended up in the Snooks, and then he decides he wants to go to the Blind Pig.'

'God,' said Star. 'I'm surprised you came out alive.'

'It wasn't so bad,' I mused, thinking of how the saloon bar at lunchtime had been only semi-menacing, with its round Formica-covered tables and its seats upholstered in the sort of rough blue nylon that would give you an electric shock if you touched metal after you'd sat down. Dockie had bought me half a shandy and we sat at one of the tables, as silent people nursing stouts and bitters looked up at us incuriously and then returned to the serious business of getting plastered.

For a long time Dockie, too, stared into his pint, and then he looked up at me and said, 'Frank rescued me, you know.'

I nodded slowly, wondering where this was going. 'Okay.'

'Frank. My saviour. He found me in an old corner of the docks, behind a stack of pallets, wrapped only in a blanket that felt like glass, with a wound in my head. Frank, it was, who saved my life, who took me to his house, put me in his bed as I babbled nothing but nonsense at him. He fed me soup and bought me clothes – just the same as you, Rosie, just the same as you.'

I blushed. 'It was nothing.'

Dockie relaxed into the rhythm of his story, as if the words had been arranged in his head for a long time. 'At the beginning, you see, my body would not do as my brain commanded. He washed me. Changed the dressing on my head hourly. Soothed me when I screamed gobbledegook. Until slowly I mended, as much as I was able to. It was Frank who brought me from death's door. If he had found me an hour later, he said, I could well have already been dead. I owe him everything.'

Dockie nodded at me. I nodded back, and cupped my half-pint glass in my hands. I wondered what Frank had looked like. I imagined a quiet bear of a man, the sort who could snap a neck but whom nobody notices until he actually does so. 'Didn't he think about taking you to hospital?'

'There was no need. He took better care of me than any of those nurses could. Little better than sadists in caps, he called them. No. Frank nurtured me, there in his small house, for weeks. Months. And when I was well enough he found me work, working for him. He had a business, supplying the shipbrokers. I swept and cleaned and mended; I was weak at first, and useless, but I learned, I became strong, and Frank was very proud of me, so he said, very proud.'

There was something rather unsettling in this tale of Dockie's that I couldn't quite put my finger on. 'He sounds very . . . altruistic,' I said.

'Left me everything when he died.' Dockie blinked. 'Debts swallowed his business and his house, but he left me his cashbox, piled high with notes.'

'So he was like a father?'

Dockie frowned. 'Not exactly.'

'But he did try to help you to find your real family, didn't he?'

'He did.' Dockie nodded. 'He put advertisements in the newspapers, went to the police, even in England, as he surmised from my accent that that was my country of origin. But there was nothing. Eventually he concluded that I had been gone from home a long time, too long for anyone to miss me, that I had been working on some foreign ship, far-distant from its native port, and had tumbled, or been pushed, into the ocean. From there, he theorized that I had been picked up by smugglers who had robbed me of my clothes and left me for dead on the docks.'

'Sounds as if he thought of everything.' I sipped my bittersweet shandy.

'And then, one day, I found a hidden compartment in the cash box.' His eyes flickered. 'A pile of clippings cut from a newspaper.'

'Oh, you mean . . . the ones you were talking about before?'

'I believe so.' He leaned across the table towards me. 'I

cannot, my dear Rosie, I cannot remember what was in those clippings, but I knew when I read them that Frank had betrayed me.'

'Betrayed you? How?'

He shook his head. 'I do not know. But I was angry – so angry I embarked on my bender, and it was after then that I decided I had to come here, to Castaway House.'

'If only you could find them, eh?' I thought of the name he'd mentioned earlier. 'What about this Clara?'

He frowned. 'Clara?'

'When we were outside the house. You looked at Star – my friend – and you said, *Clara*.'

'I had forgotten that.' He tapped the back of his head; grey hairs flew about. 'Yes, of course. Of course.'

He leaned his head against a glass case containing a model ship, and appeared to drift into a world of his own. A faint smile played on his lips.

'Dockie?' I said eventually. 'Who's Clara?'

'She is . . .' he coughed creakily. 'I can picture her. I can see her, as clearly as I can see you. Dark hair, red lips. But as to who she is . . . that, I have no idea.'

I gave up. It was probably not important, anyway. I had spilled beer on the table; I mopped it up inadequately with the mats advertising tobacco. 'You say Castaway is the key to yourself?'

He nodded.

I nodded too. 'Then I suppose it was a very long time ago that you were here.'

'Exactly so.'

'Perhaps twenty, thirty years?'

'Or longer.' He squinted at the opposite wall. 'I have no

idea of even the date Frank found me on the docks. We celebrated the day every year: the third of September – but as to the anniversary, Frank said that was unimportant, and, you see, he laid out for me the limits of my world.'

'Forty years, even.' I calculated a date, and a thought occurred to me. I leaned across the table. 'Actually, I don't suppose the name Robert Carver rings any bells, does it?'

Dockie stared. 'Robert . . . Carver,' he said slowly.

'It probably doesn't, but he was staying in the house, you see, around that time, and . . .'

'Robert Carver.' He repeated the name. 'Robert Carver.'

'You know it?'

'I know it, I know it.' He lifted his pint, tipped his head back and finished it. 'Oh, God, I know it.'

'Then who is he?' I said excitedly, feeling as if I was on the brink of something huge.

He sighed, drifting once more on the vague shapes of his past. 'I will remember. A universe is exploding in my brain.' He nodded. 'Everything shall return.'

He lumbered up to the bar to buy himself another pint with a whisky chaser, and from there his speech became more and more fragmented. He rambled about odd people he'd known in Dublin throughout his life – Frank, a cat he'd made friends with – until he seemed to need me no longer. He was just another one of the Blind Pig's waifs and strays mumbling contentedly in a corner, with the red-faced, dirty-aproned landlord on a stool behind the bar keeping a bleary eye on them all.

I recounted all this to Star, who was silent for some time, drumming her fingers on her hunched-up knees.

'It's funny,' she said finally, and then lapsed again into silence.

'What's funny?' I prompted her.

She stole a quick glance at me, and I sensed her assessing me. 'The thing is, Rosie . . . the thing is . . . people do say I resemble my grandmother.'

'Okay. Who's your grandmother?'

'I mean, not only resemble. We also have the same name. She's called Clara too.'

'Clara?'

Dark hair, red lips.

'I was named after my grandmother, you see – back when my mother was still speaking to her – only I couldn't pronounce Clara very well, and it usually came out as Star. Hence the nickname.'

'But why . . . how on earth would Dockie have known your grandmother?'

'Well . . .' And here she glanced at me again, and she took a breath and said in a rush, 'My grandmother used to live here.'

'Really?'

'That is . . . my grandfather too. They owned Castaway House.'

I laughed, but she was nodding, serious. 'What, the entire building?'

Star nodded. 'It used to be pretty grand, you know.'

'So perhaps . . .' I turned to Star excitedly. 'Your grandmother met Dockie when he came here, and that's why he remembers her. And he met Robert Carver too.'

'Exactly. I mean, that would explain why he called me

Clara.' She shrugged. 'People say I look like her, when she was young.'

'And your grandparents – they're still alive?'

'Only my grandmother. My grandfather died years ago.' Star put her chin on to her knees. 'Granny lives in Paris now. She's more French than English, these days.'

I nudged her shoulder with mine, because I knew how much it meant to Star, to let me into the secret places of her life. 'I'd like to meet her.'

'You will.' Star took another breath. 'She's coming here on Saturday.'

'This Saturday?'

'She's coming here because – well, you see, she still owns the house.'

'Hold on.' The cogs of my brain slowly turned. 'Are you saying that the landlord is your grandmother?'

'Yes.' She looked down at her lap.

I thought of all Johnny's threats over the rent, Star's evasions. 'And the flat on the ground floor?'

'That's hers. It's where she stays when she visits.'

'But . . . but you . . .'

'Look, I didn't want anyone to know, all right?' Star slid a glance towards me. 'It's the reason I'm living here, so I can keep an eye on the place for her, collect the rent, that sort of thing. She gives me an allowance, you see.'

'Oh.' I thought of her up-to-the-minute clothes, her London haircut; not funded by Johnny after all. 'I see.'

'Please don't think any worse of me.' Her hand landed on mine, clasping it. 'I mean, *I* haven't got any money. It's all Granny's.'

'Why would I think worse of you?' I folded her warm, dry fingers into my palm.

'I don't know.' She bowed her head. 'Maybe you'd think I was some sort of spoiled little rich girl.'

'So what?' I laughed. 'So what?'

She looked up at me. 'I don't want you to despise me, Rosie.'

I put my other hand to her forehead and smoothed away the crease at her brow. 'Of course I don't despise you.' I lifted her chin, and my stomach crumpled as I leaned forwards and kissed her.

At first she gasped, and then I felt her bones relax and she kissed me back. I pressed myself into her. Her lips parted, and as my tongue found hers a jolt of electricity pierced me from mouth to groin.

Finally, she pulled back from me. 'I've got to go,' she murmured, pushing herself up to standing, brushing herself down.

'What about tea?' I said, still dizzy with her.

'No time. Sorry.' She grabbed her cape and bag from the kitchen chair. 'I'll see you . . . see you soon.'

'Tomorrow.' I smiled up at her. 'The party, remember?'

She hesitated by the door. 'What? Oh yes. The party.' She swallowed, nodded a goodbye and left the room. I heard her footsteps above my head, running up to the top-floor flat.

I stayed where I was for quite a while, with Robert Carver over my head and the taste of Star on my lips. Finally, I pushed myself upright on cramped feet and went into the bedroom. The clouds were low in the sky, and the objects in the room had taken on a submerged look.

I drew all the curtains and got undressed, even though it was only mid-afternoon. I climbed under the covers and sank back into the memory of Star's lips giving under mine, her body burning heat as we'd kissed.

I pulled her into bed with me now, stripped her of her dress and her underwear, and wrapped my arms around her back as she lay on top of me, resting on her elbows, smiling down, our noses touching.

I reached underneath my nightdress and crawled fingers up my legs towards the place at the top. I caressed myself slowly, gently, and a warmth coursed through my body. I continued, firmer now, again and again and again until with a shudder and a muffled cry my back arched, my head pressing into the pillow and stars juddering up my spine.

Afterwards, I lay in a happy glow of contentment, the late-appearing sun sending a bleak yellow wash over the edge of the curtains. I thought of Star again, tenderly this time, with a shiver of anticipation for the party tomorrow.

Somehow, my thoughts travelled to her grandmother Clara, and the young woman Dockie had known. Dark hair and red lips, he had said, a memory so strong it could break through a thick wall of years. I wondered what she had been like, and how similar she was to her granddaughter, who had me dancing on the tip of her finger, again and again and again.

IO

1924

I sat squashed into the side of the motor car. Beside me, volumes of skirt crushed my trousers, and occasionally I felt a hand flutter close to my thigh. The air around me was thick with perfume, despite the roof being pulled down, and bubbling female chatter crowded out my thoughts.

'How are you there, poor man?' said the girl on the fold-down seat opposite me. 'Must be terrible having to put up with all us females.'

The woman beside me, she of the wandering hand, nudged me hard in my side. 'I'm sure he loves every second of it, don't you, Mr Carver?' She laughed loud and hard, snorting like a horse.

'I'm fine, thank you,' was all the reply I had left in me, and even that went unnoticed in the general brouhaha. I wondered, yet again, why I was here.

I'd had a troubled night's sleep, my mind going over the tale Agnes had told me in the servants' hall. The story of the servant girl Gina's fate had clearly been kept from the rest of my family, or surely I would have heard it earlier. Quite apart from the taint of suicide that would linger over the house, there was also the question of who had fathered the baby that had driven her to it.

I did not like to imagine the answer to that question,

but the idea of it refused to let me go. It had rolled like a penny round my brain as I lay in bed and watched the moonlight throwing patterns on the ceiling. I wondered also about Agnes in the basement, hunched in that rocking chair, undoubtedly failing to sleep. I felt duty-bound to at least attempt to help her by forging some sort of conversation with Mrs Bray, and it was the thought of this that drove me to get out of bed, dry-mouthed and hungover, pack my sketchbook, brushes and newly bought tin of watercolours, and join my cousin's wife in the dining room for breakfast.

'I'm surprised to see you,' she said, folding out her newspaper. I helped myself to toast and sat as gently as I could at the table. 'I heard you went off carousing with my husband last night.'

'I wouldn't have missed this for the world,' I croaked, feeling too hellish to think about my disgraceful – in every sense of the word – behaviour with those girls last night.

I attempted to bring up the subject of Agnes, but the girl herself was toing and froing with the breakfast dishes, and clearly any private talk was impossible. I decided that I would discuss the problem on the journey, as I expected the pair of us to be driven in the Brays' motor car, a shiny beast of a thing that Alec had already damaged when attempting to manoeuvre it himself. However, as we stood on the front step in the morning sunshine I saw a different one trundling round the corner.

'Are we not using yours?' I asked, turning to her in surprise.

'Oh no. We like to save on petrol,' she said, adjusting the tilt of her cloche hat on her head, as the car drew to a halt and a squeal of ladies looked out and hooted, 'A man! So typical of Clara. Clara? Where are you? Come and explain yourself!'

She smiled sweetly at them. 'Oh, you don't mind, do you? Mr Carver is my cousin, and he did beg to be allowed to join you all.'

I looked at her askance, but she did not see me. The door opened and a large woman with a big face leaned out. 'Well, if he begged!' she said. 'And in that case, Mr Carver, I absolutely insist you sit next to me. I'll protect you from all these females.'

I was already being pulled inside. 'What about you?' I said to Mrs Bray as I climbed in.

'I'm taking the next one,' she said sweetly, pointing to where another motor car was rolling up the hill. 'Mrs Darling gets travel sickness and I've promised to hold her hand. See you there.'

And so here I was, squashed into a corner of the upholstery, at the mercy of several ladies, my only male company the driver, who seemed to think it all rather amusing. The predatory woman with the large face and voice, whose name, appropriately, was Mrs Eagle, informed me that this was a ladies' painting circle, to which men were rarely, if ever, admitted, and that Mrs Bray had done me a huge favour by permitting me access. 'Although I expect you're really one of the girls at heart, aren't you?' she said, jogging me in the ribs.

Now I understood what Alec had meant by keeping my wits with me, and the mischief that had lain behind Mrs Bray's offer to me last night. All about me, the conversation rattled at whipcrack speed, from the failings of the ladies' servants to scandal about their neighbours' children, from how simply divine was somebody's wrap to a frankly disturbing conversation about politics which contained several sharp insights that would not have sounded out of place along with port and cigars round Dr Feathers' dining table last night.

I heard it all, and was made to feel fairly dizzy by it, so contented myself by watching the outlying suburbs of Helmstone fall away – new redbrick estates and then, behind them, bumpier roads, thicker trees, and our street became a country lane.

We passed drays with carts, a ramshackle farm with chickens clucking from behind the gate and cows nibbling at the grass, and then through the village of Petwick, all charming stone cottages and dogs sleeping in the road, the walls bordered with poppies and cornflowers, butter-flies darting in and out of the greenery, and I realized I had forgotten my human need for this, the simple smell of the countryside, the sight of green hills in the distance, the sense of being a small dot in a huge landscape.

After Petwick we turned off the main road and headed down a rutted lane, overlooked by willow and ash trees. The ladies had not stopped talking the entire journey, and now, as the car rumbled to a gentle halt by a fence and stile, there was a general hullabaloo of surprise and excite-ment and 'Ooh, are we here?' from several of the ladies, as if they had not noticed one single thing throughout.

Mrs Eagle, who appeared to be the organizing matron, hustled everybody out of the motor car with much more brio than was necessary.

'Now then, ladies,' she boomed, when we were all

standing in patches of shade and sunlight, before winking at me, 'and Mr Carver, of course, whom we could never mistake for a lady – and please take no offence, sir, that would never be my intention – we will be walking a quarter of a mile to our destination, and as we shall be there until two o'clock, please make sure you have everything that is yours. Especially luncheon!' she roared, which produced a general round of giggling, although for the life of me I could not understand why.

There was some twittering as the ladies ensured they had all their equipment, and Mrs Eagle then pointed her parasol at the stile and said, 'Mr Carver will, I trust, be a gentleman and look away as we ladies traverse the stile in what I am sure will be an ungainly fashion, and I shall poke him with my umbrella if he doesn't!'

I smiled tightly at her, wondering why for the life of me I would want to watch Mrs Eagle climb over a stile.

'Excuse me,' piped up the youngest of the ladies, the daughter of one of the other matrons and a pale, sickly thing. 'Will there be any – er – facilities at the place?' She blushed bright red as she spoke and looked down.

'My dear Constance, nature always provides,' Mrs Eagle boomed. 'Which means, you must go behind a tree and worry about the consequences later. Let's be off!'

I hung back, looking for the other motor car, and then decided that even when it arrived Mrs Bray would only spite me with some other witticism, and so I followed the ladies over the stile, having looked away first, and walked down a lane, the wood on one side, open meadow on the other. Spindly thistles clung to the outskirts of the wood, and bees charged about them, humming. After several minutes, we turned a corner and saw, through a clearing in the trees, a lake, which prompted much cries of 'Ooh!' from the ladies.

Mrs Eagle stopped and turned. 'Here is our muse for today,' she intoned, flinging back her hand. 'You may set up where you will, but this lake is well known for capturing a certain quality of light upon its surface, which I am sure will prove interesting to those of us who are determined scholars of the craft of luminescence, and in any case I should be very keen to see all of your results. Especially yours, Mr Carver!'

I quavered silently, wondering what she would say when she beheld my amateurish work. Nevertheless, I soldiered on, determined they would think me the strong, silent type rather than the nervous, uncertain one.

The ladies spent an inordinate age deciding where to set up their stations. It seemed of the utmost importance that each should be near their dearest friend, and they debated on the various spots around the lake at much length. I took the higher ground, at the top end of the lake, feeling more secure with the solid wood of trees at my back.

I settled myself on to a tree stump and pulled out my sketchbook. The light here was, indeed, rather special, and the lake sang in turquoise, indigo, cobalt and all manner of blues, greens and greys. I thought I would have to paint something or else risk being mocked, and so got out my jar of water, my brushes, my paints, and, fearful at first, and then becoming bolder, sketched out the shape of the lake in pencil and began splashing on colour.

'I believe this may be the best spot in the whole place,'

boomed Mrs Eagle, and I jumped. 'I do beg your pardon, Mr Carver. I too am often so rapt in my work that I barely notice the sounding of the dinner gong.'

She was thrashing her way through the undergrowth towards me, breathing heavily, her face pink. She stopped dramatically, holding on to the trunk of a tree for support. 'Now, are you one of those who refuse to let others see a work in progress? I quite understand if you are of the sensitive disposition. I, of course, welcome any number of viewings, but we can't all be as hardy as me, can we now?'

'No, no,' I said. 'It's quite all right.' I held up the page to her, which she took, holding it at arm's length as she surveyed it, allowing herself a lengthy pause in which to do so.

'That's really getting there,' she said eventually. 'I especially like the use of your pure colours.' She pointed, her finger perilously close to the still-wet paint.

'I mixed them,' I said. 'Aquamarine and turquoise.'

She raised an eyebrow. 'Is that so? I wonder you bothered. Still, a marvellous effort, Mr Carver, and I'm sure it has great potential.' She handed the book back to me. 'Also, I wanted to let you know that in general we stop for luncheon at one o'clock to let the paint dry. Not that you're obliged to, by any means, but I do encourage it, because I know that when one is creating Art the hours fly by, and one must eat.'

'One must,' I echoed, looking down at the lady artists gathered about the lake. Frail young Constance was sketching on a pad, sitting on an upturned log beside her mother, who was wearing pince-nez and peering very intently at her work. Even from this height, I heard the sound of the ladies' chatter, and wondered how they would get anything painted if they didn't stop talking. I noticed that the lakeside was, in fact, rather busy. 'Have the others arrived?' I asked Mrs Eagle.

'A while ago now, Mr Carver,' she said, chortling. 'You have forgotten the time. It's nearly midday.'

'Is it?' I scanned the lakeside but saw no sign of Mrs Bray. 'Funny how the time goes.'

'Indeed.' She plunged on past me, over bracken and daisy, thundering, 'Clara! How are you faring, my dear?'

I whipped my head about, peering through the trees, but saw nothing except Mrs Eagle's flowered behind. She must have positioned herself exactly so she was invisible to me. I wondered why this bothered me so much. Anyhow, what did it all matter? She barely gave me a thought, and I – I had no real idea as to why I was here.

The leaves rustled again, although this time I was prepared. I laid down my brush and waited for the re-arrival of Mrs Eagle on her way back to the lakeside. Instead, Mrs Bray came through the trees towards me, a satchel over one shoulder.

She stopped beside me. 'Mrs Eagle,' she said, 'has the sensitivity of a rhino.'

I was so stunned that she had spoken to me as if we were not mortal enemies that I almost forgot to reply. I stuttered out, 'I – I rather think you're doing the rhino a disservice there.'

She made a snorting sound, which may have been a laugh or may not. 'Completely put me off,' she said. 'Thought I may as well have lunch now.'

And before I had time to comprehend the enormity of this overture, she was striding past me, down to the water's edge, seating herself on a tree stump overlooking the lake.

I frowned at her, then went to put my brushes into my water jar, spilling water and dropping a brush on to the scratchy ground as I did so. I then hunted for my sandwich tin, and by the time I joined her by the lake she was eating her lunch and looking quite as if she had ceased to recall my existence.

I sat on a log and opened the tin, wondering how on earth the pair of us were going to make civil conversation.

'They're fish paste,' supplied Mrs Bray. 'Mrs Pennyworth never makes marvellously original sandwiches, but they could be worse.'

'They're delicious,' I murmured, ready to spar if sparring were needed.

She looked out across the lake. Her forehead and fringe were caught in a glimmer of sunlight; they shone in brilliant contrasts. 'When I saw you on the front step of Castaway this morning, you looked as if you were facing the firing squad.'

I bit into my sandwich. 'I suppose that pleased you.'

She twisted her mouth into a smile. 'Now why on earth would you think that, Mr Carver?'

'Just a hunch,' I said shortly.

She deigned not to answer, and we sat facing the shimmering lake in the perfect silence with which we often shared our breakfasts. I think we would have continued like that until our sandwiches were finished and we could curtly go about our separate ways, but I remembered now my promise to Agnes, and my heart sank a little.

Still, I had to try, and to try I had to engage this perverse woman in conversation. I said, 'I must say, I didn't expect you to belong to a painting circle. You don't seem the type who enjoys the company of others.'

She turned an icy glare on me. 'There's quite a lot you don't know about me, Mr Carver.'

Surely, I thought to myself, I could engage her in conversation a little better than that. I tried again. 'I'm sure you're right,' I said. 'I can only go on what I've seen. Still, I'm sure it helps the muse, to belong to a circle.'

She sighed, and closed her sandwich tin. 'If you must know, the circle's an offshoot of the Socialist Women's League. It's supposed to help the working woman engage with art, except of course working women have no time for art, and so it's only ladies of leisure who belong. Is that enough information for you?'

I frowned. 'You're a socialist?'

She waggled her head to mean, I supposed, *Perhaps*.

'Now that really does surprise me,' I said.

'Oh yes?' Her smile was tight and drawn. 'How so?'

'Well . . .' I was aware I had to tread carefully here. 'I didn't think a socialist would live in a house that needed so many servants, for example.' Or, at least, I chose not to add, she would make the effort to treat them well.

Her smile tightened still further. If I were not so sure she did not have any, I would have been convinced I had hit a raw nerve. 'You really want to know every last thing about me, don't you, Mr Carver? And then you desperately try to convince me you're not reporting back to the family. Not that I care; tell them anything you like. It's just the sneaking about that I find particularly demeaning.'

I rolled my eyes. 'I try to engage you in a reasonable discussion and you accuse me of spying. I mean, honestly, have you actually listened to yourself?'

'Ah!' She turned to me. 'You finally show some emotion. I was beginning to think you were some sort of automaton.'

'Me?' I was too astounded by her accusation to be offended. 'You're the one who's not shown an ounce of feeling since I arrived. All you've done is make snide remarks at best, outright insults at worst. It's only because of Alec that I've stayed on at all.'

'Oh, very good of you, Mr Carver. Stay in a house ten times the size of your own, with servants waiting on you hand and foot, all paid for by my husband. What a decent chap you are.'

I stared at her. Somewhere in my brain, I registered that her hands were shaking on her sandwich, but I was too angry to take much note of it. 'I honestly could not care one fig about any of that,' I said. 'I'm sure it means a lot to you, but please don't assume the same of everybody you meet.'

Cherry pink flashed into her cheeks. She threw down her tin and got to her feet. 'Don't be a hypocrite, Mr Carver. It doesn't suit you at all.'

Turning, she stormed off into the wood. I watched her go, my lungs clamping tightly shut. As the adrenalin left me, so did my air, and I found myself bent double on the log, gasping for breath and remembering the words of my doctor, the advice. Breathe slowly. In and out and in and out. I made a cup of my hands and breathed into it. In and out and in and out.

It was not a bad attack. I recovered fairly quickly, took a few draughts of water and then thought of Mrs Bray. No doubt I should leave her to it, but her words still stung me. I certainly had failings, but I was not a hypocrite, and I would not have owned my cousin's ill-omened house for all the tea in China.

I took the path that I had seen her take, high up into the woods. The trees here quickly clung together, branches intermingling above my head, bracken underfoot. Soon the lake below disappeared, and all I heard was birdsong and the distant cawing of crows in the tops of the trees at the ridge of the hill.

I climbed, holding on to branches for support, ducking under low-hanging ones, meandering up, hoping that she had done the same and I would come across her sooner rather than later.

Finally, towards the crest of the hill, the trees began to thin and afternoon sunshine reached through the gaps in the wood. I came to a drystone wall, too high to see over but with the sense of space beyond. I looked about: to my left a short distance away was what looked like a figure sitting on the wall, although that was impossible as the ridges of it were upwards-spiked stones. I made my way towards the figure and saw finally that it was a woman and she was sitting on a five-bar gate facing a neatly clipped field. I also saw that she was crying.

I stopped. If this was Mrs Bray – and who else could it be? – surely the last thing she would want was to be seen in this state. Also, I thought ruefully, I could hardly continue our argument while she was crying. Yet as I hesitated, she turned her head and saw me there.

Her face deadened into a mask, and she looked back at the field. I sighed, and then, realizing there was nothing for it, ploughed on towards her.

I reached the gate. She was some way above me, and still had her back to me. 'Are – are y-you all right?' I said, the stutter that had abandoned me all day haunting my tongue again.

She ignored me. I put a foot on the gate, which swayed rather alarmingly, and climbed up, swinging my legs over so we were both facing the field. A collection of black-faced, white-woollen sheep looked up at the commotion and then returned to grazing. From here, the field sloped downhill to another collection of trees at one side and further fields at the other. I saw cows in the distance, more sheep, and there, on the horizon, a distant puff of smoke from a train. On seeing it, I somehow felt comforted.

'Isn't it wonderful,' I began, 'to think that after we're dead and gone all this will still be here?'

There was a silence, and I thought that perhaps she would continue to ignore me until I'd clambered back off the gate again, but finally she said in a cracked voice, 'Most men, if they see a lady who clearly does not want to be disturbed, would return from where they came and pretend the whole incident had never happened.'

'Then I'm obviously an utter brute,' I said. I dug in my pocket and found an old tin, left over from last summer. I opened it out to her. 'Mint?'

She looked at the crumbling beige specks, made a tiny sigh that could almost have been a laugh, and took one. 'You are.'

'Glad we've established that, then.'

We sucked on our mints in silence. Mrs Bray cleared her throat and said in a small, quiet voice, completely unlike one I had ever heard her use before, 'The thing is, you see, I . . . well, I lost a baby.'

I paused as I absorbed not just the news, shocking enough in itself, but the fact of the confidence. I wondered what I had done to encourage it. I did not dare look at her, but I said, 'R-recently?'

'Five days before you arrived.'

I hung my head, remembering her pallid demeanour the first time I'd seen her outside the drawing room and her rasping, spiteful words, and knew she was right, I was a brute. 'I – I'm so sorry,' I said. 'If I'd known, I would never have come to stay at all.'

I sensed her shrugging beside me. 'My husband . . .' she began. 'I asked him to write to your family, but he . . . I think he would do anything if it antagonized me, and I suppose he thought allowing you to come would do just that.'

'When I get home I'll pack my bags.' I sensed that she was about to speak. 'No, I will. And I'll leave by the first train tomorrow.' I thought, with a slight regret, of Lizzie, but I would write, and we had no understanding, after all.

'Don't go.' A warm hand was placed on mine. I looked up, surprised, and saw her face for the first time. Her eyes and nose were red, her eye make-up had blotched soot-like on her face, and her bobbed hair was drooping and frazzled. 'I don't want you to go, not on my account.'

I blinked at this turnaround. It was almost as if one Mrs Bray had left the lakeside and another was up here on the gate beside me. 'It's fine,' I said. 'I'm not that enamoured of the house and the servants and . . . all those things. Really.'

She rolled her eyes. 'Oh, I just said that to upset you. You were right, anyway. I'm the one who wants it. Castaway, I mean. And all the rest of it: the servants, the never having to worry about . . . well, about anything, really.'

'Absolutely. I mean, that is, I understand.' And I did, I realized; I did understand.

'You see, Mr Carver, believe it or not, life has been better since you came to stay. Obviously, at the beginning I didn't want you there at all. But now . . . your presence seems to have a civilizing effect on both of us. If it wasn't for you being here, Alec and I would have torn each other's throats out by now.' She attempted to laugh. 'Of course, I understand that preventing murder isn't the most relaxing summer you'll have.'

I felt awful now, thinking of how Alec had denigrated this woman to me, how I had colluded. I could hardly believe that my cousin could be so callous: even if his marriage were not as sun-bright as it had once been, surely he owed it to his wife to look after her when she needed him.

'I'm just so sorry,' I said.

'Please, don't be.' Her voice was high and brittle. 'Women lose babies all the time. Mrs Eagle has lost almost as many as she hasn't, and some after they were born. Which is far worse, of course.'

'Of course it is,' I murmured. 'But all the same . . .'

'It was to be my salvation,' she said. 'You see, I've done some pretty shoddy things in my time, and the baby was going to make my life all right again. And now . . . well, the likelihood is I won't be able to have any more. He was five months in when he . . . when he went. My son. Perhaps another three more and he would have been all right.'

The gate trembled. I worried she was going to cry again. I could hardly believe nobody had mentioned it to me – but then again, I could. The servants would not have been told officially that Mrs Bray was even expecting, and as for Alec, perhaps he had been respecting his wife's need for privacy. Perhaps.

I thought of what I knew about Mrs Bray's life, before her marriage. Had she really gone to bed with half of London, as Alec had said? I thought with shame of the girl last night – the girl whose name I had never even thought to ask, and I wondered if that was the sort of shoddy behaviour that Mrs Bray had thought the baby would rectify.

But I had no idea, not really. I knew nothing. I heard a click and a scraping sound, and then I smelled burning tobacco leaves. 'I owe you an apology, Mr Carver,' she said. 'For boring you with all this dreariness.'

'Please,' I said, 'it's about time you called me Robert. And believe me, you're neither boring nor dreary.'

'I haven't been . . .' She paused, as if weighing words in her mouth along with tobacco smoke. 'I haven't been myself lately. Well, not since my marriage really.' She laughed, a coarse little hiccup of a sound.

'It's early days yet,' I said, feeling too young for a discussion about the mysterious state of marriage and Mrs Bray's place within it.

'I'm sure you know what Alec's like: he'll chase after anything in a skirt.' She sighed. 'Not that I mind. It's par

271

for the course with a chap like that, isn't it? It's when he has dealings with the servants that I'm not too keen.'

I goggled. 'The – the servants?'

'Anyway,' she continued blithely. 'I've treated you abominably ever since you arrived, and for that I really am rather sorry.'

I bowed my head, smiling at the apology I had never thought I would receive, yet confused at her abrupt change of subject. 'I'm sorry too,' I said. 'If I'd known about . . . about your condition, I would never have been so insensitive. Arguing with you about socialism.'

She waved a hand dismissively. 'Oh, but it's true, as I said. The thing is, Mr Carver – Robert – I was a red-hot firebrand in the Actresses' Franchise League before I married. And now I live a very comfortable bourgeois life and that's that, thank you very much.'

'I don't believe it,' I said. 'I saw you delivering those goods to Princes Street. And I'm sure you're fair to . . . to your servants.'

I was hoping she would clarify what she had meant earlier about Alec's dealings with the servants, but she merely tossed her head and said, 'Absolutely not. At least, not when they complain. The thing is, you see, I know what it's like to be poor – poorer than most of them have ever been – and I can't bear it when they moan about their silly little problems.'

I swung my legs on the gate and risked another stab in the dark. 'Agnes, for example?'

She groaned, but in a relieved sort of a way, as if we were moving away from tricky subjects. 'Don't talk to me about that girl. She's impossible. Rabbiting about evil and ghosts and suchlike.'

I looked at her. 'It was pretty awful what happened though, wasn't it?' I hesitated, hoping she would not think I'd been prying again. 'The parlourmaid who hanged herself.'

She shook her head. 'She didn't hang herself. It was an overdose of a sleeping draught, I believe, or something like that. Still, you know how rumours get about.'

'Oh.' But of course, Mrs Bray had known the family at the time; she would know the truth of it better than little Agnes.

'I'm sure it was awful for the girl's family, absolutely, and Alec's mother – well, she took it fairly badly. But all the same, it was nine years ago. The room's been completely redecorated. In fact, it's a fairly comfortable room, and Agnes has a hysterical imagination, no doubt egged on by the other girls. As far as I can see, the only solution is to not let it become an overriding concern.'

'All the same,' I said, 'I don't know if I'd like to sleep in a room where somebody had killed themselves.'

She tutted. 'You probably have,' she said. 'All houses have history, you know. And to be quite honest, Robert, this is really nothing to do with you.'

I paused. In the far distance, I heard shouts. It sounded as if people were calling our names. I looked at the twinkling ball of the sun and realized we had been away much longer than I'd imagined.

She turned away from me and swung herself back over the gate. 'All right,' she growled, 'I'll see if I can change the girl's room.'

I dropped to the ground just behind her. 'Perhaps it would be for the best.'

She opened her handbag. 'Would you . . . could you go on ahead and tell them I'll be there shortly? I need to sort out my face.' She gave me a swift glance. 'They don't know about the baby. You see, beneath it all I'm as terribly little England as anyone else, keeping everything under wraps.'

I nodded, impressed yet again with the weight of the confidence, and overwhelmed with the import of it. In mock solemnity I said, 'Of course, Mrs Bray.'

She pulled out her compact and flipped it open. 'Call me Clara, for goodness' sake,' she said, peering into it and pulling out a powder puff.

I turned away and crunched over fallen leaves. She had no idea, of course, that I had already called her Clara last night, inadvertently, and as I walked down the hill I found a false memory of her, leaning over me, unbuttoning my shirt, leaning into my ear and whispering my name.

I shook it away, embarrassed, and made my way through the trees to where various members of the painting party were waiting. I allowed them to berate me for having worried them so, imagining we may have fallen into the lake and drowned, a scenario so unlikely I found myself covering my mouth in an effort not to laugh.

Nothing could dampen my high spirits, and I did not stop to consider why they might be so high. Not Clara's reappearance, freshly powdered, with a spiky laugh that excluded me as she gathered the ladies round her in secret feminine jokes. Not the drive back to Helmstone, squashed yet again beside Mrs Eagle, whose hand crept up my thigh as she told me unlikely narratives of which she was the star. Not even when Clara and I emerged from our separate motor cars, waving off the others, and she said, 'What are your plans for the afternoon?' and I was forced to tell her that I was already late for tea at the Featherses', and I sensed, behind her brusque manner, that another invitation had been lurking.

Better to parse out these intimacies, I thought as I trotted up the steps to the Featherses' front door. I already had enough to ruminate on later; I was happy that I had an explanation for Clara's previous coldness, that she did not want me to leave – that, in fact, I was a bonus to the house.

We stood either side of the low wall that divided the two buildings. She stood in her cloche hat with her head bent, waiting for Scone to open the door. When he did so she turned, nodded once in almost military fashion and entered the house.

All the female Featherses were in the drawing room for tea, and I was received with alacrity, Maddie jumping up from her seat and ushering me inside.

'Thank goodness you're here, Mr Carver,' she said. 'We're in dire need of somebody to entertain us. Mother's so deathly boring, I'm afraid.'

I looked at Mrs Feathers apologetically, who was holding the sugar tongs absent-mindedly.

'I'm sure she's not,' I said.

She glanced up and smiled vaguely. 'Good afternoon, Mr Carver,' she said, and went back to peering at the tea tray.

The room, bereft of last night's party, seemed to glow in the memory of it. It was a pleasant, feminine sort of a room, with plants in pots at studied intervals and odd sticks of velvet-upholstered furniture dotted about the place. It was, of course, far grander than the little terrace I'd grown up in, but stood much less on ceremony than Castaway. I imagined Lizzie as a child here, running down the staircase, a doll clutched in her fist.

Adult Lizzie was on the sofa now, reading. I winked at her as I was ordered on to a plumply cushioned chair facing her and was rewarded with a smile. I supposed I was forgiven for abandoning her last night.

'How was your day, Mr Carver?' asked Mrs Feathers, handing me a cup.

I regaled them with the antics of the painting circle, which caused Lizzie to giggle, Maddie to squawk with laughter and Mrs Feathers to smile vaguely.

'Lizzie says you were dragged off into the darkness by Mr Bray last night,' said Maddie, shoving a slice of lemon cake into her mouth. 'What happened? Was it all terribly seditious?'

'Madeleine,' cautioned Mrs Feathers. 'You mustn't ask things like that of guests.'

Maddie rolled her eyes.

'It was rather dull actually,' I said, dangling the teacup between thumb and forefinger, remembering my stiff, caked trousers that I'd scrubbed at in the bathtub myself. I took a sip of tea; it was Darjeeling, and pleasant in a Mrs Feathers sort of a way. 'I left as soon as I could and came back home to bed.'

'I'm sure that's a lie,' said Maddie artlessly. 'And you needn't tell me off, Mother; I know that's not the sort of accusation one levels at guests.'

'Honestly, Mad, you're such an embarrassment.' Lizzie set down her teacup with a clatter. 'Come on, Robert, let's take a walk on to the balcony.' Her skirt swished about her as she walked past, scattering the scent of rosewater in her wake, and as I followed I saw Maddie stick a tongue out at her sister. I grinned at her, and she shrugged good-naturedly.

Across the room, the balcony doors had been flung open, letting bright squares of sunlight on to the polished wooden floor. I stepped out, enjoying the breeze fluttering at my scalp.

Lizzie was leaning on the iron railing. She said in a low voice, 'Sometimes I hate my sister.'

'She's a decent sort, though.' I looked down at the giddying drop of the sea. 'She was defending you last night.'

'I don't believe it. How on earth did that happen?'

I glanced over to Castaway next door. I saw with surprise that the doors were open there, too, and I squinted, trying to see if I could spot Mrs Bray – Clara – sitting at the window. 'Oh, your father mentioned some chap, and Maddie got quite heated on your behalf.'

'Not . . .' Lizzie briefly closed her eyes. 'Oh, goodness, not Freddie Sponder.'

'I believe that was it.' I stopped trying to see Clara, and turned my attention full on to Lizzie. 'You don't have to tell me anything, by the way. We're not beholden to one another.'

'Well, no,' she said, and I wondered with a jolt whether it might not be quite nice to be beholden to Lizzie. 'It's nothing, anyway. Freddie and I had been friends for years, since childhood. Always assumed, you know, that we'd end up marrying. And then one day last year he announces he's going to Egypt to work for the British Consulate in Alexandria. Said it would only be a few weeks, so I wrote, and he wrote, and then he stopped writing. Six months later we find out he's married one of the natives and is living in some one-bedroom shack above the Atta-rine Souk. I cried for seven days solid. But I'm quite all right now.'

'What a cad.' I pictured a pasty Englishman on a divan, being fed dates by a black-haired girl as bleating goats were led past on a chain through the marketplace below. Lizzie appeared to be awaiting a further reaction, so I added, 'I'd deck the coward if I could.'

'Don't be silly. I wouldn't have met you if I'd still been with Freddie, would I?' She peered at me curiously. 'Are you jealous?'

I looked at Lizzie to gauge what her reaction would be to any of my possible answers. I wondered if she had slipped her tongue into Freddie Sponder's mouth as well. I thought, on reflection, that she probably had not, and I therefore dismissed him from my mind. 'Oh, wildly jeal-ous,' I said airily, and she simpered.

'You mustn't be,' she said, leaning towards me. 'I realize now I never cared for him at all.'

'Good.' I looked over Lizzie's shoulder and saw Clara Bray step out on to the neighbouring balcony holding a long, thin drink. I wondered what was in it, but knew that whatever it was, it had to be a damn sight more exciting than Darjeeling in a china cup.

Lizzie looked round too. Clara saw us, smiled and raised her glass in greeting. I waved back. I would have brought her into our chatter, but she moved towards the other end of the balcony, where a lounge chair was set up, and curled on to it with her back to us.

'Oh, I wish I were Mrs Bray,' sighed Lizzie in a low voice. 'And then I wouldn't have a single worry in the world.'

My mind boggled at the irony in that statement, but, casting around for the only piece of information I could impart, murmured, 'Well, there's been trouble with the servants, so she's not entirely worry-free.'

'I'd adore to have servants,' said Lizzie dreamily. 'Of my own, I mean. Anyway, it's only that the parlourmaid's too scared to sleep in her room.'

'You know?' I said, somewhat surprised.

'Doris told us.' She laughed. 'Doris knows everything.'

A thought occurred to me. 'Then you must have heard about the earlier parlourmaid, nine years ago – the over-dose she took?'

'Oh yes. Well, I knew about that at the time. Although I always thought she'd drowned herself in the tub.' She glanced back into the drawing room and, satisfied that we were out of earshot, continued with relish, 'And apparently she'd got herself into trouble.'

I was rather disquieted by her gusto. 'You knew her?'

'No, not at all. I was only nine.' She squinted against the afternoon sun. 'I remember peeking out of the nursery window and seeing them carry her out, on a covered stretcher. They'd called Father for help when they found her in the morning. But Father's a professional, you know. He wouldn't tell us anything about it. Still, servants talk, don't they?'

'I'm sure they do. Terribly sad, isn't it?'

'Oh yes,' said Lizzie excitedly. She satisfied herself that Clara was at the other end of the balcony, and whispered, 'Nobody ever found out who her follower was. You know, some nasty people said it might be . . . well . . .'

'Alec?' I supplied, and she nodded.

'Only they proved it wasn't him. He'd been away at school the whole time. All the same, people do gossip, don't they? And Mrs Bray was very upset by it all. I mean, Mrs Viviane Bray. Well, of course you would be, wouldn't you, having such a thing happen in your household.'

I couldn't help but glance at Clara. Her back was to us now, and all I could see of her was the crown of her head, the dark hair smoothed like a cap across it. As I spoke to Lizzie I kept an eye on Clara Bray throughout. She looked as if she were asleep, the drink discarded on the glass-topped table beside her, her shoes neatly placed together beside the lounger, one cord of her emerald-coloured gown flopping towards the ground. I pictured her sleeping, wondering if she'd wear her usual sardonic look while unconscious as well, and continued smiling and nodding at Lizzie and giving the complete impression that I was absolutely involved with whatever it was she was talking about.

On my way out, after arranging to meet for yet another afternoon at the pictures, Doris said to me, 'If you don't mind, sir, the doctor asked if you'd pop into his surgery for a quick word.'

We were walking down the stairs to the ground floor. My lungs spasmed; I knew this would be about Lizzie, and I wished for the smallest of seconds that I could fillet her from her family, have her liveliness and innocence all to myself without the hedging about and good manners I was forced to bestow on her elders.

Then I stopped and told myself that Lizzie would not be the way she was without the support of her family. A girl without a strong background would be wild, feral – would be something, I thought, rather like the slum kid Clara Bray had so clearly been. And, I silently added with a nod that surprised the parlourmaid, that was not a desirable quality in a woman. Definitely not.

Dr Feathers' surgery was transformed from the room where we had dined last night into a large, light-filled office. Folding doors divided it from his consulting room at the back, and along the wall were several chairs that had bordered the dining table previously, interspersed with low tables which held a variety of dusty journals. Facing the chairs was a desk upon which sat a typewriter, telephone and several open files. Cabinets which had been shrouded yesterday were revealed, and it was at one of these that a sour-faced woman was rifling through. She looked up when we came in.

'Sorry,' she said, in a voice that sounded anything but. 'Doctor's had his last appointment for the day.'

'No, Miss Splendour . . .' began Doris, but the secretary cut her off.

'And to be quite honest, it's much better if you telephone. I'm sure you're on the telephone,' she said with a swift grimace, turning from the cabinet towards the desk and flashing a card at me. 'Do take one.'

I turned to Doris, who was looking fairly distressed. 'Don't worry,' I said, waving her back into the hallway, 'I'll explain.'

Miss Splendour was still brandishing the card as if it were a small firearm. I took it and said, 'Thank you. Dr Feathers asked if I could come by and see him. I'm Carver.'

'Hmm,' she grunted, looking not at all impressed. 'Well, the doctor's with a patient at the moment, so you'll have to wait. He's a very busy man, you know.'

'Of course he is,' I said, smiling broadly, and strolled about the room, looking at the paintings I had been unable to admire last night. They were mostly hunting scenes, and not at all to my taste, but I supposed they were meant to stimulate the appetite and perhaps provide Dr Feathers' patients with the impression that he was foxing out the cause of their aches and pains. I sensed the woman watching me suspiciously, as if I might unhook one of the paintings and scamper away to hawk it on the beach in the early evening sunshine.

There was a commotion behind the closed partition doors and, as it opened, I heard Dr Feathers' usual boom. '. . . Time works wonders, you know!'

A mouse-like woman emerged, clutching a handbag to her chest. She blinked at the lemon-faced secretary, who forced a smile.

'Everything all right, Mrs Corby?'

The woman blinked again. 'Oh yes, thank you, Miss Splendour.' She eyed me nervously and pulled on her gloves with a twitch. 'How are you?'

'In marvellous health, thank goodness.' Miss Splendour nodded once, extravagantly, perhaps to underline the extent of her good health. 'How's Mr Corby?'

There was a pause, and Mrs Corby said quietly, 'I'm s-sorry?'

The secretary bit her lip. 'Oh, Lord, how awful of me. I was mixing you up with someone else. Well, have a lovely evening.' She trotted behind Mrs Corby, ushering her towards the door. 'Let's hope the nice weather holds. Goodbye.'

Mrs Corby was ejected from the room as Dr Feathers came in, hands behind his back. 'All well, Miss Splendour?'

'I completely put my foot in it with Mrs Corby, I'm afraid,' Miss Splendour simpered. 'Quite forgot her husband ran off with the barmaid from the Kerrison Arms.'

'Ah. That's where the health issue lies, you see.' He tapped his head. 'Psychological. Can't tell 'em that, of course. They want a linctus that solves every problem. However, Mr Carver has no time for psychology, does he?'

'I never said such a thing!' I protested, sensing Miss Splendour's steely dismissal as her body turned towards the filing cabinet. 'And, by the way, I can hardly believe this is the same room we ate in last night. It's quite a transformation.'

I heard a sniff from the secretary, perhaps in recognition that I might not be the fraud she thought I was.

The doctor strolled into the room. 'Needs must when one lives above the shop,' he said. 'As I'm sure you know, we usually dine in the drawing room. How was your tea?'

'Excellent, thank you,' I said, although I was sure the doctor had very little idea of what tea consisted. I heard another small sniff from Miss Splendour. 'I believe you wanted to see me about something?'

Feathers nodded. 'Step this way,' he said, backing into

his consulting room. I followed, roundly ignored by Miss Splendour as I passed her by.

'I don't think your secretary was much taken with me,' I said, as he closed the door behind me. The room here, in contrast with the front office, was small and dark, with a window that looked on to a small yard. There was a reclining bed in the corner, which I eyed with trepidation, having been recumbent on many during my year of illness.

'What? Not at all. A great humanitarian, our Miss Splendour.'

I was not sure whether Dr Feathers were joking or not. 'Scotch?'

'Um . . .' I thought it prudent to accept. 'Yes. All right. Thank you.'

'Good man.' The doctor settled himself behind a huge mahogany desk, pulling out a drawer and removing a bottle of whisky and two tumblers. 'Do take a seat.'

He pointed to the chair opposite the desk. It was made of soft leather and gave somewhat worryingly as I sat on it, and I thought of all the nervous people who'd settled on its edge, hoping that the doctor would make everything all right.

Feathers handed me the drink, raised his own briefly to his lips and then steepled his hands together as if he really were about to give me a diagnosis. Instead, he said, 'Glad to hear you're having a pleasant summer here, Robert. May I call you Robert?'

'Ye-es,' I said, momentarily wrong-footed. 'Is everything all right?'

He beamed beneath his beard. 'Why do you think

something must be wrong, eh? Freud would say that was your guilty conscience.'

I coloured, although I knew I had nothing to feel guilty about. Well, almost nothing. I took the memory of the girl last night and shoved it in a dingy basement cupboard in the furthest corner of my mind, intending to leave it there for a very long time. 'I was just wondering what you wanted to speak to me about.'

'Get to the point, that's good. I like a man who doesn't flim-flam.' He peered at me from over the top of his fingers. 'You and Elizabeth are getting on well, hmm?'

Of course this was going to be about Lizzie. I swallowed. 'I think so,' I said. 'Although you'd have to ask her.'

'Oh, she thinks you're the bees' knees, as Maddie would say.' Again the smile. 'You were educated at Crosspoint, am I right?'

I nodded. 'I was fortunate,' I said, following the family line that seven years at that godforsaken hellhole had indeed been a stroke of luck. 'My grandfather insisted on my being publicly schooled. Otherwise I would have attended the local grammar, and . . . um . . . well, yes, there you have it.'

'Mmm,' said Feathers.

'I mean,' I said, swallowing, 'I'm sure Lizzie's told you all about my parental background.'

'Not at all.' I got the sense of Feathers as an animal, observing me with huge lemur eyes. 'My daughter barely tells me a thing these days. I'm told this is what happens when they grow up.'

Or perhaps, I thought, Lizzie was as aware of her

father's snobbery as Alec was, and had thought it best to stay quiet on the matter. She had thought it all very romantic and daring, and had weaved herself quite a Hollywood picture on the topic. No doubt Feathers would see it all differently, but I scorned the idea of dressing my history up in any other way than plain truth.

'My mother is Alexander's aunt,' I began. 'My great-grandfather made a lot of money from transport. You probably know about that.'

'Railways, wasn't it?' Feathers nodded. 'I remember Viviane telling me, although her family's money is much older, of course.'

'Yes,' I said, bristling slightly. 'My grandfather inherited the business, and the estate my great-grandfather had bought. He occasionally used to take his family along to the station yard. Especially my mother.' I stopped, feeling the next part of the story might be too intimate for Feathers' ears.

But he had guessed. 'And she caught the eye of somebody working there?' he said.

I nodded. 'He was the yard manager. A good job, but not good enough for my grandfather's daughter.' I had often wondered why my mother had fallen so heavily for my father; they were a shy pair, and never talked about their feelings, but once, on visiting my grandparents' house – the poor grandparents, who lived in a leaking cottage with a goat tethered in the back garden and from whose humble beginnings my father had risen – I had seen a studio photograph of him from those days. I had never realized how handsome he had been, with a sort of hunger in his eyes for more from life than it was presently giving him, a questing for a greater world than the station yard and the grease and crackle of loading coals.

'They eloped, got married and moved to my father's home town,' I said. 'That's where I grew up, until the age of nine.' The town of industry and drizzle-spattered days, where I'd spent happy childhood hours roaming the streets and searching for treasure, until I'd been picked up by some latent obligation of my maternal grandfather's and sent away to Crosspoint, an event that occurred shortly after my trip to London with Alec. I remembered the drawn face of my father at that time too, at the deaths of various family members during the attack on the Somme. It always seemed to me that all the happiness of the world had crashed in the same month, and that I as a new boy, dressed in someone else's money with glottal stops in my mouth, suffered doubly, both from the news that I would be forced to make toast for older idiots under the guise of building my character, and from the slow creep of war into our own nondescript lives.

Feathers' spectacles glinted. 'And you're going up to Oxford this autumn, is that right?'

'Yes. I won a scholarship to Magdalen.' I added, with a rush of inspiration, 'By the way, I'm due an inheritance on my twenty-fifth birthday. I believe Grandfather thought in that way my father would be unable to get his hands on it.'

Feathers said nothing, and I sat back in the soft leather chair with the sense that I had blown any chance I'd ever had with Lizzie. Finally he said, 'You are in a unique position, Robert. You have experienced life from two angles, so to speak.'

I shrugged. 'I suppose so,' I said, 'but it hasn't really affected me.'

That was a lie, but I was not going to tell Feathers about those first years of bullying at school, sobbing silently into my pillow at night, and then, through some fantastical combination of personality, cricket and a certain obtuse pride in my origins, rising through the ranks to become a sort of celebrated mascot, a representative of the world my peers misguidedly thought of as the proletariat.

'Of course, in that you have something in common with Mrs Bray. Unlike your cousin, who has had a much more privileged upbringing,' mused Feathers.

I suspected some mischief on his part in saying this, almost worthy of Clara Bray herself, but I simply said, 'Perhaps.'

Feathers nodded and tried to look solemn. 'Well, thank you for confiding in me,' he said, his eyes glittering behind his glasses. 'As Lizzie's father, I naturally have an interest in learning what your position is in life.'

My lungs tightened again. Feathers got to his feet and walked about the room, hands behind his back. 'When you go up in the autumn,' he said, and then whirled on a sixpence and glared at me, 'do you intend to remain friends with her?'

'I . . . I . . . I . . . of course,' I spluttered. 'I like her very much.'

Feathers nodded. 'Good. She's young, I know, but we are anxious for her, me and Mrs Feathers. Elizabeth is a little . . . over-trusting. We would hate for her to make a bad connection.'

'I suppose that it's my family background that concerns you,' I said stiffly.

'Oh no, no, Robert, you misunderstand me. We consider you to be a good connection. Especially now you have reassured me that you will – well, she has had a – I mean, I like to think we have given her a fairly decent upbringing, and as long as on your twenty-fifth . . . if that is certain . . .'

'Oh yes,' I said, with perhaps a sliver of a sense of how those girls last night may have felt. 'It is certain.'

He coughed. 'Then we would like you to remain friends with our daughter, in order that she doesn't . . . that she remains on the path that we consider appropriate.'

'I see,' I said, although I was not at all sure that I did.

Feathers came towards my chair and leaned on the back of it. It rocked back and forth and he looked down at me. I smelled the whisky on his breath as he said, 'Are you considering marriage? That's what I would like to know.'

I felt a headache coming on. 'Er . . . well. Er . . . of course, I'm only nineteen,' I began. 'In the future, I – er . . .'

'Yes, not now, obviously,' he said. He let the chair go and it swayed, making me feel nauseous. 'I'd expect you both to be at least twenty-one. But you're an intelligent young man, Robert. You would be a good match. Yes, that would be fine.'

'Would it?' Now he had noted his approval, I was not sure I wanted it. I said quickly, 'The inheritance due to me is – well, it's not – that is . . . I would have to work as well if I wanted to support a family.'

'Good. Can't stand these idle layabouts, living off

unearned incomes,' he growled, and I suspected an unconscious aspersion here, cast at my cousin. 'What are your plans, by the way?'

'Well, I'm reading History.' In truth, I had no idea what I would do after that, although Feathers was already nodding vigorously.

'Good, good. And of course you're bound to make excellent contacts at university. I can see you're a hard worker, Robert. Also, if necessary, Mrs Feathers and I would be happy to support you in your future endeavours. As a loan, of course. Yes, I'm sure you have a glittering future ahead.'

I had the sensation I was being drawn into some sort of agreement. 'That's very . . . very kind,' I murmured.

'Not at all.' He grinned broadly and clapped me on the shoulder. 'You are going to make our daughter very happy. Now, how about a drink to celebrate – another Scotch?'

Thoroughly dazed, I left the doctor's house half an hour later with my head whirling, under the impression that I had agreed to become engaged to his daughter without my actually having proposed at all. It was quite a magic trick; I wondered how he had done it.

I supposed, I thought, woozy on the whisky as I meandered towards the railing and looked over at the ice-blue sea, that it did not really matter, as long as Lizzie was not brought into it. Without Lizzie, it had been merely a conversation between Dr Feathers and me.

A breeze shook the air and whipped my thoughts back into shape. How could I decide an engagement with a girl's father and not bring the girl into it? The arrangement sounded practically medieval. Perhaps Lizzie would not want to marry me; arrogantly, that thought had not occurred to me until this moment.

Then I wondered if I wanted to marry Lizzie. I thought of her earlier on the balcony, with the fresh bloom in her cheeks and the sparkle in her eyes, and remembered the idea that I would not mind very much being beholden to her. She was certainly attractive, intelligent, and not at all fast; surely three very desirable qualities in a future mate. That illicit kiss in the waxworks had intimated a deep passion beating within her wholesome bosom, and the idea of being the first to draw that out in the marital bed was very alluring indeed.

Then, for some reason, I thought of Clara Bray. I saw her swaying on the wooden gate this afternoon, tears brimming her red eyes, as unattractive as I'd ever seen her and twice as beautiful. I thought of being married to her, of being able to hold her in the night, to kiss away her tears and be the one who could make everything all right.

I tried to dash away the idiotic idea, but it kept returning. Alec and Clara were fundamentally unsuited, except that they were both impetuous fools. They'd long since fallen out of love, but I . . . but I . . .

It was Dr Feathers' Scotch that encouraged my thoughts forward, placing my feelings for Lizzie beside my feelings for Clara. There was no comparison, and they had only remained hidden from me for so long because I had decided that Mrs Bray was a spiteful witch and best given a wide berth.

I loved her. I loved Clara Bray, and it was as useless a notion as any that I'd ever had. I loved her because she was wilful and brave and honest and tigerish. Maybe I had loved her since the first time I'd seen her, pale-faced and foul-mouthed on the first-floor landing, and now I was being tipsy and maudlin, which was no help to anyone. Best to think of Lizzie, with whom the future was solid and bright and who, after all, liked me a great deal better than Clara Bray currently did, despite her recent thawing.

I turned back towards Castaway House and, as I did so, I saw Dr Feathers watching me from his office window on the ground floor. He smiled and waved, and I waved back, and as I climbed the steps to home, looking forward to a night of innocent dreaming about Clara's red lips, I had the strange, distinct impression that I was not engaged to Lizzie Feathers at all, but to her father instead.

I pulled the plug and let the water swirl out of the bath-tub. In the steam blurring the cracked mirror over the wash basin I wrote my name.

From the other side of the frosted glass door, shapes moved past and bottles clanked. I heard the rumble of a joke, a swishy giggle in response, and thought that the party must have begun.

My name was already fading. I smeared Star's name beneath mine and drew a swaggering heart around the pair of us. I saw my moon-sick reflection in the smears, and wondered what the hell I'd become.

Star had been inside and around me for a whole day; I'd been grinning like a fool all morning in the kitchen of the Bella Vista, even as Mrs Hale had talked of how, if book-ings didn't look up, she'd have to think of letting me go. I'd spent the afternoon anticipating the party, resisting the urge to go up beforehand, my insides giddy with nerves.

I knew I was being idiotic. I knew this wasn't *real*, not in any proper sense. She was a girl and I was a girl, and there-fore this was no more than a silly crush – a pash, as they said in the boarding-school stories I'd devoured as a kid. And we were a hundred miles from those tales of mannish women in serge suits preying on young girls; we were just

Star and Rosie, kissing under a windowsill, sharing pieces of our past.

I tied my robe around my waist and unlocked the bathroom door. The hallway was clear, and so I padded up the gritty stairs and let myself back into the flat. I spent a lot of fruitless time trying to iron my hair straight, and then dressed in front of the sputtering gas fire, hitching fresh stockings to my suspender belt and sliding on my wool dress with the angular red and grey stripes as, in the kitchen next door, Susan and Val made cocoa and smoked and gossiped about their day at work.

I wondered what Star would be wearing tonight, how she'd have done her make-up. I wondered if she'd notice the work I'd done on my eyes, the thick black lines and the glued-on lashes. I wondered if I'd be able to speak to her on her own. I caught myself grinning once more, in the looming gilt mirror, and tried to clamp it down into something cool and aloof. It didn't work.

I checked the time on my alarm clock. I'd decided on ten o'clock, or just past, so it wouldn't seem as if I'd been waiting for that particular hour. I wanted to see Star before she was drunk, but arriving too early would seem overkeen. I was sitting on my bed, kicking my heels against the post, a chill rattling through the gap in the panes, when I remembered the promise I'd made to myself.

I threw myself backwards on to the bed, eyes closed. Perhaps I should just go straight to the party. He wasn't expecting me, after all. Yet at the same time, I thought of Dockie alone in the basement, and of how I hadn't seen him yesterday, too wrapped up in shreds of Star to worry about an old man. I also needed to square things, for myself if not for him.

I plucked from my purse the roll of notes Mum had given me yesterday. I counted out forty bob and added another five shillings of my own. Then I took the stairs all the way down. Dockie's door was ajar, and as I pushed it further open I saw that he wasn't inside.

There was still evidence of him in the room: the overcoat slung across the chair, a half-drunk cup of tea on the side. The awful reek I'd experienced the first time I'd visited him had been replaced by the acidic scent of tomato soup, still open in its giant tin on the side.

I looked behind the doorway. There was the paper bag from Bradley's, discreetly nestled by the skirting board. I looked inside and saw that my stolen shoes were still in their cardboard box, wrapped in tissue. I picked up the whole thing and put my forty-five shillings on the table. I hoped I wouldn't have to explain. Surely, with Dockie, I wouldn't have to explain.

His envelope was also on the table, with its photograph on top, the one he'd been clutching, wrapped in a blanket on the docks, when Frank had found him. I peered at the shape of a sepia ear, the blur of a baby's forehead, wishing I'd brought Mum's photograph yesterday to compare. They could be the same – possibly, just possibly. And yet, if they were, what then? What on earth could link old Dockie to my mother? I couldn't think about this right now, not with my head full of Star and my stomach filmy with anticipation.

I put the photograph back and left the room. As I was passing the bathroom at the end of the corridor I noticed a grizzled, military-type man in a crisp blue shirt leaning on the edge of the wash basin, observing himself in the plastic-edged mirror.

'Excuse me,' I said and he turned, startled. 'You haven't seen the gentleman in Flat Four, have you?'

'Rosie,' he croaked, and I realized with a shudder of surprise that it was Dockie, wearing a shirt the salesgirl had picked out for me in Bradley's. His mouth, naked without its beard or moustache, seemed to tremble uncertainly in the quavering electric light.

I touched my own chin in sympathy. 'Gosh,' I said eventually. 'You look . . . younger.'

He fingered his new short haircut. 'There was a place,' he wheezed, 'in the Snooks. Gas lamps, brass fittings, cut-throat razor in a leather case, something for the weekend, sir. Smell of hair oil. I knew I had been there before.'

'They did all that to you?'

He nodded. 'I would pay a hundred pounds to have them put it all back again.'

'What? Why?'

He stumbled past me and returned to his room. I followed him, leaving the bathroom light buzzing, as he walked to his bed and sat heavily down, putting his face in his hands. I thought of the party beginning upstairs, the booze being consumed, the dancing and the laughter, and my five-past-ten arrival time disintegrating. Pulling out the chair, I sat down opposite him and said, 'What's the matter?'

He shook his head. After a while he shifted his hands and looked at me through the bars of his fingers. 'Oh, Rosie,' he murmured. 'Sweet Rosie. My saviour. You understand, don't you, how difficult it can be when the past returns?'

'Um . . . well, yes. That is, I suppose so.'

He sighed heavily. 'I was starting to remember it all, you see. Pieces of my childhood. Sunlight on a meadow, chasing a butterfly with a net; and my mother – my mother's voice calling me to come back, lemonade in a stone jug and I, running far away.'

'I can imagine,' I said softly. 'Remembering your childhood, that would be difficult.'

'And then as the hair fell from me, I looked at the face in the mirror.' He gestured to it, as if all the answers were there, and got to his feet impatiently. 'And I wish I never had.'

'But why?'

'Frank told me, you see.' He was looking around the room; finally, he pulled the coat from the back of the chair upon which I was sitting. 'Frank, that great weasel, spoke some truth. He said to me, "Dockie," he said, "the reason you have no memory is because you wish to have no memory."'

He dragged the coat around himself.

'Look, don't go anywhere,' I said. 'Let's talk about this. Maybe I can help.'

He turned to me, his breath beery, his mouth twitching. 'Nobody can help me,' he hissed. 'You see, Rosie, I have begun to remember. As I looked in the mirror I recognized the face that looked back, and I knew one great fact: that I was a bad person.'

He snatched up the pile of money and the envelope,

whirled to the door, grasped the handle and stepped out into the passageway.

'But you can't know!' I said, hurrying after him as he stuffed the money into a deep pocket. 'Not if you don't remember properly.'

'I was a bad person!' He strode up the stairs to the main hallway, and I trotted up too, the bag of shoes still swinging from my wrist. 'You see, Rosie, I remember all this. These flagstones here – black and white – I remember them. This banister end, curled just so. There was a mirror there, where that telephone is, and a mahogany stand. There was a table in the centre, always with a vase of flowers in the middle, on a lace mat. This is what I remember.'

'And what about . . . ?'

He was moving along the hallway to the front door.

'. . . The story you had to tell?' I gabbled. 'The truth?'

'The truth!' He jabbed at his head. 'The truth is that I no longer want to remember. The truth is that I wish it would all smash to pieces.'

'What about Clara? And Robert Carver?' I said softly, as his hand rested on the door catch, unfastened so that people could come into the party as they liked.

'Never mind all that!' He flung the door open.

I thought of what Star had told me yesterday. 'I know who Clara is, and she's coming here on Saturday. She owns the house. Dockie, listen! She's your landlady.'

'It's finished.'

He was already out on the porch. As I got to the doorway, he was hurrying down the steps; I saw that it was raining, yet again. 'Where are you going?'

'Where I should have gone the minute I arrived.' He glared at the downwards slope of the hill. 'Back to Dublin.'

'But . . . but . . .'

'I thank you, Rosie, for your kindness.' He lifted a hand in farewell, as the rain slicked his newly short hair flat against his head. 'Go inside. It's raining.'

And then he continued down the path, turned left at the gateway and headed down the hill towards town. He had gone a few yards when he looked back at me and called, 'There is something of yours in the room, I believe.'

I held up the bag weakly. 'I've got it,' I said, but he had already disappeared from view. 'I've paid you back,' I added to the driving rain, before going back inside the house and kicking the door closed.

I remained in the hallway for several minutes, even after the light timed itself off. I stood in the dark beside the telephone stand, not even sure why I should be so upset. This was the business of a drunk old stranger; it had nothing to do with me. And yet I was frustrated, with him for running away, and with the whole tangled skein of wool the thing had become, and here I was, left holding the knotted ball with no idea even of where to begin.

And then from somewhere, either upstairs or downstairs or from within the walls themselves, the whistling started again. 'Oh, shut up,' I snapped, and, galvanized into action, I pushed on the light.

The telephone jumped back into life, and I noticed the blackboard above it. There was another message for me – I must have missed it earlier, while I was having my bath – and it made my blood run cold in my veins.

It said:

Rozy. Call your Mum. About harry.

I grabbed the duster and spat on it, wiping off the message so there was nothing left but chalk dust. As I was rubbing viciously, a bundle of chattering young people barged into the hall through the open front door. 'Top floor,' called one, herding a pressed and perfumed quartet up the stairs, and as they passed me, giving me curious glances, I saw that the person at the back of the line, the one doing the herding, was Adam, the boy from the dodgems.

He nudged me as he went past. 'It's you!'

I watched him go, an odd shiver of excitement in my veins. I didn't have to worry about Dockie any more: he had gone, heading for the railway station in the rain, waiting at the platform for the up-train to London, flapping at his head to erase his returning memories.

In the bedroom, I pulled the shoes from the box and changed into them, admiring the way they showed off my calves. Susan and Val had sneered at the idea of the party, saying it would be full of low-lifes, but I privately thought this was because they hadn't been invited. I picked up my cheap bottle of gin and went upstairs. As I travelled through the house, the faint sound of jangling pianos and guitars became louder, and by the time I reached the back stairs, ska music was blaring down them at full volume. Outside the open front door, on the narrow curve of the staircase, two young people were necking, ignoring everyone who had to climb over them to get into the flat.

In the bedroom there was a circle of people on the floor, one lying on all the coats heaped on the bed, smoking pot silently, all of them strangers. They nodded at me, and I continued along the corridor towards the song blasting from the Dansette's speakers.

The sitting room was dark, lit by a few leaking candles and glowing cigarette ends. The sofa had been pushed to one side and a few people were dancing in the middle of the room; the rest were leaning against the walls, drinking beer or snogging against the misplaced fridge, the kitchen units, and on the disembowelled armchair.

Then I saw Star. She was climbing out on to the roof terrace, being helped up by several friends, in her black and white op-art dress with the zip running down the front, laughing raucously. I reached her just as she was half in, half out of the window.

'Hello!' I said, waving my gin. 'Fancy a drink?'

She turned to me with a hurried smile. 'Oh, hi, Rosie. Later, okay?'

And with that, she was gone. I shrugged; that was Star. I'd leave her to her friends for now – she'd be mine later on. I walked to the sink, picked up a badly washed plastic tumbler and poured in a good measure of gin.

'I'll have some of that.'

I looked up; a man with scooped-forwards hair, wearing a parka, was smiling down at me with a shark's set of teeth. Without waiting for my answer, he took the gin bottle from my hands and poured generously into the mug he was holding. He held it up. 'I'm Geoff. Cheers.'

'Rosie,' I said reluctantly, clinking plastic to enamel, and downed half my glass in one, trying not to pull a face as it set fire to my throat.

He winked and showed me a paper bag of blue pills in

his pocket. 'Fancy one? I'll do you cheap, seeing as I've nicked your gin.'

I wrinkled my nose as I swigged some more. 'Not sure. Maybe later.'

'Don't make it too late. I might sell out.' He grinned his shark's grin and turned to the girls clinging round him. 'Here, you lot met Rosie?'

He introduced me, and we shared drinks and slurred conversation as the alcohol started to take hold. I kept half an eye on Star on the roof terrace, larking around with her friends, and, sometime later when I saw her climb down, I wandered away from the group and followed her.

I found her in the bathroom, scrubbing at her dress in the wash basin. She jumped when she saw me. 'Oh. It's you.'

She was swaying slightly. I came in and shut the door. 'Spilled something?'

'Some idiot threw his beer down me.' She squinted at the stain on her front. 'Cost me over three quid, this did.'

'Don't you mean it cost Granny?' She frowned, and I said with a nudge, 'I'm only teasing.'

'I think Geoff's just sold me a duff one.' Her voice was slippery with drink. 'It's had no effect whatsoever. I'm going to tell him to give me another.'

I walked up behind her and looked at her reflection in the mirror. 'If it is working, you'll be as high as a kite.'

'All right, Mother,' she growled.

I didn't care. The gin had layered me with confidence. I put my arms around her waist and said, 'You look beautiful.'

'Rosie . . .' she began, but with a melt to her voice that encouraged me.

I put my lips to the back of her neck and kissed it, inhaling her scent.

'You mustn't,' I heard her say.

'I'm drunk,' I whispered. 'I don't care.'

She gave a little moan and dropped her head. I ran my fingers around her neck until they met the zip of her dress at her throat, and pulled it down a fraction. I slid my hand inside, feeling my way across her collarbone.

'Stop it.' She snapped my hand away and switched her zip back upwards. She stared at the sink, and when she looked up into the mirror, her reflection was hard-boned and as cold as ice.

'What?' I felt as if I'd been slapped. 'I thought . . .'

'What if somebody came in?' she hissed. 'What if anybody saw?'

I recognized the truth in her words, and perhaps on a sober day would have heeded them, but the gin had fired me with bravado. 'Why d'you care about them?'

'They're my *friends*,' she snapped, and walked out of the bathroom, leaving the door wide open as she stalked back into the heart of the party.

I stayed a while in the bathroom, swaying as I surveyed my rogue hands, knowing Star would never describe me as a nice person, never again. It certainly wasn't what the boarding-school girls had done with their pashes, and perhaps it was obscene, and perverted, and all those things, but I was finding it difficult to care. A giggle bubbled up from me, and when Geoff walked in through the door and saw me he said, 'Hey, somebody looks happy.'

'I'm just going,' I said, woozy with gin.

He shrugged, unzipping his fly. 'Stay if you like.'

I snorted a laugh and left the bathroom, leaning against the wall.

When he came out, doing himself up, he said, 'You changed your mind about you know what?' He leaned with an elbow against the wall above my head. He smelled of musk and civet.

'Dunno,' I mumbled, feeling as if anything were possible, tonight.

'Tell you what, how about I give you a tiny bit, for free? Just to get you in the mood.'

I waggled my head to say maybe, and he pulled one of the blue pills from his pocket.

'Put out your tongue.'

I did so, expecting him to drop the pill on to it, but instead he bit off a fraction and, holding it on his own tongue, he wrapped his hands around the back of my head and put his mouth over mine.

His tongue swam into me. I felt the sour taste of the crumbled piece land beside my gum. He withdrew and said, smiling sharkily down at me, 'There you go.'

I swallowed the piece of pill and wiped my mouth with my sleeve. 'You're a cheeky beggar.'

He winked. 'Nothing ventured, eh?'

'Geoff!'

He turned. Star was weaving her way towards him, babbling about how he'd ripped her off with coloured aspirin, demanding another. She ignored me, and I wondered if she'd seen the kiss.

'Star . . .' I began, and she turned to me with a bright drunk smile.

'Oh, Rosie,' she said, as if we hadn't seen each other all evening. 'You know Geoff?'

'We're just getting acquainted,' he said, and I widened my eyes at her to tell her it wasn't what she thought.

'Good.' She winked exaggeratedly at me. 'I really couldn't give a shit,' she said in a loud whisper, and sashayed off, tipping her new pill into her mouth and knocking it back with a swig of beer.

'It's not what you think,' I called to Star, but she was gone, back into the throbbing heart of the party.

'Don't worry about her,' said Geoff. 'She's just narked 'cause she's been trying to get off with me for months. I told her, "I ain't coming between you and Johnny," but she's got a bee in her bonnet for me, know what I mean?'

I peered up at him. 'You're lying,' I growled.

He tutted. 'Shut up. Everyone knows Star's a little flirt. You know what they said about her last year, what she done with that mate of hers, Gill?'

'No,' I said breathlessly. 'What did they say?'

'It'd turn your hair if I told you.' He winked. 'She's a right fucked-up little tart; she'll go with anyone.'

A gobbet of anger fizzed inside me as I came to the realization that my kiss with Star had meant nothing to her. Of course not. She'd barely given it a thought.

I held Geoff by the shoulders and pushed him back against the wall with such force I turned the light switch on, and everybody in the room protested as they were illuminated.

'Whoa.' Geoff turned the light off, and I put my arms about his neck and pulled his head down towards me.

We kissed for a blurry, indistinguishable amount of time. I hoped Star was watching. *You're not the only one who can be a little flirt*, I thought with a sense of dirty triumph.

Geoff looked down at me, nodded towards the door of the spare room and said, 'How about we go somewhere a bit quieter?'

I knew I was too drunk, and the small sober section of my brain was murmuring, but far too quietly for me to hear. I shrugged. 'Okay.'

He winked. 'That's my girl.' Bending his head towards me, he whispered, 'I'm taking it you're on the Pill, 'cause I only go bareback, all right?'

I had a sudden image once more of Harry's huge penis listing towards me, and dashed the thought away. I lumbered towards the spare room, opened the door and stumbled inside. It was a narrow space that contained a camp bed, a wardrobe, an empty fireplace, a dormer window, a chair with a guitar on it, and Johnny and Adam on the bed, leaping apart in a confusion of limbs as I entered.

'Bloody hell,' barked Johnny, as Adam bounced towards the window in less than a second, his back to me. 'You might knock first, eh, Rosie?'

'Sorry,' I slurred. Johnny pulled down the cuffs of his sleeves and smoothed his hair as Geoff came in after me.

'Ah, Johnny mate.' Geoff swaggered in. 'Mind if you hop it? I got business to pursue.'

Johnny didn't even bother looking up. 'Get out,' he said, squeezing a cigarette from the packet on the stool beside the bed into his mouth.

There was an impasse which lasted no more than a

second, and then Geoff snorted. 'Fuck it,' he growled, and then, to me, 'Come on, darling, let's go.'

'Rosie's staying.' Johnny sparked up his cigarette with a silver-plated lighter.

'Hey.' Geoff pointed. 'You got Star. You don't need another bird.'

Johnny just ignored him, leaning back against the wall. I steadied myself against the wardrobe as a speck of sobriety entered my brain, and I said to Geoff, 'I'm staying.'

He narrowed his eyes at me. 'Your loss, darling.' He stormed out of the room, slamming the door closed.

For a while, nobody spoke, and then, by the window, Adam snorted. Johnny laughed too. I moved the guitar on to the floor and collapsed in the chair.

'What a tit,' said Johnny. 'Sells a few sweeties to his mates and thinks he's God's fucking gift.'

'Ugh.' I put my head against the side of the wardrobe. 'I don't feel good.'

'Come over here and sit next to your knight in shining armour.' Johnny patted the space beside him on the bed, and I scrambled over. 'I hope you remember I saved you from a shafting by Helmstone's biggest wanker.'

'You're so . . . crude,' I mumbled.

'You ain't heard the half of it.'

'I'll see you later, J.' A shadow blocked the light as Adam crossed the room.

'Be good.' Johnny waved Adam out of the door and put his arm around me. I looked into his eyes and saw his pupils had reduced to pinpricks. He winked at me. 'Mind you, he does sell cheap, and I'm up on the fucking ceiling, so who cares?' He cackled a laugh.

I gazed at the door that Adam had just closed behind him, and then turned back to Johnny to see if there were any clues that he was *like that*, but the only notable aspect of his behaviour was his cigarette jiggling at high speed between his fingers, as if possessed by some demon.

'Star . . .' I began, and didn't know what to say next.

'You were supposed to cheer her up yesterday, d'you remember? She came back in a right two-and-eight. Couldn't string a sentence together. What d'you do to her?'

I grunted a reply. 'She told me her grandmother owns the house.'

'Did she now?' He took out his cigarette and put it between my lips. I inhaled sloppily. Sliding it back between his own, he said, 'That's a big deal. She made me promise not to tell a living soul. See, I knew she had a thing for you.'

'I don't know about that,' I mumbled, but with less certainty than I'd felt before. 'Geoff said she . . .' And then I remembered who I was talking to, and shut up.

'What did Geoff say?' Johnny fed ash into the empty beer bottle on the stool. 'I'll lamp the fucker soon as I can stand up. He's been after her for months.'

'You and Star . . .' I said slowly, alcohol thrusting forwards words I'd never have dared to say sober. 'What is it? I mean, really? What is it?'

He shrugged. 'You tell me, Rosie. She's my best mate. My pal. But . . . Christ, y'know, once upon a time we were, like, together, properly together. And now . . .'

'Flatmates?' I said.

He nodded. 'Flatmates. That's it.' He spread an arm wide. 'As you can see, I'm in the spare room. Therefore, we're flatmates.'

I smiled, both inside and out, an excited, anticipatory sort of a smile. 'So you *have* split up.'

'Not officially. Star wants . . . Oh, God knows what Star wants. She's a closed book, that one. What you grinning for?'

'No reason.' I felt my heart beating fast and hard in my ribs. *I knew she had a thing for you*, he'd said. I'd been idiotic earlier; I saw things clearly now. 'I'm going to dance.'

'Stay away from that arsehole.' He pointed a finger at me. 'You hear me?'

I nodded rapidly. 'Don't worry. I will.'

I kissed him on the cheek, to which he tutted, and then threw myself off the bed, out of the door and back into the party. I had to find Star and tell her I knew that she and Johnny weren't together, and that . . . well, and who cared what her friends thought? The world was up for grabs, if we wanted it.

She wasn't in the sitting room, but I knew she'd be back eventually and energy was charging through my limbs; I had to use it up. The floor was a packed herd of people moving to the music, and I thrust myself into the middle of them and danced, focusing on the slithery patterns of the rug at my feet, on the smoke curling through the air, on the non-stop chattering in my brain.

Time passed. Finally, Star weaved past and I grabbed her arm. 'I've got to talk to you!' I shouted.

She looked at me. Her black eye make-up had started a steady slide down her face. I noticed that Geoff was on her other side, one arm linked around her back. She puffed out her lips and turned away.

'Star!' I jerked her towards me. Her eyes were unfocused,

and I realized that even like this I hungered for her, that I wanted her as I'd never wanted anybody or anything before. I yearned to press myself against her and run my hands through her short hair and along the slight curves of her waist and hips. Her dress was zipped up all the way to the top, and my eyes lingered on its glinting teeth and the tag at her throat.

'Get away from me,' she said, pulling her arm free.

'Come on, Star.'

Geoff leered down at me. 'She don't wanna talk to you, all right?'

'Stay out of it,' I snapped. 'It's got nothing to do with you.'

'You keep away from me,' said Star, and as the song that was playing came to a sudden end, her words reverberated in the silence that followed. 'Keep away from me, you disgusting dyke.'

There was a ripple of shocked laughter around the room. Horribly, I felt my lip wobbling. 'Wh-what?'

'She tried to molest me in the bathroom.' Star was speaking to Geoff, but her voice carried around the flat. 'Tried to touch me up. She's been wanting to do that ever since she moved in.'

Geoff sniffed as he looked down at me, a smile curling the edge of his mouth. 'Interesting.'

'Tell her to fuck off, Geoff.' Star's voice had risen to hysteria. 'Tell her I don't want her anywhere near me.'

My head was shaking with shock and anger. 'Don't worry,' I said, my heart and lungs and liver collapsing. 'I never want to see you again.'

There was a space around me now, as if I carried a deadly disease. The album had come to an end, and nobody had yet made a move to change the record. Her upper lip curving into a sneer, she spat, 'Go and find someone else to creep over, you pervert.'

She turned, as if to flounce off, tripped over the coffee table and landed in a heap on the living-room floor.

There was a second of stunned inaction, and then my contagion was forgotten as a flurry of girls thronged past me and knelt down beside Star, pulling her dress back down over her thighs, cooing, rapping out orders to the men in the room. 'Go and get Johnny.' 'Don't just stand there Geoff, get her a glass of water.' 'Come on, Star, can you hear me? Star-baby? Star?'

I remained frozen and forgotten in the middle of the sitting room. I was vaguely aware of a commotion: Johnny was searched for, Johnny could not be found, and without Johnny nothing could be done about Star. As people pushed past me I gradually came back into myself, turned and, as fast as I could, walked away, past the silent record player, past Johnny's bedroom, the bathroom, Star's room.

I was almost at the door when Johnny, coming back into the flat, collided into me with a face like fury. 'I need Star,' he muttered. 'Where is she?'

I ignored him, but one of the girls, the ribbon in her hair sliding towards her neck, said in a tone of barely held panic, tugging on his sleeve, 'She's collapsed, she's unconscious, you've got to come.'

'Oi!' Johnny said, shaking her off. 'Mind that. She'll be all right; she's just taken too much shit.'

'Yes, but she won't wake up!'

'Okay, okay, I'm coming.' He sighed, and turned to me. 'You wouldn't do us a favour, Rosie, would you?'

I snorted. 'No.'

'What?' He looked at me disbelievingly. 'You owe me big time.'

I sighed. 'Not *her*. I'm doing nothing for *her*.'

'Eh?' He shook his head impatiently. 'I don't need none of these girlie dramas right now. Listen, the landlord's about to turn up.'

'Landlord?'

'Landlady, I mean.' He fluttered his eyelids and leaned in towards me. 'Star's grandmother. The formidable Mrs Bray.'

Despite my fury, I hesitated in my march towards the door. 'What, now?'

He nodded. 'Supposed to be coming day after tomorrow. Decides she's going to arrive two days early, in the middle of the night, would you believe it? Just telephoned from the station; says she's getting a taxi and can she be met at the door.' He ran a hand over his face. 'And now Star's gone down, I'm high as the damn clouds, and if she don't get met there'll be hell to pay.'

Mrs Bray. *Clara* Bray. I'd been wondering what she was like, and now she'd arrived at just the wrong time. 'I've taken stuff too,' I said.

Johnny squinted at me. 'Nah, you're all right,' he said. 'Remember, you owe me a favour from yesterday. Never mind that I saved you from an unsavoury sexual experience.'

'*Johnny*,' whined the girl. 'You've got to come and help.'

'Bloody hell, what am I, her soddin' nurse? Ain't my fault she's a loose cannon. Go on, Rosie, it won't take you two minutes.'

I took a breath, heavily excited, despite everything, at

the thought of meeting Star's grandmother. 'All right,' I snapped. 'But it's for *you*, not for *her*, all right?'

'Yeah, yeah,' he said. 'Just go downstairs and wait for her to come, say hello, that's all. Tell her that – I don't know, Star's got the flu or something. If she finds out about the party and the drugs, she'll have our guts for garters.'

I left the flat in its uproar and climbed over the still-snogging couple on the stairs. I continued around the narrow well, along to the main part of the house and then down, all the way to the ground floor, marching to the front door and swinging it wide open.

'About time too,' snapped a sharp female voice, only the slightest bit crackly with age. 'Unless you want me to catch pneumonia, I suppose.'

I looked down at the woman standing under the portico. She was shorter than me, although she was wearing stilettos at the end of her thin, black-stockinged legs. Above that she had a sharply tailored suit, a dancer's neck, and silver hair tied into a bun. Her eyebrows were plucked into two high arches, and below them were a pair of glittering eyes, which narrowed as they took me in now. 'And who on earth are you?' she snapped.

'I'm Rosie Churchill,' I said, blurry with drink and the dregs of the pill. 'I live on the first floor.'

'Then I take it you're the advance guard.' She nodded at the two cases resting at her feet. 'You can bring these into the flat.'

'Huh?'

She ignored that, stepping on to the mat and walking along the hallway. At the door to the ground-floor flat, she turned. 'I'm Mrs Bray,' she said. 'I own Castaway House.' She plucked a key from her handbag and unlocked the door. 'Chop-chop,' she added, and as she disappeared I rolled my eyes, lifted the cases and followed her inside.

Beyond the flat door was the tiny hall I had glimpsed the other day when Star had been cleaning it. To my right was a small bathroom, and ahead of me Mrs Bray had already opened the door into the bedroom and was walking through. 'In here,' she called. 'On the chair will be fine.'

French doors were washing the bedroom with pale moonlight. Beyond them I could see the glimmering glass of the conservatory windows, whose roof jutted out below our kitchen window. A brass bedstead dominated the room, with tulips at the tips of its posts, and above it hung an oil painting of a stormy seascape. There was also a writing desk, a polished Victorian-looking thing with keyholed compartments and a proper blotting pad, and beside it a white wicker chair with an old cushion, to which Mrs Bray was now pointing.

I put the cases on top of each other on the chair, as she switched on a bedside lamp, whose base had been sculpted into the shape of an abstract female form. I saw that there was also, curiously, a much smaller bed, made up with a thin blanket, by the wall. I tried to stand upright but was finding it difficult, and so leaned casually against the edge of the door.

Mrs Bray opened her handbag and rummaged through her purse. She plucked out a coin and held it to me. 'For you, Miss Churchill,' she said, and I took it, as surprised by her remembering my name as by the coin. 'And I would like you to fetch my granddaughter, please.'

She then turned her back to me and tugged closed the drapes covering the French windows.

'She's got the flu,' I said, seeing her once more collapsed on the living-room floor with her dress round her waist. 'She's been in bed all day,' I added lamely.

'Flu!' Mrs Bray twitched the end of one curtain to meet the other. 'Hardly a reason not to meet one's grandmother, when one's grandmother has particularly requested such a thing.'

'Well, you know, she's really ill. Might be . . .' I searched my brain for a suitable phenomenon. 'Glandular fever.'

Mrs Bray cleared her throat in a highly sceptical manner and then said with a slight concessionary tone to her voice, 'I suppose I have arrived two days earlier than planned.' She turned, looked me up and down and said, 'In that case, you will have to do.'

I frowned. 'I'm sorry?'

'At the last moment, I have had to travel without my maid Louise. She has cancer, you see.'

'Oh.' I formed my face into the appropriate expression. 'I'm sorry.'

'So am I. I was forced to carry my own cases from Paris.' Mrs Bray sniffed. 'One has porters, of course, but it's not the same any more, when one has to wait by the side of the train for twenty minutes until a scruffy oik condescends to appear.'

'Mmm,' I murmured, as if scruffy oiks were likewise the bane of my own life. I thought of all the times I'd imagined what I'd say to the landlord if I ever met him, about how for two pounds a week the gaps in my windows could at least be fixed, but, faced with Mrs Bray, all I wanted to do, oddly enough, was agree with her.

She sniffed again and looked once more in her purse. 'Five pounds,' she announced. 'Is that agreeable?'

I felt I'd missed some important part of the conversation. 'Agreeable?'

'As my employee is indisposed – if one could call my granddaughter an employee, seeing as she employs herself as little as possible at my expense. I shall pay you five pounds, Miss Churchill, and not a penny more.'

'I'm afraid,' I began, trying to focus on Mrs Bray, 'that I don't quite understand.'

She looked away from me and folded her arms across her chest. 'Then you haven't been told. What I need, the reason I will pay you five pounds, is – well, I'll say it bluntly. Somebody to spend the night in the flat with me.'

My left temple had begun to throb. 'I beg your pardon?'

Mrs Bray indicated the small bed. 'This is where Louise usually sleeps. My granddaughter was to have been here. You, of course, may move this into the sitting room.' As I stared at it, struck dumb, she added, 'You can leave as soon as it is light.'

I swallowed on my dry throat. 'B-but . . . why?'

She walked to the mirror that stood opposite the bed and surveyed herself in it, tweaking at a loose hair from her tightly wound bun. 'I never sleep in this flat alone. Call it an old lady's eccentricity, if you like.' Her reflected eyes found mine, and she added, 'My granddaughter writes to me every week. I've heard all about the things the pair of you have been getting up to. I think she regards you as extremely wholesome. And now I have met you, I can see that she's correct.'

I thought of my fingers at Star's collarbone and my lips on her neck. I swallowed hard. 'Um . . . thank you.'

She turned towards me and tightened her lips. 'Five guineas then,' she said, 'and that's all the English money I have, so take it or leave it.'

I thought of what five guineas could buy. 'I'll take it,' I said rapidly.

'Good.' She looked me up and down. 'I suggest you retrieve your night-time belongings now. Knock three times on the door when you come down, and I shall let you in.'

I ran back up to my room as fast as my wobbly legs would take me. Five guineas just to go to sleep: it was too good to be true. I supposed she wanted a bodyguard, what with all the suspicious characters renting rooms at Castaway House. Not that I'd be much good in a fight, but I'd probably be quicker in a tussle than poor old Louise.

Susan and Val were both asleep in their beds, Val curled up around a giant soft elephant, and Susan on her back, her face tilted to the orange street light like the Lady of Shalott. I pulled the cardboard box out of the Bradley's bag; pieces of paper crackled beneath the box, no doubt all the receipts from the shop. I gathered my nightdress, a change of clothes, my sponge bag and alarm clock and stuffed them all on top. As I left the room I felt an odd twinge of fear, as if I really were venturing into the unknown and not just one floor down.

The hallway was very quiet. There was no indication that

any sort of party was going on upstairs at all. I wondered if Star was still unconscious, and hoped viciously that she was. I hoped she woke in severe pain. I knocked on the door, biting down hard on my lip, which was still wobbling at the memory of the things she'd said. I would never, ever think of her again.

Mrs Bray let me in. She had switched on the fancy three-bar electric fire that stood inside the fireplace, and it was warming from orange to red. 'Not a patch on the real thing,' she said crisply. 'But one can't spend a fortune getting the chimneys cleaned for the odd chilly evening, can one? The bed folds up, by the way. I believe the mattress is fairly light. Louise usually manages, and she's fifty-three.'

I spent a hazy amount of time dismantling the bed and releasing the locks, as Mrs Bray offered no help whatsoever and spent her time unbuckling her case and hanging her clothes in the wardrobe. I heaved the bed into the next room and stopped just inside the doorway to catch my breath.

There were the two square windows that looked out on to the street, their curtains open. A pair of elegant wooden art-deco-style leather-upholstered chairs flanked the vast fireplace, which had a rather impressive dragon's head in plaster hanging over the mantelpiece. Upon the mantelpiece I saw that Mrs Bray had placed five pound notes and five shillings. Despite containing tongs and a scuttle and all the other implements of fire-making I'd only read about in books, there was, just as in the bedroom, only an electric fire in the hearth. The items had all been badly cleaned – by Star, I presumed: white licks of polish smeared the handle of the poker, and the dragon's head was grey with ingrained dirt.

In the corner was a tiny kitchenette, and on the other side was a small dining table covered with a lace cloth, four spindly legged chairs and a mahogany sideboard. I pulled the bed over to the sideboard and cranked it out once more, turning it upright and locking it steady. As I straightened, I saw that above the sideboard, on the wall, were three framed poster bills.

They were old screen-prints advertising long-forgotten plays at London theatres I'd never heard of. I looked from one to the other, finding eventually one name that linked them all: *Clara Fortescue*.

'My glory years.'

I jumped; I hadn't realized Mrs Bray was behind me. She drew a triangle between the three posters, from her name in small case as part of the chorus line in *Golden Lilies*, rising to an 'Introducing' part as the 'Ingénue' in *Zing-Zing!* and then taking pride of place as 'Maria' in *Maria Gets Married*.

'Fortescue was my stage name. I thought it sounded appropriate.'

I could see she had been an actress now, from looking at her long neck, and the poise with which she held herself. She reached past me and picked up a small, oval-framed photograph on the dresser.

'That's me, playing Maria.'

The picture was poor quality, but I made out a pretty girl in heavy make-up, clutching a paper rose. It explained why Dockie may have known her name: I supposed he'd been a fan. Perhaps he'd never visited Castaway House at

319

all. Susan claimed to know all about the interior of Paul McCartney's London flat just from reading about it in magazines.

I dragged in the mattress and bedding, as Mrs Bray fitted a cigarette into an obscenely long holder that she had produced from somewhere, and lit it from the gas ring in the kitchenette. Despite my avowal of a few minutes earlier, I remembered my conversation with Star yesterday, sitting on the kitchen floor, and I found the question that had been itching inside me for several minutes rolling back to the surface.

'By the way, I was just wondering,' I gasped, as I stretched the sheet back over the mattress, 'if you'd ever known anybody named Robert Carver.'

'What?'

I turned, holding a pair of pillows. Mrs Bray had paused, in the middle of tipping the end of her ridiculously long cigarette into an ashtray on the mantelpiece.

'There's a name scrawled on the windowsill upstairs.' There was an odd expression in Mrs Bray's eyes, and I hesitated to tell her exactly what was written there. 'And – well, it's sort of complicated, but I think he might have been here in the twenties. I was just wondering if you –'

'I don't wish to discuss it,' snapped Mrs Bray. 'And if you don't mind using the bathroom now, I'd like to go to bed. I take a sleeping tablet, so I shan't wake up.'

'I'm sorry . . .' I began, but she was already walking away from me. By the time I hurried past her to use the bathroom, she was at her dressing table cold-creaming her face, and barely glanced at me at all. In her warm, modern, seashell-pink bathroom, my eyes flicked rapidly around my sallow reflection, yearning to know more about Robert Carver, aching for it, and frustrated that there was no more knowing to be had.

Back in the sitting room, I closed the door behind me and pulled the curtains closed. I had never slept anywhere so stuffed full of old, valuable things – at least, I assumed they were valuable from all the decorative flourishes that served no useful purpose. I investigated the bookshelf and the sideboard, the sculpture beneath the elaborate lamp, the nailed studs and odd Chinese patterns on the wooden chest near the window. The lock on it dangled loose, inviting further investigation, and I lifted the lid gently and swung it over.

A cloud of dust puffed out of the entirely plain interior. The chest appeared to be full of old letters and documents, and at the very top was a face-down, heavy-looking photograph frame. Curiosity impelled me; I picked it up with both hands and turned it over.

The frame was silver-plated, now blackened with age. Behind the glass was a studio portrait of a young man and woman posing in front of a velvet backcloth, beside a velvet-draped table. There were more ripples of velvet decorating the floor. Perhaps it had been the in-thing at the time, but from this distance of years it looked as if they were trapped in a giant curtain.

I recognized Mrs Bray from her photograph on the sideboard, although here her hair was cut into a severe bob, and she had decorated herself with strings of beads and a shimmering dress, slashed into half-diamonds at the ends. She tilted her head to the camera with a confident, knowing look, and I thought her resemblance to Star was in the power she knew she wielded.

I supposed that the man beside her must be Star's long-dead grandfather, easily handsome in an old-fashioned way. He wore a stiff-collared evening suit with an almost feminine arched eyebrow that suggested all this was just for show. There was a familiarity about him I couldn't quite place, although perhaps that was just the way he allowed a hint of a smile to play around his lips, inviting the looker into secret confidences.

Beneath the photograph were piles of dusty-looking envelopes and documents, which I was reluctant to disturb and which seemed to have been left there for years. I was about to return the frame to its position, when I noticed that one of the envelopes beneath it – a package really – had the words *Mrs. Alexander Bray* inscribed upon it in an old-style copperplate hand, with the address of Castaway House below the name.

There was something that hooked my attention in that package, but at first I was unsure what that something might be. I lifted up the heavy edge of it with one finger, squinting at the gummed-down underside, and I realized it had never been opened.

Odd, but then no doubt Mrs Alexander Bray had had a good reason not to open it. I looked at the photograph one last time before I returned it, fresh with the knowledge of the name of the man who was looking out at me: Alexander – Alex for short, perhaps. It seemed to fit his debonair manner.

I closed the lid, washed the dust off my hands at the tiny sink in the kitchenette and wound my alarm clock, pushing the hammer back into position and trying not to notice how few hours I had left before I had to go to work. I climbed on to the horribly thin mattress, and every twisting metal sinew of the bed base pressed into me as I leaned towards the lamp to switch it off. The moon had disappeared from this side of the house, and the street light outside was extinguished by the floor-to-ceiling curtains, thicker than the drapes upstairs. I pulled my dressing gown over the blanket to keep me warm, but I hardly needed it, away from my usual damp spot beside the window, and I wriggled my toes in the luxury of the unaccustomed heat. I was glad now that I'd taken only a fraction of that pill as, slowly, the events of the evening slid from my conscious mind and I found myself dropping deeper and deeper into sleep.

. . . And then, quite suddenly, I woke.

I lay still, disorientated by the darkness, wondering for a crazy second if I was back in Petwick with next door's dog howling at the moon and Harry snoring in the bedroom behind the wall. I remained motionless as the night filtered back to me, and, as the metal coils of the truckle bed dug into my spine, I remembered I was in the ground-floor flat and that I was being paid five guineas to sleep here.

The usual sounds of the night were absent: Susan and Val's rhythmic breathing and farting, the creaks of an insomniac tenant walking across the floorboards overhead, the bored young man who rode his moped around the hill in a constant loop. I wondered what had woken me: perhaps only a dream, although all memory of it had been lost in the sudden coming-to of my conscious mind.

I turned on to my side, hunching the blanket and the dressing gown over my shoulders. I closed my eyes and tried to go back to sleep. I was almost on the edge of it, teetering over the cliff into blackness, when somebody breathed, quite sharply, into my ear.

My eyes sprang open. I could see nothing but vague shadows looming against the curtains: the menace of a fireplace, the humps of the two chairs. There was silence, but for the steady tick of my clock. Gradually, my heartbeat slowed as I realized my drifting brain had played a trick on me and, finally, I allowed my eyelids to drop.

A sharp *crack* echoed throughout the room.

I fought with the covers and scrambled to a sitting position, my heart hammering. 'Who's there?' I said, my voice emerging as a whisper. I swallowed. 'Who's there?'

There was no answer. My heart skittered into my stomach. I screwed up my courage to crawl across the blanket towards the lamp and turn it on. I looked around, wide awake now, wishing the lamp were brighter and didn't thrust shadowy pools across the ceiling.

The room was empty, of course.

I glanced at the wall beside me that partitioned this room from the main hallway. Perhaps it had been someone on the other side: one of Star and Johnny's drunk partygoers. Maybe this was the remnants of Geoff's blue pill, crimping my heart. All the same, I remained static, one fist clutching the bed sheets, the other propping myself up in the bed. I had the odd sensation of being in a lukewarm bath and not wanting to disturb the water.

And then the whistling began.

It was not like before, a sound heard from beneath floorboards, through walls, the other sides of doors. This time, the whistling was coming from this very room, as if somebody was standing just out of my line of vision.

My breath stood still in my throat. The usual sounds of the old, creaking house were absent. I could not even hear Mrs Bray breathing next door; I might have been alone, except for the person whistling somewhere between the weak splash of lamplight and the enveloping dark.

I forced myself out of bed, my feet landing on the rug, and backed myself as I edged, crab-like, against the wall towards the overhead switch. I noticed for the first time the swallowing nature of those floor-to-ceiling curtains, like the suffocating velvet swags of the old photograph, and knew that my tormentor was there.

I jammed on the switch, and a thin, disappointing overhead light blurred out the shadows. I darted towards the fireplace, snatching up the poker and holding it in front of me. 'This,' I said in my sternest voice, brandishing the poker as I inched towards the nearest window. 'Is. Not. Funny.'

There was no response. I was aware of two sensations in my body as I pokered the curtains: the dragging, red-raw tiredness of my eyes, and the wide-awake, gibbering fear in my stomach. Above my head, rings rattled on the rail as I thrust them aside and revealed the chilly blank squares of the windowpanes.

I swallowed on my dry throat, loosened the poker and turned to the other window, jerking the curtains aside as if I were ripping off a sticking plaster. Behind them, the street lamp's orange beacon flashed down on the spiky fingers of the fence bordering the basement well. Over the other side of the road, the cliff-top railings were dimmed and, beyond, the sea and the sky were an indistinguishable squid-ink black.

My palms were clammy, my breathing hot and shallow. I rested against the window frame and surveyed my tumultuous progress around the room: the blankets tumbled on to the floor, the lampshade knocked to one side in my haste to switch it on, the curtain hanging at an angle where I'd used the poker to thrust it aside. I realized now what I should really have suspected earlier: that anyone who pays five guineas to not sleep in a flat alone must have a very good reason indeed.

And then I noticed something that made my blood freeze in my veins.

The lid to the chest had been flung open.

Still clutching the poker, I tiptoed towards it and looked down. The photograph was where I'd replaced it, facedown on top of the thick envelope. Nothing had been disturbed, except that the chest was wide open – and it was this, I realized, that had made the loud cracking sound that had sent my pulse rate soaring.

The lid was on two brass hinges. Its curved innards smiled up at me. I fingered the catch and remembered hooking it over after I'd closed the lid. The chest gaped obscenely, taunting me, telling me it could never have opened by itself.

The whistling had stopped, at least. I was sweating, although the room was chilly. I turned, moving quickly across the room, and opened the door.

Mrs Bray had left the three-bar electric fire on, and in the beady glow from its lamps I could see the dim shape of her in the bed, her face a shadow. Now I was nearby I heard her deep, drugged breathing, and knew there'd be no comfort from her. As I sat on the edge of her bed, the whistling came again, and I put my hands over my ears and shut my eyes, although the sound seemed to penetrate all the way through to my brain. Now I knew why Mrs Bray drugged herself and, of course, why she refused to sleep alone.

I thought about leaving right now, with the five pounds and five shillings still on the mantelpiece, but then I saw the small glass bottle on the table beside Mrs Bray's bed. There was scratchy French writing on the label which I couldn't read in this light.

I picked up the bottle and rattled it; there were pills inside. I considered it for a moment and then unscrewed the lid, emptied out a pill and put it in my mouth. I palmed another as a precaution, and then left the bedroom, returning to the upturned sitting room and fetching a tumbler of water from the sink to wash it down. It was enormous and almost gagged me as I swallowed it. My second tablet of the evening; I hoped it was what I thought it was, otherwise I had no idea what was going to happen.

I switched off the overhead light and climbed back into the bed, still clutching the poker. I slipped the other pill under my pillow, where I could grab it if I needed to. The curtains were still dangling open, but I preferred the sickly street light to the enveloping darkness of before.

I left the lamp on too as I pulled the covers around me, remaining upright in the bed. 'I'm waiting,' I growled, gripping the end of the poker. 'I'm waiting.'

Silence greeted me, punctuated by Mrs Bray's gentle

snores from the open doorway. The whistling had ceased too, but I remained as tense as a sniper with a rifle, waiting for my target to appear. Somebody coughed, and I froze, but I realized the sound was coming from the basement below and then, as the tablet began to seize me in its groggy embrace, I was no longer able to distinguish between what was happening in the room or outside it. There was a violent clatter and I stirred, but it was only me releasing my grip on the poker and letting it fall to the floor. I vaguely hoped I would not have to escape, because my limbs were made of lead, and as I descended into the dungeon of assisted sleep the last piece of my coherent mind wondered why Mrs Bray had put a photograph of herself and her husband face-down in a dusty, disused chest, almost as if she didn't want to be reminded of him at all.

1 2

1924

The second of August was a swelteringly hot day, the first truly boiling day there had been since my arrival. All morning the housemaids had been sighing as they went about their chores, pushing tendrils of damp hair back under their caps. I had taken my usual morning constitutional and had returned sweltering and red-faced. After lunch I was wary of going down to the beach in this weather, sure my fair skin would burn, and so now I was in the dim cool of Castaway's first-floor library, attempting to choose a book from the dusty spines lining the shelves, with the thought of settling myself in the shaded arbour at the end of the garden.

Out of nowhere, there came a tremendous clanging sound from the front door. I went out on to the landing and peered over the banister, watching Scone move ponderously across the hall flagstones and loosen the latch. Faintly, I heard a man's voice demanding to be let in, and I took the stairs down, arriving in the hallway just as the door swung open. Uncle Edward was on the front doorstep, his salt-and-pepper moustache quivering, red-cheeked and furious.

'A man could die out there!' he bellowed. 'It's hot enough to roast the devil. Robert – you still here? Where's my son? I need to talk to him.'

He strode into the house. Scone closed the door behind him with a gentle click. I held out my hand. 'G-good afternoon, Uncle Edward.'

'Don't Uncle Edward me.' He stood in the hallway, sniffing suspiciously. 'What's she done to the place, eh? Smells queer. Never used to smell like this. Where's he got to then, the so-called master of the house?' He directed this query at Scone, apparently not trusting me to give him a coherent answer.

Scone murmured, 'I believe Mr Bray went out some time ago. I'm afraid we don't know when to expect him back.'

'Typical.' He held out his arms and allowed the butler to pull off his jacket. Dark blooms of sweat patterned my uncle's shirt. He loosened his cravat also, and used it to mop his brow. 'Is *she* in?'

'Mrs Bray is also out, sir.' Scone took the items and folded them over one arm. 'But we expect her back before too long.'

My uncle scowled. I thought it must be hard for him, returning to a house he was no longer in charge of, and so I said, 'Per-perhaps we could have a drink in the garden while we wait?'

Uncle Edward narrowed his eyes at me as if suspecting a trick. 'Drink?' he said, and then glanced at Scone as if he thought the man incapable of mixing one. 'All right.'

Abruptly, he turned on his heel and walked along to the unused morning room that stood to the left of the hallway. I followed him into the little glass-fronted conservatory, and then down the concrete stairs into the garden. As a child, I had been terrified of him, forced to tiptoe round the Lancaster Gate house on the few occasions we visited. He had no idea how to talk to children, and I quickly got the impression that he thought I was an imbecile, stuttering my way into a half-formed reply at his barked-out questions.

Although I still quavered in his presence, I felt sorry for him now, mired in grief after the death of my aunt. Despite his bluster, there seemed something narrower about him, more shrunken, and as I followed him along the gravel path to the arbour, I realized that I was the taller, and wondered when that reversal had happened.

'This used to be a wonderland,' he said, gesturing to the fish pond as we passed, although I suspected he was talking about the garden as a whole. 'Wilderness, it was, before your aunt transformed it. Designed it all herself, y'know. She used to have deckchairs,' he added savagely, hitching up his trousers and sitting on one of the stone seats.

There were three benches in the arbour, forming a broken circle. I sat on one of the others. 'We didn't know you were coming down,' I said. 'I'm sure Alec would have been here, had he known.'

My uncle waved a dismissive hand. 'I didn't know I was coming down until this morning. Thought of telegramming – waste of money. And why warn him? He'll only run away, the little blighter.'

This sounded rather ominous. 'Is something wrong?'

Uncle Edward sniffed in my direction. 'There'll be something wrong if I don't get hold of the recalcitrant sod. You know your generation's problem? Too much damn peace. Soft-boiled eggs, the lot of you. What we need is another war; that'd pull everyone's bootlaces up.'

I felt horribly tired suddenly, and resisted the urge to stretch out. 'I don't think we do,' I murmured.

'Shame I missed out on the German saga.' He ran a hand over his moustache. 'I could have done with running a bayonet through one or two of 'em. How's your mother?'

This abrupt conversational switch was typical. I thought back to her last letter, the dull news of people I cared little about, and the comfort in it too, the knowledge that life back home was continuing just as it always had. 'She's fine. Well, she has her aches and pains, but . . .'

'That's her own silly fault.' Uncle Edward laid any complaints of my mother's at the door of her decision to marry my father. 'And has *she* been up to any of her witchcraft recently?'

I frowned, thinking he meant Mother, and then realized who, with a nod of his head towards the house, he was talking about. 'Oh!' I said, startled. 'W-witchcraft? No – at least – um – well, she's been rather cheerful lately.'

I meant this. Since our conversation on the gate facing a field of sheep and the afternoon sunshine, Clara had defrosted. I had been careful to keep to myself my revelation; I could just imagine with what scorn she would treat any declaration of love for her, but our tentative comradeship meant that the house in general had a distinct air of relief. Not warmth, exactly; more what one might call a cessation of hostilities.

'Cheerful!' My uncle worked at the skin round his thumbnail. 'Yes, she should be cheerful. She's got her grubby little hands on Castaway. If only your aunt had known to whom she was leaving it, eh?'

From far away, at the door of the house, I heard the

chink of glasses rattling, and sensed that we would not be on our own for much longer. I said quickly, 'Yes. I heard she knew Aunt Viviane years ago.'

'Too kind-hearted for her own good.' Uncle Edward gripped the edge of the bench. 'And she was charming. The Tutt girl. Knew what to say, the right words. All that orphan talk and crocodile tears; all she wanted was to take what wasn't hers.'

'So what happened exactly?' I asked in a hushed tone, as the tray rattled closer towards us.

'You don't know?' He shrugged irritably. 'Well, I suppose it doesn't matter now. You see, there was this silly little parlourmaid who went and killed herself and –'

The end of his sentence was cut short by a trilling voice. 'Father! What a lovely surprise! You should have telephoned: I would have picked you up from the station in the motor car,' and into the arbour, carrying a tray of what looked like gin and tonics laced with sliced cucumber, came Clara Bray, wearing a linen hat that shaded her all-seeing eyes.

I wondered if she had heard our conversation, and felt myself blushing, knowing how vicious her tongue could be, but she simply laid the tray on the centre table and handed them out. 'I bribed Scone to mix me one himself, on the condition I was to take it up to you all,' she said, stirring her drink with a metal spike. Her nails were cadmium red and glittered in the sunshine. 'What a glorious afternoon.'

She sat down on the third bench, completing our circle. Uncle Edward pulled at his shirt collar and said, 'Too damn hot for me.'

'Well, at least we have the shade here.' She put her palms flat on the bench behind her and leaned up at the dappled sun, her white neck arcing towards it. My uncle looked away, growling indistinctly. She yawned and said, 'I may have a swim later. Did you bring your costume?' She spoke with closed lids, and it was not clear to whom she was directing her question.

'Of course not,' growled my uncle. 'Can't stand the bloody beach.'

'Oh yes, I remember Viviane telling me that you never much took to the seaside.' At the mention of his wife's name on Clara's lips, my uncle pressed his own together and looked as if he'd like to murder her right now. 'How about you, Robert? Have you a costume?'

I shook my head. 'I th-think I inherit an aversion to water from my uncle,' I said, knowing as I said it that attempting to ingratiate myself with him like this was doomed to failure. 'At least, I can swim, but I've never done it in the sea.'

Clara took her drink and sipped at it. 'Now that is a shame,' she said. 'Seems to make a mockery of coming to stay in our beach house at all, if you're not going to swim.'

Her use of the plural possessive clearly incensed my uncle, whose nostrils flared. I noticed a mischievous smile on Clara's face and saw that she knew what she was doing. I sipped at my ice-cold, sour drink. 'I have to think of my health,' I murmured.

Clara pouted. 'Of course you do, darling.' The shape of her lips as she pouted provoked a tumble of emotions within me, and to hide them I turned away and studied a bumblebee hovering over the lupins behind the bench. 'How was your journey?' I heard her ask my uncle.

He harrumphed, and instead of replying, said, 'I expect you know why I'm here.'

I turned back to see Clara's left eye give a small twitch.

'Actually, I don't,' she said, and I sensed, under the smile and the charm, a touch of nervousness in the way her wedding ring chimed on the glass.

'Doesn't tell you everything, then? Thought that was the modern way.' Uncle Edward turned to me, as if I should know about the modern way. 'Newly-weds telling each other every last boring detail of their lives.'

'Then I suppose we're not very modern,' said Clara in a bright, brittle voice, and I felt so sorry for her, achingly sorry for her, married to my insensitive cad of a cousin and lost in a world to which she did not belong.

Uncle Edward harrumphed again, perhaps with approval this time. 'Well, I expect you'll find out after I've spoken to him,' he said, and turned to me. 'Only thing is, nobody seems to know where the blazes he's got to.'

'I'll find him,' I said, standing up, a little unsteadily on the gin slurring my insides. I put the glass on the tray carefully. 'I'll try his usual haunts. I'm sure somebody will know where he is.'

'My husband has a lot of friends,' said Clara lightly, picking at a thread on her dress. 'He's what you might call a social animal.'

'I know what my son's like,' snapped my uncle, and Clara's eye twitched again.

'I'll find him,' I said, more certainly. 'And I shall bring him home.'

'Thank you,' said Clara, smiling. There was genuine warmth in that smile, and I returned it. My uncle said nothing, merely cleared his drink and thumped it back on the tray, looking at the empty glass expectantly.

I walked back through the garden, up into the morning room and along the hallway until I emerged by the front door. I had already started to walk down the hill when I heard someone behind me call, 'Sir! Sir, wait!' and I turned.

Agnes was running up the area steps, red-faced and out of breath. I took a few paces back to the gate that led to the basement well and waited for her.

'I saw your feet,' she said, panting. 'I was in the servants' hall and I thought, *I recognize them feet*, so up I come. I wanted to say thank you.'

I frowned. 'What for?'

'For talking to Madam. She's allowing me to share with Jane and Harriet. We're a bit squashed, but it's all right. So thank you, sir, thanks a million.'

Now I remembered, and felt embarrassed that such a small change had wrought such a big improvement. She seemed transformed from the snivelling little mite I'd encountered on the pier a few weeks ago. 'And you're fine now?' I asked.

She laughed. 'I'm not saying as Jane and Harriet are that happy, but I don't care. See, *they* don't want to sleep in that room either. Who would? Course, Madam said it wouldn't bother her, but she ain't like the rest of us, eh, sir?'

'Indeed she isn't,' I said thoughtfully.

'And if there's anything I can do for you, sir, you only got to ask.'

'No, no,' I said quickly. 'I'm happy I could help.'

She shrugged. 'Just let me know, then.'

I turned to go, and then remembered something. 'Oh, Agnes?' I said, as she was about to walk back down the steps. 'Has anyone heard from Sally yet? You know, the girl who had your room before?'

She shook her head. 'No, sir, not a sausage.'

'Oh well. That's all. Thank you.'

I left Agnes and walked away feeling vaguely perturbed, not really sure why I had mentioned the previous parlour-maid anyway, except that something about her sudden absence bothered me and I could not quite put my finger on it.

My hair felt stuck to my scalp under my hat by the time I reached the beach. Young men turning lobster-red sat out on the sand while their sweethearts fanned themselves vigorously and smoked cigarettes. I myself had sat out here with Lizzie yesterday, hiring a pair of loungers, along with a large parasol for shade.

I still did not feel quite comfortable lazing on the beach: it smacked of indolence, and I had yet to loosen myself from my suit while taking the sun. It meant that I had become incredibly overheated, while Lizzie had looked as fresh as ever in a simple linen dress. I had not mentioned my conversation with Dr Feathers last week, and I had no idea if he had said anything to her, but her chatter had strayed more often than usual to talk of the future.

'I think peach in the dining room,' she'd said dreamily, twining her fingers with mine as they dangled on to the sand. 'I read in the *Queen* that it's quite the latest thing in town.'

'Sorry, I didn't actually understand a word of that.' Guilty thoughts forced me to leave my fingers where she'd grasped them, as stiff as five twigs.

She giggled to herself. 'Never mind. Just . . . daydreaming, you know.' She moved on to a rhapsodic discussion of some film star's delightful organza wedding dress, and I lapsed into silence, trying not to wish that my beach companion had cherry-red lips, a languid voice and a head full of secrets. That she was, of course, the one woman I absolutely could not touch.

The door to Mason & Bray's Hall of Fame was locked, but Alec had given me a copy of the key and I let myself in, unhooking the wooden planking strung across the entrance to prevent the doors blowing apart in a sea gale.

More electric lights had been fitted; they were fairly dim, but at least prevented me from knocking the royal family over this time. The entrance booth had been constructed, with a sign listing the tariffs, and the turnstile clicked as I swung through it.

On my advice, information boards had been typed up and pinned beside the tableaux. I had decided that the longer people took to go round the exhibition, the more they would feel they had had their money's worth.

'Hello?' I called as I walked in. 'Anybody there?'

However, it was fairly clear that apart from a few dozen stars of the age, I was alone under the arches. As I looked about, it occurred to me that no work had been done on the Hall of Fame for weeks; in fact, I thought, they should open it as quickly as possible, to capitalize on the summer rush before autumn set in and the holidaymakers retreated to the factories and offices of their rain-lashed lives.

I frowned at Rudolph Valentino: his robe had been pulled into an off-the-shoulder look that was distinctly lacking in masculinity. I thought of my awkward kiss with Lizzie here several weeks ago, and, before that, my second evening in Helmstone when Alec had confessed to me what a truly poor state his marriage was in. He had laid all the blame with his wife, I remembered, and I should have known then that there would be more to the story than that. I adjusted Valentino's sleeve into its proper position and, as I did so, a sheaf of envelopes fell out and fluttered to the floor.

I picked them up, shaking my head. Typical of Alec to choose the oddest hiding place for his secrets. At first, I thought they were love letters from a mistress – as Clara had suggested, I could easily imagine my cousin pursuing half a dozen girls at a time, purely for the thrill of the chase. I rather hoped there had been a discreet *affaire*: it would level the scale of my lustful thoughts about Clara.

However, the envelopes had been typed up and addressed with plain formality: *Mr. A. Bray Esq., Arch No. 231, West Beach, Helmstone*. I turned them over; jagged tears had opened them and the two words I could see at the top of the first letter told me all I needed to know and what I had already begun to suspect: *Final Demand*.

My cousin had blown the last of his mother's carefully hoarded inheritance on a venture partnered with a wasteful idiot. He had then gone to creditors, perhaps using his father's wealth as a guarantee. That would explain why Uncle Edward had arrived like a bull pawing the ground for blood.

I gathered the letters up and locked the door, squinting into the fierce sunshine, dodged between the charabancs parked along the seafront, and crossed the road between the trolleybuses, making for the cool alleyways of the Snooks and Alec's favourite pub, the Walmstead Arms. It stood in a corner of two narrow pedestrian lanes and faced a church in a sort of sneering defiance.

Despite the hubbub outside, the pub was practically empty. Alec was at the counter of the saloon bar, perching on two legs of a stool and peering into the bottom of his glass with avid intensity. I swung on to a seat beside him and said, 'I've been looking for you.'

He turned to me, his stool lurching. 'Robert!' he said, focusing. 'How the devil are you? Want a drink?'

'No, thank you.' I leaned my elbow on the bar and rested my head in my hand. Although my opinion of him had become tarnished slightly these last few days, I still felt warmed by his presence, even when he was as drunk as a lord. 'Your father's turned up at Castaway,' I said.

'Ah.' He matched my gesture, lolling his head on his hand. 'Is he in a foul mood?'

'Afraid so. Clara's entertaining him in the garden.'

'And I thought it couldn't get any worse.' He pushed his forehead on to the bar. 'They sent you to find me, then?'

'I offered,' I said, piqued at the assumption I was some sort of errand-boy. 'Glad to get out of the house, to be honest. You know Uncle Edward can't stand me.'

'It's not personal, Robert. He can't stand anyone. Apart from Mother, and she's gone, so we must all suffer the consequences. At least you're not his son. Imagine that.'

I put the letters on the bar. 'I went to the Hall of Fame,' I said. 'These fell out of Valentino's sleeve.'

Alec stared at them, but made no move to pick them up. 'I'm broke,' he said in a weary tone. 'No. Broke doesn't sound too bad. I'm in bloody serious debt.'

'How much?' I asked softly.

'Took a mortgage out on Castaway.' He put his chin on the bar and twirled his glass. 'All for the business, you see. It just seems to . . . swallow up money. Bump knows the figures, but he keeps saying everything will be all right once we start ticking over.'

'But you've received a final demand.' I tapped the letters. 'It was at the top – I didn't sneak a look.'

Alec waved a hand as if he hardly cared either way. 'I named Father as a guarantor, without his knowledge. I expect that's what all this is about. Oh, God, I don't want to lose Castaway. I can't, Robert.'

'But Uncle Edward can pay, can't he? I mean, I thought he had money.'

'He won't care if Castaway gets sold. He hates the place. Reminds him of Mother.' He bit his lip. 'I may have to get rid of some of the servants. At least there's some give there, eh?'

'Scone?' I said, thinking of the man's devoted service to the house.

'Costs me an arm and a leg, Scone does.' Alec stormed the letters into his fist and slid off his stool. 'Well, one may as well get things over with. Coming, Robert, to see my final humiliation?'

'If there's anything I can do . . .' I began, but Alec was already stumbling out of the door and into the Snooks.

I caught up with him, and together we walked in silence until we emerged back on to the promenade. Alec slouched, hands in pockets, along the front.

'My wife seems to have thawed towards you,' he said, quite suddenly.

'I know,' I said. 'It's incredible. I think it's because I survived the ordeal of the painting circle's day trip.'

He snorted a laugh. 'I'd be careful if I were you. She's only ever friendly when she wants something.'

'Oh no,' I said. 'I think she's just been rather unhappy.' I spoke without thinking, forgetting that she'd blamed her husband as the cause of her unhappiness.

'Told you I was sleeping around, did she?'

I blushed. 'Er . . . no. Well, not exactly.'

'God, she didn't tell you about the baby?' Alec stopped, and saw the truth in my face. 'The woman's unbelievable. She'll use anything to lever her way above me. She has absolutely no shame. I suppose she told you I was a cad about the whole thing?'

'She was upset,' I said, shame-faced. 'Crying.'

'Crocodile tears,' he snarled. 'She never gave a damn about the baby. *I* cared. I was over the bloody moon when she told me she was expecting. I mean, come on. Does Clara appear the maternal sort to you?'

I felt it was not up to me to answer that, and so I remained silent. We crossed the road towards the bottom of Gaunt's Cliff. As we began climbing, Alec said, 'That baby was the one thing that was going to make our marriage all right again, and she killed it.'

'Don't be silly,' I said automatically.

'Don't argue with me, Robert. I know.' He ran one hand

along the rail. 'She wanted to go out dancing. I told her not to, not in her condition, but she went anyway, and she fell over.'

'An accident,' I murmured.

'Not in the least. She threw herself down the steps, and that was that. She's had plenty of practice in getting rid of unwanted encumbrances, I'm sure.'

'I'm sure that's not true,' I cried, but Alec was far ahead of me and not listening anyhow. I followed him up the hill, wondering how my cousin could be so blind. I had seen how upset she was, and nobody would fake that, surely. But he had other things on his mind than his wife, and when we arrived back he allowed Scone to manoeuvre him towards the library, where Uncle Edward had chosen to wait.

Alec slouched up the stairs, never looking more like a schoolboy than he did at that moment. Halfway up he turned and raised a hand towards me. I waved back and he pulled a face, before continuing up the stairs. I heard the click of the library door closing, and hoped he could sober up enough to withstand the bawling out he was going to get.

I found Clara still in the garden, under a parasol stand, reading a book and reclining on a cushioned lounger beside the fish pond. I hovered awkwardly until she said, 'Are you going to stand about like a butler all afternoon? Because if you are, you may as well order yourself to pull up a chair and sit down.'

She waved a hand towards the stone summerhouse. I made my way towards it and disturbed a spider's web in the corner. Inside was half a ping-pong table jammed against the wall, more folded loungers, mouldering mattresses, a very tired-looking child's hoop, a few pairs of galoshes, a mackintosh and an ancient, yellowing newspaper. I pulled out the lounger, dragged it along to the side of the pond and then returned for the mattress, thumping it with my hands to clean it, sending up puffs of dust. Clara coughed.

'You're not conducting surgery on the blessed thing,' she said.

'It's filthy,' I mumbled, cringing at the primness of my voice. I lay the mattress on the carcass of the chair and then balanced delicately on top.

Clara raised the book to her eyes and appeared to be reading avidly when she suddenly said, 'You found my husband, I take it? Propping up some bar, I suppose.' She sighed, still hidden behind her book. 'I expect it's about money. It usually is, with Alec.'

'I'm not sure,' I murmured, unwilling to be the messenger between them. 'Still, if it is, I'm sure Uncle Edward will help him out.'

She lowered her book. 'He's been worrying the end off of that leash for years,' she said. 'Your uncle's not a fool.'

'Whereas Alec . . .' I began humorously, hoping we could share some sort of fond affection for him.

'He's not a fool either,' she said sharply. 'He's a child. He never considers the consequences of anything. He thinks, he acts, and the world can go to hell for all he cares. But still. Let's not talk about him. What do you think of the garden, Robert?'

'Um . . .' I looked about me, shading my eyes with my hand. 'It's very nice.'

'Alec's mother designed it all,' she said. 'She used to have tons of parties out here.'

I leaned forwards on the lounger. 'Ah yes, I'd heard about those.'

Clara flopped her book on to the paving stones. 'She told me all about them. Always sounded like some sort of dream: candles lighting the paving stones, cut flowers in bowls of water, the women in those sumptuous gowns, men flirting with other people's wives.'

As she spoke I had an image, not of the party, but of a raggedy-haired child sitting on an upright chair with a china cup and saucer in her hand, listening to my aunt Viviane's cut-glass voice weave romance out of the air.

I had a moment of revelation. 'It's you,' I whispered. 'You . . . you're . . . so like her.'

I thought she would dismiss me with a snort, but instead she smiled, a flickering, secret smile that drew the two of us into a private circle. 'When I was a child I thought she was everything a person ought to be,' she said. 'I studied her like a scholar. How she sat, how she held her drinks, how she talked.'

'Do you mean,' I said, 'that you're trying to emulate her?'

She laughed, and again it was a private, enclosing laugh. 'Not at all,' she said, 'but the unconscious mind is a wonderful thing. Have you read any psychology? Quite fascinating. You see, consciously I'm absolutely aware that Viviane Bray was as much of a fake as me, albeit in a rather different way.'

'What do you mean?' I said. 'What did my aunt do?'

'Another time, darling.' She sniffed and looked around.

'I'm too hot out here. I must prepare myself for my husband's approaching bankruptcy.'

'It may still be all right,' I murmured. I watched her walk to the edge of the path, where it wound round a hedgerow and led eventually back to the house.

She looked back at me, and her dark eyes sharpened. 'If we are to live in straitened times,' she said, 'then I'll make sure I go out with a bloody bang.'

A quiver of a smile graced her lips and she disappeared from view, leaving me to wonder what on earth she had meant.

Alec remained in the library, holed up with his father, for the rest of the afternoon. Dinner was the usual strained, awkward affair, made even more difficult by the presence of my uncle, who found fault in everything from the potato salad to the temperature of the wine. Alec stayed hunched in his chair, picking at his food and chugging from his glass, and it fell to Clara and me to make conversation.

'How is Lizzie, by the way?' asked Clara, after several minutes in which nobody had spoken at all.

'Lizzie?' For two dreadful seconds I found myself quite unable to recall who Lizzie was or picture her in any way. 'Yes. Lizzie. She's – um – she's well.'

'What a sweet girl,' said Clara absently. 'I quite forgot to have her over for tea. You must invite the family to our garden party to make up for it.'

Alec's mouth set itself into two grim lines. 'What garden party?' he said.

'The end-of-August garden party. Your mother used to throw such marvellous ones, or so I've heard. I thought I'd revive the tradition.'

346

Alec stared at the stem of his glass. 'I don't think that would be quite appropriate,' he said coldly.

'No, darling, I insist.' Clara smiled with all her teeth. 'We'll invite everyone.'

Alec gripped the edge of the tablecloth. 'We'll discuss the details later.'

Uncle Edward coughed. 'Probably a good thing to have a blasted party. It'll be the last one you'll have for a while.' He threw his napkin on the table and got to his feet with a great deal of noise. 'Bit of a long day. Think I'll go up now.' He left without waiting to hear our muted chorus of 'Goodnight'.

We sat in silence as the servants cleared the cheese plates and brought in coffee. Alec helped himself to port, forgetting to offer me one. After the servants had withdrawn, Clara lit a cigarette and said, 'You may as well tell me now. I'll find out soon enough.'

'Please excuse me.' I scraped back my chair.

'Stay,' said Clara, and although it was absent from her voice, in her eyes I saw the quavering plea.

I stayed. Alec was too drunk to care either way. He turned his cigarette tin over in his fingers and stared at it intently.

'I s'pose you're having the time of your life,' he mumbled at his wife. 'Love to see me fall.'

Clara blew smoke at the ceiling. I looked at it, wishing, as I had so many times this summer, that I could escape to the electric light fitting myself.

'As we're yoked together in this,' she said, 'I actually do have your best interests at heart.'

Alec snorted.

She eyed him and said, almost softly, 'Tell me the worst.'

He looked up at her, as cold as I'd ever seen him. 'We'll have to sell some of Mother's furniture. Get rid of the car. And most of the servants, including Scone.'

'Fine.' She tapped ash into the tray.

'I'll have to find some sort of employment.'

She sucked on her cigarette. 'Yes,' she said thoughtfully. 'There, I agree with your father. I think it'll be good for you.'

'And we'll have to sell Castaway.'

'No.' There was no pleading in her voice; it sounded like a statement of fact.

He shrugged. 'No choice, sweetness. We're going to move into a serviced flat in London and Father's going to get me a job through one of his cronies and we're going to live bloody well happily ever after.'

'You're not selling Castaway.'

I was sure Alec did not see her hands shaking on her cigarette, but I could, as she said, 'Your mother would never have allowed it.'

'Don't you dare mention my mother.' He jabbed a finger. 'Castaway is not your house. It's mine, and I can do with it what I like.'

She banged her palm flat on the table. 'It'll be chopped up into flats or turned into an hotel or . . . or something hideous like that.'

'It's only a house, Clara. It's not a baby.'

She received the words like a slap in the face. She flicked a glance at me, and I saw tears trembling in the corners of her eyes. 'You'd regret it,' was all she said, swallowing hard.

'You ought to be careful, Clara.' His face reddened. 'I raised you up from the gutter; I can drop you back down again.'

She blew smoke towards him. 'If I go down,' she said in a voice as smooth as coffee, 'you'll be coming right down with me. Dearest.'

Alec uttered an oath and saw me finally. 'Enjoying the show?' he snarled.

I stared at him, surprised, and said, 'Oh, come on, Alec.'

He cursed again and left the room. A few seconds later the front door banged so resoundingly on its hinges that the entire room rattled.

For a full minute, silence reigned, except for the hiss of Clara's cigarette being extinguished. I considered my options. Either, I thought, I could leave the room on a pretence of neutrality or I could plant my flag now. Then I heard a swallowed-back sniff from Clara and knew, just as I always had, that the choice was no choice at all.

'I don't know about you,' I said, getting to my feet, 'but I need a very stiff drink.'

She widened her eyes so the tears would not fall, and reached blindly back to the bell pull by the fireplace.

'Not here,' I added, and her hand dropped.

Clara drew in a breath; of course, she saw in an instant the partisan nature of my statement. She nodded and stood up, turning to face the mirror that hung over the mantelpiece. She patted her perfect hair, her eyes in the reflection as black as coals. 'I know somewhere,' she said in a murmur.

She moved swiftly into the hall. I heard her talking to Scone, to whom none of what had occurred could be a

349

secret, and by the time I joined her in the hallway she was already dressed for outside. I collected my hat from its peg, and together we walked down the steps in the warm, scented night air.

She did not speak to me the entire way down the hill. Only her heels clattered angrily as I kept pace with her. Dr Feathers' waiting room was lit as we walked past, and I saw the doctor in the window. I raised a hand to him in greeting, and he nodded, arms behind his back, and I wondered what he thought of my accompanying my cousin's wife into town, not five minutes after the master of the house had gone this same way.

We continued along the seafront, past the entrance to the Snooks. The midsummer sky was still indigo; a few stars twinkled, but true darkness had not yet set in. We walked all the way to the east end of the town, towards the small harbour, and crossed the road just before it. A terrace of whitewashed houses stood facing the front, and from the basement of one I heard the faint pulse of live music.

Clara stopped at the top of the steps and turned to me. 'Thanks, Robert,' she said. 'You've been an awful brick about the whole thing. I know it can't be easy, stuck between Alec and me.'

I shrugged. 'I want you both to be happy.'

She shook her head. 'When two liars marry each other, it's never going to end well.' She grimaced. 'And d'you know what? I'm fed up of lying.'

I frowned, because it seemed to me I had never seen her so honest. 'Are you lying now?'

'All of this . . .' she drew a line around her black beaded

dress and her emerald wrap with one finger. 'All of me is a lie. The only thing of me that I have that is still true is down there.' With the same finger, she pointed to the basement.

I peered. Through the barred windows I saw hazy movement. 'What's down there?'

She inclined her head, saying, 'Come and find out,' before turning and heading down the steps. I paused, and then followed her. She knocked rat-a-tat-rat-a-tat on the door and then waited. I hovered on the steps as the door opened and a burst of music and sticky warmth emerged. I heard a voice say, 'Sweetheart! You're back!' and as she leaned in I saw two masculine arms embrace her.

Clara smiled up at me and disappeared beyond the doorway. I hesitated and then climbed down the steps and entered the room.

It was stiflingly hot inside and almost pitch-black – or, at least, after the milky light from the street lamps outside it seemed so. The room was crammed with people, and they all seemed to be talking and moving at once, making the place appear a many-headed, buzzing insect. At the far end of the room, on a raised platform, a band was thumping on a piano and playing strings and horns. I saw with a jolt of surprise that they were Negro.

A hand pulled at mine; it was Clara's, and she tugged me through the throng to a small bar on the right where a man – perhaps he of the embracing arms – was serving drinks. He sported a thin, elegantly twisted moustache and eyebrows arched even more sardonically than Clara's.

'This is my cousin, Robert Carver,' said Clara breathlessly. 'Robert – a good friend of mine, George Basin.'

The man put down the glass he was holding, wiped his hands on his apron, and shook mine. 'Glad you persuaded her out the house,' he shouted, over the noise of the band. 'We been missing her down here these past few weeks.'

'Stop your flattery,' said Clara, but her lips and eyes flashed all the same. 'And get us a drink. What'll you have, Robert? Gin? It's too hot for anything else, isn't it?'

I nodded, too ambushed by my surroundings to care much what I was drinking. There were couples dancing in the middle of the room, in front of the band. The singer, his eyes screwed tight shut with concentration, belted out a fast jazz number and the couples twirled apart and together. Bodies banged against bodies, hemmed in by the narrow walls of the club, and Clara handed me my drink and I knocked it back, needing the dumbing effect of the alcohol to cushion the novelty.

'Like the whangdoodle?'

I looked down. A short man wearing blue-lensed glasses was shouting up at me.

'The band,' he added at my bemused expression.

'The band? Oh – yes, very.' I did not add that I had almost no experience with bands, apart from the Salvation Army in the park on bank-holiday afternoons.

'From London,' he said with satisfaction. 'They play all the top places there, you know. Clara! Nobody told me you was here.'

Clara embraced this man too, kissing him on both cheeks, and introduced me to him as Mr Eli Golden, the proprietor. 'Eli saved me from death by boredom,' she said. 'When I moved back here I thought I'd never go dancing again, and then I met Eli.'

'She's a great little hoofer.' Eli winked at me. I presumed he thought me her lover, and I blushed, glad of the darkness. I remembered what Alec had said, about her fall after dancing, and wondered if the accident had happened here, perhaps on those stone steps outside.

Still, she appeared unaffected by the memory now. 'Want to dance?' she said, and I heard, in the exuberance of shouting, and the sentences clipped of necessity, a coarse echo of another voice, one that spoke without irony, with literalness, in harsh, unaffected tones.

I shook my head. 'I can't, I'm afraid.'

For answer, she took my empty glass from me, laid it on the counter and pulled me into the middle of the throng. I was jostled on all sides by moving bodies, but I managed to grasp Clara's right hand with my left and put my other to the small of her back, which was damp with sweat. I had no idea what to do now, but I managed to sway in time to the music as she darted away and towards me, her hips shimmering, her lips mouthing the words to the song, perfectly in time, as if the rhythm of the band was beating out the pattern of her heart.

Towards the end of the song she was claimed by other friends, both male and female, and I retreated gratefully to the edge of the dance floor. I ordered another drink and leaned on the bar, craning my neck to watch her dance, cursing when other couples lumbered in front, obscuring my view, and I wished now that at some point during my wasted adolescence I had taken lessons, at least, and wondered why nobody had ever pointed out to me that an ability to dance was worth a hundred Latin declensions or a matchless spin-bowl.

There was a commotion near the stage, and a great deal of applause and whooping. 'Here she goes,' said George Basin behind me, and when I queried him he said, 'Your cousin. They always get her up on the stage when she's here.'

The singer bowed and made way for Clara, who scrambled rather inelegantly up on to the platform. She passed her drink down to a friend in the crowd, and there was a general hushing sound as dancers stopped moving and chatterers turned to see what was going on. The double bassist twanged a few notes, the pianist floated a melody over the crowd, and Clara opened her arms wide and sang in a voice as deep as the sea outside the door: '*Your love won't give me no roses . . .*'

The couples on the dance floor nodded to each other and struck up into a new rhythm, swaying together. The chatterers resumed their chattering. I remained where I was, one elbow on the bar, my face welded to the sight of Clara Bray, her eyes limpid with feeling, her voice dredging all my unused emotions up from the bottom of my heart and flinging them out across the crowded floor.

And I knew then that I would always love her, no matter what happened in the future or who she'd been in the past. My adoration was unselfish; it was not dependent on subclauses, it merely was, and that knowledge was enough to make me happy.

'Good actress, ain't she?'

George Basin was grinning at me. I was irritated he had interrupted my contemplation of Clara, and so I ignored him, but he hardly seemed to care.

'Yeah,' he continued. 'I reckon she could have been one

of the stars, you know, in the pictures and that, if she hadn't a got married. When she sings it makes you feel all sort of mushy inside, know what I mean?'

I nodded dumbly, and returned my attention to the stage, smug and safe in the knowledge that, however good an actress she was, I knew the real Clara Bray, who had cried on a five-bar gate and trembled as she smoked a cigarette; and as she climbed down from the stage to adulation and cheers and joined me, breathless and excited, I saw her eyes glowing and knew she could not be more real. I longed to take her in my arms and kiss her, and contented myself with saying idiotically, 'Bravo! Very well done!'

'I expect you think I'm a terrible show-off,' she said to me, as the band struck up again. 'Well, you're right.'

The weight of the people thrust her against me. I thought I could feel her heartbeat, but realized it must be my own, thumping like a rabbit's inside my breast. 'Th-thank you for bringing me here,' I shouted back.

She smiled and flung her arm out. 'This was my life,' she shouted. 'In London. Until I met Alec. Now I'm an old boring married woman.'

'You're not, absolutely not. Well, married yes, but that's it.'

She touched my chin. 'Bless you. Sweet Robert,' she said, and my insides twisted, because this was the most affection she had ever shown me, and whether it was alcohol-induced or not, I didn't care.

We stayed a while, as she introduced me to friends I had no interest in, and I laughed and joked with them all the same, and before the party had ended she said she was achingly tired and did we mind leaving. I shook hands with everybody, and as we climbed back up the basement steps to the street, I watched her bottom as it rose up the steps, shifting in its swathe of silk.

'I know you're looking where you shouldn't, Robert Carver,' she mumbled as she walked up.

'I'm not!' I said, so loudly I convinced myself. 'I was making sure you didn't fall.'

We reached the street level and crossed over to the sea-front side. Clara touched the railing and looked out at the masts rattling on the boats in the harbour. 'I did fall,' she said quietly. 'The last time I was here. It's how I lost the baby. I was a silly fool. I should have been more careful.'

I leaned on the railing beside her. 'Accidents happen,' I said quietly, remembering Alec's cruel words earlier.

'They do. They do.' Her eyes were dark shadows in her face. 'How wise you are for someone so young.'

I was sure she was mocking me. 'We're not so far apart in age, I'm sure,' I said stiffly.

'Oh, but I'm married. It ages one considerably. Don't you do it, not for years.'

'The thing is,' I said, 'I've sort of – well, it seems I've promised Dr Feathers that I'll propose to Lizzie. After university, that is.'

'Oh dear.' She laughed. 'What a pickle you've got into.'

I frowned. 'Maybe I want to marry Lizzie.'

'Maybe you do.' She leaned back, holding on to the rail for support. 'But she won't be peaches and cream for ever, you know.'

'When you're in love,' I said loftily, 'that doesn't matter.'

'Exactly.' She spoke with a sigh. 'Exactly.'

We stood beside each other in silence, looking at the fat

moon bulging through the gaps in the masts. The night still held the heat of the day, and I kept my jacket tucked under one arm, the sweat from the club gently cooling away.

After a while Clara said quietly, 'I wonder if Alec will want a divorce.'

My heart quickened, but, attempting nonchalance, I said, 'On what grounds?'

'He can trump something up. Get himself photographed with some floozy; it won't hurt him too much.' I heard her fingers tapping the rail; her wedding ring clinked on the iron bar. 'It's only the truth, anyhow. Love, honour and obey? I don't think he waited until we'd stepped on to the honeymoon train before he was at it with the dining-car stewardess.'

'I thought you didn't mind?' I said carefully.

She turned her beautiful face towards me. 'One puts up with things,' she says. 'But sleeping with the servants; that really was the last straw.'

I leaped into a realization. 'It was Sally, wasn't it? The girl who disappeared.'

'Left a note under my door on the night she high-tailed it to whatever hole she'd crawled out of. Told me they were in love!' She laughed scornfully. 'Said he was going to leave me and marry her. I mean, I never liked the little strumpet, but I didn't think she'd be that stupid.'

'Is that why she left?' I watched Clara straighten with a slight pulling-together of herself, and I knew that when we went back to the house we would never speak like this. I wanted this moment to pause for ever, the two of us suspended in time.

'I presume so. I expect she's still waiting for him now to ride up and sweep her off her feet.' She shook her head. 'That was the night I went out dancing. I was so angry. I couldn't speak to him about it; I still haven't. And then I lost the baby and he blamed me. Me, if you please! If only he'd bothered to keep his trousers fastened, I might still be carrying his precious goods.'

'Lord.' I looked away from her. I was still sure there was not a malicious bone in Alec's body, but that did not mean there was no harm in it. I murmured, 'You were right. He is a child.'

'And here I am, boring you again with my woes.' She laughed.

'Not at all,' I said lightly. 'Although, of course, you're forcing me to take sides here.'

'Well,' she said with a mischievous curl to her mouth, 'I'm quite sure Alec has put his case across also. It's only fair I should have the chance to do the same.'

I turned to walk back along the promenade. 'I'm surprised you care what I think.'

She came alongside me and took my arm. 'We're chums, aren't we? You and me.'

'We are?' I asked, genuinely surprised, and overwhelmed by her small hand inside the crook of my arm.

She laughed, but said nothing. After we'd walked a few paces she said, dreamily, 'Do you know what I really want to do right now, Robert?'

'What's that?'

She chuckled. 'Go for a swim.'

'Oh. Well, I'm sure that would be terribly dangerous.'

'Mmm.' She paused. 'Let's go.'

'What?'

But she was already moving past me, down the steps and on to the beach. I hurried after her, catching up as she was bending down to unbuckle her shoes. She kicked them off and hooked her fingers into their open mouths.

'You're not going to swim now?'

She turned to me, her eyes flashing. 'But don't you feel all hot and uncomfortable after Eli's club? This is the perfect remedy.'

'They say never to swim in the sea at night.' I was anxious now, running along beside her. I wondered how I could prevent her. 'The tides are unpredictable.'

'Oh, Robert,' she sighed. 'Have you never wanted to do anything unpredictable?'

Yes, I called silently, *Yes, Yes, Yes*. Aloud, I answered, 'Of course I have, but when one's an adult, one can't continually act upon desire.'

She stopped, slightly ahead of me, her shoes dangling from one hand, her bare toes curling on the boards that led to the beach huts. 'Well, if you don't now,' she said, 'you never will.'

An excitement clutched at my heart, a yearning chasm of feeling; and just now, tonight, I felt as if all things were possible, that Clara Bray was standing here in front of me, wanting me to swim in the sea with her, and that she was right, that if I did not do it now, then I never would.

Still, I was unable to express this to her. 'I haven't a costume.'

She smiled at me, and there was a world of mystery in that smile. 'Alec has,' she said. 'In the beach hut. I know you're taller, but I'm sure you can squeeze in.'

I followed her around the corner to the line of huts. She took a key from her bag and fiddled with the padlock on the door. 'I expect this will be the first thing to go,' she said breezily as the lock gave and she pulled open the door. 'Once the new regime kicks in.'

I watched her climb the step and shut herself inside. I took a few paces back, watching the moonlight wash in over the sea. Nobody was on the beach; even as I turned towards the prom, I saw nobody about on the seafront road. I thought of Alec and wished him far away.

Clara emerged in a navy swimsuit with white piping that accentuated her waist and hips. I took in the curve of her thighs, the soft swell of her knees, all in a second's glance, as she said, as if seeing her almost naked was an everyday occurrence, 'I laid Alec's out for you. It might be a little snug.'

I went into the hut and closed the door, shutting out all light except for slivers that crept in round the edges. It was very snug in here too; in fact I worked out that I had approximately three feet of space to manoeuvre myself in. Towels, draped on a line suspended from the ceiling, flapped round my head as I groped about and felt the straw lines of the wicker chairs Alec and Bump had reclined on, stacked one above the other with, on top, a woolly mesh of material I took to be Alec's swimsuit.

There was also a narrow dresser upon which paints and brushes had been thrown carelessly, Clara's underclothes flung provocatively on top of it and my aunt Viviane's gold locket placed carefully to the side. I risked picking her garments up and holding them to my face, inhaling as much of her scent as I could, before I worried that I had taken far too long already, and hurriedly pulled off my clothes, bundling them beside hers in place of my own body.

Alec's costume was tight, and I had to stretch the material considerably to pull the straps over my shoulders. I thought I probably looked an idiot, but when I emerged from the hut Clara was already by the shoreline, her toes touching the waves. When I joined her she was lost in a world of her own, but jumped back into a smile when she saw me.

'Ready?' she said.

'We mustn't go far out,' I warned. 'Besides, I'm not a strong swimmer.'

'And your health. I know, I know.' She held out her hand. 'We'll go together.'

I took her hand, and although I had felt her hand more than a few times tonight, there was something intimate in this holding, facing the wash of the sea and its wildness together.

It was colder than I'd expected. Clara gasped, and I squeezed her hand.

'We should run,' she squeaked. 'It's better if you run.'

'I'm not . . .' I began, but she was pulling away from me, and in order to keep up I quickened my pace. The water splashed over my calves, my thighs, and then I heard Clara scream gently as it lapped her stomach.

'After three,' she said. 'One, two, thr—'

The end of her word was lost as her hand left mine and she launched herself into the sea, thrashing her arms, swearing at the cold. I took a breath and joined her.

The shock of it on my chest, my groin, my lungs and

stomach took my breath away. I remembered strokes from Briggs, the teacher at Whitemere Baths and pounded on, cutting into the rolling waves and kicking hard until finally the cold released and I drifted on a tide of the warm licks of the sea.

Clara joined me, her face wide with delight. 'Tell me this wasn't the most brilliant idea,' she said, bobbing in the water.

'We mustn't go too far out,' I said. 'Make sure we can still touch the seabed.'

She gave me an exasperated look. 'Robert . . .'

I gave in. I smiled. 'Yes,' I said, 'it was the most brilliant idea.'

She laughed delightedly and flung herself on to her back, arcing her arms left and right over her head. She was a strong swimmer, much stronger than me, and I allowed myself to gently float, watching her swim away from and towards me, just as we'd danced in the night club a few hours earlier, and I knew I would never forget this, that perhaps this, here, was the pinnacle of my life, of the reason for my having stayed alive throughout the attacks, the air gasped for and found, all to watch Clara Bray swim in a moonlit sea.

Her voice was sudden in my ear; I had not even noticed she was beside me. 'The first time I ever saw Castaway House,' she said, dancing in the water, her eyes bright, 'I knew it was meant to be mine.'

I kicked my toes and turned to look where she was pointing, towards the ghost of the pier, a dark grey against the black night.

'Dad had taken me and Billy on to the pier,' she continued, in a voice changed by the darkness into something grainier, huskier, rawer, 'to get us out from under Mum's feet – because she was dying, you know. I saw the tip of it, all buttermilk yellow, and I asked him who lived there. He said, "Viviane Devereau," and I thought that was the most beautiful name I'd ever heard. Then he told me she was Mrs Bray now, with a husband and a son, and do you know what I thought, Robert? I thought to myself, *One day, Clare my girl, that house is going to be yours.*'

I shivered suddenly and swam a few strokes back and forth to warm up. 'So you had ambition.'

'I was a little mercenary, is what I was.' She spread her arms wide in the water.

'You were only a child,' I said. 'It doesn't mean anything.'

'Listen to me,' she said. 'Just listen.'

And I listened, as we drifted on the spangled sea, to the tale of her mother dying, and then Billy, and her dad out all the time drinking. She told me how she'd find herself walking up the hill just to look at Castaway House and imagine the lives going on within it. How she'd finally spotted Viviane Devereau and thought the woman matched the name, with her lined velvet coats, her fur wraps, her laced boots.

Clare Tutt, on the other hand, was barely brought up at all: she took herself to school when she felt like it, ate tea at the neighbours in rotation, let the house turn nasty with filth. Occasionally her father would come home and cling to her, telling her he loved her, say he was going to look out for her, that good times were just round the corner. In the meantime, she hatched a plan to get to know Viviane

Devereau. She never called her Mrs Bray, her real name. For Clare, she existed without husband and son, floating in her own sea of perfection.

The house was a holiday home, used at weekends and in the summer, and so Clare learned the family's rhythm to perfection. She waited until Viviane came down alone one weekend, and followed her on the Saturday as she went into town; lurked in her shadow across all the floors of Bradley's and then, on the route to her home, raced along the back streets, emerging at the head of the cliff to collapse on the road, just a few yards from the house, claiming to be faint from hunger.

Most women on that street would have sidestepped the little girl and carried on, but Viviane was kind and got one of the male servants to take her down to the kitchen and feed her on leftovers from lunch. She then asked for the little girl to be sent up to the drawing room to see her benefactress.

Clare, who everyone knew as a foul-mouthed, slummy tearaway, who ruled the kids of Princes Street with a sharp tongue and a hobnailed boot, transformed herself that day. She became a poor little motherless child, a wide-eyed girl who loved school but was unable to go, beaten by her inebriate father, scorned by her neighbours. Viviane drank it all in like a mother's milk, and in return talked to Clare, told her of her husband with his important City job she did not quite understand, and her naughty son whom they were hoping school would straighten out.

She invited Clare to visit again another day, and Clare, who had secreted a silver teaspoon in her pinafore pocket before she left, nodded shyly and said that that would be wonderful. When she got home, she squirrelled the tea-spoon away in her private box of treasures and vowed that she would be a better fake daughter to Viviane Devereau than her real son had ever been.

Over the next two years she made a habit of Castaway. She would start in the basement, where the servants would feed her, and she charmed them with her wit and inno-cence, and the breath of outside air she brought into the dark space. She would then go up for tea with Viviane, and they would discuss the book Viviane had lent her the week before, or Clare would show a bruise she had received fighting with the Princes Street boys and tell her it was from her father's fist, and Viviane would press a coin into her hand and tell her to buy meat or some other wholesome comestible.

When war was declared, Clare shared Viviane's fear for her male relatives who had signed up, and when the first casualty lists were announced, she held her hand as Vivi-ane went through them and shuddered with relief when all the names were unknown, and comforted her at the deaths of distant nephews and cousins three times removed.

In all this time, she never met Alexander Bray, the golden disappointment of his parents, expelled from school after school for misbehaviour, the child who had shown such intelligent promise but was now wasting it in his asso-ciations with undesirable friends. Sometimes she would arrive to tales of what Master Bray had got up to the night before, but it seemed that he stayed away from the draw-ing room, perhaps aware of the cuckoo in its midst.

And then, one day, everything changed.

She arrived at the house to see an ambulance pulling away, and went down to the basement to find the servants grouped round Cook's deal table, the girls white-faced and trembling, the men cupping glasses of brandy. It seemed that sharp, lively Gina Scott had killed herself the previous night, and nobody could understand why.

Rumours flew round the table. She had a condition – nobody explained this to Clare, but as a Princes Street child she knew exactly what that meant. She had been let down by a man, they said; had family trouble from back home in Shanker; perhaps she'd always been touched in the head but had never let on. The other girls asserted they would leave – said nobody would take a position in a house where such a thing had occurred. Mrs Bray should have known, they said. She'd been too involved in her own life to worry about the servants.

And here they stared at Clare, as if she had been the cause of Viviane's distraction. Clare faced them out, declared her sorrow at Gina's death – which was genuine, because she'd been her favourite of the female servants, and if any one of them should have killed themselves she would rather it had been dumpy Maggie, with her pockmarked face – and asked to be taken to Viviane.

It was a mistake. She should have left and returned on another day, not allowed her presence to be associated with Gina's death. But she was young and lacked empathy, and could not understand why Viviane would be so upset. Yet she was – almost hysterical in fact, and her husband had arrived from London to comfort her, and Clare's presence in the drawing room as a witness to this was extremely unwelcome.

'Oh, Clare,' sobbed Viviane when she saw her. 'It's too awful. It's all my fault.'

This was typical of soft-hearted Viviane. Clare took a step forward, discomfited by Mr Bray's hand on his wife's shoulder. 'Of course it's not,' she said, worldly wise at her grand age of fourteen. 'You couldn't have known this would happen.'

'I should have,' she cried. 'I could have stopped it all.'

Clare thought she was being silly, in her usual Viviane-like way. 'Please don't be upset,' she said, holding out a hand; a rather dirty little hand, she saw now.

'I'd rather you didn't touch my wife,' said Mr Bray stiffly, and Clare took her hand back as if she had been shot.

'I – I'm sorry,' she said. 'Should I go?'

'Yes, go,' he said. 'Go and don't come back.'

Clare looked from him to Viviane, whose shoulders were still shaking, but who said, in between bursts, 'Oh, Edward, it doesn't matter.'

'It does matter. It matters a great deal. We know you've been stealing from us, you ungrateful little girl.'

'I . . .' She wanted to tell them it had only been one tea-spoon, two years ago, but then she wondered if she should admit even that.

'Taking money from my wife's purse. You knew where it was kept.' He indicated the drawer where Viviane did, indeed, keep her purse. Clare knew this because Viviane drew it out every week to hand over a few shiny coins.

'She – she gave it to me.' She saw Viviane shaking her head desperately. 'I don't steal.'

'The teaspoon,' Viviane croaked. 'It all started then.'

And now Clare understood Viviane's treachery: the

367

handing out of money, unsanctioned by the bullying husband, and when he had found out, perhaps today, she had lied — undone by the discovery of Gina's body and its implications, but lied nevertheless — and implicated Clare in crimes she had not committed.

'You're lucky my wife doesn't want to call the police,' he said. 'I'd have you thrown in gaol, minor or not.'

She left then, still protesting her innocence, dragged out by the same male servant who'd carried her in on the first day. This time his hand was on the scruff of her neck, and as he tossed her on to the front steps she shouted, loud enough for Viviane to hear through the first-floor windows, 'I'll get you back! You'll see! You can't get away with this!'

The money had never been spent; it had been hoarded in the box of treasures. She went home that night and counted it all up into wavering columns. In the morning she dressed, rolled the money inside a change of underwear, tied the whole thing into a shoddy-looking parcel and told Dotty to say goodbye to her father when he staggered home later. She took the first train to London and went to visit an old Princes Street friend of hers, Lil, who was seventeen and making her way on the stage. Lil took her in and fed and watered her, taught her how to dress and make herself up, changed her name and shoved her on stage in baby-doll clothes in a grubby revue. She encouraged her to take lessons in elocution, deportment and the classics. Clara Fortescue found she had a talent for the stage, and as she got older the theatres became smarter and the men who pursued her became wealthier.

By the time she caught the eye of Alec Bray she had already received three proposals of marriage.

'And how could I say no to him?' she said, looking up at the stars. 'He'd already promised me Castaway, without knowing I was a Helmstone girl. He said his mother was dying, and leaving it to him. He said it would be our home, that he was fed up with London, that all he wanted was a quiet, seaside sort of a life.'

We had drifted back to shore now and were lying half in, half out of the waves. Occasionally the water would unplug us from the sand, forcing us to dig our toes in and push ourselves back up again. Goosebumps speckled my arms, but I felt none of the cold.

I traced her profile with my eyes. 'So you married him for Castaway.'

She shrugged. 'He was attractive, naturally. He could be charming. Back when he was still wooing me, he brought me to Helmstone for the day. We were both a dreadful pair of liars, of course. I pretended I'd never been before, and he pretended the house was rented out. Didn't want to let his parents know he was pursuing an actress. So we bought day tickets on the train and came down here, and it was lovely.' She sighed. 'We went looking for crabs over by the rock pools, and I found a little shell with a mother-of-pearl inlay. I scratched our initials on to it and gave it to him, said it would bring us good luck. He promised to wear it next to his heart for ever.'

'And does he?' I asked, suddenly nervous of the answer.

She snorted. 'The very next day he told me he'd lost it. Said not to worry, he'd buy me a diamond ring instead.'

She shook her head. 'That was when I knew I'd be a fool to lose my head over him. I accepted his proposal the week after. You know, with clear eyes and the conscience of a gold-digger.'

My heart was leaping inside my chest. She did not love Alec. Perhaps she'd never loved him. She'd married him for his house, and the security that came along with it. Possibilities lapped my feet with the incoming tide.

Clara propped herself up on one elbow and looked down at me. 'It's so nice to talk to you,' she said. 'It's like talking to a brother.'

'Like Billy?' I mumbled, crushed.

'Of course. You can be Billy.' She smiled. 'We're sort of similar, aren't we?'

'Mmm.'

'I mean, neither of us fit in. We always have to play the part.' She sat up and hugged her knees. 'And now Princes Street won't have me either, so I'm sort of stuck. Nobody wants me, you see.'

I do, I thought. I held out my hand and said, 'Brother and sister, loyal to the end.'

She wrapped a fist round my little finger and smiled at me sadly. 'Absolutely.' She glanced down and grimaced. 'Lord, there's sand everywhere.'

She jumped to her feet and attempted to brush herself off, showering me with grit.

'Hey!' I said, standing up too.

'Sorry.'

In the thick moonlight, I saw that she was plastered with the stuff. We both were; I felt it in my hair, under Alec's swimsuit, at the backs of my knees.

She looked away from the beach and frowned. 'I'll have to rinse off.'

I looked about. 'How . . . ?' I began, and then saw that she was darting up the slope towards the beach hut, shouting, 'I'll only be a minute!'

I waited for her, brushing off sand, until I heard her voice in the dark call, 'Up this way, Robert.'

I made my way up the slope to where the beach huts hulked darkly before their wooden boards. 'Where are you?' I asked.

'Here – at the end of the huts.'

Now I saw her, silhouetted against the furthest hut. Beside it, a tap jutted out of the ground, with a bucket below it. She held out a towel, and I took it.

'I need you to do me a favour,' she said. 'I want to clean up, but I need somebody to guard my privacy. Would you do that?'

'Of – of course,' I said, not really sure what she meant.

'Thank you.' Her face was in darkness, but I thought I saw her smile as she began peeling off the straps of her costume.

Now I understood and, alarmed, I spread out the towel and turned my head away, towards the high, blank sea wall where, in a few hours, fishermen would start hoisting out their trolleys to display their catches of the morning. I heard water gushing, and resisted, hard, the temptation to look round.

'I'm sure it's fine,' I heard her say, 'but you can never be too sure, can you? One doesn't want to be arrested.'

'N-no.'

'I'm so glad we're friends now, Robert. God, this water's

cold. You know, I do feel as if we have a sibling-like connection. Right, all done.'

I felt the towel pulled from my grip, and when I turned she was wrapping herself in it, her costume slung on the tap like a victory flag. 'Do you want a go?' she said. 'It's very refreshing. I'll grab you the other towel.'

We reversed our roles. She held the towel high over her head, so high I could see her calves and ankles. As I pulled off Alec's swimsuit, I heard the rumble of a motor car overhead and realized how much closer we were to the seafront road up here, compared to our idyll at the shore. I felt awkward and stupid, rinsing myself in freezing water, and the only positive effect, apart from ridding myself of sand, was that it also rid me of any latent desire. We were two silly kids, playing on the beach in the early hours of the morning, drunk and tired, and that was perfectly all right.

She thrust the towel at me when I had finished and then, shivering and giggling, we ran into the hut. I pulled the door closed, murmured, 'I'm frozen solid,' and turned to her. I could barely see her in the darkness, but I heard the squeak of the stacked wicker chairs and I thought she must have pulled herself on to them. Her leg banged into my shin. I stumbled forwards and brushed against her hair as I righted myself.

'Sorry,' I mumbled.

'That's all right,' she breathed.

The space between us was changing. It had changed the moment that the door closed on us, but I was only just beginning to realize. The musty air in the hut crackled. I heard her short, high breaths. I bent down before I properly knew what I was doing and placed my lips on her forehead.

She lifted her face. My lips found the tip of her nose and then her mouth. I kissed her, tugging at her bottom lip with mine, and, just as Lizzie had done to me, I pushed my tongue between her lips and Clara parted for me with a gasp.

I could not hold my balance. I sank to my knees. She bent her head towards me; her hair brushed my face and we kissed and then, when she released me, I said, as though possessed, 'I worship you.'

She breathed heavily. 'Then worship me,' she whispered, and took my hand and traced it across her neck and down over her breasts. I felt her nipples and kissed them, and cursed that I could see nothing of her except a shadowy outline filtering through the wooden slats in the beach-hut door. The damp towel was rough about her sides; I kissed her stomach and she moaned. 'Worship me,' she said, and pushed my head lower, in towards the dark, salty heart of her. I felt my way, not even knowing what I was doing, guided by her hand and her whimpers, and, when I found the nub of her, caressed it with my tongue, over and over. She moaned louder and the wicker chairs squeaked and trembled, their legs rattling, and my knees grew numb on the gritty rug on the hard wooden floor. Sand on her thighs scraped my face, sand that she had missed, and her ankles crossed behind my neck, pulling me closer, and as I held on to the wooden struts of the hut to keep me stable, she bucked once, twice and again, and the wicker chairs creaked dangerously, and the beach hut shook, and she called out in a voice I'd never heard from her, 'Oh bleedin' fuckin' fuck,' and then all was still.

I gasped for breath. I kissed her thigh, found sand plastered to my wet cheeks. In all my dreams I had never . . . and the smell . . . and I was overwhelmed . . . and I sank down to sitting, gulping in the sweat-drenched air.

Then the chairs creaked again, and she knelt over me, pushing me backwards on to the rug. I felt my feet catching in the legs of the chairs, and my head knocked against the tip of a shoe as her hand felt for me, guiding me into her, and as she sank herself down around me all the stars illuminated inside my head and I thought, *Not yet, not yet, not yet*, and she moved up and down and up and down, and it was the dance and the swim and everything, and now I knew why I was alive, it was this, and it was so, so sweet.

I exploded in a confusion of sound and light and the chairs collapsing into the side of the hut and the shoe bruising my face, and then Clara was bending over me, our sweat sliding together, whispering something I could not hear, and I was barely aware of anything any more. She pulled herself away from me, her breaths hot and heavy, and the hem of her dress brushed my chest.

'You'd better get dressed,' she said, and, feeling as if I was a being landed from another planet, I extricated my legs from those of the collapsed chairs and staggered to my feet. Clara turned her back as I dressed, unsteadily, breathing hard. The hut stank of our act of love; I could hardly stand upright in it.

She turned to me as I was doing up the buttons on my shirt. She shook her head. 'Let's hope Scone went to bed as I told him to,' she said, looking at me, and I mumbled, 'I love you.'

'Oh, do be quiet.' She touched my nose.

She opened the door of the hut and looked out. I saw the pale silver of sunrise tinting the eastern sky. 'I love you,' I said once more, to her back.

She looked at the ruined chairs. 'I'll have to damage the lock. Kids are always breaking into the huts.' She shook her head. 'And you're not going to tell me you love me again, all right?'

'But I do love you,' I said dumbly. 'I worship you.'

She sighed. 'This has been lovely,' she said. 'But it's not going to happen again. Do you understand that?'

I nodded.

She smiled, and looked at my shirt and refastened my buttons. I felt her fingers at my throat and my spirit soared.

'You've a wonderful girl in Lizzie,' she said. 'And I want you to think about her. Will you do that? For me?'

'All right.' I could think about Lizzie. Thinking about Lizzie meant nothing to me any more.

'Good. Then we'll go up the hill, you'll go to your bedroom, sleep, and in the morning we'll have breakfast as normal. All right?'

'Of course,' I said. In a few hours I would see her again. I hardly cared under what circumstances.

'Then I'll remember this night with great pleasure,' she said, smiling. 'Now, will you be a dear and break the lock on the door?'

I did as she asked. I was her pack animal, her beast of burden; I would have done anything for her. Together, we walked up the steps towards the seafront road, she slightly behind me, cautiously looking left and right.

'Wait.'

Her fingers touched my back. I stopped, just below the

level of the road, and peered along the street. I saw, in the distance, a figure shambling along towards us. His gait was unmistakable, and my soaring spirit splattered into a muddy puddle.

We hovered, my heart pounding, as Alec approached our hiding place. He was drunk; that much could be seen even from so far away, but it did not mean he would not see us. I felt sordid now, and idiotic, abusive of my cousin, who had never shown me anything but love and friendship. Clara had had her own reasons for making her husband a cuckold; I had none but my own witless desire.

Alec appeared to be shouting at some unknown adversary. '. . . I was never good enough for you, eh?' came the tail end of his cry, carried on the breeze towards us.

Clara's shame radiated from the bent top of her head. I wondered if we could explain ourselves away, but then I thought of the broken lock on the beach-hut door, and the collapsed wicker chairs, and the stench that must still permeate the tiny room. I shuddered, seeing Alec's hurt and my disgrace and, worse, what would happen to Clara if she was found out; and I knew she was right and that this must be the only time, and if we escaped with this I vowed I would not even look at her again. Perhaps, I thought, we could creep down the steps now, but he was almost upon us and he might catch some movement with the corner of his eye. In fact, were he just to cast his glance a little over, he would see us in plain view: two cringing lovers biting their lips.

As he got closer I realized that Alec's opponent existed only in his inebriate mind. 'Can't bear it . . . Mother . . .' I heard him say, banging his fist on the rail. A sob broke from his throat. '... Not my fault ... Castaway ... It's not ...'

He was upon us now, and I held my breath. 'Not Sally ...' he slurred. '... Mustn't mention Sally. I'm not listening, Mother, d'you hear? Not listening.'

And then he was moving past us and was gone.

We waited, without moving, for a long time. When Clara did look up at me, her face was cold and set. I knew that when we did finally start to walk towards the house, when we could be quite sure Alec was lying unconscious on his bed, we would not talk about this. We would not talk about anything.

Her flinty, coal-edged eyes pierced mine, and their message was clear: that even though she may have allowed me to love her, briefly, I was only at the threshold of understanding Clara Bray. I also knew that if she had her way, I never would get to know her at all.

13
1965

I was dreaming, I thought.

I couldn't be sure. I was in the sea, with the full moon turning the waves from black to white. My face was sticky from dried salt, my hair was stuck tight to my head, and there, a short distance away, a girl was drifting, lifting an arm to wave.

It was Star, of course. I swam towards her, the tide pushing against me, but I knew I was a strong swimmer, that I could beat the crush of the sea, and so I forced myself onwards. 'Come here!' she was calling. 'It's lovely. It's beautiful.'

'Wait for me,' I said, my voice odd, enclosed as if I were in a cupboard. Her white arm was beside me, and I grasped at it, lifting her clear.

It wasn't Star. It was Mrs Bray – a younger Mrs Bray, an image from a photograph, with sharp dark hair and all-seeing eyes, a tilted chin and a beaded dress. She was wrapped in a velvet curtain, which was dragging her down under the surface of the sea.

I made a huge effort and pulled her shoulders up towards mine, freeing her of the velvet cage. I thought I heard her laughing, but when I finally brought her near to me, her neck lolled back and I realized that the eyes were seeing nothing at all, because she was dead. She'd been long dead: her face had that green, sour look, and her limbs were withered from the relentless pound of the salt in the sea.

A great sense of desolation overcame me. It was horrible, awful. 'It's all gone wrong,' I tried to cry, but my lips were gummed closed by the water, and the more I tried to move them, the more they stuck fast.

And then there came a great battering, clanging sound, on and on and on, and I groped my way out of murderous sleep into the dim half-light of a strange room, and the sound of my alarm clock's hammer bashing the bell over and over again.

My limbs were as mummified as my lips had been in my dream. The blankets seemed to be pressing down on me, restricting even the tiniest movement. I creaked an elbow upwards, pushed aside the top sheet, freed my hand, groped along the floor towards the demented sound, found the switch and, at last, stilled the awful noise.

I lay for a while, coming to, remembering where I was: Mrs Bray's sitting room, flat on a thin mattress, the steel coils underneath poking up and misshaping my flesh. I gazed at the unfamiliar shapes of the furniture and finally remembered what had happened last night: the slam of the chest cracking open, the whistling in my ear, and the sleeping pill I'd taken from her bottle by the bed that had dragged me down into the groggy sleep I was now trying to wake up from.

My tongue felt thick with fur, my throat was parched, and there was another hammer in my head using my brain as a bell. I supposed this was what people meant by a hangover. My eyes were sandy with grit; I felt sleep struggling to claim me again. With a huge effort, I padded my hand on the floor, found the clock and pulled it upright.

It was half past six.

Bugger, said the voice in my pounded brain. I had exactly zero minutes before I was supposed to be at work, and Mrs Hale had been talking yesterday about letting me go. I threw back the suffocating covers, collapsed on to the floor, pulled myself upright once more and staggered towards the bathroom.

Mrs Bray was still asleep, breathing lightly. Unlike me, she seemed perfectly at ease inside the cocoon of her drug; make-up-less, her face had taken on an innocent look. She had a certain resemblance to those sculptures of royal ladies I'd seen on cathedral tombs, lying in marble over their casket, serene in death, as unlike the lolling body of my dream as could be.

I dressed in the grey light whispering over the tops of the curtains, my hangover creasing out any fear of the shadows. I fumbled my way into stockings and dress, switched my greasy hair into a ponytail and gulped down a cup of tepid water from the sink. I picked up the Bradley's bag that I'd crammed my belongings into last night, and it tore, sending the scrappy, oddly yellowing receipts from inside fluttering across the floor. I sighed, kicked the bag under the bed and heaped my clothes on top of the covers, intending to pick them up later.

As I stood there, a voice behind me whispered in my ear,

'*Rosie.*'

My guts vaulted. I turned, and there was Star behind

me, still in her clothes of last night, as pale as a drowned girl flung up by the sea. She put a hand out and supported herself on the counter of the kitchenette.

'Huh,' she added, and I turned back in silent fury to pick up my handbag as she mumbled, 'I've been chucking up for hours. I want to die.'

'Good.' Her words of last night bounced from floor to ceiling and back into my head. *Disgusting dyke. Tried to touch me up. Pervert.*

She seemed too gone even to comprehend what I was saying. She trudged towards the bed, kicking her shoes off, and climbed under the covers, my belongings on top rippling under the wave of her body. She curled up against the pillow.

'I never want to see you again,' I hissed, and was rewarded with slow, heavy snores.

I was in an even fouler mood now, as I left her sleeping and marched past Mrs Bray into the hallway. Not only that, but I could see she wouldn't wake for anything, not a slammed-back chest or an eerie whistling. Bitch.

Outside, I shivered under the frosty blue sky and hurried up the entrance towards the Bella Vista.

'You're fifteen minutes late,' snapped Josie as I walked, feeling like death, towards the basement stairs. 'I wouldn't be surprised if she didn't give you the old heave-ho.'

'I've had a bad night.'

'You're young. You wouldn't know a bad night if it slapped you round the face.' She sucked archly on the end of her cigarette. 'Tell you about my back trouble, did I?'

I grunted, and went down the stairs to the kitchen. There were already a couple of guests sitting in the breakfast room when I arrived, the commercial traveller sort, one filling in his newspaper crossword in pencil, the other smoking an unfiltered cigarette and staring at the ancient, Riviera-type poster of Helmstone in a dazed sort of gloom.

I knew Mrs Hale was going to skin the hide off me; it was now twelve minutes to seven, and I opened my mouth as I pushed aside the beaded curtain, ready with my tale of the demanding landlady and the truckle bed, the spooky occurrences, the sleeping pill still trudging through my brain.

'Rosie!' Mrs Hale turned from the stove. 'Thank goodness you're here.'

'Yes, well, I've had a terrible night,' I began, pulling my apron from the hook before she could tell me not to bother.

'Mmm. Now then.' She headed past me towards the curtain. 'You're going to have to run the ship until I get back.'

'What?' I paused, in the midst of tying my apron strings.

'I have to go and see Father. He's in a terrible state. You'll be all right, won't you? Both the gentlemen just want the regular breakfast with tea; you know where everything is by now. You can leave the washing-up until after I come back.' She frowned. 'Although I don't think we've enough cups, so you're going to have to do those as you go. Well then, I'll see you in a while.'

And before I even had time to breathe out, she was gone.

'What?' I said to the empty space. 'What?' But there was only the rattle of chairs being pulled out, and when

I peeked through the beaded curtain I saw that there were more people in the breakfast room: a retired couple looking round expectantly, bright with morning. I closed my eyes and leaned my head against the teapot shelf, the world still swirling merrily from behind my shut lids. Through the other side of the curtain I heard a woman call out, 'Excuse me! Is anyone coming to take our order? We've a train to catch, you know.'

I opened my eyes, switched on the electric grill, pulled the frying pan from its hook, set it on the stove and reached for Mrs Hale's tub of lard. I had a feeling it was going to be a long morning.

Sometime later Mrs Hale came back to quell the angry chorus of hotel guests demanding their breakfasts. She found me in the kitchen, slapping broken fried eggs on to two plates. 'I'll take those out,' she said, swooping down. I heard her trilling to the guests about the 'new girl' and how she, Mrs Hale, had had to tend to her aged father, and, as I smelled the aroma of burned toast yet again, and pulled out the grill pan to throw the charred squares into the pig bin, I heard the guests laughing themselves into being good sports about the whole thing. Then I realized the hot-water urn had run out of water, so I ran to the sink to fill jug after jug to pour into it, and I knew it was going to be another fifteen minutes before we had hot water for tea, so I set the kettle to boil as well and looked around at the bomb crater of the kitchen – plates tipped into the sink, still covered in bacon rind and baked beans; used teacups precariously balanced on top of each other; two broken eggs splattered on to the floor with a dish cloth dropped on top so I wouldn't slip up on them; the cutlery tray running dangerously low – and I saw it was only eight o'clock, and wanted to burst into tears.

'I've five minutes before the doctor arrives,' said Mrs Hale as she came in behind me, setting to at the stove. 'Come on, Rosie, chin up. That isn't the attitude that won us the war.'

'Is he all right?' I mumbled as I stared, overwhelmed, at the mess.

Mrs Hale thrust a dish mop into my hand. 'He had an awful night. Didn't sleep a wink.'

'Me neither,' I said, taking a breath and searching for forks in the sink. 'It was my landlady, you see –'

'He's convinced he saw a ghost,' she continued, throwing bread under the grill and spooning more lard into the pan. 'It's his nerves, you know.'

I turned and stared at her. 'That's really odd,' I said. 'Because last night –'

'I don't know if I mentioned it to you,' she continued, taking the milk from the fridge and sniffing it suspiciously, 'but he was shell-shocked in the war. He was at a guest house in Southend when a bomb hit.'

'Mmm,' I said, frantically dumping plates in the water, bacon rind and all, and rinsing them clean. 'But about this ghost –'

'He was still in hospital when we got the news about Anthony. My youngest brother – he was in the Air Force. Shot down somewhere over the Mediterranean. Anyhow, we never recovered the body. It was the last straw for Father, as you can imagine, coming on top of the bomb blast. He changed overnight – almost never goes outside, you know. Scared of his own shadow.'

'Mrs H.!' Josie's strident tones could be heard from somewhere in the stairwell. 'Doctor's here!'

Mrs Hale stuck her head through the curtain and called, over the heads of the seated guests, 'I'll be right up.' Returning to the stove, she plucked out the toast and stuck it in the rack. 'Now then, Rosie, will you be all right for a bit? I'll be back as soon as I can. It's Lizzie, you see: she thinks she's helping, but she just makes things worse.'

'I'll be fine,' I said weakly, thinking that in two and a half hours everything would be over.

'Of course,' she murmured as she left the room, 'it's the whole Robert Carver business that's to blame.'

I whipped my head round. She was already pushing aside the beaded curtain. 'Robert Carver?' I said, and followed her out into the breakfast room. 'What about Robert Carver?'

'Hmm?' She glanced back at me absently. 'Oh, ignore me. I'm talking to myself.'

And, with that, she climbed the stairs up to the ground floor.

The second half of the morning passed as badly as the first. By the time all the guests had left, in varying degrees of bad humour, the kitchen and the breakfast room were a quagmire of dirty plates, burnt pans, knives on the floor, skewiff tablecloths, broken teacups and butter pressed into the floor tiles. I knew I should get on and clean the place, but instead I pulled out one of the chairs, sat down, and put my face in my arms on the table.

'Oh dear, oh dear, oh dear.'

I peeled my face half an inch off the table and saw Josie's violet-coloured nails tapping the door frame. Her nostrils flared as she took in the room, her lips twisting with satisfaction.

'Don't,' I mumbled, returning my face to my arms. 'Just don't.'

She snorted, and I heard her heels clacking past me. 'You stay there,' she said, one nail pressing into the soft flesh of my upper arm.

I eased my head up further and rested my chin on one fist, twisting so I could see her. She battled with the beaded curtain and disappeared into the kitchen. 'Christ on a bicycle,' I heard her say. 'You ain't half got your work cut out here, eh?'

'Thanks,' I murmured. I heard her rattling pans in the kitchen. Louder, I said, 'How's Dr Feathers?'

'Not long for this world, I wouldn't wonder.' The smell of lard frying in the pan returned to haunt me like last night's whistling. 'Mind you, he's always seemed that way to me. He'll prob'ly outlive us all.' She cackled, faintly.

'Mrs Hale said he'd been shell-shocked. In the war.' I was thinking of Robert Carver, of course, but I didn't know how to bring him up.

'Straw that broke the camel's back, if you like.'

I heard bacon sizzle and, despite myself, my stomach growled with hunger.

'According to my mum,' Josie continued, 'he wasn't the same after his wife left him back in the twenties.'

'I thought she'd died.' I gazed up at the tourist poster of Helmstone, much as the commercial traveller had done earlier. The artist had bleached white the promenade and printed a turquoise sea under a searing sun.

'Died a few years ago. But they'd been separated for

years; she went off and joined the Quakers, something like that. Never did get to the bottom of that story. Mrs H. don't like to talk about it. Right then.'

She marched back inside the breakfast room and put down in front of me a bacon sandwich and a cup of tea. 'Get that inside you,' she snapped. 'Quickly now, before it goes cold.'

A tear sprang into my eye. 'J-Josie . . .' I began.

She flicked a glance at the clock over the tiled-in mantelpiece. 'I got to get upstairs. Mrs H. says, when you're finished, I'm to pay you your wages. But she wants all this cleaned up first.' Josie patted her old-fashioned hairdo. 'I saw you was looking peaky when you walked in this morning. Anyway, eat up, chop-chop.'

'Thank you!' I called, but she ignored me, carrying on up the carpeted stairs. I turned my attention to the bacon sandwich and thought I'd never eaten anything so delicious in my life.

Sometime later, I pulled off my apron and made my way to the lobby. There was a commotion going on behind the door of Dr Feathers' room, but Josie was back at her desk, serenely reading her library book and smoking a cigarette as if nothing untoward was happening.

'Is he all right?' I said, as, distantly, I heard the old man shout, 'It's him, I tell you, it really is him!'

Josie glanced up at me. 'I told you, he ain't been all right since 1926.' She snorted and twiddled the dial on the safe. 'Mrs H. wanted me to check you'd cleaned up properly down there, but I ain't doing them stairs again, so you'd best tell me the truth.'

I briefly shut my heavy eyelids. 'It's fine,' I said, thinking of the grease spots still clinging to the tiles and the encrusted, unidentifiable scab of burned-on food on the cooker.

Josie raised one eyebrow. 'Fine,' she echoed, and dumped a collection of coins on the counter. 'Mrs H. wants to give you an extra five bob for your trouble, you know.'

'Oh, great,' I said, thinking that five bob was nothing for all the work I'd done today.

'And don't you be sarky, young lady.' Josie separated some of the money and pushed it across the counter towards me. 'She's a lot on her plate, has Mrs H.'

'I know, her father,' I muttered.

'And this place.' Josie rolled her eyes. 'Nobody wants to come and stay here any more. It's all day-trippers these days. I said to her, you know where you should have a hotel? Spain. That's where they all want to go these days, all the moneyed lot. The middle classes. Hot weather, cheap food.'

'I can't see Mrs Hale in Spain,' I said. 'They live under a jackboot, don't they?'

'And they eat garlic.' She sniffed. 'But that's where the living is now. Not these English seaside places; they're rotting in their graves, you mark my words. Even twenty years ago this place was something – even during the war, when you couldn't swim in the sea. Not now. I said to her, not even these Mods and Rockers want to come here; town ain't even good enough to throw some deckchairs about in.'

From behind Dr Feathers' door I heard a female voice – either Mrs Hale's or her sister's, say, 'Now then, Father. You know what happened last time.'

'Course,' Josie was saying, 'this road used to be the best address in town, back when my cousin Agnes was working next door.'

I stared at her. 'Your cousin worked at Castaway House?'

'Didn't I say?' Josie picked up her cigarette and took a drag on it. 'It was only for a year or so. She was parlour-maid; left after all that scandal, you know.'

'What scandal?' Vaguely, I remembered a pencil moustache and a purple headscarf: a couple on the front, muttering about long-finished occurrences I hadn't had much interest in a week ago.

'You know . . .' She sighed and frowned. 'What was his name? That fella.'

I took a breath. 'Not . . .' But I knew; of course, I knew. 'Robert Carver?'

'That's the one.' Josie clicked her fingers. 'Robert Carver.'

I leaned across the counter. 'What happened?' I said urgently.

'Well.' Josie's eyes flashed, at the pleasure of having a new audience. 'According to my cousin –'

'Rosie!'

I turned. At the entranceway to the Bella Vista was Star, colt-legged and ashen-faced. As she shuffled towards me I saw her hair was sticking up around her head, and she had a stippling pattern of spots across her forehead.

I rolled my eyes and turned back to Josie. 'Never mind her,' I said. 'I want to know what happened with Robert Carver.'

'Listen, Rosie.' Star put a hand on my arm and I looked

at it, surprised she wanted to be so close to me, after everything she'd told me last night. Despite myself, a flash of memory returned: me, with my lips to her neck, and the moan as she surrendered.

'D'you mind?' I said, as coldly as I could. 'I was in the middle of something.'

'It's important.' Her voice stuck on a frog in her throat. 'Please.'

'You two get on,' said Josie. 'I'm off to see if Dr F.'s gone mad.'

'Wait, Josie!'

But she lifted the flap of the counter and walked towards the door, opening it without knocking. Faintly, I heard her say, 'Now. How about a nice cup of tea?'

I glared at Star, although a small part of my brain was very pleased that she looked so sorry for herself. 'What d'you want?'

She lowered her eyes. 'I can't remember saying what I said last night.'

'Lucky you.'

'But I've been told a hundred times what it was.'

'Yes. I thought that was considerate, in front of all your friends.'

'I'm so sorry.' She steadied herself on Josie's desk. 'Really, you must believe me, I'm so sorry.'

'No, it's fine.' I snatched up my bag. 'It's better to know what you actually think of me. At least I'm aware. Anyway, I must go. Bye.'

'Wait.' Her hand hovered an inch from my arm. 'Don't go. I'm . . . I'm doing this all wrong.'

'I don't care,' I said, although I did care, and my stomach was collapsing all over again at the memory of her assault on me.

'But listen, there's something else. Someone's been asking for you.'

I narrowed my eyes. 'Who?'

'This chap. Knocked the whole place awake this morning. Granny answered the door to give him short shrift, and he said he'd come for Rosie Churchill at Castaway House. He works on the seafront.'

Although a large part of me wanted to walk away from her right now, I was intrigued. 'Who was he?'

'He cleans the seafront in the mornings. He said there's an old man who's got into one of the abandoned arches and won't leave. Apparently he told them that the only person he'd speak to was you.'

I breathed out. 'Dockie,' I said. So he hadn't left Helmstone after all last night. 'The man from the basement.'

'He was wondering if you'd go down and have a word with him.' She looked at me with red-veined eyes.

I eyed her sourly. 'Thanks for the message,' I said coolly, and I walked past her, along the lobby, and down the stairs to the street. I turned left and was annoyed to see Star still trailing along in my wake. 'No need for you to come,' I snapped, looking away and seeing the back of Lizzie's curly-haired head and her large body in the frame of the Bella Vista's ground-floor window.

'I'd like to.' She bit her lip. 'If that's all right.'

I wondered what her game was. 'It's a free country.'

Star was babbling away as we walked downhill. 'It's so great you stayed the night with Granny,' she was saying. 'She never sleeps alone in the house; it's one of her things.

I told her there's no need to keep coming, but she says she wants the house to know it still belongs to her. She's a bit odd like that. So thank you.'

'I owed a favour to Johnny,' I said shortly. 'And she paid me five guineas.'

'Come on, Rosie. I can't bear this.'

I stopped and faced her. I had never seen Star looking so miserable. 'I don't know what the matter is,' I said. 'You've told me what you think of me. What else is there to say?'

'But I don't think that. Of course I don't.' She ran a hand through her hair. 'I mean, I saw you kissing Geoff —'

'That was nothing,' I snapped, blushing. I'd been trying to forget about that, and my less-than-perfect behaviour last night. 'Anyway, *you* walked away from *me*. In the bathroom. And then you told everyone I'd tried to molest you.'

'Of course I walked away from you!' she said heatedly. 'I was shit-scared.'

'Of me?' I said sarcastically, although I felt I was starting to understand her, and the fears that ran a wild river through her mind.

'Not of you.' She leaned against the railing hanging over the angle of the promenade. 'I need to tell you something.'

I formed another glob of sarcasm on my tongue, but was unable to flick it out. I sighed. 'Go on then.'

'It's about . . . remember a few days ago, when we were talking about secrets?' She glanced in my direction to see that I did. 'I had this friend last year, you see. She was part of our gang.'

'Gill?' I said, and she looked up, surprised. 'Johnny said

you'd had a row. And Geoff . . .' But I didn't want to mention what Geoff had implied.

'It wasn't a row. We . . . well, we did things together.' She peered up at me. 'Do you understand?'

I attempted a cool nod, while her last sentence ran hot rings through my mind. *Did things together. Did things. Together.* 'Um . . . I mean . . . Yes.' I felt myself blushing. 'Yes, I do.'

'I'm telling you because I owe you. If anyone found out . . .' She shuddered. 'As it was, they started saying things. Suspecting. We couldn't handle it; neither of us could. She moved away, up to London. The next week I got together with Johnny, and I thought that was the end of it.'

I thought of Gill; I wondered what she looked like, and what they'd done together. An obscure, unpleasant sensation – jealousy, maybe – wriggled through my gut. I smiled as if I was used to hearing such revelations. 'So why are you scared now?'

'Because you moved in. And . . .' She turned her huge eyes on me. 'And we were friends. And I knew that . . . that to you it was all just a funny game. You were kissing Geoff, and I thought you would tell everyone about us, and I've been so scared, Rosie, of you finding out the truth.'

I frowned at her. 'What, the truth about you and Gill?'

'No,' she said, almost wearily. 'The truth that . . . that I think . . . For God's sake, I think I'm in love with you, all right?'

She turned and moved rapidly down the hill, clamping her arms across her chest, and I stared, stunned, before chasing after her.

'Wait!'

'It's okay.' She was at the kerb, looking left and right before hurrying across the road. 'You don't have to say anything. I owed you an explanation. That's all.'

'Star –'

'It's this way.' She pointed across the road. 'He's just down here, beside the pier, apparently. The chap said he'd be looking out for us.'

'Listen to me.'

But she was already darting beside a coach parked on the promenade. I followed her, and found myself in the middle of a rambunctious works outing, a driver in a braided cap attempting to herd them all. 'Four o'clock!' he was bawling. 'And if any of you sods're late, I'm leaving you here!'

The crowd laughed and heckled him. 'Don't have too many pints of mild, Jack!' shouted one, a plump blonde woman in lashings of make-up. When she saw us she yelled backwards, 'Out the way for the girlies, you lot!' She turned to me and winked.

I weaved hurriedly after Star through the bunch of people as they argued with each other about whether they ought to go straight to the pub when it opened or down to the fun park first. 'I want a donkey ride!' called one, to hoots of laughter. By the time I emerged, Star was walking down the steps to the concrete walkway running alongside the abandoned arches built into the promenade wall.

'Please wait,' I called, but she was already talking to a man wearing overalls leaning against the seafront wall and smoking. She pointed at me as I approached, refusing to meet my gaze.

'You Rosie?' The man put out his cigarette on the wall behind. 'Friend of yours, is he, this fella?'

'Um . . . yes, sort of.' I didn't care about Dockie right now. I cared only about what Star had just said to me.

He indicated the rusted lock hanging loose from the door. 'Kids broke in a while ago, coming in to get up to all sorts. That's how he got in. Thing is, kids're all gone by morning, but this old fella's still here.' The man shrugged. 'I told him I'd call the police, but he ain't bothered. Just said he won't leave till he's spoken to you.'

'I'll be off then,' murmured Star, toeing herself backwards, away from us.

'No.' I glared at her. 'Wait for me.'

She allowed the sunlight to pepper her lashes until, finally, her eyes met mine. Her tongue fumbled on syllables. 'D-d-d . . .' she began, and I wondered how I'd never noticed her stutter before. Finally, she shrugged and said a simple 'Okay', before heading towards the horizon.

I watched her go, my heart somersaulting in my ribs as the man squeaked open the door for me. 'Be careful in there, all right?'

'Careful?' I said vaguely, my head still with Star and her hunched form padding across the sand. I watched her as I stepped across the threshold of the arch.

'Don't get spooked.'

And then the door swung shut behind me, and I was alone, with just the dim light entering through the frosted windows either side of the doorway to guide me.

The air smelled old and musty. There was the sharp tang of damp, and of ancient wet bricks. As my pupils slowly adjusted, I made out sandy stone slabs on the floor and a curving ceiling overhead. I took a step forwards, narrowing my eyes to see the ground, and, from nowhere, loomed a bare foot.

I stopped, my heart lurching. The bare foot continued upwards; it belonged to a leg abandoned just above the knee.

I gasped, and as the rest of the tunnel lifted from the gloom I saw ten – no, twenty – bodies, some sprawled on the ground, others collapsed against each other. Glassy eyes stared; gashed mouths beseeched, and it took me three terrifying seconds to realize that the eyes were glassy because they were made of glass, and the gashed mouths had been painted on, and that I was, of course, in a store-room of shop-floor mannequins.

I breathed out heavily. My heart was still going like the clappers, and as I waited for it to calm down I saw the false moustaches and wigs, mildewed dresses and red nails. It looked as if the window displays of several boutiques had got together for an epic battle. Bodies lay across the width of the tunnel; others, somehow remaining upright, loomed at me from their positions against the slimy tunnel walls.

I couldn't see the end of the archway; the faint light from the windows didn't reach that far, and so I took a ginger step forwards and nearly skidded on a black wig. 'Dockie? It's me, Rosie.'

There was no answer. I continued onwards. I passed a bald dummy with the faint outlines of spidery lashes, clothed in mouldering rags, the flat shape of a guitar glued to her hands. There was another in what seemed to be the soggy serge of a Great War uniform.

At the end of the tunnel to my right, a further tunnel doubled back towards the seafront. I turned into it. 'Dockie!' I called. 'Where are you?'

The windows at the end were almost obscured with nailed boards. I inched forwards, and stumbled on a body lying on the ground. My breath froze in my throat, but it was only another mannequin, this time in a dirty robe, its arms stuck straight out in front of it. A headdress lay trampled into the ground beside it. Its glass eyes were missing, and it gaped at me blindly.

'Dockie?'

I remained where I was, hardly able to see a thing but for dark outlines in the gloom. I had never wanted to be anywhere else quite so much as I had now. 'Dockie?' I said again, fearfully. Perhaps I had missed him; perhaps he was back in the other arch.

'Rosie.'

My name was a sob. I whirled around. There were bodies everywhere: on the floor, against the walls; there was even one slumped on the steps in front of the nailed-shut windows beside a boarded door.

I narrowed my eyes at the body and then said tentatively, 'Dockie?'

'Rosie,' it murmured, and I rushed towards him, the faint light picking him out, his face in his hands, rocking back and forth on the step. I cast aside a large piece of plasterboard and crouched on the ground below him. I held out my hand and he gripped it, hard. 'Dockie,' I whispered. 'It's okay. I'm here. It's Rosie.'

'Rosie.' He squeezed the life from my fingers with his calloused hand.

I breathed out. 'You didn't go back to Dublin.'

He shook his head. In a cracked voice he said, 'I walked along the beach. I saw the number above the arch, number 231. The lock was open. I came in, and ... and I saw ... I saw *that*.'

He pointed with one flailing finger, and I looked around, expecting to see him indicating one of the silent bodies lining the walls. Instead, he was pointing at the plasterboard I'd just tossed aside.

'What is it?' I reached over, almost toppling, and picked up the board. It was half of a sign, its paint mostly worn away, faded and cracked by damp, but still readable. It said:

SON & BRAY'S HALL O

'I saw this,' he said shakily, 'and I remembered.'

I frowned at the sign. *Bray*, I thought. 'Remembered what?'

He took a wheezy breath. 'Everything. Everything returned, as if it had never been away.'

'And now?' I put the plasterboard down, but more reverently this time, leaning it against the wall.

'I still remember.' He gripped my fingers harder. 'But I am afraid, my dear Rosie, that when I leave this place I will forget again. Perhaps it is just being inside these walls that has brought it back. That's why I need you here, do you understand? I will tell you who I am. You must be my memory, Rosie; you must give me back to myself, in case I forget.'

'I thought you ...' I paused. 'You told me you didn't want to remember.'

'When I was born on the docks . . .' He sighed. 'I wanted to forget. I wanted to begin again; a new life, if you will. Every flash of my past was ignored, every hint of my previous existence that I could have chased, that I could have worked on, I let rust away, until nothing was left.'

'But Frank?' I said. 'You told me he betrayed you.'

Dockie nodded. 'A lonely man, Frank. No family, few friends. He wanted – no, he needed somebody to care for. And there I was, as vulnerable as a newborn baby, believing everything he chose to tell me. Or not tell me.'

I breathed softly. 'Do you mean he knew who you were all those years, and never told you? That's awful.'

'He saw the truth in the newspapers; he clipped the stories out, perhaps intending to show me one day, perhaps later putting them out of his mind. I think he convinced himself that it was best all round, that I really had wanted to escape my past. And you see, Rosie, in a way he was right, because I sensed, deep down, that I did not want to know who I was. It seemed easier, under the circumstances, to start anew.'

I thought of myself, frantically packing a bag and running away to Castaway House. 'I think I understand,' I said quietly.

'I have had a good life, Rosie. I want you to know that. I have been happy. Simple, uncomplicated. Perhaps that was all I'd been looking for.'

'What about Frank?' I asked.

'Without Frank, I would have died.' He shrugged. 'He also allowed a great injustice to stand uncorrected, but he was not to know that. And now you must help me to apologize.'

'What injustice? And who must you apologize to?'

'To so many people.' He shook his head. 'But firstly, and most importantly, to my wife.'

My brain whirred. 'Your wife?'

He nodded. 'Clara, my wife.' He gestured to the plaster-board. 'My name – my real name, of course – is Alexander Bray.'

'What?'

He nodded again, surer this time. 'My name is Alexander Bray, and Castaway House is my home.'

I thought of two people standing in velvet, and I shook my head. 'Alexander Bray's dead.'

'Not any more.' Dockie creaked up to standing. 'Not any more.'

It couldn't be true. Of course it wasn't true. He was a mad old man, and he'd got hold of the name some-how and had convinced himself that a fantasy was the truth.

'Maybe we should – um – talk to a doctor.'

He whirled around and beetled his brows. 'I thought you were my friend, Rosie.'

'I am! I just meant . . . perhaps you're not well. You've spent all night in this creepy old place, for a start.'

'You said Clara was the landlady of Castaway.' He jabbed a finger at me. 'Where is she now?'

'Er . . . er . . . Paris.'

'Then I need you to help me. You must help me. Now, more than ever.'

'Okay, okay,' I said, holding up my palms. 'What do you want me to do?'

'She will be on the telephone, no doubt. I need you to

find her number, call her and inform her that her husband has returned. I shall reimburse you, of course.'

He walked past me through the tunnel, stepping over the body on its back, its robes adrift. I hurried after him.

'You might forget,' I said hopefully. 'You know, tomorrow. Or in five minutes. All of this . . . memory stuff, it might go.'

'That is why I need you. You are to be my memory. You will tell me who I am. Agreed?'

He was still shuffling down the tunnel, wincing and coughing. 'I will,' I said, already deciding that I wouldn't. I wondered where on earth he'd got the idea he was Mrs Bray's husband.

I followed him through the forest of mannequins, up one tunnel and down the next, and finally we emerged, squinting in the chilly sunlight, beside the beach. The man from the council gave Dockie a ticking off, to which he listened not one jot. I spotted Star standing on the beach, facing the sea; Dockie, I realized, was claiming to be her grandfather.

'I have to talk to my friend,' I said in a breathy rush. 'Before we do anything else, I must talk to her.'

He nodded and tapped his head while muttering, 'I am Alexander Bray. Alexander Bray.' He eyed me. 'Speak to your friend, my dear. Go.'

Star sensed me coming, and turned to watch me padding across the sand. 'I've been thinking,' she said, with a fake cheerful tone plastered over her deathly pale face. 'Let's just forget what I said. You know. Totally hungover, talking nonsense . . . I mean, we're still friends, right?'

My head was spinning with Dockie's fantastical claim.

'Yes, yes, of course,' I said distractedly, and she looked rather taken aback. 'But listen, something else has cropped up.'

'What's that?' She frowned, flummoxed.

I indicated Dockie, still pacing the area outside the arch and tapping his head. 'See that man over there?'

'Yes, the crazy old chap who called me Clara. What about him?'

'You know I told you he'd lost his memory? Well, it's returned.' I bit my lip. 'The only thing is, he's insisting that his name is Alexander Bray.'

'What?' She stared at me. 'It can't be. That's my grandfather's name.'

'I know. He's saying that Clara – your grandmother – is his wife, and that he owns Castaway House.'

She shook her head. 'My grandfather's dead. He died before I was born.'

'Well, I tried to tell him that, but he wouldn't listen.'

'Then he really is crazy.' She puffed out air with her lips. 'But he knows Granny? How could he know her?'

'Perhaps a fan? You know, from your grandmother's actress days?'

'Yes, maybe.' She nodded slowly. 'I ought to tell her. She might know who he is, if he's been . . . God, following her or something.'

'Okay. Let's deposit him somewhere and then you can talk to her.'

'You're on.' As we walked back across the sand I felt her relax, perhaps in the knowledge that I hadn't flounced off at her revelation. But there was something else here too, and it was only as we reached the concrete walkway and shook sand from our shoes that I realized what it was: the balance of power had shifted between us.

'Incredible,' Dockie was murmuring to Star as we approached. 'You look so like my wife.'

'Not that much,' I said, and then added rapidly, 'I mean – that is – maybe she did, once. But Mrs – I mean, your wife . . . she must be much older.'

He frowned at the sea-rippled sand. 'Ah. I hadn't thought of that.' He brightened and smiled at us. 'And now, back to Castaway House so you can make that telephone call.'

'Yes,' I said, glancing at Star. 'I was wondering: it might be better for you to wait for us somewhere.' I looked about the beach, as if the answer might be under the shadow of the broken pier.

'I shall wait at the house.' He limped ahead of us towards the steps that led up to the promenade. 'I still have that little room. I will stay there while you telephone my wife, and you shall tell me what she says in consequence.'

'Of course, she probably won't be in,' I said to his back, as he wheezed up the steps. 'Or – I don't know – she'll be ex-directory, or something.'

'I know you will do your best, Rosie. I trust you.'

'I will,' I said weakly, turning to pull a face at Star.

At the top, Dockie gripped the rail and looked over the seafront. 'It must be over forty years. I remember all this, you know. A penny to go on to the pier, the Punch and Judy man in his striped booth. Oh, those shows were a treat.' He chuckled, and then turned towards the huge climb of Gaunt's Cliff.

We walked slowly up the hill, Dockie having to pause for breath every so often. Star walked behind, not wanting to get involved. I wondered how this was going to end. No doubt there were authorities who dealt with this sort of thing. I hoped there wouldn't be straitjackets or injections. I didn't like the thought of Dockie in a pea-green room with nurses in masks holding him down as a doctor in glinting spectacles approached, telling him this wouldn't hurt a bit.

Suddenly he said, 'Her name – is it still Bray?'

'Um . . .' I glanced at Star, who shrugged. 'Yes. Yes, I think so.'

'Then she has not remarried. I imagined she would have. That would be bigamy, I suppose. Or have I been declared officially dead?' He shook his head and, as if musing on this for the first time, murmured, 'I suppose this will be rather a shock for her, after forty years.'

Star rolled her eyes. We crossed the road opposite the Bella Vista. Dr Feathers was back in position sitting by the window; next to him was Lizzie, talking volubly at her father, who appeared not to be listening. As we approached he pointed a trembling finger in our direction, and I smiled and waved.

However, he did not smile or wave back. He turned, and appeared to be speaking to someone in the room behind him. Lizzie switched her gaze to the window, and a second later Mrs Hale's dim face appeared behind her. They were all looking in our direction. Mrs Hale leaned in between her father and her sister, knocked on the window and motioned for us to stay where we were.

'What's going on?' said Star, arriving beside me on the pavement.

'I have no idea.' I looked at Dockie, who was standing, transfixed, staring into the window.

Mrs Hale appeared in the doorway to the guest house. She hurried down the steps and along the path. There, she clung on to the rotting pillar beside the empty gateway, stared at Dockie and said in a hoarse whisper, 'Tell me it's not you.'

I flicked a glance at Star. Dockie was still staring in through the window, but finally he tore his eyes away, looked at Mrs Hale and said, 'I beg your pardon, my memory is not what it was. Do I know you?'

She shook her head faintly, one hand to her mouth. 'You can't be,' she croaked. 'You can't be.'

Dockie pointed towards the window. 'I recognize *him*,' he said, indicating Dr Feathers, who was still peering out, talking wildly to Lizzie, who was also staring. 'But for the life of me I cannot remember who he is.'

'It's D—' I began, but Dockie cut me off with a wagging finger.

'No, Rosie, do not inform me. It will be better if I remember alone. And I shall. I shall remember.' He turned and walked towards Castaway House, shaking his head and muttering.

Mrs Hale was backing up the path. 'I must . . .' she began. 'I have to . . .' And she turned and went up the steps to the guest house, still glancing back.

I looked at Star and she looked at me, and, silently, we followed Dockie up the steps of Castaway and on to the covered porch. He pointed up at the stained glass over the door. 'Art nouveau,' he said wonderingly. 'Her name was Viviane. Long white hands. A frail voice. I suppose – yes, I suppose she was my mother.'

'Let's go in,' I said, unlocking the door.

'Absolutely.' He clapped his hands. 'I loved Castaway, you know. More than anyone else, I think. Here we are. The hallway. Oh yes. Here we are.'

As he strode ahead of us into the hall I turned to Star, who shrugged at me helplessly. He stopped at the telephone plinth and shook a pile of coins into his hand. Placing them on top of the A/B box, he said, 'That should be enough. Paris, you said? International Directory Enquiries. Clara Bray, that is her name. I shall await your answer downstairs.'

'I'll do my best,' I said guiltily, hoping Mrs Bray would not come out of her flat at this particular moment.

He put a calloused hand on mine. 'I know you will.' He walked slowly, painfully, towards the end of the hallway and turned to go down the stairs, lifting his hand in a wave.

I looked at the coins he'd left, scattered untidily below the phone, and then, like some haunted animal, I unwillingly lifted my eyes to the blackboard above.

There was no message. My shoulders sank, and at the same time I felt oddly disappointed – as if maybe, after all this time, Mum had decided I wasn't worth the effort.

'Will you come with me?' Star indicated the door to the ground-floor flat, that same uncertain quaver on her lips. 'Tell Granny together; then we'll have done our duty, after all.'

'Yes.' I shook myself free of the looming dread that blank blackboard gave me. 'Of course.'

Star knocked, and Mrs Bray answered promptly, in full make-up, a dogtooth jacket and the stilettos of yesterday. 'There you are,' she said. 'Have you sorted out whatever unholy mess you promised to untangle?'

This was directed at Star, who simply said, 'We need to talk to you.'

Mrs Bray raised an eyebrow, stood back from the door and said, 'I'm in the garden. I telephoned Bradley's earlier for some groceries. Perhaps you could bring some tea out to the terrace.'

Without waiting for a reply, she turned and marched through the open French windows into the conservatory and from there disappeared into the garden. Star turned to me. 'That's Granny,' she said. 'On her terms or not at all.'

I followed Star into the sitting room, where she went to the kitchenette and filled the kettle at the sink. 'It's okay,' she said. 'I can manage.'

'I just wanted to . . .' She looked up at me as I spoke, and I took her hand. 'I don't know, say that everything's going to be all right.'

A hint of a blush spread across her cheeks. 'I wish I'd never said anything.'

'I'm glad you did,' I said, and her blush deepened. I squeezed her fingers and then left her making the tea. As I walked back out of the room towards the conservatory, an idiotic grin widened my face.

The two doors of the conservatory had been propped open with stone flowerpots, letting a breeze in that rippled the neatly made bedcovers. There were two wicker chairs in the conservatory, and a glass-topped table. I walked through it, and out on to the open terrace that looked over the abandoned garden. There, Mrs Bray was seated at the ironwork table. As I came out she turned, held a hand to her forehead so she could see, and said, 'Oh, it's you.'

I sat down opposite her. 'I had a very strange night,' I said.

She switched her gaze straight through me. 'Did you?' she said archly, taking a pull on her cigarette. 'I slept like a baby.'

'I noticed.' I ground my knuckles into my fist, determined not to be intimidated. 'Somebody in the room was whistling in my ear.'

'How odd,' remarked Mrs Bray. 'Are you sure you didn't dream it?'

'I didn't sleep a wink,' I snapped.

'Until you took one of my pills.' She eyed me thoughtfully. 'You forgot to screw the lid back on. I do notice everything, you see.'

I leaned forwards on the table. 'Then you must have noticed the chest. The lid? It flew open by itself.' She gazed, as if bored, in my direction, but I saw one eyelid flicker slightly. 'You knew all this would happen, didn't you? That's why you wanted me to sleep in the flat.'

Mrs Bray's look could have put out a fire. Icily, she said, 'You took the money, didn't you?'

My guts wobbled at that look, but all the same I growled, 'Yes, and now I think I was bloody cheap at the price.'

My landlady looked as if she was whipping up a retort, but there was a clanging sound from the conservatory and

Star emerged on to the terrace, unsteadily holding a tray in two hands. She put it down between us, and tea slopped from the pot on to the saucers piled in front of it.

'You don't need to say.' Star flung herself dramatically into a chair. 'I know Louise would have done a better job.'

'I wasn't going to say that at all, my dear.' Mrs Bray picked up the pot. 'How's your glandular fever?'

'What?' Star frowned. I widened my eyes at her and she nodded. 'Oh. Oh. Yes. Much better. I think it's just a touch of – um – tonsillitis.'

Mrs Bray poured out cups of weak tea and handed them round. 'The thing is, I'm so terribly ashamed that a grandchild of mine could be such an awful liar.'

'I'm not lying,' said Star in an affronted tone. 'I feel like death.'

'Then you're lucky you've such a good friend in Miss Churchill.'

They both turned to look at me. I reddened, and looked out at the untidy heap of the garden, the ferns trailing over the broken paving stones, the hedges hiding what I knew from my view from above were bird-muck-spattered benches, the overgrown path leading to the abandoned pond and the stone storehouse. 'We ought to tell her,' I muttered.

'Tell me what?' Mrs Bray shifted slightly on her chair.

'Oh, it's ridiculous,' said Star. 'It's just that Rosie's met this old man, a bit gaga, you know. Says he's lost his memory. He's renting a room in the basement; moved in last week.'

'Causing trouble, I suppose.' Mrs Bray sniffed. 'I presume Mr Clark can deal with it. It's what I pay him for.'

'It's not that,' I said. 'You see, this morning I found Dockie – that's what he calls himself – in one of the old arches on the beach, surrounded by all these dummies –'

'Dummies?' she said sharply. 'What sort of dummies?'

'Oh, I don't know.' I shrugged and thought of the mannequin in the dirty robe, another in uniform. 'I suppose like a waxworks.'

'I see.' Her lips twisted thoughtfully. 'Continue.'

'Um – well . . . He's now saying he's recovered his memory, and that he's – er – well – that he's your husband.'

Mrs Bray stopped, in the middle of sipping her tea. Her eyes burned into mine. 'I beg your pardon?'

'He told me his name was Alexander Bray and that you were his wife.' I glanced at Star. 'He's downstairs now. In the basement.'

Mrs Bray glanced sharply towards the basement well jutting out below the rim of the terrace, as if a phantom might be about to rise up from it. Her teacup rattled uncontrollably on its saucer. She put it down with a clatter on the table and held a hand to her chest. Her face appeared to have lost all its colour. I wondered if we hadn't just done something irredeemably awful.

'It can't be,' she whispered. 'It can't be.'

'We think he might be a crazed fan,' said Star. She turned to me. 'But then – didn't Mrs Hale next door seem to recognize him just now?'

'Please.' Mrs Bray held up a hand to silence us. She got to her feet and walked unsteadily into the conservatory, her silhouette disappearing into the bedroom.

'I thought she'd laugh,' whispered Star, a slight look of horror on her face.

I looked at the chair Mrs Bray had vacated, thinking hard. I pictured her going to the chest and lifting up the hinge, taking out the face-down photograph within. 'Your grandfather – he is dead, isn't he?'

She shrugged. 'That's what I've always been told. Granny never talks about him. She doesn't even keep photographs.'

'Except the one in the chest.'

Star looked up at me, her fingers to her mouth. '*Shit,*' she said. 'That's the . . . you'll think I'm mad, but I call it the haunted chest. The lid of it won't stay down. Even if you pull the catch closed.'

'That happened to me last night,' I said excitedly. 'Scared me half to death.'

'Maybe the photograph . . .' began Star. 'Perhaps my grandfather's haunting her.'

'How can he be haunting her if he's alive?'

Star motioned me to lower my voice. I turned. Mrs Bray had reappeared in the doorway to the conservatory, carrying her long cigarette holder. She walked slowly back to her chair, sat down and fitted a cigarette from her purse into the end of the holder. She handed me a silver block of a lighter, and I sparked up a flame for her. Her hands were still shaking. She looked at least ten years older.

'I thought Grandfather was dead,' said Star quietly.

Mrs Bray looked at her with her coal-dark eyes. Eventually she said, 'Your grandfather, my dear girl, was not Alexander Bray.'

Star frowned. 'I don't understand.'

'My husband was not your mother's father. Clear?' Mrs Bray looked swiftly at me and then back at Star. 'You mustn't tell your mother. She'll be devastated at being a bastard. All her progeny ill-begotten. How many is it now? Five? Six?'

'Five, just as it's been for years,' said Star. 'So you mean you . . . that is . . . ?'

'Really, my dear, I thought you were a woman of the world,' said Mrs Bray. 'I imagined it wouldn't take too long to work it out.'

Star's mouth hung open. 'So who was he? My real grandfather?'

The truth tumbled to my lips. 'Robert Carver,' I said, before I could help myself. 'It's Robert Carver, isn't it?'

Mrs Bray's eyes flared. She expelled smoke into the sunshine and then nodded.

Star turned to me. 'You mean, the writing in your kitchen? And the picture? R. C.?' She looked at her grandmother. 'And you're telling me now?'

'I'm sure you've had your secrets, my dear.' Mrs Bray eyed Star thoughtfully. I saw Star's cheeks bloom red. Mrs Bray waved her cigarette holder; a plume of smoke wafted towards the basement. 'But anyway, with all this . . . Of course, the story was fairly famous at the time. It was in all the papers, you know; even the national press got hold of it. Not that anybody knew I was expecting, thank goodness. Funny, how your mother never had an inkling. That's partly why I had her grow up in France, where nobody gave a fig.'

I took a breath. 'The newspapers,' I said, and they both looked at me. 'When I first saw him, Dockie, he was talking about newspaper clippings, and how they'd set him off remembering. He said he'd put them somewhere safe.'

I frowned, as an odd image occurred to me: a clipped-together pile of receipts at the bottom of a bag, curiously yellowed with age.

I scraped back my chair with a gasp.

'I didn't think,' I muttered. 'I was too distracted . . . oh, God.' And I ran back through the conservatory and the bedroom to Mrs Bray's sitting room, where this morning I'd dropped a flutter of what I'd imagined were shop receipts on to the floor.

They were still scattered all over the place, and as I crawled about the room picking them up I wondered how I could have mistaken them, these newspaper clippings that were the key to Dockie's soul, the story Frank had hidden from him all those years ago, the articles that had briefly fired the engine of his memory and sent him all the way here, to Castaway House.

As I gathered them I scanned each one, and the news they contained stunned me. I piled them all into my hands, smoothing them flat again, and then hurried back on to the terrace, attempting to absorb the astonishing information within them. Mrs Bray and Star looked up as I came in. 'He had these,' I said, passing them over. 'Is it true? What it says in there?'

Mrs Bray spread a dry finger across the crackling newsprint. Her eyelashes fluttered as she nodded. She bit her lip, and if I hadn't been so sure of the sort of person she was, I would have sworn she was holding back tears.

'What do they say?' asked Star, and Mrs Bray handed them to her. Star looked over them and murmured to herself, 'Oh my God.'

Her grandmother sighed. 'I'm going to tell you,' she

said, her hand fluttering as she rested the cigarette holder on the ashtray. 'I think it's about time you knew what happened between my husband and Robert Carver. You need to know, after all, so we can decide what to do next.'

'Can Rosie stay?' asked Star.

Mrs Bray looked at me, and I had the odd sensation that she understood me, more than anybody else ever had before. 'Yes,' she said. 'She may.'

Star handed the newspaper clippings back to me, and I folded them into my lap. Mrs Bray gripped the arms of her chair, as if preparing herself for an uncomfortable journey, and began to tell us a story.

14

1924

I watched Clara Bray sleeping, as the dawn tipped salmon pink over the sky.

She was naked, one arm slung over her face. I had pulled the curtains back a notch to be able to see her properly, and took her in, one inch at a time. It had been hot in the night, and she had pushed the covers down to her waist. The locket she wore round her neck dangled on the pillow. Its engraving, I had come to realize, was of a bird amid foliage, and was quite beautiful. I supported myself on one elbow and studied her small breasts, the soft swelling of her stomach. Our love-making was always dark-edged, of necessity; I knew her body by touch, but not by sight.

Breathing gently, I eased the covers away from her waist and looked within, at the flat planes of her hip bones, and the mound of dark hair that continued to startle me with its raw beauty. The French photographs, passed round under the desks at school, had never shown me that.

She snorted, and shifted in the bed, and I dropped the covers back and assumed a just-woken pose. I rolled sleepily around as she blinked awake, and smiled at her. I kissed her and she sighed.

'Good morning,' I whispered.

'Wh-what time is it?' she mumbled. She blinked again, and saw the sunrise curling through the gap in the velvet curtains. 'Oh, fuck. Why didn't you wake me?'

She scrambled for her robe. 'I've just woken,' I lied, as her body disappeared inside its sheath of green silk. 'It's still early.'

'Housemaids get up at five,' she hissed. This had been the pattern of her moods: the daring night-time escapades up the stairs, the giving over of the future to the joy of the moment, and then afterwards, as her guilt set in, the foul temper and the paralysing fear. Never mind that Alec might have gone to her room in the night and found it empty – it was the morning after when she was afraid.

'They probably know anyway,' I murmured. 'Servants know everything.'

It was just as well that she was too wrapped up in herself to listen to me. 'And the garden party,' she muttered. 'They'll be waking me at seven.'

She left without a backwards glance. I listened hard, but could not make out the creak of the stairs as she went down; she was practised, she said, from her years padding about backstage, but I wondered how many other stairs, in her previous life, she had crept down, leaving somebody behind, sleeping alone.

I lay back on my pillows, working up a feeling of elation. I had obtained what I wanted: I had become Clara's lover, and knew her as intimately as any man ever could, so I could not understand why a sense of triumph was so hard to come by. I took my nightshirt out from under my pillow and pulled it on, the better for decorum when Scone entered with my tea and toast, and then went to the window and hooked the curtains back, looking out at the garden, where I'd sat by the pond with Clara that day, never dreaming she would allow me to do to her all the things I had.

Perhaps my sense of anticlimax was due to the way that, if she did not fall asleep first, she leaped out of bed the minute the deed was done, leaving me in the soggy cool of the bedclothes and the sense of having been discarded in some way. Maybe I felt some residual guilt over deceiving Alec, although consciously I knew that their marriage was over in all but name. My robe was hanging over the chair; I pulled it on, put my hand in its pocket and found the newly familiar square metal tin, shaking out a cigarette. I lit it, standing by the window. The smoke smothered my lungs, but once I had inhaled a few times they adjusted, and I enjoyed the way the tobacco curdled my brain. I leaned my forehead against the cool of the pane.

Beyond the garden wall, on the other side of the lane, the fields that stretched to the cliff were about to be built upon. Much of the grass had already been churned over into uneven furrows of dried, caked earth, and canes had been stuck into the ground all the way along to the end of the field. Bungalows, according to the local gossip, to house the town's expanding population, stretching all the way from here to Shanker along the coast.

There was a knock on the door. 'Come in,' I said, and the smoke and the tiredness lifted my voice to a pre-pubescent squeak. I coughed, a nasty taste in my mouth.

Agnes entered with my tray. She was looking at the bed,

and jumped when she saw me by the window. 'Oh! I didn't know you was up.'

'It's a beautiful sunrise,' I said, indicating the window and trying to hide my own shock – not only that it was Agnes, and not Scone, who had nearly caught me in a state of *déshabillé*, but that it must also be later than I'd thought. Clara had done well to leave when she had. 'Seems a shame to waste it.'

'Yes, sir,' she said, disinterestedly, placing my tray on the stand, and I realized that sunrise to Agnes would be associated with hard work. 'Mr Scone was busy, so I said I'd take up your morning tray. He said all right, seeing as how I been so trustworthy.'

'Well, naturally,' I said, wondering if it should not be more the case that I was the trustworthy one. 'By the way, have you found another position?'

She shook her head. 'Not yet. It's all right. I can afford to take my time. My mum'll take me in for a bit. There's a bit more money now my brother's working.'

'It's such a shame,' I mused. 'After all that bother before, to then have to leave anyway.'

'Oh no. It's much better this way. Mrs Bray's written us all good references. I'm going to go for head housemaid.' She glanced at the door, adding in a low voice, 'And somewhere I won't have to wear a cap.'

'I see,' I said. I had overheard the female servants grumbling before about the cap situation; I expected they saw it as a mark of their servitude.

'By the way, sir, the reason I asked if I could take your tray up, is – well . . .' She looked again at the door, one ear cocked for noise. 'D'you remember you was asking about Sally that time?'

'Oh!' I said, startled. The events of the past few weeks had pushed all thoughts of other people from my mind. Since Clara had begun entwining her feet with mine under the table, digging her toes into the hollow of my ankle as the servants moved implacably around, the idea of the missing parlourmaid had vanished just as the girl herself had. 'I mean, I do, vaguely.'

She jerked a hand into her apron pocket and brought out what had been a small oblong of paper, torn in two. 'I don't know if you're still interested,' she said quietly, 'but see, Harriet was cleaning out the library yesterday, and she found this in the waste-paper bin. She comes to me and says, "That Sally that done a runner, wasn't her surname Trent?" And I says, "Yes it was," and she gives me this and asks, what do I think then?'

I took the torn pieces from her. Since the imminent sale of Castaway had been announced, and with it the fact that all the servants were to be let go, there had been a looser atmosphere to the house. I had heard uproarious laughter bubbling up from the kitchen, and the indiscreet passing on of gossip had been much more pronounced. Thankfully, I had neither heard nor seen evidence yet that they knew about Clara and me, no stifled giggles or side-long glances. Perhaps, despite my statement of earlier, Clara's whipcrack speed at stealing in and out of my bed had indeed fooled everybody.

It seemed as if the torn scraps had once formed an envelope – empty, but with Alec's name on the front, and on the back a return address: *Mrs. B. Trent, Draker's Farm, Petwick Lane, Petwick.*

I looked at it. 'Are you sure this is Sally's mother's address?'

'I'm sure that's Sally's surname, and I think she talked about growing up on a farm.' Agnes frowned. 'I know it's not very useful, but you was asking me if we'd heard from her, and I did say if I could help you out I would.'

'Thank you.' I pocketed the torn envelope into my dressing gown. 'But of course, if her mother wrote to Al— to Mr Bray – all I have to do is ask him.'

'Yes, sir.' Her eyes fixed on the tray. 'You could do.'

As I looked at her, I realized something. 'You knew,' I said. 'Didn't you? You knew about . . . about the *affaire.*'

She blushed scarlet. 'He told you then,' she said. 'I didn't expect him to tell no one. I thought it was his little secret.'

The way she said that showed me exactly what she thought of my cousin. 'That's why you were scared of sleeping in Sally's old room, isn't it?' I said. 'You thought he might . . . well. Take advantage of you.'

'He used to sneak up the back stairs.' Agnes pursed her lips. 'Sally told me all about it. She thought he was in love with her; said he was going to marry her. Then one day she vanishes. Snap.' She snapped her fingers for effect.

'What happened to her?'

'I told you before, I ain't never heard from her since.' She shrugged. 'But as you said, most likely Sir will know.'

I patted my gown pocket. 'Thank you,' I said. 'Thank you, Agnes.'

She nodded. 'I like you, Mr Carver. You're much nicer than them other two.'

At breakfast Clara darted about, bright and clipped, barely glancing at me. All week she had been preparing manically: meeting Mrs Pennyworth, chattering on the telephone in the study to suppliers, the delivery boys scooting down the area steps, crates piled high in their arms. She left the room almost as soon as I'd sat down, saying she had to fly into town to catch Bradley's as soon as it opened, and I nodded and smiled and read the news-paper, and tried to pretend I did not long to still her in my arms and kiss her eyes.

Alec, still undressed, slouched into the room and slumped into his chair as I folded back the last page of the paper. 'Morning,' I said, and he mumbled a reply and poured himself a large cup of coffee. He had lost weight recently, and his skin looked old and grey. It occurred to me that it had been a long time since I'd seen the relaxed, cheerful cousin I remembered. Every time I saw him my conscience was pricked, although I was sure he could have no idea about Clara and me. Alec was not the sort to suf-fer in silence. 'Hangover?'

He glared at me, red-eyed, and drank his coffee. 'Aren't we smug this morning?' he said bitterly.

'Not at all,' I said cheerfully. 'Got a touch of a headache myself. Drinking Scotch with old Feathers next door.'

'Well, as long as you haven't any real problems.' He smeared butter on to his toast and crunched into it, send-ing crumbs flying.

I resisted the urge to point out to him that Alec's ver-sion of a 'real problem' was having to sell Castaway, get rid of his servants and abandon his life of leisure, none of which had ever been written in my stars, and never would be. Scone replaced the coffee pot and I nodded my thanks.

'I heard Uncle Edward found you a job in town,' I said, tucking into my sausage and egg.

'Working in finance.' Alec uttered the words with such loathing he might as well have been talking of gutting fish. 'And we'll have to stay with the pater temporarily. Which Clara is going to absolutely adore.'

I swallowed on a dry throat. I was trying not to think of Clara and Alec's future in London together. 'Maybe they'll grow to be fond of each other.'

Alec snorted. 'Pigs might fly.'

I leaned across the table. 'Listen,' I said, checking first that Scone and Agnes were not in the room. 'Is anything else bothering you . . . apart from all of the above, that is?'

He shook his head. 'I think I've quite enough to be getting on with, thank you.'

'What about . . .' I wondered how to put this. 'The servants?'

'We're going to get new people in London.' Alec nodded. 'Just one, rather. The flat will be so small it's all we're going to need.'

'No. I mean past servants. Are any of them – I mean . . . ?'

'I have absolutely no idea what you're talking about, Robert. And if you'll excuse me, I have an inheritance to put on the market.'

He whisked up his cup, retied his robe and flapped out of the dining room. I watched him go, then pulled out the torn envelope again. I thought of Agnes, and Sally Trent, and Gina Scott the dead parlourmaid, all of them sleeping in the same room at separate times. I tapped the envelope pieces on the table, and came to a decision.

I pulled on my old suit jacket, the one I had arrived in at the start of summer, and walked into town. The morning was already heavy with heat, and outside the station a queue of taxis reflected the fierce light with their shiny metal bodies. I climbed into the first one, leaned against the leather back of the seat and turned my face to the sun as we trundled away out of town, past the stuccoed villas and the neat redbrick semi-detached houses, bumping over potholes and through a glade of overhanging trees.

I had imagined Draker's Farm to contain a fat pig snuffling in a sty and pails thick with cream. However, as we approached, I remembered the ramshackle farm we had passed before, travelling along this very country lane with the ladies from the painting circle, the first time Clara had opened up a sliver of her heart.

It was into this farm that we turned, along a fenced lane. Two gloomy horses peered out from their paddock, sniffing the air. On the other side, cocoa-coloured cows chewed yellowing grass and turned sad eyes upon us. The air was one of general desolation, not helped by the rickety track we drove along, and the farmhouse now approaching, which looked as if it were missing an entire roof.

'Will you wait here?' I asked the driver as we drew to a halt in front of the house.

He cranked up the brake lever. 'If you pay,' he said, pulling a newspaper from the window ledge and breaking into a tobacco-stained cough.

I got out into a chicken's dust bath, spattering my

trousers. I glared at the birds as they pecked around me, oblivious, and made my way to the door. The roof was not completely gone, I saw now, but many of its tiles were, and the barn beside it looked as if it might fall down at any moment.

The front door was of an ancient, thick wood, possibly oak. There was a bell with a pull, but when I tugged at it no chime emerged. I knocked on the wood, and my knuckles barely made a sound.

'You gotta go round the back way,' I heard a rumbling voice from behind me call. I turned and saw a beefy man in the field next door, manhandling a vicious-looking ploughshare. 'They never answer that one.'

'Thank you,' I said, aware of how timorous my voice sounded. I walked carefully round the side of the farmhouse, resisting the temptation to pick up, petticoat-like, the bottoms of my trousers as I trampled the dusty ground, pursued by curious chickens.

The back door was more modern than the front, but in worse condition. Flakes of faded green paint peeled from the frame, and the glass panels were thick with grime. I knocked. After a while a dark shape appeared, and the latch squeaked back.

A hollow-cheeked woman with grey hair escaping from under a cap looked out. 'Good morning,' I said. 'I'm here to see Mrs Trent. My name's Robert Carver.'

'Whassit about?'

'Her daughter,' I said.

The woman grunted and closed the door. I waited in the full beam of the morning sun, sweating gently, for several minutes until she returned and beckoned me in.

'Wipe yer feet,' she said, and then, as if the thought had just occurred to her, 'Please.'

I wiped my feet on the mat. I was standing in a large kitchen, with roughly plastered walls and dangerously tilting beams overhead. There was a table piled with vegetable peelings at one end and several accounts books at the other, and a cat was sat in the middle. Along one wall was the range, and along another were a stone sink and counter. On a dresser with mismatched crockery stood a crib. Narrow leaded windows let in a minuscule amount of light. I shivered, despite the heat of the day outside.

'Siddown,' said the woman. 'I'll just get missis.'

I sat, abruptly. The cat landed on my lap with a yowl and I pushed it on to the floor. After a while a plump woman with a tatty shawl came into the room. 'All right,' she announced, leaning against the sink and looking down at me. 'You might as well get it over with. What's my bloody Vera done now?'

'I'm sorry?' I said.

'Is she being kicked out the laundry?' The woman picked up a cloth from the floor and threw it into the sink. 'Well, you can tell her from me, she ain't coming back here. I've had enough, all right?'

'It's not Vera,' I said. 'It's about Sally.'

The woman straightened, and frowned at me. 'Sally?'

It only occurred to me now that I might have done irreparable wrong coming here; that the family might already have written the girl out of their lives, and I, coming here to reopen those wounds, would hardly be welcome. 'I – er – I – er . . .' I began.

'What about my Sally?' said the woman. 'And who the flamin' 'eck are you, anyway?'

'Is it him?' I heard a distant voice say, and then feet came thumping down the heavy wooden stairs overhead, and a breathless, untidy, disappointed girl bundled into the room and stared at me.

She hung on the doorpost, her pale eyes lowering, her nose wrinkling, and as I got to my feet I saw the tangled, gingery hair, the freckles blasting her face, the bloom of fresh youth in her cheeks, and now I understood it all, from start to finish and everything in between.

'Sally,' I said. 'You're Sally.'

'I thought it was *him*,' she said, and kicked the doorpost.

Her mother turned to her. 'If it was him, do you think I wouldn't tell you? It ain't going to be him. It's never going to be him, all right?'

'I'm his cousin,' I said, and they looked at me as one. 'I'm Alexander's cousin. Robert Carver.'

The girl took a breath. 'You got a message?'

'I'm sorry,' I said, and saw the sag again in her eyes. 'He doesn't know I'm here.'

'So you found out,' said the mother. 'Well, I hope you can tell him to do right by my girl.'

From the crib standing on the dresser across the room came a sound like a factory whistle. Sally walked towards it and bent over. 'Don't you ever stop crying?'

'They don't,' said her mother, flipping a tea towel over one shoulder.

Sally lifted from the crib a dribbling comma of a baby and joggled it up and down. 'So now you seen her before her father,' she said. 'Pr'aps that'll make him come by, eh?'

She was young, not more than seventeen. 'I didn't know about . . . about the baby,' I said. 'I don't think anybody knows, except for Alec.'

'I didn't tell nobody, except when I run off, 'cause then I was getting so big I couldn't hide it.' With one practised hand, she pulled out a chair at the kitchen table and sat down. 'I didn't even tell *him*. He never noticed, or he pretended not to.'

I sat down too and looked from the girl to her mother. I pulled out the torn envelope and showed it to them. 'Is that what you wrote to him about?' I asked.

Mrs Trent leaned over to look, then turned to the sink and rattled water in the kettle. 'Twice, I written to him now. First time after she was born, then again last week. Course, he don't want to know. I said to her, "That's what Upstairs is like."'

'He's bankrupt,' I said, cringing because Alec's version of poverty was a rich tapestry of wealth compared to Sally Trent's life. 'He's having to sell the house.'

'I don't care about the money,' said Sally. Her mother harrumphed loudly and dumped the kettle on the stove. 'I just want him to visit.'

'I'll speak to him,' I said, aware of how pitiful my promise sounded. 'He ought to do something. Or perhaps I could . . . I don't know. Tell my uncle.' Although as I said it I knew no good would come of that.

Mrs Trent did not believe me anyhow; I saw it in the twist of her mouth as she put the cups and the teapot in its knitted cosy on the table. Sally chattered brightly about Alec as the baby drooled against her neck.

'He loves me,' she said simply. 'I know he does.'

'Hush, you silly girl,' said her mother. 'Why won't you see the truth? He's got a wife, and no doubt he'll have other kiddies soon.'

'He doesn't love his wife,' said Sally. 'They hate each other. Everybody knows that. So why wouldn't he love me?'

Mrs Trent gave me a look. 'Always living in a fantasy world, that one,' she said. 'Best we can hope for is some bloke comes along who don't mind too much she's already got a nipper.'

'Josh would marry me.' She dandled the baby on her knee. 'But we don't love Josh, do we? Because he has eyes that look different ways and he only talks about furrows.'

I wondered if Josh was the fierce-looking farmhand I had seen earlier, and felt rather miserable that this would be Sally's best hope. I could understand why Alec had been attracted to her. She had a certain vitality in her features, a zest for life that he would have needed. A child, Clara had called him. A child who had no idea of the harm he could cause.

As I was leaving them, Sally said, 'Wait a minute, I got something to give you,' and passed the baby over to her mother. She went up the stairs, and when she returned she was holding something in her hand.

'Will you give this to him?' she said, passing it to me. 'My brother took it with a Box Brownie just after she was born.'

It was a small photograph of the baby in its crib, taken outside somewhere; I saw the blur of grass behind it, and the sunshine slanting across its forehead. On the back, in scratchy ink, somebody had written in best copperplate, *Baby girl Grace, born 23rd June 1924.*

I swallowed, put the photograph in my wallet and said, 'I'll see he gets it. I'll . . . I'll talk to him.'

'Good luck with that,' called Mrs Trent from the sink.

Sally smiled at me. 'I know he'll marry me in the end,' she said. 'He just needs to come round to the idea, that's all.'

'Ye-es,' I said. 'I hope so.' There, at least, I was speaking the truth, even if hope was a rather poor truth to feel. I left her standing on the porch, holding Grace. She waved the baby's hand at me as the taxi pulled away, and I waved back, wondering if I would ever see my – what would she be? My second cousin, perhaps – again.

When I arrived back at Castaway, the house was in pandemonium. I paid off the driver and went through the wide-open front door. Two men were carrying a trestle table into the house and along the hallway, the floor protected from their boots by newly laid raffia mats.

Scone was in the hall directing the men along towards the garden. 'Everything all right?' I asked him as I passed him on the way up to my room.

'Tip-top, sir,' he replied wearily. Scone would be leaving Alec's employ directly after the house was sold. He had a family in Shanker awaiting him with baited breath, and, according to the servants' rumours, for a much-increased salary. As a consequence, although he was still completing his duties, I sensed that he very often could not be bothered to accommodate the Brays' little whims, of which this party was surely one.

I bumped into Clara coming out of her room, attired in an ivory dress with a red felt corsage at her hip, and swinging a green satin pochette. 'Oh, there you are,' she said. 'I thought you weren't going to turn up at all.'

429

Her hair had been reset, her eyes outlined in emerald, and her lips were coral pink. She was beautiful, but not as beautiful as the woman I sometimes saw in the early dawn, her face cold-creamed and de-masked. I wanted to put my lips to her neck and kiss it, but I knew that would end badly for me, so I simply said, 'Don't be silly; I'm just off to change.'

'I thought you might be with Alec.' She raised an ironic eyebrow. 'But apparently he's incapable of turning up to his own party on time.'

There was a commotion downstairs: it appeared one of the tables' legs had come off. Clara sighed dramatically and hung over the banister to shout instructions. As I passed her I murmured, 'I think you're in your element,' to which she gave a sniff of derision.

I went to my room and looked out of the window. Servants were hurrying about, setting out fold-up chairs in semicircles. Another was stringing lanterns along the trees that lined the path. Clara was certainly doing her best to bring back to the beating heart of the house a sense of her mother-in-law, at least with regard to emulating the dazzle of my aunt Viviane's garden parties, and I thought of the little girl in a dirty dress and loved her more fiercely than ever.

I changed into the new linen suit I'd had made, at great expense, from Mr Solomon's shop in the Snooks, and smoothed back my hair with a comb. I had a new set of handkerchiefs; I folded one red polka-dotted number and tucked it into my breast pocket. I put my hands in my pockets and smiled at myself in the full-length glass; a debonair sort of a smile that said I would sail through life without letting it trouble me much, that I would hear all the rules and disobey them just the same, that I was the sort of man to enter a room and hold all the people there in the palm of my hand.

I looked at the mirror with a sense of recognition, not of myself, but of someone else. It took me a few minutes to realize to whom I had committed this act of homage: it was Alexander Bray, of course, but not as I knew him now. The Alec Bray who winked at me from the mirror was the charmer who had whisked me round the Natural History Museum on a whim one day, not the man who currently bore his name.

I heard the bell sound, the click of Scone opening the door and the rumble and squeak of male and female voices. I watched out of the window as they were led into the garden, and Clara came towards them and embraced them extravagantly with many kisses. I waited a while, enjoying the small observations I made, and then extricated myself from the window and went to the door.

There were several people in the garden now, milling about and quaffing champagne. I took a glass from the white tablecloth-covered bar, and meandered round the edges of the garden, along the path to the arbour, drifting and eavesdropping. There appeared to be a lot of theatrical types here, visiting from London. I passed by a couple discussing 'dear Dickie's latest outing', which apparently had been 'an absolute scream', especially when 'Sophie's scarf caught on the flies, quite by accident, you know, and she nearly bought it in full view of the plebs in the gods.' They smiled at me as I walked by, and I nodded and did not have the slightest clue what they were talking about.

By the fish pond at the end of the garden I saw Eli Golden, proprietor of the night club I had visited with Clara, still wearing his blue-tinted glasses and talking to a handsome man I finally recognized as George, the barman from the club. I was rather surprised Golden had brought along his employee, but I supposed they must be chums, especially as they seemed to be in fits of laughter about some private joke they chose not to share with me as I went past.

On my way back along the path I heard my name being called from the arbour, and on entering saw, to my dismay, Bump sitting next to a scrawny girl with a disdainful expression.

'Carver!' he roared. 'Not seen you since that debauched night at the Majestic, what?'

'Indeed.' I felt ten years older since that shameful evening. 'I'm surprised you were invited today, to be honest.'

He stared at me with his piggy eyes. 'And why on earth shouldn't I be?'

I was no longer intimidated by him, and it was a pleasant thought. 'If you haven't been told, then it's not my place to say.'

I was about to move on when he said, 'Not that damn Hall of Fame nonsense? So Bray's lost a few shillings on it, what does that matter?'

'It was more than a few.'

'He should never have invested more than he could afford to lose.' Bump looked at the girl, whose attention appeared to be elsewhere, and pouted. 'You don't want a job lot of waxworks, do you, Adne?'

'Well, I think it's a damn shame,' I said, which was as

diplomatic as I could be, considering I had put quite a lot of my own time into the project for free. 'Alec's rather upset about . . . well, the whole thing.'

'Oh, the Bray'll be all right. Chaps like him always are. Listen, Carver, let me introduce you. Robert Carver, an artistic chap. Lady Ariadne Tarnish, daughter of the Duke of Dellsway . . . oh, and my fiancée.'

Her hand, when I shook it, was like a bunch of twigs. 'Congratulations,' I said, to which she sniffed and yawned.

'Heard the buffet's been laid out,' said Bump. 'I forward the motion we investigate. Sweetest?'

Sweetest avowed that she would rather stay where she was, and so Bump and I left the arbour together. 'Dull as ditchwater,' he said regretfully, 'Still, her old man's absolutely stinking. We're going to honeymoon in India. Shoot a few Bengal tigers, what?'

The buffet table was groaning with cold hams and roast chicken, egg salad and pickles, salmon en croute, cheese straws in dainty pots, crudités arranged in concentric circles around a centre of artichoke hearts. Bump stuffed his face and took another glass of champagne from a platter held out by the under-housemaid Harriet, who'd been run ragged all morning by the upper servants. He winked at her and I turned away in disgust.

'Robert!' I heard a female voice cry, and I turned my head to see Lizzie walking towards me, her parents and siblings following along behind.

I smiled automatically 'Lizzie!' It was surprising how her eyes still gleamed when she saw me. I had barely thought of her these past few weeks, despite upholding our rendezvous as regularly as a shift in the office, allowing her to linger outside the rings on display in the jewellers' shops in the Snooks, smiling indulgently as she coyly discussed children's names as if all these topics of conversation were as irrelevant to our friendship as the clouds that occasionally fluffed across the powder-blue sky. I had even kissed her, although more for show than anything else, and all the time my mind had been somewhere else entirely.

'Afternoon, Robert.' Feathers pumped my hand up and down. 'Splendid feast, eh? And what a beautiful garden, don't you think, Tamsin? Of course, back in Viviane's era there were parties like this all the time – we used to dance until dawn, didn't we, dearest? Before the war, you know. Those were the days, eh?'

'Yes, dear,' said Mrs Feathers vaguely, gathering her older children round her like fence stakes bordering a precious flower. I saw Nanny in the background, draped in the younger Featherses and warning little Anthony not to steal food from the buffet.

'Daddy's always talking about the olden days and how wonderful they were, and I don't believe a word of it,' said Maddie. 'Hello, Robert, we haven't seen you much lately. What've you been getting up to?'

'N-nothing really,' I said, with the disquieting sense once again that Maddie knew exactly what I'd been getting up to. 'How have you been?'

'Bored,' she said. 'I want a beau, like Lizzie. At least it would give me something to do in the evenings.'

'Now, dear, you know you're too young,' murmured Mrs Feathers.

'Modern girls always want to grow up too fast,' said

Dr Feathers. 'What's wrong with being a child? That's what I'd like to know. By the way, Robert, have you seen your cousin? I wanted to ask his opinion on these damn-fool bungalows.'

'Um . . . he's about somewhere,' I said, sure that Alec would not give two hoots about the damn-fool bungalows. 'Perhaps by the fish pond?'

'I see. Well, I'll catch up with you later.' He walked off, and Mrs Feathers drifted after him, pulling along the others in her wake, and then there remained only Lizzie and the guilty sense, not that I had betrayed her, but that I had hardly thought of her as I was doing so.

She was holding a glass of iced lemon water and was sipping from it, her parasol balanced on one shoulder. 'It's terribly hot, isn't it?' She squinted out from under the umbrella. 'Father says it's going to thunder later.'

'I don't think so. Apparently Scone has the weather entirely under control. Had a word with the man upstairs, you see.'

Lizzie giggled; I had learned her ways over the recent weeks, and now I was able to scatter conversation about her that made it appear as if I were utterly engaged in whatever topic she had brought to mind.

'Doesn't Mrs Bray ever feel the heat?' She nodded to where Clara was standing with a group of friends, resplendent in her ivory shift, her head thrown back with laughter. 'She looks so lovely.'

'Not as lovely as you,' I said automatically, with the vague sense that I was being a complete cad.

She sighed happily. 'Do you know who her friends are? They look awfully glamorous.'

I recognized Eli Golden and George from the club, but there were two women I did not know. One was very tall, with a sharp black bob and charcoal dress, and the other was wearing men's flannels. 'Theatrical people, I expect,' I said. 'Would you like to meet them?'

'Oh no.' She shook her head vehemently. 'They're not my sort of people at all.'

'Don't be such a goose.' I took her by the arm and dragged her across the lawn, because I had been loosened from Clara's side for long enough and I yearned to be near her.

'Ah!' As I approached the group, Clara turned to me. 'I was wondering where you'd got to.'

'Sorry, old thing.' I sensed that Lizzie was hiding behind me. 'I was talking to Bump. Did you know he's turned up with some titled fiancée you couldn't imagine him less suited to?'

'God! He's not even invited.' I saw she was halfway tipsy already on champagne. 'I ought to kick him out for what he's done.'

'Is that Lord Mason?' said the woman in the bob, in an accent as coarse as the seabed. 'He used to come and watch me nightly. He's a depraved beast, that one.'

'Anyway.' The woman in the flannels turned to me and held out her hand. 'This isn't getting us introduced. I'm Mary Garrett, and I take it you must be Clara's husband?'

I heard a cough from one of the men. 'Not at all,' I said with an easy smile, my heart racketing hard, aware of Lizzie behind me, 'I'm Robert Carver, Alec's cousin, and this here is my friend Miss Feathers, who lives next door.'

I shoved Lizzie in front of me. 'How do you do,' she

said in that same tight, nervous voice she'd used on me the first time we'd met, and I saw the amused confusion on Miss Garrett's face at the odd combination we must make.

'And this is Miss Lilian Marshall.' Clara indicated the tall woman and beamed at me, and I saw that the shift to her evening persona had begun, the one that, relaxed by alcohol, would flirt with me in secret and whisper in my ear about the night-time adventure to come. Strangely, I felt more restrained than ever before, conscious of Lizzie, awkward beside me.

'I looked after this little one when she first came to London.' Lilian put her arm about Clara's waist. 'Put her on the stage, I did, at the mercy of all them horrible men.'

'Until I was rescued,' she said with an ironic twist to her mouth.

Behind me there was an almighty crash, and we all turned to see Alec stumbling through the glass doors, falling down the steps and landing in a heap at the bottom. Scone rushed to help him up, but Alec waved him away, getting to his feet and announcing, 'I'm quite all right! No need to panic.'

He staggered towards the bar, and Clara pushed a high, brittle laugh out into the air. 'And as if on cue,' she said, 'my knight in shining armour.'

I turned to Lizzie and was surprised to find her gone. I saw her parasol nodding its way along the path towards the fish pond. I blinked, confused, and George said, 'I think we scared your friend away.'

'Oh, she's tougher than she looks,' I murmured, although I had no doubt something had upset her, perhaps to do with the unusual ladies. She probably thought they'd been sneering. Later, I would talk to her, but my head was already cocooned in champagne, and I had not the slightest inclination to do so now.

'I wish I were young again,' said Mary Garrett. 'To have all that life ahead of you. Everything opening up. I remember that feeling, as if the whole world were yours for the taking.'

Lilian leaned on her shoulder and looked at her adoringly. Clara said, 'Before it clamps you up and begins chewing you to pieces.'

'I don't think you even believe that,' I said.

She pouted. 'Oh, darling, I've been trying for years to be a cynic.'

'Cynics don't mean what they say,' I observed. 'They're children, desperate for their innocence to be restored.'

'Do you know, I think you're right,' said Miss Garrett. 'Only I'd never thought of it like that.'

The conversation wound back and forth as the afternoon became evening. People drifted away from and joined our group, and the servants lit the lanterns strung between the trees, and the candles on the steps, and the evening sky became thick with the day's heat, with just the breeze from the sea to relieve the humidity. I found myself making jokes, and the jokes being appreciated, and the conversation skittered from the theatre to politics to London to the differences between men and women, and I felt a little of what Miss Garrett had been trying to describe, that soaring delight in the world, the feeling that I could go down any path, take any life that appealed to me; and as champagne became cocktails, I realized with a pure clarity that the life I wanted was this one. Not the peaceful silence of back home, nor even the perfect elegance of Castaway, but this: parties and lights and rattling conversations with people who had slipped the moulds society had laid out for them, and did not care at all.

At one point I walked away from them, with the vague intention of finding Lizzie; however, as I looked into the arbour I saw inside not Bump, but Alec in his shirtsleeves, sitting on one of the benches, an empty glass beside him, and looking at the sundial in the middle. I stood at the entrance and said, 'Cheer up, old thing.'

He looked at me, startled, and then said, 'Oh, it's you.'

I refused to be swayed by his glum mood, so I sat beside him and said, 'The party's going well, anyhow.'

'Is it?' He appeared not to care either way. He patted his jacket pockets and said, 'Blast. I've left my cigarettes inside.'

I took out my own tin and gave him one. He cupped his hands around the flame as I lit it. 'I know you think losing Castaway is the end of the world –' I began.

'Not another lecture, Robert, I can't bear it.' He took a deep drag and sighed out smoke.

'I haven't even given you one lecture yet,' I said, rather offended.

'Well, everybody else has. Made my own bed, must lie in it, et cetera, et cetera. Actually doesn't make me feel better one iota.'

'I wasn't going to say any of that.' I lit my own cigarette. 'I was going to say, it's good to appreciate what one's got, even if that is considerably less than before.'

'What have I got?' said Alec bitterly. 'I'm a failure.

Mother was the only one with any hope for me, and now I'm selling her house before she's even cold in her grave.'

I rolled my eyes. 'You've your health,' I said.

He grunted.

I added, although the words stuck in my throat, 'You've a beautiful wife.'

'Who hates my guts. That's going to be fun, trapped in some God-awful flat in Ealing or somewhere hideous. Home from work at six, "Hello, dearest", sitting on opposite armchairs, staring at each other and pretending everything's fine.'

'You can always divorce her,' I said lightly. 'Or . . . or separate or something.'

'I wouldn't give her the satisfaction,' he said. 'I'd just be playing into her hands.'

I didn't really understand, but Alec was talking with a drunk's logic. I added, 'I know somebody who'd be glad to see you at the end of the day.'

'Really?' He said this with no hope.

'Yes.' I swallowed. 'Sally Trent.'

There was a pause. Alec looked at the stone bird pecking at the edge of the sundial. Finally he said, 'Have you been checking up on me?'

'You didn't tell me you'd been . . . with her,' I said. 'You didn't tell me she'd had your baby.'

He turned to me, his eyes red-rimmed. 'Oh, I'm sorry, am I supposed to tell you every detail of my life? I mean, what the hell business is it of yours, anyway?'

'None whatsoever. Look, it doesn't matter how I found out, but I've seen her, and I've seen the baby. She's called

Grace.' I took out my wallet and held the photograph towards Alec, but he turned away.

'Don't come the moral high ground with me, Carver. I know what happened with you and the call girl that night at the Majestic.'

'I'm not coming any moral high ground,' I said steadily, containing my anger. 'She asked me to talk to you. She says she's not interested in money. She just wants you to visit her and the baby.'

Alec was still turned away, staring at the hawthorn bush behind the bench. 'We were still living in London,' he said. 'Clara and I, before I had to get rid of the flat. We had the blazes of a row – she told me the full story, how she'd only married me to get her hands on Castaway. I stormed out, came down here alone. Sally'd always been . . . well, I'd always noticed her. She made it easy for me.'

Quietly, I put the photograph back into my wallet. 'I can imagine,' I said softly.

'Went back to Clara. Forgave her – after a fashion. We moved to Castaway permanently; I thought it would make her happy, but she wasn't. And I continued with Sally. And you don't need to tell me it was wrong. I know it was wrong. She was sixteen. A servant. Everything that everybody knows is utterly immoral. You won't understand me for a second, Robert, but I seem to have this compulsion to wreck my own life. It's as if it was what I was meant to do.'

There was another silence. Overhead, the lanterns swayed in the thick breeze. From somewhere beyond the arbour I heard a woman's high, bright laughter. 'And Gina?' I said. 'What about her?'

He looked at me. 'Who's Gina?'

'The other parlourmaid. Nine years ago.'

'Not the one who . . . ?' He shook his head impatiently. 'You're behind the times, Robert. I've already been accused of that one. Not guilty. I thought you'd know me better than that.'

'What do you mean? You did the same thing with Sally.'

He held up a finger. 'First time. With a servant. I know there shouldn't have been a first time. But still.'

'And she's had your baby.'

'What do you want me to say?' He got to his feet. 'I'll go and visit her, all right? I'll buy a bunch of flowers and I'll go off to that godforsaken farm and see her bloody baby.'

'She thinks you're in love with her. She thinks you're going to divorce Clara and marry her.'

'She's deluded! I never told her that.' He frowned. 'I'm sure I never told her that. Look, what does it matter?'

'It matters to her, apparently.'

'Oh, God.' He sank back down on to the bench, head in hands. 'I don't want to think about it. Why are you making me think about it?'

'You can't just forget about your responsibilities.'

'Can't I? Who says I can't?'

'I mean – even if you wanted to. The things we do always seem to find us again, in the end.'

Alec still had his head in his hands. 'You have no idea what it's like, being me,' he growled. 'So thanks for the advice, but no thanks.'

'You're right,' I said, and my lungs constricted as anger tightened my breaths. 'I don't know what it's like to be you. Growing up with a silver spoon jammed so hard inside your mouth that you think having to work for a living is somehow demeaning.'

'How dare you?' snapped Alec. 'How dare you?'

I pointed in the direction of the house, the other hand on my chest to calm it. 'You have an army of people who spend their entire waking hours ensuring that your butter dish gets to the table at the correct temperature, and you have no idea how any of them actually live. Your daughter is going to grow up in poverty because you don't want to take responsibility for her.'

'Honestly, Robert, you wouldn't know what it's like to actually feel alive, would you?'

'What are you talking about? I appreciate everything that I have, and you . . . in your little bubble of privilege, with a mother who thought you were a gift from Heaven and everything you've ever wanted handed to you on a plate –'

'And I've lost it all!' he shouted. 'From Mother downwards.'

I took a step towards him. 'You have everything,' I said through gritted teeth. 'You still do, you just don't appreciate any of it.'

And with that I walked out of the arbour and dived back into the gentle sway of the party, almost knocking a lantern with my head as I went. I stormed down the path, hardly knowing where I was going, until an arm caught mine and a voice said, 'Come this way.'

I was wheeled about. I looked down. Clara was holding my arm, drunk and giggling. 'We were talking about hoops,' she said. 'You know, racing them down the road, and I remembered we had one in the summerhouse, and I've been told to go and fetch it. Only the thing is, you see, there are giant spiders in there and I'll scream if I walk into a web, so you'll come with me, won't you, and defend me against the beasts. Are you all right, darling?'

I swallowed. My lungs were tight. My head felt swollen. 'I'm fine,' I said. 'I'm absolutely fine.'

As we walked I calmed down a little. Clara waved and blew kisses at people as we passed. 'Fabulous party!' somebody called, and she simpered and said, 'Thank you, thank you,' as if she were a film star at a premiere.

The summerhouse was dim and cooled my head somewhat. We banged about in the dark, and I tore down spiderwebs. 'It's in here somewhere,' murmured Clara, groping her way along. There was one small window, and through it I saw the shimmer of coloured lights and odd pieces of people passing by like flimsy butterflies.

'Ah! Here it is.'

She stood in front of me. The hoop bounced between us. I bent and kissed her softly.

'You smell delicious,' I murmured. Damn Alec; how could he not give thanks every day that he was married to this woman? If only I'd met her first.

Clara giggled quietly. 'Champagne always makes me feel naughty.'

I took the hoop from her hands and put it aside. 'I thought you were always naughty.'

She glanced sideways at the ping-pong table. I followed her gaze to its dusty surface, and then my hands were racing over her body and under her dress, pulling at her silk underwear. With a small, giddy shriek she kicked off the shiny, soft thing and it scudded into the dirt on the ground. I picked her up, carried her to the table and set her on it, but she turned round and whispered, 'Like this.'

I took her from behind as she grasped the edge of the table for stability, and I held the soft warmth of her belly as I plunged into her again and again. Outside, a girl laughed and there was the tinkle of glass against glass, and although I was inside Clara I was thinking of Alec, and my victory for those few short minutes was complete.

I shuddered to a climax and lay, sweating and panting, inside her for a while. When I withdrew, I folded myself over her and kissed the back of her neck. 'I love you,' I murmured.

'Be careful,' she muttered. 'My dress.' She rearranged herself, found her underwear in its dusty heap, brushed off the dirt and pulled it on with a quick wrinkle of her nose.

'That was lovely.' She raised herself on tiptoe, and I kissed her. I pulled myself on to the ping-pong table and trapped her with my legs; I wished I could lie down on its musty surface and go to sleep with Clara in my arms.

'Come away with me,' I said suddenly.

She looked at me. 'Robert . . .'

I rubbed a patch of dirt from her shoulder. 'What am I going to do after the summer's over?'

'I told you,' she said, as if speaking to a child. 'I can't leave him. How would we live?'

'We'll find a way – I love you –'

'I'm not going to be your mistress,' she snapped. 'That life's gone. I'm respectable now.'

'He'll divorce you,' I said, ignoring what Alec had told

me only a few minutes ago. 'He'll do the honourable thing. And then we can be married. And I don't care if you can't have children. We can adopt. We can adopt five.'

Her eyes slid away from me, and she pushed my legs apart so she could leave. 'It won't work.'

'Why not?' I jumped down from the table. 'Listen. In six years I'll come into money.'

She picked up the hoop and walked to the door. 'Not enough,' she said shortly, easing open the door. 'If you were going to be as rich as Bump Mason, I might think about it.'

'You're not serious, Clara?' I followed her and put a hand on her back.

'I told you I was a mercenary.' She shrugged. 'When my father-in-law dies, Alec'll be able to buy back Castaway, or a house ten times the size.'

'You mean . . . you're going to stay with him – for that?'

'Yes.' She looked at me with a glittering gimlet eye. 'For that.'

I bent towards her and put my face to her neck. 'I don't believe you,' I whispered.

'Well, that's your problem, I'm afraid.' She bounced the hoop between us. 'We should get back, don't you think?'

There was a noise beside us, a footfall, and I looked up. Dr Feathers was walking away from us rapidly, his arms pumping left and right.

'Oh, Lord,' I said. 'What did he see?'

'Two friends who've retrieved a hoop from the summerhouse,' she said brightly. 'Now come on. I'll tell them we got waylaid chatting to people.'

I followed her back along the path, but I knew what he

would have seen. And I knew that I had to speak to Lizzie before her father did.

She was nowhere to be found. I saw Dr Feathers with his wife and family in a small huddle, and I hurried past them, my face burning. Eventually Harriet told me Lizzie had been seen leaving by the front door, and I raced down the hallway, emerging on to the covered portico.

She was across the road, leaning on the rail and watching the promenade below, her parasol folded into pleats.

'Lizzie!' I called, and walked over to join her.

'There you are,' she said, as if we had made an arrangement to meet and she had been waiting for me all this time. She pointed up towards where the cliffs overlooked the sea. 'Shall we take a walk?'

'Absolutely.' In the evening gloom it was hard to make out her face. 'Are you all right?'

She did not answer and, my heart pounding, we climbed up to the very top of the cliff and crossed over to where a tamped-down path led along the edge towards Shanker, three miles distant.

'I feel it's going to rain in a minute,' she said. 'My brain's so tight I can hardly think.'

'Maybe that's the cocktails,' I said, attempting a smile.

'I've only drunk lemon water,' she said shortly. We stopped now, at a small promontory, and looked over the darkening sea. Below, waves lapped against the rocks and, further along, the promenade started and lights twinkled back to the town.

I swallowed, and grasped the bull by the horns. 'Have you spoken to your father?'

'My father?' She frowned. 'Not since we arrived. Why?'

447

'Oh.' I sank into relief. Perhaps he would say nothing. Certainly, he would be unable to name the act itself to his daughter, of that I was sure.

Lizzie looked away from me towards the glooming sky. 'I saw you, you know.'

My breath froze in my throat. I paused until I could be sure of eliminating my stutter, and then said calmly, 'What on earth are you talking about, my dear?'

'When you introduced me to the gang, those fearsome ladies and funny gentlemen. You didn't know I was watching.'

In a second, I realized she knew nothing of the summerhouse, and my breath bobbed back into warmth. 'Please enlighten me, Lizzie; I don't know what you mean.'

'I saw the way you were looking at her.' She turned to me now, although I could not make out the expression on her face. 'Mrs Bray. I saw the way you looked at her, and I realized I've been an utter fool.'

'I think you are,' I said lightly, 'because you're talking rot.'

'You're in love with her, Robert. I saw it as plain as day. You're absolutely dotty over her, and I'll tell you something. I may be a fool, but you're a bigger one.'

'Come on. She's my cousin's wife, for heaven's sake.'

'Exactly.' She pressed her hands together over the bamboo handle of the parasol, digging it into the soft ground. 'You can't get in between a married couple; or, at least, not when they're still in love.'

They're not, I wanted to say. 'You've really got hold of the wrong end of the stick, honestly. Listen, how about

I come round tomorrow and we can chat about it then, when we're not in complete darkness?'

'I don't want to chat,' she said, with a sudden burst of spite, and turned on her heel, marching back down the hill.

'Wait, Lizzie!' I hurried after her.

'All we do is chat,' she shouted over her shoulder. 'All I ever did with Freddie was chat, and look how that ended up. And, of course, I'm the idiot who fell for both of you.'

I caught up with her at the junction; she had stopped where the grassy path became the road of Gaunt's Cliff. 'Listen,' I said, and unpeeled one of her hands from the bamboo handle. Her palm had indentations where she had dug her nails into the flesh. 'You know you're always thinking things like this. And you're always wrong.'

'That's because somewhere, deep down, I knew you didn't love me the way I love you.' She glared at the windows of Castaway, brilliantly lit as if for a play. 'At least Freddie had the decency to move to another country before he fell in love with someone else.'

'Honestly, it's not what you think,' I insisted. 'Listen, I'll knock on your door tomorrow afternoon. Three o'clock.'

She paused, and said in a brittle voice, 'You really don't care whether you break my heart, do you?'

'Please stop this, Lizzie.'

'One of Father's friends wants to marry me. He's made it quite obvious on several occasions. He's totally gaga over me, Robert. Quite doolally.'

'I'm sure he is. But listen —'

'He's forty-five years old and he owns a perfectly decent

place with an acre of land. I'm sure I'll be very happy.' She withdrew her hand from mine and held her palm to the sky. 'Oh dear. It's started to rain.'

She crossed the road back towards the house, and as I followed her the Feathers emerged en masse, the doctor, at the front, wielding a crow-like umbrella. He eyed me coldly, before saying, 'Come along, Lizzie, it's time we were getting back.'

'Bye, Robert!' called Maddie as she was hustled along the path by her father. Lizzie joined her family group and was absorbed into their midst. As they walked up the steps of the house next door I shouted, 'I'll see you tomorrow,' but she did not turn round.

I sighed, but I knew that in the end Lizzie would be all right. I would go there tomorrow and break off the whole thing, but in a calm, planned-out sort of a way, saying that we were still too young for this sort of commitment and that I would be gone within a couple of weeks anyhow. She had always known something of the truth, as she had said, and besides which, our friendship had been a schoolkid-ish, innocent sort of affair; it was nothing the passage of time would not heal.

Then there was the problem of Clara's obstinacy, but I would get round her one way or another. I had to. Buoyed by optimism, I hopped back inside the house to find a flurry of excitement as umbrellas were brought into service and handed out to the guests in the garden. Many people had already left; however, among those who remained the rain was causing a sort of high-pitched camaraderie, involving much celebration of 'good old England', and demands for more rum punch. I looked round for Alec but could not find him, and then Clara announced, to whoops and cheers, that an evening buffet would be set up shortly in the dining room and everybody began to bundle inside the house.

I borrowed an umbrella and made my way back to the arbour. As I'd thought, Alec was still there, sound asleep on one of the benches, protected from the rain by the overhanging hawthorn bush.

'Come on, old stick,' I said, nudging him in the side. 'You're going to get drenched.'

He muttered and turned on to his side. 'Robert,' he mumbled.

'Look,' I said, 'I'm sorry about our row. I'm really rather fond of you, old chap. And – well, I know under the circumstances this is silly, but I'd hate you to think badly of me.'

His eyelids fluttered open briefly. In a voice dredged from the bottom of the sea, he mumbled, 'It's all too late. It's too late for me.'

'Exactly. You probably ought to be in bed. Don't forget, I know what pneumonia's like.'

His hand groped for me, and like a baby he clutched his fingers around mine. 'Never meant it . . .' he said. 'Think the world of you, Robert.'

For the first time since that night with Clara in the beach hut, guilt caught in my throat over the many nails I had struck into the coffin of my cousin's marriage. 'And I do of you,' I said softly because, at that moment, it was true.

'Tell Sally . . .' he murmured, and gave a little snore and drifted back into sleep. I tried to pull him upright, but he was a dead weight, and I thought that at least out here he was causing no trouble. On an impulse, I reached into the jacket pocket beside his breast and removed his wallet.

The photograph of the baby was still in mine; I took it out and placed it inside Alec's. As I did so, my fingers brushed on a rounded, brittle item pushed deep into one of the wallet's folds and, piqued by curiosity, I drew it out.

It was a small seashell, its innards worn into an iridescent mother-of-pearl by the tides, and, just visible in the dim light filtering through from the house's blaring windows, were two tiny etched letters: *C. A.*

I held it in my hand for a second or two and then, deciding not to think about it any longer, I dug it back inside the fold and slid the wallet into the pocket of his jacket, which I arranged over his chest like a very inadequate blanket. I wondered what it was he had wanted to tell Sally, and if it had been an instruction for me or a decision for himself. Perhaps not tomorrow, because he would have the hangover from hell and be in a consequent foul mood, but the day after, I would try to talk to him again.

The crowd that remained was being herded into the dining room, with Clara at its head, waving a sparkling umbrella like a tour guide. I followed the partygoers but felt out of step with their antics now, and Clara roundly ignored me, handing out drinks to all, her coarse laugh pealing out like a worker's bell. I remained on a window seat, watching the rain pelt against the area steps below, until there was a call to repair to the drawing room and utilize the gramophone. I, not wanting to share Clara any more, bade goodnight to all and wound my way upstairs.

I listened to them from my room, the women's darting shrieks and the men's rumbling laughter. As time crept on, I heard effusive farewells, and Clara's tinkling laugh, and the stairs creaking, and the front door opening and closing. I put out my lamp and tried to sleep, but when the thunderstorm started I found it impossible to concentrate. Instead, I pulled back the curtains and watched lightning lash the sky, counting the seconds until the boom shook the panes. Twenty seconds first, then ten. It was coming closer. I remembered Alec out in the garden, but surely he would have woken by now – perhaps he had even joined the party.

I realized that there was no more noise from downstairs, but I thought that maybe a few old friends remained, smoking and drinking and chatting. I imagined them lounging on the sofa, occasionally rising to change a record, and Clara on the floor perhaps, her back to a chair, her legs folded under her, discoursing and arguing and snapping out any opposition.

My image of her there was so intent that when a small body curled beside mine in the bed I jumped out of my skin. She put her arms round my waist, and they were so cold I drew her to me and folded her into the warm bedclothes. Her hair had escaped its set; it tumbled about her face. I lifted her chin and made out her features in the dark. 'Are you all right?'

She nodded once. 'Hold me,' she whispered. 'I just want you to hold me.'

'Of course.' Together, we lay propped up on the pillows and watched the storm rage outside. I thought of her lanterns, tossed to the elements, ruined in puddles of rainwater, and it occurred to me that we were the same, Clara and Alec and I: flakes of paper blowing in the wind.

I imagined I would stay awake until the dawn, holding Clara and watching the storm, but I must have fallen asleep, because I was woken by Scone bringing in tea and toast. Clara was gone.

I looked at the fresh rounds of crunchy toast and my stomach vaulted, remembering all the cocktails of the night before. 'I won't be down for breakfast,' I mumbled, pulling the covers up over my head and not even hearing Scone's reply, so quickly did I fall back asleep.

I woke, much later, to a vague commotion in the house. People were running up and down stairs; from the study I heard the telephone peal, not just once, but several times. There was excited chatter; I heard Scone's low voice, questioning, and one of the maids answering squeakily. I was struggling to a sitting position when there was a knock on the door and Agnes came in, her cap in disarray, her face flushed and anxious.

'Sorry, sir,' she said breathily. 'Didn't mean to disturb you, sir, but Mr Scone wants to know if you've seen the master at all. 'Cause he didn't come back last night, see, nor this morning, and now it's midday.'

'Is it?' I rubbed my eyes and saw the clock. 'Good Lord. Don't tell me he's still out in the garden.' I laughed.

'Garden?' She looked at me as if I were mad. 'No, sir, he ain't in the garden.'

'I didn't think so.' I yawned and stretched. 'I found him there last night, sound asleep in the arbour. Looked so peaceful I thought I'd leave him.'

'All right.' She looked about, as if unsure what to do now. 'I'll – um – go and tell Mr Scone.'

'He'll be back in a moment, I'm sure,' I said. 'You know what he's like.'

She fiddled with a hem on her apron. 'Yes, sir. I'm sure you're right, sir. It's only Mr Scone don't usually worry so.'

'I'm sure everything's fine,' I said, although after Agnes had gone a sense of unease asserted itself. I imagined Alec stumbling out of the house, perhaps going towards the town, and then . . . maybe he had just fallen asleep somewhere and, for whatever reason, had been unable to make his way back home. I thought of Bump, and his suite at the Majestic. It was quite within the realms of possibility that Alec had gone there, and was continuing the party right now, with no thought of the rest of the household.

I dressed and went downstairs. The dining room was empty, but I found a maid and asked for Mrs Pennyworth to make me up some sandwiches. When Scone arrived with them I said, 'Any word from Mr Bray?'

'No, sir.' He paused. 'We are getting rather concerned.'

I put an entire egg-and-cress sandwich in my mouth. 'Why?'

'I saw Mr Bray last night in the hall.'

I looked up. Scone never usually volunteered any unnecessary speech.

'After everybody else had gone home,' he continued. 'Before the thunderstorm broke. He was holding the large red umbrella from the stand and said he was going to look at the sea.'

'Then there's your answer. Went out to look at the rain

and then decided to go on for a drink somewhere. A few of those places will open if you know the correct knock, I believe.' I grinned. 'I'm sure my cousin knows them all.'

'Undoubtedly.' Scone brushed invisible crumbs off the table into his gloved hand. 'However, he certainly has not been home yet. The door was still unbolted when I came down this morning.'

'Come on, Scone, you know Alec as well as I do. He's probably still asleep somewhere, dead drunk.' I took a huge draught of lemonade to ease my parched throat. 'Where's Mrs Bray?'

'Mrs Bray is at the police station.'

'What? She's that worried?'

Scone did not look at me. 'She is convinced he met with some sort of accident in the storm.'

I knew the cause of her anxiety: guilt over her place in my bed last night had sped her on to the police station, exaggerating her wifely concern. 'She's mistaken. In fact, I shall go out now and endeavour to bring him home.'

Scone paused. 'Please do,' he said. 'Sir.'

The storm had abated, but a fierce wind whipped along the cliff, nearly taking my hat with it. The sky was iron-clad and menacing, and I bent my face to the ground and marched onwards. The beach was empty bar a few brave souls; I saw a man swimming in the sea, and stopped to squint in case it was Alec on some mad adventure, but as soon as he emerged I saw this was an elderly man, with tough, leathery skin, built like a bird of prey.

The receptionist at the Majestic gave no sign of recognizing me, but said he would call up his lordship immediately. I hovered in the lobby under the giant chandelier, remembering the last time, and my shame as I had run out, and how none of that seemed important any more.

'Carver!' Bump emerged from the wheezing lift doors and came towards me. 'I've a head like a pumpkin on me today. Still, I expect you're bright as a farthing. Bet you hardly touched a drop, you weasel.' He clapped me on the back, sending me stumbling forwards a few paces.

'Actually, I did,' I said, but he was not listening. 'Anyway, I was wondering if I could pick my cousin up. I know it's a bore, but the house is in panic and Clara's gone to the police station.'

'What's that?' he said. 'Do you want a drink? Or tea? Coffee?'

'No, no drink. I'd just like to take Alec home, to be honest.'

He frowned. 'Why would Bray be here? Heard he's got a perfectly good bed at home, what.'

My stomach dipped. 'You mean, he didn't come to you last night?'

'I bloody hope not,' he said. 'I was out for the count. God, you didn't think it was the same set-up as last time, did you? When one's fiancée is staying on the floor below, it rather hampers one's movements somewhat.'

I had forgotten his fiancée. 'Then,' I said, 'where is he?'

He scratched his head. 'You said Clara's at the police station?'

I nodded. 'She's worried he may have been caught up in the storm last night.'

'I'll ring the station now,' he said. 'See what news they can give me. Come upstairs.'

I travelled with him in the lift, my unease mounting.

The suite was transformed from before; now all was neat and orderly. Bump placed me on the sofa, facing the armchair where I had been humiliated, while he sat at the desk and placed a call to Helmstone police station.

'Hello,' he drawled. 'Lord Hugh Mason-Chambers here. Listen, I'm calling about a friend of mine, Mr Alexander Bray. Apparently he went missing last night. Just wondering if you had any news.'

There was a pause, and then, 'Hello. Morgan, isn't it? Yes, I'm fine, just down for the weekend with my fiancée. Oh, thank you. Now, I'm calling about Mr Bray . . . Yes, that's right . . . I see . . .'

He scratched notes on the pad in front of him. Despite my hatred of him, I was impressed by his urbanity, his languid 'Lord Hugh Mason-Chambers here', and the way his courtesy title unlocked doors.

He replaced the receiver in its cradle and turned to me. 'It's not good news,' he said, and my stomach dropped further. 'A dog walker this morning found a discarded shoe on a ledge of the cliff. And on the rocks by the water, what appeared to be the shreds of a red umbrella.'

I found my hands were shaking. I pushed them into the sofa. 'Perhaps it's not his.'

'Perhaps.' Bump sighed. 'Although it seems as if the shoe is. I suppose Clara's identified it.'

'He may have stumbled.' I clutched at straws. 'He could be unconscious a few yards further along.'

'They're doing a search of the area now. Lifeboat's already gone out, apparently. Although the Inspector says if the accident happened last night it . . . well, it may be too late.'

'Oh, Lord.' And then I thought of Alec's misery yesterday, his talk of losing Castaway, his complaint of a worthless life. 'I hope he hasn't done anything stupid.'

'What are you saying?' snapped Bump. 'Because that's rather a strong implication, and I'm not sure I like it.'

'I don't like it either,' I snapped back. 'But we may have to face facts.'

Bump got to his feet and walked to the window. 'Bray wouldn't kill himself,' he said. 'And if you knew him at all you'd understand that.'

'I didn't say he had.' The word *kill* buzzed about my brain like an angry wasp.

'Then what are you saying?' He turned towards me.

'I'm just trying to understand what happened.' I stood too. 'I should go back to the house. See if I'm needed.'

'Yes,' he said dismissively. 'Go.'

I took the lift down to the ground floor. As I walked back to Castaway, the wind battering my senses from my body, a great dread bubbled within me. I knew Alec was not a depressive sort, and yet I could not deny that he had been in the blackest of moods yesterday, the sort of mood when an impulse could strike him and he might act on it. I thought of our argument, and I prayed that nothing had happened to him bar a minor accident. I trudged up the cliff as if walking towards my doom.

Scone met me in the hallway.

'I'm sorry,' I said. 'I was convinced I knew where he would be. I was wrong.'

'That's quite all right, sir,' he said. His tone was almost kind. 'There's a policeman in the dining room interviewing everybody. I said you would be back shortly.'

I looked at the dining-room door, which now, unlike every other occasion, was firmly closed. 'Do you really think . . . ?' I began, looking about, expecting Alec to walk into the hall with tales of another mad escapade ringing from his lips. 'It seems like a joke.'

'I can assure you, sir, it is not a joke.' Scone turned away. 'If you wait in the library, I shall call you when you are needed.'

'Yes. Yes, of course.' I curled a hand over the snail end of the banister. It was beautiful, I thought. It had never occurred to me before just how beautiful it was. 'Is Mrs Bray here?'

'She arrived back about half an hour ago.'

I looked up the stairs and he added, 'She has given instructions not to be disturbed. I'm sure you understand.'

'Of course,' I said automatically, knowing that she had not meant to include me in that instruction but unwilling to test the theory just yet. I sat in the library with a dry mouth and listless hands. I held a book on my lap but was unable to concentrate on more than a line. I waited anxiously for my interview with the policeman, wanting it over with and wishing it would not come at all.

I heard men talking in the hallway, voices I did not recognize. Nobody came to get me. Sickly yellow afternoon light filtered through the windowpanes. It seemed disrespectful, somehow, to switch on the electric lamp. The rain began pattering again. Summer was over. Alec was . . . He was . . . but I would not think of it.

I was finally called into the dining room a couple of hours later. 'Sorry to keep you waiting, sir,' said the policeman at the table, who'd introduced himself as Dawes. 'Thought we'd do the servants first. Hope you don't mind.'

'Not at all,' I said faintly, sitting opposite him.

He asked me a few basic questions – my name, my age, what my purpose was in the house – and then pushed an item resting on a white handkerchief over to me. 'Can I ask if you recognize this, sir?'

I stood up to view it and saw a wristwatch face, smashed to pieces and reassembled as much as possible. I felt queasy. 'Is it Alec's?'

'It appears to be. So you don't recognize it?'

I sighed. 'Couldn't say, I'm afraid.' I sat down again, light-headed. My chest was tighter now than it had been for days, weeks. I coughed. 'Was it on the cliff?'

'On the rocks by the water's edge. I take it you know about the umbrella?' When I nodded, he added, 'We found bloodstains on the spokes, protected from the rain.'

I thought I might be sick. 'Surely . . .' I began. 'Is there a chance . . . ?'

'I'm sorry. The boat's been out all day, and they've found nothing.' He shot me a look. He was only a few years older than me – the same age as Alec, perhaps. 'We should prepare ourselves for the worst.'

Oh, God, I found myself thinking, *please let it have been an accident*. He slipped and fell; it was a terrible night. I could not bear the thought that he might have done this to himself, alone.

'I'm sorry to have to ask you this, Mr Carver, but how has Mr Bray seemed to you recently? Has he been in good spirits or . . . or not?'

'He was . . .' I looked at the table. 'He had some financial problems . . . I mean, that's not a secret . . . and . . . and he's been drinking quite a lot recently. But really, I can't believe he would . . . it must have been an accident, mustn't it?'

'That's what we're attempting to find out, sir.' He consulted his notes. 'Now, Mr Scone says he came across Mr Bray in the hall last night at quarter past one. Did you see him after that time?'

I shook my head. 'The last time I saw him, he was asleep in the garden. There's a sort of sheltered part out there. He was on one of the benches.'

'And that would have been at . . . ?'

I thought. 'Perhaps nine o'clock?'

He scribbled a note. I wanted to curl up in a ball and hug my misery inwards. Instead, I had to answer more questions, about yesterday's party, about what time I had gone to bed, about whom I'd seen and whom I'd talked to.

'Thank you, sir. Just one last thing.' He frowned at his page. 'Now, you say the last time you saw him was at about nine o'clock. However, we have two witnesses who say they saw you walking up the cliff outside the house at half past one last night, with Mr Bray.'

I blinked. 'I'm sorry?'

He glanced up at me. He looked awkward and embarrassed. 'You deny being there?'

I coughed, my brain whirling. 'Of course I deny it. I went to bed at about eleven o'clock, as I told you. They must . . . they must be mistaken.'

'And your relationship with Mr Bray? It's a – er – that is, do you get on well?'

'Absolutely. We're cousins and friends. At least, I'd like to think so.' As I spoke, I realized that we were talking about him in the present tense, and wondered, with a sick feeling, whether it ought to be changed to the past. 'Look, I don't know why anybody would say they'd seen me talking to him, but it wasn't me.'

'I see.' He folded his notebook closed. 'I have to tell you, sir, that it is possible your cousin was not alone on the cliff edge last night; if, indeed, that is where he was.'

Words stuck in my throat. 'Wh-wh-what do you mean?'

'There are very faint indications that there were two people on the cliff.' He paused. 'A lot of the grass there has been churned up. That could be due to any number of reasons, but one of them is that there may have been some sort of a struggle.'

'Are – are you saying . . . ?' But my mind did not want to grasp what he was saying.

'It's early days yet.' He got to his feet and smiled at me. 'But we'll find out what happened to your cousin, don't you worry.'

There was rather a menacing tone, I now realized, to his voice as he edged round the table to open the door. 'It wasn't me!' I said.

'Of course, sir,' he said blandly, smiling with reptilian eyes, and stepped out into the hallway. As the front door closed on him, I took a breath and found there was none to be had.

I gripped the edge of the table. A vice was closed about my chest. Air. I needed air. I heard the familiar rasping sound of my throat attempting to capture oxygen. I got to my feet and knocked over the chair.

Then Scone was in the room. 'It's all right, sir,' he said. 'Sit down.'

I heard him righting the chair, and then he planted me upon it. He put a hand on my back and commanded, 'Breathe here. One . . . two . . . three . . .'

Slowly, the panic subsided. My fingers relaxed their grip on the table. Breath entered my body. My lungs shuddered with their exhaustion. 'I'm sorry,' I croaked.

'I wouldn't speak if I were you.' He disappeared momentarily; I heard him unstopping the carafe of water that sat on the sideboard. 'Drink this.'

He put a glass in front of me. I sipped at it, returning to myself inch by inch. 'Thank you,' I whispered. 'If you hadn't come in . . .'

'I heard you in the hallway. It's that whistling sound. I know it well.'

'Whistling?'

'I was gassed in the war.' He put a hand over his right lung. 'It got in here. The other lads, they used to laugh at me, for the sound my chest made when it got bad. Like an out-of-tune whistle, they said. Used to spook them at night, apparently.'

'I never realized you had . . . similar trouble,' I said.

'Feels as if an elephant's sitting on your chest?' He nodded. In Alec's absence he seemed to have assumed some sort of second-in-command role, almost father-like. 'It's because of the worry over Mr Bray. I'll tell Agnes to bring you some tea in the library.'

I allowed Scone to manoeuvre me upstairs and sit me back in the same chair.

When Agnes came with the tea she said, 'How are you, sir? Mr Scone says you was took bad.'

'Two witnesses . . .' I began faintly, but was unable to continue. 'Maybe he's out there, unconscious. Lost his memory.'

'Yes, sir.' She put the tea tray on the rosewood coffee table beside the fireplace. 'Maybe writing it all down will help.'

I looked up at her. 'I'm sorry?'

She shrugged. 'Helps me when I'm feeling out of sorts. A diary or an account or something.'

'Oh.' I nodded. 'I see. Thank you.'

When she had gone I sat at the writing desk by the windows that looked over the back garden, dim in the afternoon gloom. I held the pen above the ink pot, but was unable to order the jumble of emotions into a coherent sequence of events. I stared at the blank paper, and then in a fit of anger took up the letter opener and gouged the paper into jagged squares, scoring into the blotter beneath.

'What witnesses?' I crunched the pieces into my fist. 'What damn witnesses?'

My words sprang me somehow into action. I had to do something. I had to talk to somebody. I got to my feet, leaving the letter opener and the screws of paper on the desk, and walked to the open door. Immediately to my right, at an angle, was the drawing room, its own door shut tight. I raised my fist and knocked on the wood.

I heard nothing for a long time, but instinct told me she was inside. Eventually the handle gave a creak and the door opened a notch.

'Clara.'

Her face was slivered by the gap in the door.

'Let me in. I need to talk to you.'

'No.'

But my foot was in the doorway, and I was stronger. Finally, she relaxed her hold and I entered the drawing room.

I had barely been inside this room since coming to Castaway; it had always been Clara's domain, a feast of gold and blue, with her vibrant paintings hanging from the rails and a huge, listing gilt mirror over the fireplace. My aunt Viviane's heirlooms were scattered about: statuesque women holding lamps, a studded chest with Chinese letters inscribed on its borders. I felt too masculine here; too much of an unwanted intruder.

Clara was still wearing the make-up she must have put on this morning, but her eye pencil had blotched about her face, and the bobbed set of her hair was frizzing in wild strands. She stood in the middle of the room, clutching that locket about her neck, and said, 'What do you want?'

I spread my palms wide. 'Just to talk.'

'We've nothing to talk about.' The whites of her eyes were scratched with red. 'I don't want to see you again.'

'Clara . . .'

She turned away from me.

'I'm as upset and worried about all this as you are –' I began.

'No, you're not.' She spat the words through dried, flaky lips. 'This is exactly what you wanted, isn't it?'

I almost laughed with the absurdity of that sentence.

'Of course it isn't. He's my cousin. And my friend. I don't want any of this.'

She turned back to me, her face screwed into a tight little ball of misery. 'Alec is the only man . . .' she began, her voice shaking. 'The only man I have ever loved, and I treated him worse than a mangy dog.'

'You and me,' I said in my softest voice. 'It has nothing to do with all this.'

She came towards me. 'I love him! Don't you get it, you imbecile? You were nothing to me, Robert. I only did it to . . . to . . . well, I don't know why I did it, and now he's gone, and there's nothing I can do.'

She lapsed into tears; hideous, weeping sobs. I took a step towards her but she held a hand up, the other still clutching the locket, Viviane's locket that Alec had given her, with a scrap of his hair inside. 'Stay away from me! I swear it, I'll scream if you touch me.'

'I'll give you some time,' I murmured. 'We'll talk later.'

'We're never going to talk. I never want to see you again.' She pointed at the door. 'I want you to pack your things and go. Do you understand me?'

'You don't mean it.'

Her face transformed, gargoyle-like, and she rushed at me. 'Get out! Get out! I never want to see you again!'

'Clara . . .' But there was no talking to her. I hurried out of the room, closing the door behind me, and heard the key turn in the lock as soon as I was gone. I backed away into the library next door, my heart beating hard, my breaths rackety and hollow. I held on to the back of the chair as tears squeezed from my eyes. I had no one to blame but myself.

I had been living a fantasy – a fantasy that Clara secretly loved me but was trapped inside a farce of a marriage, undertaken purely for financial gain. She had lied to me, yesterday in the summerhouse a hundred years ago. She was not a mercenary; or, at least, if she was, then she was one who also loved her husband.

And then I thought of the seashell I had discovered in Alec's pocket last night, the shell Clara had found for him and etched their initials into, the shell that had not been lost at all, that had never been lost, that had instead, just as he had promised her, been kept beside his heart.

I saw it now, saw the whole truth: here were two people who loved each other dearly but had done their best to wreck all the tenderness out of their marriage. Stupid, stupid fools, but not as stupid as me for being strung along by all the spite they'd expended on each other. I remembered Lizzie's words of yesterday, and the truth she had told about Clara and Alec and their mutual love. I recalled the way I had dismissed her own heartbreak, as if such an emotion could be overcome by force of will, and I sank to the floor, hunching myself beneath the writing desk as if the room were too large and unsafe a place for my shattered soul.

I remained there a while, the back of my head against the cold wall, and then, as if galvanized to one last action, I scrabbled my hand upwards on to the desk, retrieved the letter opener and began gouging into the wooden underside of the windowsill.

The work took me some time, and calmed me, in an odd sort of way. At that moment, it seemed as if it was of the utmost importance that I finish the task, and that I could do nothing else until it was completed.

After the letters had been etched, I was still not satisfied, and so I retrieved the ink pot and pen from the desk and, as if I were a master craftsman, began a careful blacking in of my work. It was tricky going: ink dribbled on to my face and my hands, spotted my suit and the floorboards, but I knew that none of this was important; creation was the thing, and this was far more vital than a watercolour of a lake or a sketch of a gull on the crest of a wave.

Finally, it was done. I raised my weary eyelids one last time to take in my art:

Robert Carver
is innocent

And then slumped, exhausted, against the wall, dropping pen and pot to the floor and closing my eyes.

Immediately, I fell asleep and dreamed of Clara standing on the peak of a giant, pallid skeleton of a diplodocus. Beside me was Alec, who took my hand and with his other pointed upwards. 'Look away, Robert,' he said. 'She's going to jump off.'

A hand touched my shoulder and I came to, startled. It was Scone, on his knees, crouching under the desk to reach me. 'I'm afraid the police are back, sir,' he said, taking in my appearance with a sympathetic waggle of his head. 'They would like another word with you in the dining room.'

I staggered downstairs, feeling as if I had been woken in the middle of the night, although the clock in the hall said it was only seven o'clock. Dawes welcomed me into the room and took a seat beside the window. At the table now was a dirty-looking middle-aged man straining out of his shirt buttons. He indicated the chair beside him and said, 'Mr Carver, do have a seat. My name's Inspector Morgan, and we just have a few more questions for you, if you don't mind.'

I shook my head and sat down. I felt as if I had been drained of all life. 'What do you want to know?'

'I want to know about Mrs Bray,' he said, and I kept my face as still as I was able. 'What do you make of her?'

I attempted as regular a voice as I could. 'Well, she's – um . . . she's my cousin's wife.'

Morgan cleared his throat. 'Yes, we know that. I want your impression of her.'

I was weary of this; I wanted the day to be over, so I could begin anew tomorrow. 'Of what relevance is this, anyway?'

'You see, Mr Carver, we've been talking to a lot of people today, and the general idea is that . . . well, I'll be frank. That you are in love with Mrs Bray.'

'They're mistaken. We're friends.'

'I don't doubt you're friends. Just as you're friends with her husband, your cousin. But you've entertained hopes of it being more than that, haven't you?'

I shook my head. I wanted to laugh at the irony. 'Not at all.'

'She's very beautiful.' He winked at me in an unpleasant manner. 'I'm sure half the town is in love with her. There's no shame in it.'

'Well, I'm not.'

'Not even the tiniest bit attracted to her?'

'No.' I sighed.

Morgan looked at his assistant, who was writing more notes. 'Get that, did you?' he said, and was rewarded with a nod. 'Good. Now we've cleared that up, how about your relationship with Mr Bray, your cousin?'

I breathed, relieved to get away from the subject of Clara. 'It's good, I suppose. He's been very generous in letting me stay here.'

'Hasn't he just?' Morgan looked about him. 'Nice place he's got, eh? A lot nicer than mine, I'll tell you that for nothing.'

'Mmm.' I had no idea where this was leading.

'Yours too, I expect.'

'It's bigger,' I said coldly. 'But I don't set much store by material possessions.'

'You're an unusual young man, then.' Morgan stared at me in the manner of a dead fish. I had the feeling he did not believe a single word I said, but I could hardly betray Clara to this odious being. Besides which, I supposed it would not make much difference whether he knew of our affair or not. 'Most people would be wildly envious. I mean, he's your cousin, and he's got ten, fifty times what you got.'

'I shall inherit some money when I'm twenty-five,' I said.

'Let's face it though, it isn't going to be enough to get you all this, is it? I bet you were jealous of him, weren't you? Beautiful wife, gorgeous house, all these servants at his beck and call. Didn't appreciate how lucky he was, did he?'

'Maybe he didn't,' I said. 'But I've never been jealous.'

Morgan put his head to one side. 'So what were you arguing about yesterday evening in the garden?'

My head ached. I put my elbow on the table and rested my forehead in my palm. 'What argument?'

'Oh, a few people heard you going at it hammer and tongs.' He chuckled. 'Apparently you told him . . . what was it, Dawes?'

I heard a riffle of paper.

'That he'd grown up with a silver spoon jammed inside his mouth, sir,' Dawes said. 'Oh, and that he lived in a little bubble of privilege, everything he'd ever wanted handed to him on a plate.'

'Bubble of privilege.' The Inspector sniffed. 'I don't blame you. I'd have felt the same, being you.'

'I only said those things because he was feeling so damn sorry for himself. Look, let me explain.'

'No need. So you deny you were jealous of your cousin?'

I saw Clara then in my mind, and felt her beneath me and around me, and now I understood why every time I'd found elation so hard to come by: I had been her substitute for the man she really wanted.

'Yes. I deny it,' I said quietly.

'All right then.' Morgan nodded, and leaned ever closer towards me. I smelled his celery breath. 'Seeing as we've cleared up the first argument, what about the second one?'

'There was no second one.' I shrugged. 'In fact, I think that's the only argument we've ever had.'

'On the cliff top between about half past one and two o'clock,' said Morgan as if I had not spoken. 'Do you mind telling me the details of that argument, sir?'

I sighed again. 'I told him,' I said, nodding at Dawes. 'Your witnesses must be mistaken. The last time I saw Alec was in the garden, and he was asleep under a bush.'

'I know that's what you've told us, but I'll be frank, Mr Carver, I don't believe you. Now. Two separate people say they saw you walking up the hill outside the house, towards the top of the cliff, just before the thunderstorm broke. You deny that also?'

'I do. Absolutely, I do.'

'Very well. Now then. I don't suppose you've seen the *Evening News* tonight, have you?' When I shook my head, he said, 'See, I took the step of releasing a statement to the press, and on the cover of tonight's paper there's an appeal for witnesses. Anybody who was near the cliff top last night, before or during the thunderstorm.'

I looked at him. He was smiling broadly.

'Of course, there are always the cranks who call up saying they know everything, but we've weeded them out. However, there was one man – I won't tell you his name, and he's unknown to you anyway, but I have to say we very much appreciate his help, especially considering he's a married man, living in Shanker, who apparently has a lady friend living in Helmstone. He says he sneaks across the fields to visit her, in case he gets spotted on the road.

'According to him, the storm had just begun, and he was hurrying on his way to be warm and dry, when he spots what he thinks are two lovers embracing on the cliff edge. Not wanting to disturb them, he skirts round the outside, and it's only when he's level with them that he realizes that they're not embracing, but having a fierce argument.'

I shook my head. 'That wasn't me.'

'The person facing towards him fits the description of your cousin. Now this man, presumably Mr Bray, shouted to the other person, 'I know what you did.' Those words were quite clear. Our witness made good his escape, not wanting to pry, so to speak, and it was only on reading the paper this evening that he realized what he may have witnessed. And so, like a good little citizen, he called us up and told us everything.'

Dark hands were clamping about my lungs. 'I wasn't there,' I croaked. 'I swear to you on . . . on everything I hold dear, it wasn't me.'

Morgan smiled. 'Accidents happen,' he said. 'I'm sure you were just having a right old barney and he slipped. I know you probably feel terrible, but you'll feel a darn sight worse if you don't tell us now what happened.'

'I was in bed,' I whispered, as the breath leaked from my throat. 'I was in bed all night.'

'And you've a witness to that?' he asked, and I closed my eyes and thought back to Clara's small, cold body curled in beside mine, and wondered when that had been. I tried to ignore the two policemen facing me, the chilly width of the dining room around me, and found myself back inside last night, alone in bed as the thunderstorm shattered the sky.

I swallowed on a hard, dry ache in my throat. 'This argument on the cliff top,' I began, and both Dawes and Morgan looked up keenly. 'Did it . . . That is, is it certain to have happened just after the storm began?'

Morgan gave his inferior a quick glance. Dawes nodded. 'Within a matter of seconds. A minute at most.'

Then it was no use. Even if Clara were to tell these men she had betrayed her husband on the night of his disappearance and slept with me, her testimony would be worthless. She had come to me a good half an hour after the storm had begun. I wondered, with a sense of disquiet, where *she* had been at that time, but then dashed the thought away. Clara loved Alec, a thought that pierced my heart like a shaft of ice. She would never have hurt him.

And then I wondered, with a growing unease, if she realized the same about me. Clara would not think me guilty, surely? So we had no alibi for each other; what did that matter? She must know who I was and what was real and that, however bad it appeared, I would never, ever, ever have pushed Alec off the cliff edge, never in a hundred years.

I shook my head. 'In that case I've no witness, I'm afraid.'

I took a breath and heard the rasp in my throat. Scone was right, there was an answering whistle in my lungs, an awful, off-kilter wheezing sound. The Inspector got to his feet and put a hand on my shoulder, and the band round my chest tightened further still. 'Then I'm afraid, Mr Carver, that I am going to have to arrest you on suspicion of attempted murder and that you are going to have to come with me now to the police station. The cuffs, Dawes.'

I heard the rattle of metal and saw two silver bracelets gleaming, and my lungs revolted, and I began coughing and coughing; and as I was jerked to my feet in a haze, my arms pulled behind my back, and my chest constricted tighter and tighter and ever tighter, I begged Clara to come to my rescue. Never mind if you don't love me, I beseeched, just come downstairs and tell them you know me and that I would never do harm. Please, Clara, please.

But she did not come. The front door opened as if by itself, and I was bundled through it and out into the dark, unforgiving night.

I expect you to have been rather surprised when, on seating yourself at the breakfast table in the morning with a fresh pot of coffee at your elbow, Scone handed you this parcel and you saw that it was from me. I expect you are, even as you read this, half-angry, half-astonished at the nerve I have in writing to you at such a time. I suppose you are tempted to hand the whole thing to one of the maids to burn. I hope you do not. I sincerely hope you do not.

Every day that I have not spent in the sick bay I have worked on the manuscript you now hold in your hands, hunched over the tiny table in my cell, peering at the paper in the weak light that shows through the barred window high up in the prison wall. It has certainly been a distraction from the clanging of tin mugs on bars, the screams in the night from the madman in the cell next door, the potato slops and shrivelled grey meat that passes for food.

I apologize; I had not meant to be indelicate, but I have no strength to rewrite this letter and, besides, this place hardens one. Even as a remand prisoner I have become hardened, and what once would have seemed unbearable now seems very commonplace indeed.

You are no doubt by now impatient with my waffling, and drumming your fingers on the tablecloth, waiting for me to get to the point. You see, Clara, the one thing I have here is time, and I forget that in the outside world, life moves much faster. If, as my lawyer believes, I am soon to be released, then I imagine I should be made rather breathless by the screaming hurry with which people demand things done.

I will be honest: that day cannot come soon enough. My cell walls stream with damp, and my health is failing here. I have had several asthma attacks, none serious, but I am still waiting for the latest bout of bronchitis to clear up. Luckily I am no longer in the sick bay, which is not so much a place for convalescence as an opportunity to obtain any diseases currently missing from one's collection.

Now I know I really must press on, or you shall screw up this letter and hurl it towards the fireplace. How are you, dear Clara? I hope you are not overwhelmed with fear and despair and anger. I hope you are sleeping well. I hope you still have the use of the servants, that the sale of Castaway has been temporarily suspended.

However, most of all, I hope that you believe in me. I hope that you know that the reason my case will probably never come to trial is not just lack of evidence, but the indisputable, incontrovertible fact that I am innocent.

Surely, Clara, you must know that had there been some sort of accident, that had Alec fallen from the cliff in my presence, I would have owned up to it immediately. I may have behaved poorly on any number of occasions, and this memoir here is proof of that, but I have never evaded my responsibilities.

I am certain that you have realized that whoever the two witnesses are, they must be somehow mistaken — or they are lying. Clearly, somebody did have an argument with Alec on the top of the cliff; this person to whom, apparently, Alec said the words, 'I know what you did.' I am aware that the papers have made much of this, which no doubt has caused you great distress, but for me, those words have another significance. Were Alec talking of a recent incident, I am convinced he would have said, 'I know what you've done.'

I am sure, then, that he was referring to something that happened many years ago. To what that is, I have no idea, any more than I know to whom it was he addressed those words. I wish I did! To think that this person is smugly comfortable somewhere, hoping that I hang . . . but it is no use speculating. I cannot think whom it may be, but if I ever find out, I will curse them to the end of their days.

This, then, is the reason I have written to you — not just this letter, but this entire memoir, from the very day I arrived at Castaway to the day I left. I could not give two hoots if the entire population of the country thinks me guilty as hell, if even Uncle Edward is so convinced he refuses to stump up my bail money; what matters to me is that you know me to be innocent. This package you hold in your hands is the only way I can show you; everything in it is true, and when you have read it you will know me as well as, if not better than, I know myself. You may then judge for yourself what sort of a person I am, and see if this sort of person would have his cousin fall off a cliff and hush up his part in that.

I love you, Clara. I love you to distraction, and I always will, and it is the thought of convincing you of my innocence that has kept me going throughout the long nights of coughing and the terrifying attacks on my lungs. Now this is finished, I can only hope that you read it and, even if you will not love me, then at least you will understand me.

You may think it strange, but this summer at Castaway has been the happiest of my life. Now that autumn is here, and chilly grey clouds scud across the tiny window of my cell, I go there in my mind and wander the dark polished wood of its hallways, or drink a gin Martini in one of the shaded arbours in the garden. I like to think a piece of me will always remain there, watching the comings and goings of future inhabitants and hoping some of them, at least, experience the depths and heights of passion. Because I have realized that it is this, after all, that makes one feel alive, and to feel truly, properly alive, as opposed to simply existing . . . well, I would take that route now, every time, and run straight into a moonlit sea.

Yours ever, and ever,
Robert

15
1965

After Mrs Bray had finished speaking, a silence descended on the terrace. I drifted on a tide of the past: a garden party in full bloom, candles lining the pathways and champagne spilling from tipsily held glasses. Then, later, a storm crashing into the cliff top and two men struggling on the edge. Robert and Alec, as Mrs Bray had called them. Two cousins who'd been in love with her, who had fought over her, one plunging into the frothing sea and the other, standing there and watching him fall.

Overhead, a late-season bee buzzed lazily by the hydrangeas. I watched its looping gait around the unruly garden, circling a collapsing gazebo, as my eyes came to rest on Star. She was staring at the tea table, the sun haloing a brilliant circle on the top of her head. The light bounced off the hot metal of the table, and Mrs Bray took a sip of tea. Four cigarette ends lay crumpled in the ashtray, two apiece from Star and her grandmother. She had been speaking for almost an hour, and I thought of Dockie in his bedsit downstairs, waiting for me to telephone the woman he said was his wife.

Dockie. Perhaps, perhaps, Alexander Bray. I tried to marry the two images together, of the young husband stumbling over a cliff edge at midnight, and the scratchy-faced old man with a voice like plum brandy.

'And there you have it.' Mrs Bray pulled a face at her tea. I supposed it was cold. She set it down in its saucer and nodded at the clippings I still held in my lap. 'You hold the conclusion to that sorry episode in your hands.'

I looked again at the topmost piece of newsprint and, oddly, found a tear in my eye for somebody I'd never met and never would.

'CASTAWAY HOUSE' SUSPECT DIES IN CUSTODY

POLICE SAY NO FOUL PLAY SUSPECTED

IT HAS come to our attention that Mr. Robert Carver, who was arrested by police in connection with the disappearance of his cousin Mr. Alexander Bray of Castaway House on September 2nd, has died while on remand.

Mr. Carver, who had a long-standing health problem, was found dead in his cell last night. He had apparently suffered an attack of the lungs, which was so sudden that by the time the doctor was summoned Mr. Carver had already been dead for several minutes.

Mr. Carver's cousin Mr. Bray is still missing at sea. It is presumed that he fell from the cliff near his family home during a violent storm. Hopes for his survival have dwindled to almost nothing in recent weeks.

I flicked through the rest of the cuttings, heading backwards in time, from 'CASTAWAY HOUSE' DISAPPEARANCE:

ARREST IS MADE going all the way to SEARCH FOR MISSING MAN CONTINUES.

'It's awful.' Star spoke for the first time in an age, and I was reminded that it was her grandfather, her real grandfather, who had died in prison.

'Are . . . are you sure?' I said cautiously, thinking of the scrawling under the windowsill, the proclamation of innocence. 'Are you quite sure it was him? Who pushed your husband off the cliff, I mean? I know he was arrested, but all the same . . .'

I expected her to snap at me, but instead she settled her hands in her lap and said, 'It was him. I'm not saying it was deliberate; I think it was probably an accident. After all, there's nobody else it could have been.'

'But . . . but . . .' Mrs Bray's eyes scorched mine, and I lapsed into silence. I was being idiotic, after all, to decide on somebody's innocence based on no more than a hurried self-portrait and some words scratched into a windowsill. And yet I still couldn't quite believe that Robert Carver had done what he was supposed to have done.

'Anyhow, it was my fault.' Mrs Bray nodded sharply. 'Two cousins who had a perfectly wonderful relationship, and I broke the whole thing for no other reason than my own selfish needs. I thought I was being so clever, you see. I thought I understood how the world worked, and all the time I was just a child, stamping her foot because she couldn't get her way.'

'I can see now why you've never got on with Mother,' said Star quietly. 'Seeing as her father was . . . well, you know.'

'I think we're just very different. But they do have similarities, which is . . . unfortunate. However, it's because of your mother that I now own all of this.' She trailed a tal-oned hand towards the glass-paned conservatory, the peeling walls, the cracked window frames, the attic roof. Her lips twisted into an odd smile. 'But then, I'd always been convinced that Castaway would be mine, one day.'

'Didn't you inherit it?' asked Star.

She nodded. 'Only because my father-in-law bought the house outright, to prevent it being sold. You see, when I discovered I was going to have a baby, I threw myself at his feet, said it was Alec's child, naturally. He was a broken man by then; he left me the house in his will, in order to provide for his grandchild.' She blinked, vulture-like, at the peeling frames. 'Unfortunately, financial considera-tions meant I had to turn it into flats. Perhaps one day it will be whole again. Perhaps when you inherit it, my dear.' She looked at Star, who seemed taken aback.

'Oh, not for years yet, Granny, surely.'

'Well, I'm not leaving it to your mother. She'll turn it into some sort of dreadful charity or something.' She sniffed at me, her eyes snapping as if she'd forgotten, momentarily, that I was there. 'You probably think I'm a cold bitch.'

'Oh!' I grimaced. 'I don't know why you care what I think.'

'I don't know why either. There must be something about you, Miss Churchill.' She frowned as she thought. 'Purity, perhaps.'

'I agree,' said Star, and I eyed her sceptically, but she was nodding.

'Well, for what it's worth,' I said, 'I don't think you're a cold bitch. I think you did what you had to do to survive.'

Mrs Bray inclined her head, as if in acknowledgement of the truth of that statement, and then said, 'He wrote to me, you know. From prison. Just before he died. A huge wad of notes about what had happened, what he had and hadn't done. It arrived the day after his death was announced. I couldn't bear to read it; sealed it all back up again. It's still around, somewhere.'

An idea rolled like a marble in my mind. 'Could it be in the chest? The one in the sitting room?'

'Oh, it is!' squealed Star. 'I've seen it. Yes. When I was cleaning. An unopened packet. Years old.'

'Then it's *him*,' I said in a whisper.

'Who's him?' Star frowned at me.

'Robert. Robert Carver.' I looked at Mrs Bray with some trepidation. 'That's why the lid's always open. He wants you to look inside.'

'For heaven's sake,' snapped Mrs Bray. 'It's a faulty lid.'

'And the whistling?' I looked at her, saw the quiver in her eyelid again. 'And the reason you won't sleep alone?'

She sighed. 'I thought,' she said in an old, tired voice. 'I thought it was Alec. Blaming me for what I'd done. Cursing me. Being the same annoying shit he'd been when he was alive.'

There was a pause. 'He is alive,' I said quietly.

Mrs Bray's lips folded in on themselves. She placed one hand to her throat. I thought she was struggling to speak, but then from beneath the collar of her dogtooth jacket she pulled free a gold locket dangling round her neck on a chain. 'He gave me this on the day he proposed,' she said in a soft croak.

'What's inside it?' asked Star, and Mrs Bray stretched her hands behind her neck and, in a surprisingly agile movement, unhooked the chain. Star received it in her palms and studied the engraving, as I leaned over her shoulder. It was of flowers and leaves, with a small bird at its centre.

'It's beautiful,' I murmured.

Star gently opened the clasp. Pinned beneath an oval of glass, on a bed of blue paper, was a twist of blond hair.

'You say he's alive,' sniffed Mrs Bray, somewhat sourly. 'To be honest, I'd rather he were dead.'

Star shifted the locket from one palm to the other. 'You can't mean that, Granny.'

'I certainly can. Better dead than being alive for forty years and never once letting me know.'

A tear glimmered in the corner of her eye. 'He says he lost his memory,' I said. 'Perhaps when he fell from the cliff.'

'Bully for him. If only I'd been so lucky.' She dashed away the tear.

Star leaned across the table and folded the locket back into her grandmother's hand. 'He thinks you're in Paris,' she said softly. 'You don't have to see him if you don't want to.'

Mrs Bray swallowed. 'I may be many things, my dear, but I am not a coward. I shall speak to this man, and if he is ... I can hardly say it. If he does turn out to be my long-lost husband, then ... do you know, I cannot imagine what I shall do then?'

'Have a stiff drink,' I suggested, and saw a glimmer of a smile play about her lips.

'Miss Churchill,' she said in her usual, brisk voice. 'You ought to fetch this man immediately. Before he forgets who he is once more.'

I stood up, and Star made to move too, but Mrs Bray

said to her, 'I'd like you to stay here.' In an awkward tone, she added, 'I'd rather not be on my own until he comes.'

'Okay.' Star hovered, halfway to standing. 'I'll just see Rosie out.'

Mrs Bray nodded a reluctant assent, and I followed Star back into the glare of the conservatory and then the gloom of the bedroom. She took my hand and made a movement with her head. 'This way.'

She led me through to the sitting room, still in uproar from the night's adventures. The blanket from the truckle bed had been kicked on to the floor; my belongings were scattered across the rug from where I'd emptied out the Bradley's bag. I half expected the lid of the chest to be wide open again, but it was firmly closed, the catch still connected.

Star let go of my hand and sat cross-legged in front of the chest. She eased open the catch and swung the lid back. A puff of dust flew out, just as before. The photograph was still on top, face-down, and she lifted it out and wiped its glass with her sleeve. She prodded the young form of Alexander Bray and said, 'What do you think?'

I bent over her, looked past the velvet swags and the old-fashioned clothes, in towards the angle of his jaw and the set of his eyes. I placed Dockie's worn-out face over the top, removed the red veins that contoured his nose, the leathered texture of his skin, the weary lines to his mouth, and nodded. 'It's him.'

For several seconds we both looked silently at the beautiful, oblivious couple in the velvet studio, and then Star said with a sigh, 'I suppose I ought to prepare Granny; tell her that he really is her husband.'

'You should show her this as well.' Dropping to my knees, I searched through the dusty files until I found the thick envelope at the bottom. Lifting it free, I gave it to Star, who snatched it from me.

'This is it,' she said in a whisper, turning it over. '*That's* why his name was familiar. I saw this before, when I was cleaning.'

On the reverse of the envelope was a scratchy brown indentation, inscribed with the same hand that had written the address. It said: *Sender: Mr. R. Carver Esq., Marstone H. M. P.*

I fingered the package. 'He wants this to be read,' I said. 'That's what all this is about; not a punishment. A plea.'

'I'll take it to her.' Star brushed off the dust and held it against her chest. From her sitting position, she looked up at me, and I saw a new, vulnerable light in her eyes.

'You're beautiful,' I whispered, lifting her chin and turning her face towards mine. Dipping my head towards hers, I kissed her on the lips, Robert Carver's letter pressed between us like a ghost.

I left her there cross-legged on the floor, and staggered, giddy and hungover and a hundred per cent alive, out of the flat and down towards the basement. The world was opening up before me; I felt a sort of soaring delight, a feeling that I could go down any path, take any life that appealed to me, and I marched down the passageway, entered Dockie's room and realized that he had disappeared.

I walked into the empty room. Sheets and blankets were curled into a ball at the end of the bed. The bright sunlight of the garden barely penetrated the highest corner of the basement yard. Dockie was not there.

I shivered in the sudden chill and headed back down the corridor. I looked into the bathroom, but there was no sign of him. A cracked slice of soap rested on the side of the tub, and shavings decorated the wash basin. A rubber shower hose was lying on the floor like a subdued beast. The mousetrap was empty.

I ran up the stairs to the hallway. I wondered where I would go, if I were him, and realized I had no idea who he really was. I pulled open the main door and trotted down to the pavement, walking past the Bella Vista before hesitating inside a plank of sunshine and looking both ways.

'Rosie!'

I turned. Mrs Hale was coming down the path next door, hair askew from its bun, cardigan buttoned up lopsidedly, one stocking wrinkling around her ankle like the jowls of a dog. She came up to me and put a hand on my arm. 'That man . . .' she said breathlessly. 'Oh, Rosie, I'm all in a flap. You see, he looks so much like . . . at least, it may not be, but my father's convinced of it, ever since he saw him last night. Thought he was a ghost, but of course he's not, and then you were here with him, and . . . I suppose you have no idea what I'm talking about, do you?'

'I do,' I said. 'He's Alexander Bray, who fell off the cliff forty years ago, and he's been missing ever since.'

Mrs Hale clutched my arm tightly. 'That's impossible,' she croaked.

'He lost his memory.' I tried to release her grip on my arm, but she was too strong. 'But listen, I need to find him. He's gone off somewhere, and he's confused enough as it is.'

'But . . . but . . .' Mrs Hale opened and closed her mouth

several times. 'Has he said anything? About . . . about the past?'

'Not much. Not yet.' I frowned at her. 'What do you mean, anyway?'

'Nothing,' she said quickly. 'I was just wondering. Goodness . . . what a shock. What an utter shock.'

And then a memory of this morning slivered back to me. 'Earlier, in the kitchen,' I began, 'you mentioned Robert Carver. You said the reason your father was upset was the whole Robert Carver business.'

'Did I say that?' She tucked an escaping strand of hair back behind her ear. 'I was in such a state, I'd no idea what I was saying. He'd been awake all night, you see, yelling the place down about ghosts and so on.'

'But Robert Carver,' I insisted. 'You knew him, didn't you?'

She nodded. 'He was Lizzie's beau, for a few months. He became . . . part of the family, almost. He was wonderful. I was quite in love with him, you see. He had no idea of course; I was only a child to him.'

'And then he was arrested for murder,' I said.

She looked at me sharply, and nodded. 'It was such a shock. For me.'

There was a strange cadence to the way she'd said that, and I peered at her. 'You thought he was innocent, then?'

'Of course I did,' she murmured. 'Of course I did.'

I looked up and down the hill. 'Dockie will remember – Mr Bray, I mean. Now his memory's returned, he'll be able to tell us who pushed him off the cliff.'

'Oh, Lord . . .' Mrs Hale put a hand to her eyes. 'He will, he will.'

It was such a shock, she'd said. *For me.*

For me. And an idea crept like a thief into my mind.

'You know, don't you?' I said. 'You know who tried to kill Mr Bray, and it wasn't Robert. Robert Carver was innocent.'

She grasped my sleeve. Urgently, she said, 'I didn't know at the time. Not for years afterwards. I mean, I believed he hadn't done it, but I had no idea of the truth. I wouldn't have let him die in prison, Rosie. You must understand that. By the time I found out, it was all too late.'

I faced her, my breath tight in my lungs. '*Then who was it?*'

She sniffed and, instead of answering, turned round. I followed her gaze; she was looking towards the Bella Vista, at the ground-floor window.

And there, looking out at us, his head shaking uncontrollably, was her father, Dr Feathers.

'No,' I said. 'No.'

Mrs Hale was still looking at her father. 'You must tell him, Rosie, you must tell Mr Bray that it was an accident; it was such an awful accident. He never meant it to happen.'

I watched him too, resting on his stick, his head wobbling anxiously. 'Robert died in prison,' I said in a croak. 'And your father let that happen.'

'I didn't know, I swear I didn't know, not until after the shell-shock, when he was in hospital. And what was I to do then? Betray him, after twenty years?'

'But Robert died.' Sorrow tugged at my throat. 'He died.'

Mrs Hale turned back to me, words spilling over themselves as if, now that the dam had burst, there was no way of keeping them in. 'He was petrified, you see. My father, I mean. The next day, the day after Mr Bray went missing, the police came round to ask us if we'd seen anything, and he told them he'd seen them walking up towards the cliff together – the two cousins, that is.'

'Mrs Bray told me there'd been two witnesses,' I said softly. 'That's what made them arrest Robert.'

'The other witness, that was Lizzie,' said Mrs Hale, and there she was, behind her father, holding on to the back of his chair, large and square and beetle-browed.

'You mean . . . ?' I stared at Mrs Hale's sister. 'She lied to the police? I thought he was her beau.'

Mrs Hale ran a hand through her straggling hair. 'He broke her heart. She'd already been heartbroken once, and she couldn't bear it a second time. He never knew what a vengeful streak she had in her; he thought she was sweet, docile. That night, she was furious with him. Wanted to hurt him as he'd hurt her. She looked out of the window and saw our father outside, talking to Mr Bray. By the time the police came to interview us, she'd already spoken to Father, and he'd convinced her it was Robert she'd seen instead. She didn't lie on purpose, but I suppose it was . . . convenient for her, to think that. It's one of the reasons we don't get on now.'

'This is . . .' I was inarticulate with rage and injustice. Now I saw what had made Dockie take this journey, across sea and land, all the way back to Castaway House. 'He's got away with it. For years.'

'No, Rosie, not at all.' She shook her head firmly. 'Not at all. Mother found out what had happened, you see, and she left him for the Quakers. Then there was the bomb during the war, and the news of Anthony being killed, and of course his business had been failing before that . . . No, you mustn't think he got away with it. In fact, it's almost as if he's been cursed, for years. We all have, actually.'

'It wasn't your fault,' I said.

'The sins of the fathers . . .' She shrugged. 'You will at least try to explain, won't you? He can't go to prison now. He hasn't much longer left, anyway.'

I looked at Dr Feathers in the window. As he saw me, he attempted to smile, and raised one wavering arm in a salute.

'I need to find him first,' I said. 'Mr Bray. I don't know where he is.'

She pointed. 'I saw him go towards the cliff top.'

'What?' I whirled away from her.

'It's only dangerous if you go too close to the edge,' she said. 'He wouldn't do that, would he?'

'I don't know.' I began marching up the hill. A few paces on I turned, and looked back. Mrs Hale was still staring after me, clutching her hands to her chest. I smiled at her and called down, 'I'm sure everything'll be all right.'

She nodded uncertainly. I waved at her, and then continued upwards.

The sun streamed into my eyes as I walked. I passed a woman wheeling a pram up the hill, bent double with the effort, overheated in her autumn coat and headscarf. The squeak of the pram's wheels was the only nearby sound, except for the faint squawking of gulls.

I crossed over to the cliff-top path that wound beside the fences of the bungalows. Hard ridges had formed from the mud churned up in last week's storm. As I puffed my way upwards, the sky blue and brilliant above me, I saw a dark figure beyond the path, standing right on the very edge of the cliff, looking down to the crashing waves below.

'Dockie!' I called, but my voice was whipped back into my mouth by the breeze sifting over the cliff. I picked up my pace, passing the glassy-eyed bungalows. A line of washing flapped; flags of terry-cloth nappies and a cream-coloured blanket, doubling over itself in the wind. A low table held a jug with remnants of lemonade; a dead wasp floated on its surface while others foolishly buzzed about the sticky rim.

I drew level with him; he was facing the sea, his arms by his sides, leaning into the wind to hold him upright. 'Dockie,' I gasped, 'please come back from there.'

He turned, his red eyes leaking tears. 'I remember,' he said hoarsely. 'I remember everything.'

'I know. I know about Robert Carver. But listen, come back from there. It's dangerous.'

He remained where he was. 'The story in the news-papers,' he croaked. 'The story Frank hid from me; they arrested him for my murder. My cousin. My friend. Arrested him, and he died in prison.'

'Dockie . . .'

'All these years, Rosie. Can you imagine? All these years I willingly let my memory rust away. Oh, Frank played his part all right. My head injury was helpful. But I could have known, if I'd searched hard enough inside myself. I could have brought it to the surface, but I thought only of myself. It never occurred to me that an injustice may have taken place.'

I saw he wasn't going to budge an inch, so I took a few steps closer towards him.

He shook his newly shorn head, eyes glinting. 'It was *him*.' He pointed a finger back towards the house. 'The doctor. He was the agent of both our destructions.'

I thought of what Mrs Hale had wanted me to say. 'Perhaps it was an accident,' I said quietly.

He narrowed his eyes. 'I feel as if a curtain has been pulled back across my mind. I see it all.'

I took another step closer to the edge. Below me, the rocks lurked with ragged jaws. 'What do you see?' I said.

'A party. Me, drunk and unhappy. Maudlin, self-pitying. I lean on the rail, outside the house, and *he* comes up the road. Never liked me, you know. Pretends to all right, but underneath considers me an idle good-for-nothing.'

He breathed heavily, and I took one more step and held on to his wrist, my heart beating fast now as the base of the cliff loomed into view. 'Go on.'

'He smells of drink. Must speak to me most urgently. Asks if we may take a walk. As we climb, tells me that my wife and my cousin are . . . that I am being made a cuckold of. His duty to inform me of the fact.'

The breeze was stronger out here on the edge of the cliff; a gull swooped nearby, calling plaintively, and I ducked out of instinct. Dockie appeared to notice nothing, except for what was occurring forty years in the past.

'I'll have none of that. Not Robert. Not my cousin, my friend. Oh yes. He insists. His eyes a flash in the lightning. His beard dripping rain. The storm curdles my anger. I shout. I curse. You worthless worm, you care nothing for me! You care for nobody but yourself. I know . . . I know . . .'

And now I too was in the past, as thunder raked the sky

and two men stood on a cliff top, drunk with rage. 'What?'
I whispered. 'What?'

'*I know what you did.* You killed Gina Scott, and you
allowed me to take the blame.'

I paused. 'Who's Gina Scott?'

Dockie narrowed his red-rimmed eyes. 'I always suspected. Killed more patients than you saved, that's what
I've always thought. You were treating her for sleepless-
ness, prescribed her Veronal. You wrote the dosage down
wrongly, didn't you, and she died. Then you spread the
rumour she was having a baby, so her poor parents would
imagine it had been suicide. And everyone . . . everyone
would think it was my fault.'

'Oh, Dockie.' I gripped his arm tightly. If he fell now,
so would I.

'My collar, grasped.' Dockie put a hand to the shoulder
of my dress, gripping it hard. 'Shakes me like a dog.
Ungrateful little boy. I've only ever tried to help. We dance
at the edge, like this, just like this.'

My toes curled on a daisy that grew at the edge of
the cliff. Marvellous, that this yellow-hearted dash of life
could thrive on such a bitter spot. 'Put me down, Dockie.
Please, put me down.'

'And then his hands at my chest, the ground disappears
and I fly through the air.' He lifted his other arm high,
raising his head. 'Still holding my umbrella, I was. Exhilar-
ating, beautiful. Alive.'

The wind buffeted my hair around my face. Far below,
I could hear the sea calling me. *I'm waiting*, it hissed as it
coursed around the rocks. *Come, come, come.*

Dockie swayed on the edge of the cliff as he spoke, as

495

if in a dream. 'The sea and the stones, pounding me, pounding me. I struggle, I drift; and then later, much later, asleep and awake, with the constant motion of the sea. They argue over whether to throw me back or save me. A foul smell from my head, like fish guts and stale beer. My clothes soaked through with the blood and the seawater; cut from me. Everything taken, except for a photograph. It's worthless, let him keep it. It's ruined, anyway. I must never tell a soul who picked me up, or they will rip me from throat to groin.'

'Dockie!' I shouted in his face, as fragments of earth under my feet crumbled sixty feet down to the sea. 'Come back, Dockie . . . Alec.'

His eyes found mine. 'Huh?'

I felt time swing slowly back to the present. I spoke as firmly as I could. 'Put me down, Alec. Put me down.'

He frowned, confused, but his grip on my shoulder relaxed and I was able to take a step back away from the edge.

'Come with me.' I held out my hand.

He looked at me, and then, hesitantly, he grasped my hand and slowly, slowly, I led him back to the path. As my feet felt the solid ridges of the hardened mud, my legs wobbled and gave way, and I sank to the ground beside the bungalow fences, shaking as uncontrollably as Dr Feathers.

Dockie looked down at me. 'Rosie,' he murmured. He put his own hand out towards me. 'Dear Rosie.'

I grasped his weathered fingers and allowed him to pull me back to standing. 'My dear girl,' Dockie was saying. 'My dear, dear girl.'

I took a few deep gulps of sweet air. I looked up at him and said, 'Your wife. She's not in Paris.'

He stared at me. 'Where is she?'

I pointed back the way I had come. 'She's at Castaway House.'

He put a hand to his chin as he stared towards the brow of the hill. 'She is?'

I nodded. 'She's waiting for you there.'

He looked down at himself. 'But I can't.' He glanced at me, terrified. 'I cannot see her like this.'

I put a hand to his sleeve. 'You look fine. Honestly.'

He touched his short hair, attempted to smooth it down, although the wind blew it back into tufts. 'Will she forgive me, Rosie? I have been gone so long.'

'I think . . .' I shrugged. 'I suppose you'll have some talking to do.'

He took a step along the path and I followed him, matching his pace with mine. Dockie put a hand into his pocket and brought something out, worrying it over and over in his fingers as we walked. 'She must forgive me,' he murmured. 'She must.'

I looked down and saw that he was rubbing a small sea-shell, twisting it back and forth in his hand. 'You had that before,' I said. 'When you were turning out your pockets in the hallway, that first day I met you.'

'I have no idea if it is the same one, even.' He smiled to himself. 'My talisman. My good-luck charm. My Clara.'

I let him ramble on without asking more questions. In the distance, the tip of Castaway rose to meet us, and Dockie suddenly cried, quite from nowhere, 'Sally! I had forgotten Sally. Now she – she will never forgive me. I am quite sure of that.'

'Sally?' I squinted up at him, and in a rush I remembered the photograph: a dash of a baby's head in a quarter-inch of sunlight. My heart picked up a pace. 'My – my grandmother . . . her name was Sally.'

He touched his scalp. 'It's too late for Robert, though. Far, far too late.'

'Did she live on a farm, do you know? Married a man named Josh Brewer? Had a daughter named Grace?'

But I was babbling, and Dockie was not listening. There would be time, I supposed, later. I hoped there would be time later. I put my arm through his, and we reached the house together. Mrs Hale had gone inside; the doctor was missing from his spot by the window. Lizzie, too. I wondered what thoughts were on all of their minds.

The front door was still open from earlier, and when we crossed the threshold sunlight thrust through the coloured lozenges of glass above the door, painting a motif on the hall flagstones. Blooming beneath my feet in green and red was the legend of the house.

I knocked on the door to the ground-floor flat, and waited, my heart thumping. Dockie pulled down his cuffs and slicked back his eyebrows. After a while Star opened the door and looked out.

'Is everything all right?' she said. 'You've been gone for ever.'

'I went for a walk,' he intoned in his rich plum brandy of a voice, and only I heard the nervous shake in it. 'May I come in?'

Star nodded. 'She's in the garden.' She came into the

hallway. I noticed she had the package still clutched to her chest. 'She said you're to go on through.'

Dockie looked at her. 'Alone?'

Star nodded. 'Alone.'

'Well, then.' He turned to me and held out his hand. 'Thank you for everything, Rosie. I am so utterly grateful.'

I ignored the hand, reached forward and enveloped myself in his hug. 'Thank you,' I whispered.

'What on earth for, my dear?'

'Never mind.' I wiped a hand roughly across my eyes. 'Go on now.'

He nodded at both of us and disappeared inside the flat. Star pulled the door closed and looked down at 'Castaway House' in red and green flooding the floor. She toed the pattern. 'What a day, eh?'

'Absolutely.' She looked up at me and I said, 'Let's go for a swim.'

She grinned at me. 'Meet you back here in five minutes?'

'You're on.'

Star raced past me up the stairs as I went up one flight and pulled out my key. The flat welcomed me warmly in through its door, the sunshine lighting the scrolled coving at the ceiling and the flecks of old colour in the wallpaper. I found my swimming costume in the suitcase beneath a pile of unused summer blouses and stripped off, pulling it on and throwing an old dress over the top.

Before I left I took Robert from his hiding place and looked at the sketch. I traced the contours of his face and kissed his forehead. After I put him back I checked my appearance in the mirror; my hair was still scraggy and my eye sockets hollow with tiredness, but there was a new expression there I couldn't quite fathom.

I waited for Star in the hallway, listening for the out-of-tune whistling but hearing nothing at all. Dockie's coins were still on the box below the telephone, and I gathered them into a neat pile. The blackboard above was still empty of messages.

I picked up a sixpence and rolled it between my finger and thumb. I thought of Mrs Bray's words earlier. *I may be a lot of things, but I am not a coward.*

Well, what about Rosie Churchill? Was she a coward, who ran away when things got tough? I took a breath, lifted the receiver and slid in the sixpence, then dialled the telephone number I knew off by heart.

I closed my eyes as the phone rang, and wished I'd drunk a glass of water first, because my throat was parched, and then I heard my mother in her telephone voice say, 'Petwick 287,' and I knew there was no going back.

'Hello?' she said now. 'Hello? Is that you, Rosie?'

I pushed the A button and heard the coin clanking into the box below. 'Yes,' I croaked, and swallowed. 'Yes, it's me. It's Rosie.'

There was silence, except for the hammering of my heart. Finally my mother said, as if continuing an entirely separate conversation, 'After you left the other day I searched your room.'

She hesitated and I held my breath.

'I found your jewellery box.'

I breathed out and a long *Haaaah* sound spat back into my ear. The secret bottom of my jewellery box was where I'd stored all the notes from Harry. I hadn't thought to throw them away. Mum wasn't a snooper; at least, she never had been before.

'Rosie.' Her voice cracked, and a sob emerged.

'Mum . . .' I clutched the telephone wire in my other fist.

'I should have known.' She laughed in an odd, bitter sort of a way. 'When I met him at the Dashwoods' party they said to me, they said, "Be careful of that one, Grace." Didn't listen, of course. But I never thought he'd try it with my own daughter.'

'I'm sorry,' I whispered, cringing at the inadequacy of the words. 'I'm so, so sorry.'

'Oh, Rosie.' Again, the laugh. 'Oh, Rosie, you've nothing to be sorry for.'

'I . . .' I began, not knowing what to say next, because maybe she hadn't realized what the notes signified, and now I'd have to explain, and I had no words for that.

'He's gone,' she said. 'For good. So you can come home now, and start school again, and all those things, all right?'

'He . . .' The air was getting stuck in my throat. I tried again. 'I let him . . . Ah . . .'

'Rosie. Darling.' My mother's voice softened suddenly, like a crumpling flower. 'God, Rosie, you don't think I hold you responsible, do you?'

'I sh-shouldn't have . . .'

'Listen to me,' she said firmly, and now she was like my mum of old, laying out the world for me, a piece at a time. 'It wasn't your fault. You were innocent.'

'Innocent,' I repeated, and said it to myself, inside my head. *Rosie Churchill is innocent.* I felt an insane urge to giggle.

At the corner of the half-landing Star appeared, wearing a green dress with thin straps and a floppy sun hat, the handles of a straw bag slung over one shoulder. She stood there watching me, and I knew she understood.

'Of course. Now listen, I've been thinking. How about I come to your place tomorrow afternoon? And you can make me a cup of tea, and we'll just have a nice chat. What do you think?'

I nodded, although she couldn't see me, and thought of Dockie, and the photograph, and his talk of a girl named Sally. 'I've loads of news. Good news, I think.'

Mum sighed through the wires. 'I've missed you.'

'I've missed you too.'

After I'd hung up I leaned against the G. P. O. list of exchange numbers framed beside the telephone and waited for Star to reach my side.

'You okay?' She touched my bare arm.

I smiled at her. 'Yes, I am.'

Together, we walked down the hill in the sunshine. I peered at a bright orange scarf wrapped around something sticking out of the top of her straw bag.

'What's that?' I asked.

'Oh, it's to protect the envelope.' She waggled her eyebrows at me. 'Granny let me have it.'

'What? Not . . . the package from Robert?'

She nodded. 'She wants me to read it first, so I can tell her if there's anything upsetting in it.'

'Wow.' I looked down at the beach, the families setting up camp beneath the unexpected sun, the donkey-ride woman further along in her deckchair, the metal edging of the pier winking in the light. 'She really trusts you.'

'She does.' She nudged me. 'Of course, I'll let you read it too. She'll never know.'

'Oh, *Star*.' I was pleased all the same, and put my arm inside hers. 'And you mustn't forget our date tonight. The One-Two, remember?'

She looked down and blushed. 'I wouldn't,' she murmured, and I felt again the glimmer of power just within my grasp.

I put my shoulders back straighter, and as we crossed the road to the promenade I said, 'Oh, look, there's Johnny.'

We walked down the steps, plunging across the filmy sand. 'This is okay, isn't it?' murmured Star, in a sort of wonder, a giggle just under her breath.

I was bright with a new sort of confidence. 'Yes,' I said. 'It is.'

We nudged each other, sand sinking between our toes as we walked to where Johnny was lying on a towel in shorts and a vest, wearing sunglasses.

'You two made it up?' he said, as we unrolled towels and kicked off our shoes. 'I've got the hangover from hell, so don't disturb, all right?'

Star wriggled out of her dress and stood before me in her black-and-white swimsuit. 'You coming, Rosie?'

'Um . . .' I looked down at the bag Star had dumped on to the towel. 'All right. Just give me a second.'

'I'll see you in there, okay?' She turned and ran off towards where children were squealing in the waves.

I bent down to the bag, sand spattering the outsides of it, and pulled apart the fringes of the orange scarf. Inside was the envelope; it had already been unpeeled and I inched out the first few pages. The topmost one appeared to be a letter; I saw *Dear Clara* in an elegant copperplate hand. The second one began:

> *Both trains were packed: all the way from Birmingham New Street to London, and again on the connecting service to the south.*

'Go on, bugger off,' murmured Johnny from behind his sunglasses. 'I'll make sure it don't go nowhere, okay?'

'You'd better.' I gently pushed the pages back and returned the envelope to the bag. I stood up and squinted out towards the shoreline, making out Star's head bobbing in the waves.

I stepped out of my dress and kicked it on to the towel. I walked towards the glinting blue line of the sea, dodging past the families reading newspapers and the kids building sandcastles. As I stepped into the sea I gasped as the cold water hit my shins.

'You've got to run!' Star shouted from a short distance away, her lips wide, her eyelashes wet. I took a breath, waded in up to my thighs and then, with a wild scream of abandon, launched myself into the sea and began swimming, the sunshine hot on my head and the gulls wheeling and calling somewhere far overhead.

Acknowledgements

Thank you Judith Murray, and all at Greene & Heaton.
Thank you, everyone at Michael Joseph and Penguin.
Thank you, Stella Kane and Laura Longrigg.
Thank you, Grit Lit and Rattle Tales in Brighton.
Thank you Sam, my first editor.
And most of all, thank you for reading this book.
I hope you've enjoyed the journey.

He just wanted a decent book to read ...

Not too much to ask, is it? It was in 1935 when Allen Lane, Managing Director of Bodley Head Publishers, stood on a platform at Exeter railway station looking for something good to read on his journey back to London. His choice was limited to popular magazines and poor-quality paperbacks – the same choice faced every day by the vast majority of readers, few of whom could afford hardbacks. Lane's disappointment and subsequent anger at the range of books generally available led him to found a company – and change the world.

'We believed in the existence in this country of a vast reading public for intelligent books at a low price, and staked everything on it'
Sir Allen Lane, 1902–1970, founder of Penguin Books

The quality paperback had arrived – and not just in bookshops. Lane was adamant that his Penguins should appear in chain stores and tobacconists, and should cost no more than a packet of cigarettes.

Reading habits (and cigarette prices) have changed since 1935, but Penguin still believes in publishing the best books for everybody to enjoy. We still believe that good design costs no more than bad design, and we still believe that quality books published passionately and responsibly make the world a better place.

So wherever you see the little bird – whether it's on a piece of prize-winning literary fiction or a celebrity autobiography, political tour de force or historical masterpiece, a serial-killer thriller, reference book, world classic or a piece of pure escapism – you can bet that it represents the very best that the genre has to offer.

Whatever you like to read – trust Penguin.

read more
www.penguin.co.uk